D1528073

SHADOWS
OF
VERIHDIA

VERIHDIAN WARDENS - BOOK ONE

Shadows of Verihdia

NIKKI ROBB

ISBN: Paperback: 9798848407570
ISBN: Hardcover: 9798352518571

This novel is a work of fiction, any similarities to real people and events are entirely coincidental.

Cover and Interior Formatting by Rachel McEwan
Map Design by Melissa Nash
Court Mark Designs by Alison Turjancik

Printed and distributed by Kindle Direct Publishing
First Printing Edition

To everyone who isn't sure where they belong.

Content Warnings

Shadows of Verihdia is a new adult fantasy novel that contains descriptions of drowning, nightmares, choking, being restrained, and explicit sexual scenes. This novel also touches on feelings of intense guilt, including inter-familial guilt. There are brief mentions of previous body issues/negative body image, suicidal thoughts, and domestic violence. Readers who may be sensitive to these elements please take note.

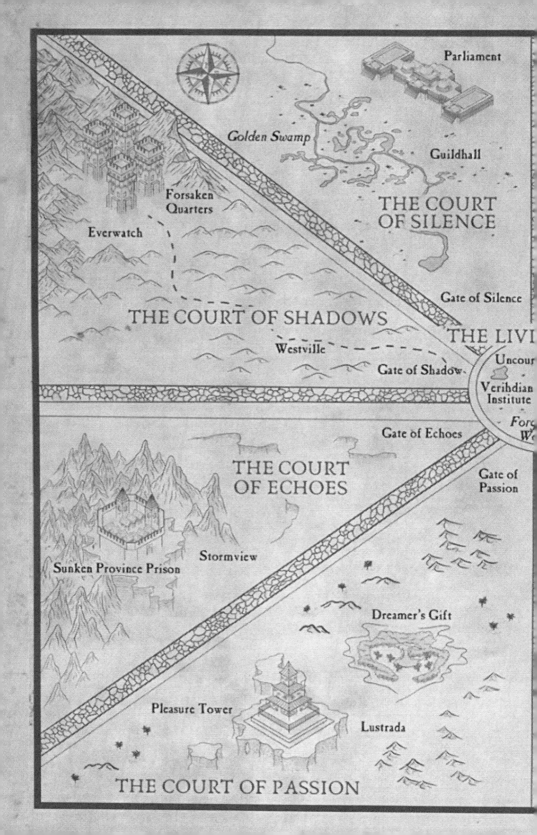

PROLOGUE

*D*rowning is such a painful way to die. I should know… I do it every night. They're only nightmares, of course, and nightmares can't hurt me. At least that's what I tell myself each morning when I jolt awake, expelling the nonexistent remnants of my death from my burning lungs.

It started when I was young - not long after I started classes at the Institute. Each night when my eyes would close, sleep would come to carry me away with a promise of blissful rest, but instead, I would find myself drifting alone in the middle of a wide open ocean. There was no surface and no ocean floor, at least none that I could reach. Each night I'd swim in a different direction, arms flailing as I fought to keep conscious long enough to find safety. But I couldn't find what wasn't there. It was only me and the water. Water that consumed me, stealing my breath and replacing it with scorching salted liquid. This happened every single night, deprived of oxygen until my body was wracking with painful tremors, my throat tightening in pain, my lungs screaming and begging for one gasp of fresh air - one single ounce of a reprieve. But night after night, it never came.

And night after night, I would drown.

I used to think I was cursed, that I was being punished for something. But what could I have done that warranted this kind of torture?

I knew there had to be a reason behind it. Dreams have meanings after all. Maybe I was sent adrift in the nothingness of the open ocean because of how adrift I felt in my own life. Was I drowning in my indecision? The harder I looked for an explanation, the worse my dreams became. Soon, I stopped trying to make any sense of them and just learned to survive. Well, 'survive' was a strange word for it. Maybe, 'coexist' was more appropriate.

Eventually, I got used to it - the pain, the fear...dying. It was just another night, another dream, another death.

What does that say about me?

ONE

There are seven Courts in Verihdia, and in each Court, there is a Warden. These realms - entirely separate worlds in their own right - are connected only by a thin veil of Mythica, or magic. Each Court has its role to play in the dynamic and delicate structure of our world, and despite their formidable individual power, they rely on the small circle of land that lies nestled directly in the center for their survival. This circle of land, kissed ever so briefly on each edge by the veils that offer entrance to the worlds that lie beyond, is known as The Living Lands. A lush landscape of modest homes, very few luxuries, and at its center - appropriately lying the same distance from each Court - The Verihdian Institute.

The Institute's hallowed halls were at some time home to every living soul in Verihdia, save for the Wardens that preside over the Courts. You cannot grow to be a contributing member of Verihdia without the guidance and education that can only be found within its walls. At least that is what we had been led to believe.

This unassuming circle of land was minuscule in comparison to the vast landscapes of the Courts that lie beyond the Mythica shrouded borders, but even so, I had not yet seen the entirety of what The Living Lands have to offer.

Sometimes the sheer immensity of Verihdia kept me awake at night, tossing with sleepless rest as I was confronted with the thought of how much of this world I had never, and possibly would never, see. Until you are Pledged to a Court, you are not permitted to cross the veil into any of the seven realms. However, any member of the Courts may enter The Living Lands freely if they choose to do so. Not that many do. Why would they, when the only thing offered here is the education they have already received and hundreds of Uncourted students desperately attempting to discover which sin they are best suited for? While I knew that there was so much more to this world than I could even begin to comprehend, I made myself a comfortable life here in The Living Lands.

This is where I'm from. Well, it's where I grew up. I don't know where I'm from. None of the children at the Institute know where they were born. That's how it works in Verihdia. That's how our Courts continue to thrive.

'Let no single thing influence the Pledge.' And to the governing faction in The Court of Silence, that includes family.

Perhaps they're right. If I knew which Court my parents belonged to, I couldn't imagine I'd willingly Pledge anywhere else. Even without knowing them, without a single memory of their love or affection, I still find myself desperate to know them. I would, without a doubt, choose their Court just so that I could be granted a semblance of a family that had long since been stolen from me. The Court of Silence made the right choice in taking away that interference. I could admit that - even if I hated it.

At least I have Axel.

My brother. My mirror in every way that counts. When I was ripped from the arms of whatever mother I had, at least I was not ripped alone. My mother gave up two children that night, and two children joined the sea of hundreds of newly minted orphans in the heart of The Living Lands to be raised and cared for by the Uncourted at the Institute.

"You are a million miles away, Lexa." A familiar voice managed to drag me back to reality. I forced my eyes to center on his face as Chandler rested on his arms above me. Our bodies were still joined beneath the white cotton sheets. He stared at me with his brown eyes questioningly. "You couldn't possibly be thinking of something else right now." He grunted, unmoving. I felt a flush creep up my neck and reach my cheeks.

"Of course not, Chandler. Please, don't stop." I whispered, letting my hand rest on his cheek. His warm skin felt painful against the cold touch of my palm. He watched me for a moment more before he moved within me again, and this time I forced away thoughts of Verihdia and its unfortunate traditions - compelling myself to focus on nothing but the way he felt inside of me. His thrusts became erratic and he swore under his breath as he neared his climax. I ran my hands absentmindedly across his back and forced out soft moans. It wasn't a displeasurable experience - it never was with Chandler. However, neither of us were destined for The Court of Passion, and we had long since confirmed that we weren't a truly mated pair, so our joinings lacked that blind, intense desire that was often referenced during our studies of that Court in particular. Refusing to let my mind wander anymore, I feigned ecstasy as Chandler sheathed himself twice more before shuddering and spilling himself inside of me. I thanked Buyhay, the Goddess of Life, for my contraceptive tonic, as I did after each of our joinings, and sat up as Chandler shimmied his pants back up to his waist. His labored breathing filled the silence in Chandler's dormitory. It was several moments before he spoke again.

"That was great." *It wasn't.* But we would never be honest with each other about that. We found comfort in each other long ago which manifested in a physical connection. We didn't dare hope for more in this life and sins of desire were best left in The Court of Passion.

"It was. Thank you." We both recognized the half-truths in which we spoke to one another, but we chose not to acknowledge it. We were only allotted so much in The Living Lands, and with one final week until the Pledging Ceremony, it was clear that we both felt the weight of the impending event firmly on our shoulders. After the ceremony, there was a strong possibility that we might never see each other again. It was imperative that we soak up the small bit of comfort we had created for ourselves - while we still could.

"Are you nervous about tomorrow?" He asked. Even if he hadn't brought it up, the approaching date had rarely drifted very far from my mind. The Final Compatibility Trial.

Throughout a student's time at the Institute they are exposed to each of the seven Courts of Verihdia and tested on their compatibility with each of them. It is a specialized program that allows each child of The Living Lands to experience - albeit in a watered-down capacity - the best and worst each Court has to offer so that at the Pledging Ceremony they can make an educated and well-researched decision. The Final Compatibility Trial is a Mythica-induced challenge that, when completed, reveals the Court the student is best suited for.

The result we receive at the Final Trial follows us until the day we expire.

"A little," I admitted. Truthfully, I hadn't allowed myself a moment to truly think about the implications. In all my time at the Institute as my brother, my friend, Riley, and Chandler found themselves gravitating towards a specific Court, I never quite felt at ease with any of them. Even though this was how the Pledging process had been run since the very inception of the Courts, it truly baffled me that anyone felt completely confident in choosing to spend their lives dedicated to a Court they've never seen, never even experienced. Perhaps that's why I still hadn't made up my mind. At this point, only a week until the Pledging Ceremony, every graduate at least had an idea of which Court they planned to Pledge their life to. Except me. The decision haunted me so heavily that I resolved long ago to choose whatever Court the Final Trial deemed me best suited for. It was easier that way. Why make a choice when this Trial could make it for me? However, a nagging feeling in my chest kept gnawing at me, asking the question 'what if the Trial is wrong?'

"I guess I can see why. This is pretty important to you, right? Since you don't know yet?" He crossed the floor and sat down on the large black armchair in the corner of the dark room, leaving me to sit alone on his bed. I adjusted my skirt, sliding it to rest comfortably on my soft curves, and swung my legs over the side before looking at him. His sandy blonde hair was tucked behind his ears, and his shirt was unbuttoned just enough to offer a peak at his toned chest. His physique was impressive, and honestly quite intimidating. His Mythica manifested in such a way that improved his physical strength, to a formidable degree. It was something he often showed off. He stood a little taller than seemed natural, and his muscles bulged as his power ran through his veins. He was one of the children who knew which Court he wished to Pledge to within the first year of schooling.

The Court of Shadows.

Known for their trickery, Shadow Pledges were often seen as liars or thieves. Assisting others only when it benefited them. Their silver tongues were frequently used for trapping innocent Uncourteds into unfair bargains. They covet what every other Court has but cannot obtain, so instead, they settle for their secrets. Why Chandler felt so drawn to such an envious Court was beyond me. Although, I guess I too often felt the sting of jealousy at the way he so clearly had a vision and direction for his life. Perhaps I wasn't one to judge.

"Yeah. I suppose that's true. I bet you feel like this is more of a formality at this point for you, huh?" He smiled, and I had to admire his beauty. He had a strong chiseled jawline and his pale skin was virtually unblemished. If I was one to indulge in the sins of The Court of Passion, he would be a worthy partner.

"Of course. I've known where I belong since I was a child." Again, the envy gnawed at me. He was so sure of himself, so sure of his place in this world. I bit my lip, letting the thought fade away. Maybe I did belong in The Court of Shadows after all.

"You're not nervous at all that you may get a different result?" I don't know why I asked it, but by the time I had thought better, it was already through my lips.

"Not at all." He spoke assuredly, but I could see the slight twinge behind his eyebrow as he looked out the window of his dorm room to the courtyard below. This time of year the students had finished their school work and traded their books for flying discs and balls that were being tossed from hand to hand as they joyfully bounded across the green expanse.

He was holding back. I saw the fear dancing behind his eyes, subtly, as if it was merely a whisper. If I didn't know him the way I did, if I didn't have an intimate relationship with fear, I wouldn't have noticed it.

Before I could stop myself, I felt the dark cloud of my Mythica ignite within me.

Why are you lying to me, Chandler? What are you afraid of?

The silent question floated across the space between us until it found its mark in Chandler's mind. His eyes snapped towards me unwillingly as his mouth opened and words spilled out, despite the vehement protest in his eyes.

"If I don't receive a Court of Shadows result, I'll choose it anyway, even if that means I risk being rejected and labeled Uncourted." The words tumbled from his lips as if being torn from the very depths of his subconscious. Which they were. His clouded eyes blinked once...twice and suddenly his gaze focused on me, filled with fury. With a harshness lacing his tone, he exclaimed, "Lexa. I told you never to do that to me again." His fingers gripped the armrests so fiercely that his knuckles turned white from the strain.

I was no stranger to this particular response. My Mythica often elicited strong reactions. And none of them were ever positive. All it took was a silent and simple question, and I was able to learn an individual's deepest fears, desires, and guilt. There was a time, long ago, when I had not yet learned to control my Mythica when its use created massive rifts among the other students at the Institute, and even some of the Uncourted Instructors as well. I have long since learned to control it but still tried to limit its use - seeing as people often didn't appreciate my prying. As evident in the rather furious, handsome man who sat across the room from me.

"I'm sorry, Chandler. I could tell you were hiding something from me... I just–"

"You decided I had no right to my secrets?" He snapped. I let my chin fall, and turned my eyes to the ground below me, anxiously twirling a strand of my long black hair between my fingers.

"The Court of Shadows deals in secrets too," I whispered in defense.

"The Court of Shadows takes secrets in payment, Lexa. And they are always freely given." He was right. I nodded slowly.

"I'm sorry. It won't happen again." He scoffed before standing abruptly from his chair and stalking towards the door. Opening it with a quiet rage, he looked back at me.

"Listen, I need to get some sleep before the Trial tomorrow...so..." he paused.

"Yeah. I should get going anyway. It's late." I slid off the cotton sheets that adorned his bed and dashed across the floor towards him. At his full height, he stood a solid nine inches taller than me. I was of average height for a female, it wasn't hard to tower over me, but Chandler often cast a large shadow on those who stood in his vicinity - in more ways than one. I tossed one last look at his umber eyes, completely emotionless, before dipping through the door. It closed behind me without so much as a moment of hesitation. The sound of the deadbolt echoed through the empty hall and I winced.

Way to go, Lexa. Burn every single bridge in your life, why don't ya?

The journey to my quarters was not a long one, but I managed to prolong it by taking painfully slow steps through the halls of the massive Institute. Vaulted ceilings and ancient gothic architecture combined to solidify this building as the most gorgeous venue in the entirety of The Living Lands. The two-story tall windows that decorated the halls allowed the moonlight to flood through, casting wicked shadows on the floor that seemed to reach out for me with each shame-filled step.

One week. That's how long I had left in this beautifully tragic building. Even if I was labeled Uncourted at the ceremony and forced to remain in The Living Lands for the rest of my days, I would never again be a resident of the Verihdian Institute. One week left of the life I had grown accustomed to. One week left of the simple existence I had learned to love despite its many glaring flaws. One week until I made a choice that would decide which of the many futures I had envisioned for myself would come to fruition.

Suddenly drowning in my dreams every night was the least of my worries.

TWO

*M*y best friend's hand in mine was the only thing grounding me to this plane of existence as we walked in silence to the Observatory Sanctum where the Final Compatibility Trial would take place.

"Lex, if you grip my hand any tighter you're going to be escorting me to the healer's office." Riley Wynn, my closest and dearest friend, aside from my flesh and blood, smiled at me slyly. Their usually angular pixie-like features softened as they looked at me. Their dark blue hair was pulled back into a small bun at the back of their head, drawing attention to the shaved sides. They, like the other students in the hall on their way to the Final Trial, wore the Institute-required white cloak with golden trim. I pulled my hand from theirs and apologized half-heartedly. Although my friend had already clearly shown an aptitude for the healing Mythica best aligned with the members of The Court of the Undying, and I didn't think they would mind a trip to the healers on campus, I truly did not intend to hurt them.

"You look like you're going to faint." Their hazel eyes were tinted with worry.

"I'm ok, Riley. Really. I just... today is important to me." They nodded in understanding but didn't push. I appreciated that about them. To this day, Riley and Axel remained the only people in my life on which I hadn't used my Mythica. I intended to keep it that way. Although I spoke the truth about my nerves to Riley, there was another reason I was so tired, so dead on my feet. An explanation that I kept safeguarded even from them. My nightmares. Thrashing in water, lungs burning, no escape. I hadn't had a good night's rest for as long as I could remember; some nights were worse than others, and last night was particularly difficult. Even now, I still felt the echoed sting of the salted liquid in my lungs. But that was my burden to bear. If I had it my way, Axel wouldn't know about the nightmares either, but I couldn't hide them from him when he was my roommate all through childhood. He was the exception. I didn't need anyone's pity or worry. These dreams were as much a part of me as anything else.

"Do you think the rumors about the Trial are true?" They asked casually, bringing my focus back to their face.

I hope not. I thought. The rumors about this Final Trial began when we were old enough to know of its existence and each speculation was more outlandish and terrifying than the last. Some say we were set to face off against a giant creature in battle and how we chose to deal with it would determine our suited Court. That thought always delighted the wannabe warriors of The Court of the Vanguard. Gladiator battles and bloody fights of honor in their Chaos Colosseum were not only commonplace but a near requirement there. But that option seemed to worry those who showed an aptitude for The Court of Passion. What were they going to be expected to do? Seduce the creature?

Despite the many rumors and the amount of Uncourted in the Living Lands who had gone through the Final Trial, no accurate account of what to expect had ever been given. Walking through these halls with my best friend among the other students in our Pledge class, it was obvious that we all knew we were walking into the unknown.

"Lexa! Hey! Wait up!" An instant flood of calm washed over me at the rich sound of my brother's voice.

"Axel, I was worried you were going to sleep through the whole thing. We knocked on your door." I smiled at him as he squeezed in between Riley and myself. Looking at my twin, it was impossible not to see myself. We shared so many things in common. Not to mention the unique convention of our names. We were often teased for it growing up, but I loved it. It felt like I had a piece of him always with me, right there in my name. Like looking in a mirror. Something that I'd surely be thankful for when we were separated after the Pledge. I looked forward to asking my parents if there was any significance behind the choice when I met them.

If...I meet them.

Shaking that off, I studied my twin. His bright blue eyes, clear complexion, and dark black hair were almost an exact match to mine. We were nearly identical aside from his lean muscular frame compared to my thick and soft curves and the slight tan that he achieved by spending hours out in the sun in the courtyard with his friends playing games. His nose and jawline were more defined than mine and he often sported a dark shadow of a beard on his face. He threw a muscular arm around me and smiled one of his 'I know I'm charming, and you love it' smiles. I elbowed him in the ribs before leaning into his hug.

"Eh, you know I'm not too worried about this whole thing today. I'm pretty confident in my Pledge." My twin was Vacant, an individual without Mythica, so he understood at a young age he would need to work hard to find a place where he truly belonged, since he had no abilities to assist in the decision, like Riley. When he heard that even those who could wield Mythica in The Court of the Vanguard were not permitted to utilize it during Gladiator fights, he knew he would do anything he could to become a Verihdian Gladiator. Gladiators were a bit like celebrities in Verihdia. Each year, they'd hold tournaments at their home colosseum in The Court of the Vanguard. The news of these tournaments spread far and wide, citizens eagerly placing bets, and cheering for their favorite to survive each combat. The Verihdian Institute was honored to host one Gladiator event a year. Folks from every corner of Verihdia would gather in our small ampitheatre that was transformed into a venue fitting of a battle royale. The first time we were old enough to attend, I saw the light in my twin's eyes as he watched the bloody performance with glee. It was love at first decapitation.

He trained, and he worked tirelessly to sculpt his body into the perfect machine. Did I particularly enjoy the prospect of him fighting to the death in a colosseum filled to the brim with blood-hungry monsters who would want nothing more than to see him fall prey to an opponent? Absolutely not. But at least he knew without a doubt what he wanted. The same could not be said for me.

There's that envy again.

I felt my twin's gaze on my face, studying me. Despite my attempt to cover up the dark circles under my eyes this morning, I know he saw them. He pulled me closer, and squeezed my shoulder, pity coloring his expression. He knew me too well.

"Axel, we were just talking about what we're expecting from this Trial. What do you think it's gonna be?" Riley linked their arm through Axel's and the three of us continued down the hallway, arm in arm.

"Something terrifying. The Uncourted wouldn't be so secretive about it if it wasn't something to fear." He had a point.

"I think it's some elaborate joke to scare us when in reality it'll be as easy as any other test we've taken before, " Riley was quick to retort. Axel's eyebrows furrowed at that.

"If it was easy, it wouldn't be a proper test of character. After this, we are supposed to know, beyond a shadow of a doubt, which Court we should choose at the Pledging." Axel's voice softened in this rare moment of seriousness. "This isn't like the tests we've taken before."

"I know. But I can dream, right?" Riley shrugged, but their face contorted in such a way that reminded me of my own hesitations. I leaned into Axel's side and reached around to squeeze Riley's arm comfortingly. Less than a week until we decide. And no matter which Court I chose, the three of us would never again be together like this. At least never in this capacity. Axel was set on The Court of the Vanguard and Riley's heart and talents truly belonged to The Court of the Undying. In less than a week, we would separate, and begin living the lives we had trained for, leaving the Institute, and the people we met here, behind us. I squeezed tighter.

"Well if it isn't my worst students." My heart warmed at the familiar authoritative voice. I turned my head in the direction of the call to see Oliver Thorne, Institute instructor, leaning up against a pillar. His short-cropped dark hair was peppered with grey, and his blue eyes were such a dark hue they almost looked black from a distance. He wore a casual white tunic over dark pants and draped on his shoulders was the same Verihdian Institute robe that we wore. The robe, like ours, was a bright white with gold trim with the crest of the Institute proudly embroidered on the breast.

The shield of the crest boldly displayed the Court Marks of all seven Courts of Verihdia, and framing the shield from behind was a U-shaped sprig of laurel leaves.

"Admit it, you're going to miss us." Axel taunted, removing his hands from around Riley and myself to shake the instructor's hand. Oliver laughed, deep lines forming in his cheeks and just beside his eyes as he joyfully shook.

"My life will certainly be a lot less interesting without you three around." He scanned each of us fondly, nodding slightly as he made eye contact with me.

"Do not lump me in with those two. I'm a great student!" Riley protested in jest and the four of us fell into a fit of laughter.

"So are you going to finally tell us what to expect in that room?" Axel asked, and I watched Instructor Thorne's face carefully as he considered it.

"Let's just say…" His gaze flicked around the hall, leaning in so we were the only ones who could hear him, an edge of seriousness to his voice. "I hope you're ready to run for your life." In unison, our heads lowered to survey our choice of footwear. The boots I was wearing were comfortable, but I never had to run in them. Panic seized my heart.

And then Oliver laughed, bending slightly at his waist and resting his hands on his knees. Axel let out an incredulous laugh.

"You're just plain evil, old man, you know that?" Riley's hand lashed out, gently slapping Oliver on the arm.

"I couldn't resist." He said, hands up in a defensive position. "Listen, you don't need to worry. The Trial won't throw anything at you that you are not capable of." His gaze landed on me.

"Axel, Riley, mind if I speak to Lexa for a moment?" Oliver clapped Axel on the back, giving him an encouraging smile before reaching out to squeeze Riley's hand in his. "Remember to trust your training." Axel and Riley murmured their thank yous, and started down the hallway, with the several other students who were shuffling in that direction.

"You seem nervous, Lexa." Instructor Thorne was, without a doubt, my favorite teacher. Not because I particularly loved his subject - Court Conditions - his Mythica granted him the ability to manipulate weather, so each day the temperature in his classroom was designed to mimic the climate of a different Court so that we knew what we were getting ourselves into. I learned quickly not to bring my books with me on The Court of Echoes days, seeing as the entire room became a raging thunderstorm. No, I liked him because he had this uncanny ability to always understand me, to read me better than even my brother sometimes.

"I am." He nodded, running a hand through his salt and pepper hair. "Whatever it tells me today, that's where I'll Pledge." I made that promise to myself a while ago, after years of hearing Riley, Chandler, and Axel declare their intentions so confidently.

"You haven't felt drawn to any Court at all?" It wasn't accusatory, or confrontational. He just wanted to know. Another reason I appreciated him.

"Not one that's strong enough to devote my entire life to it." That's the issue really. Of course, I had found things I liked and admired about each Court, that was the intention with all these courses. But I also found things I disliked. Nothing felt quite right.

"I understand." I didn't know if Instructor Thorne was Uncourted by choice or by necessity. He could have Pledged to a Court that rejected him, or maybe teaching here was always his passion. His Mythica certainly made him an excellent addition to the teaching faculty here.

"What was your result?" It wasn't necessarily a taboo topic, in fact, most people were thrilled at their results and shared them with anyone who would listen. But I have noticed that Uncourted people don't often share that information freely. I worried, only briefly, about betraying Oliver's trust with this question, but my urge to know the answer was stronger than the fear of asking it.

His eyes narrowed and he watched me carefully from behind the curtain of his dark eyelashes.

"Would knowing my result settle your nerves?" He asked calmly. Would it? I thought about that for a moment. Did I want to know if he chose Uncourted on purpose? Sure. Would it make me feel better? I'm not so sure about that.

"Probably not," I answered truthfully. He exhaled through his nose and nodded gently.

"Then forgive me for not sharing." He leaned forward placing a hand on my shoulder and applying the slightest bit of comforting pressure. "Trust your instincts in there, Lexa. Do not do what you think is correct, do what you know you must." A tear slid down my cheek as I nodded, letting his words sink into me.

"Thank you, Instructor Thorne." He smiled softly, a twinkle in his dark blue eyes.

"Please, my favorite students get to call me Oliver." I wiped the tear from my cheek with the back of my thumb.

"I thought you said we were your worst students." I joked and his shoulders rose and fell with silent laughter.

"Worst and favorite are not mutually exclusive." And with a wink, he started down the hallway, away from the Observatory. I watched him go, counting his steps, prolonging the moment of calm that he had brought me. But it couldn't last. The hallways had begun to clear and it was time for me to complete the Final Trial. The twenty-five years I spent living in these halls have all led to this. I turned away from Oliver and began my trek into the rest of my life.

Our Pledge class shuffled into the Observatory Sanctum, the large room with a magnificent glass ceiling was used for many things throughout the years, classes, socials, and lectures…but today the space had been completely emptied. There were fifty-six students in my Pledge class, and as we filed into the room, we instinctively spread out and found our own spot in the space. I weaved through my classmates to catch up to Riley and Axel who had found open space next to each other. I slid in between them.

Idle chatter filled the silence, but the tension in the air was palpable. I glanced around the Observatory at the faces of my classmates. People I have known for a quarter of a century, my entire life - people with fear and uncertainty etched on their faces. A look that no doubt also graced my own features. A classmate, Callum Andras, was nearly jumping out of his skin with excitement, while others looked pale and anxious. My eyes landed on the familiar muscular frame of Chandler Mills. I knew I should probably be feeling the weight of our fight, but I guess in order to feel heartbreak, your heart had to be involved in the relationship. In our case, it certainly wasn't love between us. Friendship though. Definitely friendship. So instead of crushing heartbreak, I felt guilty. Guilty that I caused discomfort to someone who often brought comfort to me. Guilty that I often sought out physical connection with him while offering no emotional bond beyond friendship. He didn't look at me, but I could tell by the tension in his shoulders that he knew I was watching him, and he was forcing himself to ignore me.

Perhaps his heart was involved. I could always find out.

I banished that thought the moment it arrived and made myself a silent vow. I would not use my Mythica on Chandler Mills, ever again. Just as I had declared that to myself, the double doors on the far side of the Observatory Sanctum swung open, and in walked The Seven.

The Deans of the Verihdian Institute, known as The Seven, are Uncourted individuals who at the time of their Pledging were offered a position as Court liaisons to The Living Lands. It happened so infrequently and was considered to be the greatest honor ever bestowed on an Uncourted. Each member of The Seven was hand-picked from their class by the Wardens themselves and offered the position at their Pledging Ceremony. They of course had the choice to decline and instead Pledge to a Court, but no one ever said no to a Warden's offer. The Seven are the only Uncourted individuals who bear the Mark of a Court and therefore are the only Uncourted individuals who are permitted to travel through the veils. Their primary purpose at the Institute was to create the curriculum and ensure that each student was appropriately exposed to each of the Court's traditions and cultures so that they could make a balanced and well-educated decision.

The Seven strode through the double doors, shoulder to shoulder, displaying the image of a completely level playing field, even now. They had substituted their usual casual tunics for long hooded cloaks, the colors representative of their Courts, with the embroidered Crest of the Verihdian Institute on their breasts. They came to a stop at the head of the room and the silence that followed their arrival was one of eager anticipation. We rarely saw The Seven all together, and by rarely I mean that we had only seen them all in the same room once before. The year we began our specialized Court education. They entered the space, much like they did now, cloaked and hooded, and described the purpose of the Court Compatibility Trials, the Courting Ball, and eventual Pledging Ceremony. Back then it seemed so far away as if it was the responsibility of someone entirely different in a completely different world. And yet, here they stood again, prepared not to usher us into our training, but out of it.

The figure in the long red cloak lifted their hands to remove their hood. Damon Howden, the Dean of Echoes, lifted his head to scan the crowd before him. His bright eyes were a stark contrast against his dark brown skin as he studied us, scanning us methodically as if he could see right to the very soul that resided inside.

"Congratulations Pledges. Today you embark on the final leg of your lifelong journey of discovery." Damon spoke clearly, and dispassionately as if he barely believed the words he spoke. To be fair, members of The Court of Echoes were known for their lack of empathy - or really any emotion other than the pure unbridled anger that seemed to motivate all their actions. It was apt that The Court of Echoes held dominion over the Sunken Province Prison, home to the most vicious and vile criminals in all of Verihdia.

"Today, you complete the Final Court Compatibility Trial." This time, the soft dulcet tone of voice came from Vitrola Gorgan, the Dean of the Undying. She lowered her powder blue hood at a glacial pace and smiled slowly at us. My eyes had barely settled on her before the pink-shrouded Dean of Talisman chimed in. "Today you will learn where you belong," he cooed as if comforting us with the very sound of his voice. I felt Axel's hand squeeze mine at that statement.

Where will I belong?

I gave Axel a reassuring smile that I knew could not have reassured a stranger, let alone the one person who knew me as well as I knew myself. His eyes clouded with worry and his lips downturned slightly with the promise of a frown, but I leaned into his arm and turned my face back to The Seven at the front of the room so I would not be subjected to his burning gaze any longer.

"By now, you not only know the history of Verihdia and the Courts, but you understand their importance in our way of life." This was Keegan Morsoe of The Court of Silence. I wondered if Keegan specifically requested the line that spoke to the Court's importance, seeing as the governing faction of The Court of

Silence quite often felt the need to remind every living soul of its crucial purpose in our survival. His brilliant hazel eyes complimented the golden thread of his cloak. I could have sworn I saw a glint as his gaze passed over us.

"It is imperative you remember, that while we encourage you to take your result today into account, the final decision is entirely yours," Salazar Forwright of The Court of the Vanguard spoke proudly, his broad chest puffed out, his bright smile on full display as he lowered his royal purple hood. A comforting statement in theory, sure. Although, it wasn't exactly true. We'd heard the same spiel hundreds of times, but if history had taught us anything, those students brave enough to attempt Pledging against their Final Trial result, were more often than not rejected and forced to live as Uncourted for the rest of their lives.

"You will be tested today in ways you never imagined. You will be forced into positions you have only ever dreamed of." The euphemism that flowed easily from the painted mouth of Bellamy Vicious was not unusual. In fact, getting through a conversation with the Dean of Passion without an innuendo would be the odd occurrence. Bellamy's black cloak, eye makeup, and pitch-dark painted lips made them look alluring and mysterious. That was the point after all. "Lay down," Bellamy whispered. "Now." The demanding tone also was not uncommon - members of The Court of Passion were not shy when it came to giving commands. Or following them.

For a brief moment, the Observatory Sanctum was filled with the sound of fabric rustling and joints cracking as we lowered ourselves onto the cold stone floor. From my new position, I was forced to look at the glass ceiling. It was early morning, just before the rise of the sun, so the remaining night sky mixed with the morning light beautifully in an exchange of focus. I could still make out a few of the constellations.

It was Lilith Hargrove, the Dean of Shadows, who was the last to lower her hood. The dark green fabric pooled around her powerful shoulders as she surveyed us with an antagonistic gaze. I tried to focus on her, but my heavy head kept falling back to look at the ceiling. A thick fog slowly began creeping its way along the floor, blanketing all of us in a shroud of darkness. Whatever this Mythica was, I don't think I'd ever come across something like it before. It covered us and my eyes suddenly became very difficult to hold open.

"When you are finished with the Trial, you will wake to find a small stone resting on your chest. Open it immediately, and then exit the Observatory. Do not wait for any other Pledges. The Trials will affect everyone differently. Some of you may finish within the hour. While some may not complete it for days."

Days?!

I tried to swallow my shocked gasp, but the unsettled murmur that traveled through the crowd at the same moment told me I wasn't alone in my discomfort at that tidbit of information. I did not enjoy the prospect of losing those days, days that I could use to spend with my brother, with Riley, even with Chandler if he let me. I silently begged that my test would be completed in a swift and timely manner, but I couldn't wallow in that worry for long because the cloud of Mythica above me had taken hold. Sinking into the depths of my mind, beckoning me to join it in the recesses of my subconscious.

"Good luck." Lilith's voice was the last thing I heard before it all went dark.

Lexa

THREE

My senses came back to me in waves. First, I could taste. Salted wind thrashed against me, assaulting my tongue as my mouth hung open begging for breath that seemed to elude me. Then, the smell. The strangely raw and rich and yet familiar scent of the ocean, rushed through me just as I heard the distant cawing of seagulls and the casual crashing of waves against a shore. My heart constricted for a moment as I fought the panic that threatened to crest. My hand pressed into my chest, the pressure calming me. This wasn't like my nightmares. I wasn't drowning. I was alive. Then, I could see it.

I stood alone on a miniscule island in the middle of a vast, unending sea. If I took more than a couple of steps in either direction I would be greeted by the dark waters with which I was more than acquainted. The coarse black sand beneath my feet was warm, the sensations felt so vivid, so real. The mist off the waves gently caresses my cheek, as the warmth of the sun in the sky pressed into my skin like a welcome embrace.

I tried to call out, but my voice did not come. I couldn't produce a single sound. My mouth hung open as I strained against my invisible barrier. I clawed at my throat in frustration as tears threatened to fall from my ocean-colored eyes.

It's a test.

My hands fell to rest at my sides and I forced myself to take deep calming breaths. This was why I was here. To be tested. To be pushed. To determine the true grit of my character.

With fresh resolve, I wiped the cresting tear away with the back of my hand and turned to analyze my surroundings. The sunless sky prepared to turn to night as it stretched across the canvas above as far in every direction as I could see. I felt my heart pound against my chest as if it was asking...what now?

I don't know.

"Lexa Cromwell." My name echoed through the expanse, the sound seemingly coming from every direction, in no particular tone, as if every sound around me had forged together to create the words. The cawing of the seagulls and the crashing waves joined the wind to speak to me in a disconcerting cacophony.

I tried to speak again, but still, the words did not come. Instead, I thought the words in silent response. The way my own Mythica was wielded.

I am Lexa Cromwell.

A benefit, I decided, of using my internal voice was that the fear that coursed through my veins was easier to hide than if I were speaking aloud.

"Do you know where you are?" The strange melody asked.

The Final Court Compatibility Trial.

As I thought the words, I turned on my heel to survey the area behind me. Still, nothing appeared. Nothing but the wide-open immensity of the ocean. I took a moment to study it. The dark blue expanse looked beautiful, peaceful even, from my position, but the chill that descended my back reminded me of the vicious nature of these waters. This ocean was a familiar antagonist for me, now watching me as a passive spectator. Perhaps it was pointless, but I stood tall, refusing to show the waters any of the fear it had spent my entire life instilling in me.

"Technically, you are correct." The words taunted in jest. I furrowed my brows at the insinuation.

And literally correct as well, I believe. Seeing as that is exactly where I am.

I bit back through the channels in my mind, attempting to avert my gaze from the lazy waves.

"Perhaps." The whispered sounds grew to a quiet crescendo before falling off into a calm hum again.

What is my Trial?

I don't know how long I awaited a response from the cacophony, but it felt like several minutes. I counted how many times the waves crashed onto the black sand at my feet. Two. Three. Four. Ten. Twenty.

"Only the greedy judge freely. Only the vain elude their part. Only the jealous benefit from the choice." The sounds danced around me, ebbing and flowing with the waves. *"While the passionate use their heart."* The wind picked up to a terrific speed, and the black sand my bare feet stood on was being ripped from its resting place to join the storm of wind around me. *"Only those who want in excess, judge with selfish need. While those who tire of the expense of time, judge to end the deed."* The sand continued in its torturous torment of my skin as the wind thrashed it around and around until just before me it came to a climax in two large funnels of dark sand and damp air spiraling ferociously. My arms reflexively rose to shield my eyes from the storm. *"The moral judge with deeper knowledge, understanding every pledge. And the raving, with hearts of black, instead judge for revenge."*

The black sand settled as the wind died down to reveal two individuals kneeling on the ground in front of me. Their naked forms were hunched over in shame or pain. Perhaps both. Their hands were tied tightly behind their backs and their sand and grime-covered hair fell over their faces in a curtain of fear.

If I could scream, I would have.

What is this? What did you do to them?

"They have sinned, Lexa Cromwell, and now you will choose their punishment.

Release. Jail. Or Death." The waves crashed, the birds cried and the wind carried the sound to my ears in a taunting barrage. I could have fallen to my knees right then, and if I didn't know that at this moment I was being tested, I might have.

What are their crimes? I asked the wind in a futile attempt to postpone the task asked of me.

"You have four minutes."

My heart rate spiked again. Four minutes. In four minutes I needed to decipher these men's sins and decide their fate.

You're being tested, Lexa. I reminded myself. *This isn't real.*

"Please… please let me go." The whimper came from the man on the left, for the first time since appearing in the cloud of sand, his eyes rose to meet mine. He had a handsome face, but it was ragged from weeks, maybe months of neglect. His shirt hung open to reveal a deep and fresh wound, evidence of an attack of some kind. His dark brown eyes clouded with tears that fell freely, carving a path through the dirt that had collected on his cheek. "Please." He sobbed.

My fists clenched at my side. This is why I was here. I had a task, and I needed to complete it. With a deep breath, I let my eyes drift closed, and I reached for the well of Mythica that lay deep inside me and mentally caressed the edges of it, coaxing it to the forefront of my mind.

What did you do? What are you guilty of?

I am no stranger to using my Mythica to learn about people's fears and desires. However, uncovering guilt was a facet of my power that felt too personal, even to me. It felt like I was ripping the flesh off to reveal the soul beneath, I didn't like the power it gave me over someone else. With fear, there was a possibility that I could assist them in overcoming it. With desires, I could try to give them what they wanted, or find someone who could. But once I knew someone's guilt. I couldn't absolve them of that. I couldn't change what they had done. I could only hold this truth over them, and that wasn't typically the type of power I wanted to wield. However, today, it is exactly what I needed to do.

His face contorted in pain, and the veins on his neck bulged as he fought against the truth that I was coaxing from his lips.

"I…" He stuttered, biting his tongue to keep from spilling the secrets of his worst deed. "I…" He cried out in pain as my Mythica gripped the truth within him and pulled. "She wanted to leave me. I couldn't let her. I couldn't let her leave. I could have been her everything, but she wouldn't hear me. I didn't mean to kill her." His cries filled my ears but I didn't dare let them affect me. A murderer. He was a murderer. Did that mean he deserved death himself? I saw the guilt that I had drawn from him plastered on his red face as he cried and fell forward into the sand. His shoulders heaved with his pain. The corrupted love he felt for this woman was etched on his face, his soul, in his very breath. It had driven him to a place so dark and empty that he would never return. A scoff drew my attention away. I turned to the other bound man, he seemed cleaner, as if he hadn't spent as much time in captivity as the sobbing man next to him. His eyes remained on the sand below. His body sagged with defeat. This man has already accepted his fate. I could see that.

And you, sir? What is it that you are guilty of?

His eyes rose to meet mine and I gazed into the empty void behind the blue of his irises. There was no fear, there was no desire. Only guilt, and unlike his companion, he gave it freely.

"I was not the father I should have been. I was not the father she deserved." I let his words sink in. Guilt, of course. But a crime? "I could have saved her. I can't live on without her. Please." Begging for death. His crime must be despicable.

Is that why you are held captive?

He bowed his head and frowned deeply but offered no explanation.

Sir, explain why you are bound here before me.

Again he remained silent. The wind began to pick up and I knew my time was running out. I needed to make the right choice here. I needed to get this right. My entire future depended on it, and I supposed the futures of the men at my feet as well.

Tell me, damnit!

I screamed through my mind. I wanted to force him to understand that if he didn't tell me he might die unjustly, but I wouldn't let my emotions drive this moment.

I knew what I had to do. There was a facet of my Mythica that I so rarely explored, mostly because it truly frightened me. I could bring this memory to the forefront of his mind, and force him to relive it, for my own personal viewing. It was an ugly power, the type that could bring strong-willed individuals to their knees before their own trauma. It was a dangerous tightrope that more often than not led to destruction. I had learned long ago not to utilize this dark corner of my Mythica. However, with the time running out, and our futures hanging in the balance, I knew there was no other choice.

I reached inside the well again, pushing deeper within my soul to the darkest depths where the worst of my intentions lie to grab ahold of the power I needed to get my answer. The dark tendrils of Mythica climbed up through my senses clouding my vision until all I could see was a shadowed silhouette of the man before me. I tilted my head, locked eyes with him, and uttered one simple phrase.

Show me.

The man screamed as if he had been hit by a tidal wave that began to sink him below its massive weight. He cried out to the sky in desperation, begging Kamatayan, the Goddess of Death, to make it swift. The shadows behind my eyes cleared and then I joined him in his nightmare.

A younger, cleaner version of this father stood in a small room. The floors were a dark brown wood that creaked under the weight of his anxious pacing. The walls were empty canvases of beige, and one solitary window was the only light source, bathing the room in an amber hue. I took a breath, as the man before me mindlessly picked at his fingers in front of him, his eyes fixed on the singular exit.

The wooden door swung open, the man stopped his pacing as a beautiful young woman entered timidly through the doorframe. Her features were soft and gentle, but the resemblance was undeniable.

"Hello," the father squeaked out, his words bubbling into nervous laughter. The woman visibly relaxed at the sound of his voice, her eyes softened as they embraced. I bit my lip to restrain the cry that threatened to spill from my chest. My desperate desire to embrace my father consumed me.

Just as I regained composure, the room dissipated into smoke and the memory shifted.

The father led his daughter on a tour of their new Court - Silence, I deciphered, based on the swamp lands that the two traipsed together.

The memory shifted again, and again, and I watched as these two strangers became a family. My heart swelled with pain because I knew how this story ended.

Then he came into the picture, the other bound man, but in this memory, he was not the blood and dirt-covered pleading man I saw, he was suave, put together, a perfect gentleman. That is the role he assumed. That is the lie they believed. I watched with regret as this father saw his daughter fall in love with a monster in disguise.

Flashes of moments, the tiniest of aggressions, a minuscule argument, unexplained bruises, withdrawal...She was slipping away.

And yet he said nothing.

He said nothing when this man's anger proved volatile, he said nothing when his daughter's smile disappeared, he said nothing.

And then it was too late.

His guilt was overwhelming, tangible, I nearly choked on it as he cried over her grave. He saw the signs, he watched it happen, and he did nothing.

The memory shifted once more, this time in a dark prison cell, the father crept in silently, his bare feet padding across the cold stone floor towards the sleeping man. His eyes burned with a dark fury. How dare this man sleep peacefully, when his daughter was dead?

He raised the silver dagger above his head, a rage-filled expression coloring his face as he brought the blade down, thrusting it into the sleeping man's chest.

The man screamed, the sound drowning in blood, but despite that, there was no satisfaction etched on the father's face, as he realized there was no revenge great enough for *what this man took from him. In a moment, he turned the dagger towards his own heart, I gasped, nearly intervening before I remembered that this was just a memory.*

Guards called out, rushing into the cell, grabbing hold of the father, and tossing his dagger to the ground. He cried out with a type of pain I could only ever imagine, as the vision slipped away. His scream echoed through the smoke, imprinting itself on my soul.

I fell from his vision with a force that nearly toppled me to the sand below. His quiet wince was the only sound that reminded me I was no longer in the desperate fractured memory of self-hatred. But his pained screams still softly played in my mind.

Do you regret attempting to murder this man?

I asked, my eyes trailing to the other man's chest, seeing the burning red evidence of the attack.

"I only regret that I was not successful in ending either of our lives that day." The other man scowled but did not respond.

I shook my head and fell to my knees before this father. This man so deeply hated himself for not protecting his daughter, for his failure, that he sat here before me, begging for death. He felt the sharp sting of a loss so deeply, that I wasn't sure his blackened soul could ever recover, and I saw on his face, in his eyes, that he never wanted to breathe another gasp of the air that his daughter would never have the chance to taste again.

I didn't notice that tears had begun crawling down my face until they landed on my lips and the salty taste stung my lips.

"Time's up," the sounds returned in whispered dissonance. I stared at the men before me. A murderer, and a broken man.

"What is their punishment?"

I knew what the 'correct' answer would be. The lawful answer that the governing faction of The Court of Silence would expect. And I knew the passionate answer, the one that defied logic, but made the heart feel healed. I knew what the wrathful Echoes or the jealous Shadows would require. I could tell you the many different combinations of punishments that could align me with any Court of my choosing. However, I didn't dare listen to what I thought they would want from me.

Do what you know you must. Oliver's words pulsated at the back of my mind.

Then, I gave the only answer I could.

Jail the murderer. Allow him to spend the rest of his life alone and be forced to do nothing but think of his crimes.

The dark brown eyes of the man on my left widened in shock.

"You won't see me killed?" He asked as if he had just won some incredible gift.

You deserve to sit with your guilt. Forever. I hope when you close your eyes you are haunted by her eyes, I hope when you see the scar on your chest you are reminded that you survived because his dagger could not penetrate a heart you don't have.

His eyes darkened and his mouth opened as if he planned to speak again, but he disappeared in a cloud of black sand, leaving only myself, the broken man, and the wind.

"*What of this one?*" The man's gaze did not leave mine. The vision of pain was so visceral I thought I would never feel a moment of reprieve again as long as I live. His hollow eyes did not cry, not anymore. He had used them all. There was nothing left of him.

Kill him.

Two words. Two words and everything changed. His blue eyes for the first time since arriving on this island flooded with emotion. One that I could name easily. *Relief.*

He looked up at the sky and I watched as he took a shaky breath before turning his gaze back to me. As the wind and sand began to pick up again, encircling us both, he nodded to me through the cloud around him, and I saw him mouth his own two words back to me.

'Thank. You.'

Then he was gone.

And I was alone.

The waves crashed casually against the shore of the black sand-covered island. The night sky now blanketed the canvas, and in the darkness, there was no voice in the wind, there were no prisoners in the sand, there was no witness to my tears.

Darkness flooded over me, cradling me in the warm embrace of nothingness and suddenly gone was the island, gone was the ocean, gone was the Trial and I heard two words calling me back. "Good Luck." I sat up with a start, unleashing a gasp so loud and deep it felt vaguely like I was awaking from my nightmares. It wasn't until I felt the eyes of Lilith Hargrove fall over me that I realized where I was. I placed my palms flat against the cold stone floor of the Observatory Sanctum to ground and steady myself. Whispers of the black cloud of Mythica were still enveloping the ground and the students that lay on it.

"Lay down Pledge, the Trial has begun." Damon Howden's declaration burned into me from across the room.

"I...I, what," was all I managed to squeeze out of my mouth. It felt strange having use of my voice again.

"Damon, calm down, will you? Look, she has her stone already." Keegan stepped forward and placed a hand on Damon's arm. My head was still spinning when I glanced down onto my lap to see what the Dean of Silence was referring to. The small obsidian sphere sat nestled in my lap, its inky depths swirling with smoky tendrils of color as if the Courts themselves were fighting to determine which one would claim me as their own.

"My my, that's the fastest anyone has ever completed the Final Trial. Even faster than you, Lilith." Bellamy's seductive timber sang with the taunt, and it certainly found its mark. Lilith's eyes darkened with distrust as she studied me. For a moment, I thought she might attack me, and maybe she would have if we had been the only ones in the room. I didn't want to think about that.

"Well? Go on girl. Break the stone. Get your results." Lilith's voice was stiff, quick, and unyielding, but it was not difficult to notice the disdain lacing every single word.

Gripping the sphere in my hand, I turned my attention away from The Seven who stood watching me expectantly. They received the results themselves after the Trials concluded, they would know what was in my sphere no matter what, but something about them watching as my future showed itself to me made me feel exposed in a way I never had before. Lifting the sphere to eye level I studied the object as the streaks of color danced and chased each other within the orb. The moment before I crushed the stone to my forehead I could have sworn I saw a wave of pure white crash inside the darkness within.

I did not have time to confirm the strange image though, because as the sphere cracked, the smokey tendrils spilled out and enveloped me in a rainbow of possibilities. Each one grazing my skin, begging to be let in. Then my vision blurred.

Fragments of images were all I could see, bits and pieces of the future my result had planned for me. First, a dark black ocean, raging in a storm that would not relent. Next, a massive shadowed figure floating just beneath the surface. Then a broken building with shattered windows and moss-covered doors. Followed by a whispered plea in a voice I couldn't place. *'Find me.'*

Once again, I was dragged back to the Observatory with a gasp, my shoulders quivered with my uneven breaths. For a moment all I could see, taste, and hear was that raging ocean. The salt still burned my lips. It felt as real as my nightmares had. And yet, I knew it couldn't be.

"Well? What was your result?" Lilith's agitated question drew my attention back to The Seven who stood patiently waiting to hear the result of the fastest Final Trial in our history.

"It's... it's supposed to be obvious right? I'm supposed to know without a doubt which Court I'm best suited for?" I asked, my voice hoarse and unsure. I silently wished I could think the words again so as not to depend on my shaken voice to relay my question.

"You saw fragments of pictures, moments in time right?" Vitrola Gorgan spoke slowly and deliberately. I nodded. "Each stone gives a personalized result, but they all will point to one of the Courts. What did you see?" Her lips turned up in the corners at an achingly slow pace.

None of the images I saw made any sense. I had studied the different Courts my entire life, I knew their traditions, their landscapes, their weather patterns. I knew what I would have seen if my result had aligned with any one of them. A few of the Courts had small oceans, bodies of water, but none that looked like that. None that felt so vast... so consuming. So familiar to the image I often dreamt of. Perhaps it was a blessing that The Seven were still here. They would explain my result. Because it had to mean something.

"I... I saw a raging ocean. An abandoned building... a storm..." I stopped myself before recounting the final part of my stone's message. Those two words were still echoing in my head. I don't know why, but it felt like a secret for me and me alone.

A long moment passed in silence as a few members of The Seven exchanged knowing glances, but Lilith's gaze remained locked on mine. Her disdain for me was painted clearly on her face.

"Are you sure that is what you saw?" Vance asked, he ran his hands cautiously down the front of his blush-colored cloak.

"I'm positive," I responded. Damon and Salazar shared a hushed exchange, far too quiet for me to hear from my distance across the Observatory. Keegan's eyes studied me as if he thought he could find some sort of lie in my body language. Lilith still did not tear her eyes from mine.

What are they hiding?

I didn't dare use my Mythica here, despite the voice within me that begged for me to rip the truth from their silent judging stares.

"What does it mean? What Court am I suited for?" My voice was desperate. I needed to know. Whatever the result told me is what I would choose. I had promised myself that. I couldn't make good on that promise if I didn't know what Court the vision had referred to.

It was Lilith who spoke first. "It means that you are destined to be Uncourted," Lilith spoke with a clear tone, an edge of declaration to her voice so that I would not doubt her words. *Too late.*

Uncourted? Uncourted. Has anyone ever crushed one of these stones before only to be told they belong to no Court at all? I hadn't heard of any instances. It didn't make any sense. The Seven all looked at me with what I assumed to be pity in their eyes. The poor Uncourted girl. Her incredible speed in the Final Trial was not due to anything other than the lack of need to truly test her. She didn't need any more time. We knew where she belonged. Nowhere.

But still even as I began to accept the possibility that Lilith presented, the images within the stone replayed in my mind, beckoning me to reconsider. I pressed my lips firmly together and banished the thought. The Seven would not lie to me. They just wouldn't.

"Uncourted," I repeated, trying to grow accustomed to the taste of that word on my lips. It was my future after all - I should be comfortable with the feel of it on my tongue.

"I'm sorry for your unfortunate result," Vance spoke softly. "But remember the choice ultimately still lies with you." Vance's reminder was met with warning glances from both Damon and Salazar. Vance lowered his head slightly before exiting the room and Vitrola, who had a solemn look etched on her face, followed close behind. One by one they left the Observatory until Lilith was the only member of The Seven who remained. Her harsh gaze was relentless. I didn't speak. I had no words. Instead, I watched her and tried to understand her. To see her words for the lie I so desperately wished they were. Normally, I would use Mythica here, but I couldn't do that. Instead, I relied on my knowledge of body language. One thing was abundantly clear by the burning gaze, the angled brows, and the crossed arms. Lilith Hargrove was furious with me.

But why?

Moments later she turned on her heel and left the Observatory through the double doors leaving me, and fifty-five of my unconscious classmates, alone.

I didn't hesitate after that to leave back the way I came only minutes ago.

Goddess, how was it only minutes ago? So much has happened.

I left the Observatory and didn't dare look back. I rushed to my room and found myself entranced and staring at the dark wooden wall when a knock at my door sounded many hours later.

"Lexa! Let me in!" My brother's jovial tone meant one thing and one thing only. He had gotten the result he was hoping for. I took a deep breath. How was I going to tell him? Was I going to tell him the truth of what I'd seen, of what I had to do in my Trial? Was I going to tell him I was destined to stay here for the rest of my life? "Lexa! Come on! I know you're in there. Twin thing, ya know?" I smiled for the first time since before The Final Trial and moved to open my door.

Axel spilled in quickly, clasping his hands together and spinning around in an effervescent display of pure unbridled joy.

"I've done it! I am suited for The Court of the Vanguard! Can you believe it?! All that hard work and I did it! I may be a Verihdian Gladiator yet!" His blue eyes danced with euphoria. I laughed slightly at him as I sank onto the end of the bed. My heart swelled with pride for a moment before a dark cloud of envy shrouded the enthusiasm. My brother was going to Pledge to the Court he fell in love with, and they wanted him there. He belonged there. I didn't belong anywhere. Not even here.

"I'm so happy for you, Axel." My words were not imbued with the emotions that should have corresponded with my words. Instead, they fell flat in the room, utter despair flowed through me.

"Lex…What's wrong? What was your result?" He moved until he was on his knees on the ground in front of me. His hands rested gently on my knees.

"I don't want to ruin the moment. I really am so proud of you." He beamed at that, but then the concern crept back into his expression.

"Don't change the subject, Lex." A strand of his dark black hair fell in front of his eyes, I watched him study me. He knew me better than anyone, but I'm not sure even the closest of bonds would allow him to discern what it is that truly ailed me.

"Uncourted," I spoke the word again and it tasted just as stale and harsh as it had the first time. Axel was quiet and his eyes darted across my face, searching for the lie he and I both wished was there.

"You're kidding." It wasn't a question or an accusation. He spoke the words as if he could will them into truth if he said it confidently enough.

"I wish I was." And it was the truth. I didn't have my heart set on any particular Court, but I have never doubted that I would find a home in at least one of them. Maybe my time in the Institute, never quite feeling at home or comfortable with any of them was the first sign that I didn't belong. I should have listened to that nagging voice inside.

"You're not going to choose that though, right? You can still pick something else." His reminder was more demanding than Vance's had been earlier. "You can't stay here. You can still choose a Court. They'll accept you! You have Mythica!" He wasn't talking to me anymore. Not really. He was throwing his suggestions at me, furiously hoping one of them would stick.

"They could reject me," I whispered. It was the unfortunate risk of choosing to Pledge outside of your result. Of course, as everyone so graciously points out, you always have the final choice in which Court to Pledge to, no matter the result of our Final Trial. However, the Warden and Dean of each Court reserve the right to reject the request - and they often do. Why would the Warden of a Court, whose job it is to keep their Court strong and satisfied, ever allow someone in who didn't belong? In every Pledge class, there's one or two brave enough to attempt to Pledge against the result. And for the last 10 years, every single one of them had been rejected. Every. Single. One. Axel knew it as well as I did. Although he wasn't thinking logically at this moment.

"It's ok, Axel.. shh. It's ok." I reached up and placed my palms on either side of his face. His expression was full of the hurt I refused to let myself feel. Not here. Not with him.

"It's not. You don't deserve this."

Then why is it happening?

"At least this way you can always come to visit me." I joked in a foolish attempt to lighten the mood. "You know I can't risk being rejected. I want to learn about our parents." He nodded at that. Once you Pledge to a Court and it is accepted, you are given a golden envelope. This envelope contains the identities, and Court, of your parents. Students whose Pledge is rejected on the day of the Ceremony do not receive this envelope. If I were to Pledge Uncourted then I would get to know who they are and which Court they belong to. That's worth it to me.

I've desperately wanted to know the truth about my family from the moment I could acknowledge the reality of the situation. I've wanted to know them so badly that I've even made questionable - horrible - decisions to preserve that chance for myself. I used to fantasize about the night I Pledged to a Court and received that coveted golden envelope. In my fantasy, I always chose the same Court as them - although which Court it was shifted nearly every time - and we were finally free to become the family that we could have been.

With Axel standing firmly with one foot in The Court of the Vanguard and my future pointed squarely at the Uncourted village just beyond the marketplace in The Living Lands, I knew my dream of living as a family was all but shattered. But the thing I was holding on to was that I could still know who they were. I didn't want to jeopardize that by attempting to Pledge outside my result.

"This isn't fair." He leaned forward until his head rested on my shoulder. I held my arms around him. My brother. My other half. It wasn't long ago that he fell ill and I was forced to think of the possibility of a future without him in it. It was a future so dark and lonely that I'd give anything to avoid it. Almost anything. So now, when I had the chance to hold him, to truly embrace my twin, I took it. With the results of The Final Trial behind us, I couldn't help but feel the overwhelming weight of this new reality pin me firmly to the ground. We must have stayed there for hours because by the time a second knock sounded at my door the sun had completely crept beneath the horizon outside my window.

Axel pulled back on his knees and moved to the bench that sat beneath the window. His icy eyes glistened with the remnants of tears.

"Come in," I called, shakily.

Riley bounded in with a giant smile plastered on their face. The Court of the Undying no doubt. They were happy. I was envious.

Speaking of envy. Chandler took cautious steps through the open door behind Riley. His expression was one of complete and utter content.

Everyone around me is getting exactly what they want. What they deserve.

I couldn't help but wonder if this was all happening because I chose to kill the innocent man in the Trial. My choice was not one born from logic or anger, not even empathy. I just understood him. I knew what he needed. Perhaps that choice was what led me to the result I got. Perhaps that moment was the reason I will be stuck to live the entirety of my life within the confines of The Living Lands. Maybe taking Oliver's advice led me to this bleak future. Despite all that, I couldn't bring myself to regret my decision, even now.

I have no idea if the men I met in my Trial or the crimes they did and did not commit were real or if the entire thing was nothing but an elaborate illusion. Some Mythica wielders have been known to possess the type of power to conjure images like those that I saw during my Trial.

Even so, it felt so real. The mist off the ocean, the taste of salt on my lips, the rough sand on my feet, the wind caressing my face, the guilt. Oh gods, the guilt I felt when I used my Mythica on that second man - the broken man - it had felt so real. Raw. While I can logically assume that those men never existed, their crimes were simply a figment of some illusionist's imagination, and the island was nothing more than a location with the sole purpose of throwing me off center, fostering a tense environment to test me - I couldn't shake the shadow of pain and guilt from the broken man that I knew would follow me to the day I die. I had no doubt about that.

"Did someone call for a healer?!" Riley exclaimed boastfully. I stood to wrap my arms around them, holding them in my embrace tightly, hoping they could not sense my own growing jealousy as I hugged them.

"I knew you would get what you wanted, Riley. This is amazing news!" Riley beamed proudly.

"What? No hug for me?" Chandler asked from his position near the door. I released Riley and eyed him questionably. Last we talked he was kicking me out of his dorm, now he was asking for me to embrace him?

"Only if you tell me your result." I teased. I could tell by his stance, and by the fact that he wasn't destroying everything in his path that he received exactly the result he had not only hoped for but expected.

He only nodded happily at me. I rushed forward to toss my arms around him.

"The Court of Shadows will be lucky to have you, Chandler." He relaxed into my hold and his fingers trailed lazily up and down my spine. I placed my lips near his ear and whispered "I'm sorry about yesterday." His hold tightened on me.

"Already forgiven." I released a sigh I didn't even know I was holding at that. Chandler and I may not be a mated pair, but that didn't mean that his company wasn't important to me. That I didn't value his companionship. Because I truly did. So when I pulled back from Chandler's embrace, my smile was genuine.

"What a freaking doozy, huh?" Riley asked, plopping down on the mattress. "You get what you wanted, Axel?"

Axel had somehow managed to compose himself in the few moments since our solemn embrace and the mask of joy and pride was well and firmly in place.

"You know it!" He smiled and Riley reached their hand out to pat him on the back.

"Alright, that leaves you, Lex. I've been dying to know what you'd get. Wait, don't tell me, let me guess!" Riley flipped onto their stomach and smiled brightly like we were at the beginning of a game that led to four winners. Axel and I shared a glance, both of us knowing that I had not won today.

"My money is on Talisman." Chandler pitched in as he slid down to the ground with his back against the wall and found a comfortable sitting position.

"No way, unless that's what you actually got? No, it's Passion, isn't it? I've got a sneaking suspicion that you're a freak in the sheets. Chandler, please feel free to chime in." Riley continued.

"No, Chandler, do not feel free to comment on that," I interjected with a laugh. There was a huge chance he'd confirm the exact opposite, plus my brother was sitting less than five feet away from me. I desperately needed to avoid that particular line of conversation.

"Well... what is it?!" Riley's anxious question hung in the air. Their smile was bright and their tone was celebratory. I couldn't bear to look at the faces of the people I cared about most in this world looking at me like I needed pity. So maybe it was because of that, or maybe it was because I still hadn't found a way to say the word without it resulting in a bad taste in my mouth, that I said what I did.

"It's a surprise." Axel's gaze flashed to mine, and one of his eyebrows arched in challenge. I ignored him.

"Come on! You can't do that to me, I'll go wild!" Riley whined. I laughed and plopped down on the bed next to them.

"We've gone twenty-five years without knowing which Court I was best suited for. We can go five more days." Riley scoffed but eventually gave up. I was thankful for that. Five more days of pretending would be nice. The more I thought about this plan, the more I liked it.

Chandler and Riley began discussing the details of their Trials. Riley had to climb a mountain with limited resources and had come across several injured individuals along the way. They had to decide how and when to use the very few resources they had. They beamed when they talked about how they were able to create medicinal pastes from organic matter to help the injured and barely had to dip into the resources they were given at all. They had used their Mythica to mend the truly horrible wounds, and used their own experience and training for the rest. I really was proud of my friend. There was not a doubt in my mind that they belonged in The Court of the Undying.

Chandler recounted the task he was sent on in his Trial. A woman came to him, asking for help finding her son. He helped, for a price of course. He really was well suited for The Court of Shadows. Coveting what he didn't have, and finding a way to take it.

Axel practically exploded with excitement as he regaled the tale of his gladiatorial match. A colosseum was full of spectators chanting his name, screaming for him to fight, to kill, to win. He won. Of course, he did. I didn't like to hear about the circumstances under which he won though. One bad fight, that's all it would take for me to lose my brother forever. Well, lose him even more than I already would. I had a taste of what it would be like to lose him not too long ago, and I never wanted to feel that again.

Their chatter continued late into the night, I told them that if I recounted my Trial for them, then it would give away the result. My little way of keeping my secret close to my chest for as long as I could.

Riley and Axel left just before midnight together. Axel had either forgotten about my predicament or was doing a fantastic job of hiding it because he only smiled at me and hugged me the way he always did before heading to his room. Riley squeezed my hand and asked "You'd tell me if it was Undying right? You would... You'd have to. Right?" I only laughed.

Then it was only Chandler and me. He turned to me, the afterglow of his result still prominently showing in his every move, and pulled me in for a kiss. It was quick, abrupt, and before I was even able to fully comprehend and sink into it, he pulled away again.

"Today's been... Gods. It's been perfect, you know? When everything is as it should be?"

I nodded because I didn't trust my voice not to betray me.

"I needed to make things right with you. I know you didn't mean to use your Mythica on me again. And everything is just so perfect. I need us back where we belong too." His fingers caressed my arm. His eyes trailed the length of my body. It wasn't hard to guess where his mind was headed.

Maybe I could use the distraction.

I stood on my toes and kissed him again, this time taking my time to melt into it, forcing the events of the day to the back of my mind.

Make today disappear, Chandler. Make me forget. Please.

He answered my silent plea by lifting me into his arms, my breasts flush against his broad chest. My legs wrapped around his waist and I could already feel his growing erection through the layers of clothes that separated us.

He carried me to my bed and laid me down on my back. Pulling away from our kiss, he looked down at me from his position above me. Always above me.

"You know how to make me feel good, Lexa." He murmured, resting one hand on the bed near my head, and loosening the fastening of his pants with the other. Moments later his length sprang free and pressed into me over the material of my clothes.

"Why don't you take those pants off and let me show you how a member of The Court of Shadows can fuck." I nodded, ignoring the sting that I felt at his confident declaration, and hooked my fingers in the waistband of my pants, sliding them down my legs until I could kick them off onto the floor. He wasted no time before wrapping his fist around his length and guiding it towards my center. "Are you ready for me, Lexa?"

I knew by the resistance that he was met with at my entrance that I was not. He groaned in frustration.

"Not yet, baby. Well, let's see what I can do about that, huh?" Chandler dragged one of his hands down my body until he reached the point between my thighs that begged for attention. With one hurried finger, he slid directly into me, ripping a pained moan from my lips. He swallowed the sound with his mouth on mine.

"That's right baby, I can take care of you," he whispered against my lips. His breath smelled faintly of the peanut treats we had all shared a few hours ago.

"Why don't you make sure I'm taken care of too, ok baby?" he withdrew his finger from within me and wrapped his fingers around my wrist, guiding it down until my hand closed over his length. He moaned.

"Yes, that's it." He closed his eyes and thrust his hips, his erection sliding through my fingers. I watched him carefully. Studying his reactions. Despite our lack of sexual connection, I truly did want to make this an enjoyable experience for him. For both of us.

He continued his thrusts into the curve of my hand for a few minutes in muted silence, cursing every few moments and offering words of encouragement. It felt like ages before his hand returned to my apex. I found myself lifting my hips to meet his fingers again. He slid one inside, and moved quickly, timing the thrusts of his hips into my hand with the movement of his fingers inside of me. I allowed myself to focus on nothing but the feeling of his hands where I needed them most, banishing any thoughts of the Trial, or the Pledging Ceremony. At this moment, Chandler was giving me exactly what I needed. Exactly what I craved. A distraction. I knew that I was offering him exactly what he needed as well. A celebration.

He pulled his finger out from my folds, now slick with my arousal, then moved to position himself above me and his hand replaced mine on his length.

He settled between my legs and directed the head of his hardened member to my opening. It slid in easily this time, an inch, two, more. He slammed into me and cried out.

"Goddess!" He began moving, pulling out only to thrust inside of my sex again. Over and over, methodical, rhythmic. And it felt good. My mind wasn't drifting to thoughts of the Ceremony or the broken man who I sentenced to death. No, my mind wasn't analyzing every facet of the vision I received from the stone. I wasn't thinking about those things at all. Definitely not.

Chandler's pace quickened and his breathing became labored and I knew he was close to a climax. I adjusted my hips against him, hoping, begging for friction to rub me where I so desperately needed it.

Oh goddess, yes there.

A wave of pleasure rippled over me as my adjustments forced just the right amount of pressure on the sensitive bundle of nerves.

Oh, so this is what it can feel like.

My eyes rolled back in my head and I let this new sensation wash over me. But just as I felt the beginning of my own climax building, Chandler thrust into me one last time before spilling himself inside. I whimpered involuntarily at the loss of friction against my swollen bud. His body collapsed on top of mine.

"Goddess, you make the best sounds, Lexa." He murmured against my neck before planting a single kiss there and pulling away. Unsheathing himself from me completely. Leaving me unsatisfied, and desperate, especially after getting just a taste of the desire that Bellamy from The Court of Passions keeps talking about.

He stood from the bed and pulled his pants back over his hips and secured them. He leaned over the bed and placed a stiff kiss on my forehead. Transactional.

"I'm going to miss this after The Pledging Ceremony, Lexa." This. Not me. He will miss this.

I smiled at him meekly before he exited the room, leaving me behind with nothing but the night sky and my thoughts.

FOUR

*W*hy *did I choose this color?*

I stood alone in my room in front of the full-length gold-framed mirror. Tonight was the last event before The Pledging Ceremony tomorrow. Then, it would all be over. Riley, Chandler… Axel. This time tomorrow, they would be arriving at the veils of their new Courts, ready to embark on a brand new adventure.

Their new life.

Without me.

I had spent so much of this week practicing how I would tell them. Forcing myself to say the word Uncourted as often as I could until it didn't feel foreign anymore. It hadn't worked yet.

Meanwhile, Riley and Chandler packed the entirety of their dorm rooms into bags that sat patiently waiting by their doors. They couldn't wait to get out of here. I don't blame them.

Tonight was The Courting Ball. Once an extremely important part of the Pledging process, but rarely anymore. The ball is thrown for two purposes. The first is to celebrate the last night as Pledges. Never again will any of us be students. Never again will any of us walk the halls of The Verihdian Institute as Pledges. Some may never see this building again in their entire lives. This was a final celebration of the twenty-five years we lived and learned within these halls, with these people.

The second, and far less common purpose of the Courting Ball was to allow the Wardens of each Court a chance to meet and entice certain students into Pledging to their Court.

After the Final Trials, the results are sent not only to The Seven, but directly to the Wardens of the Courts along with an assessment of our strengths, weaknesses, and Mythica - or lack thereof - conducted here at the Institute. The Wardens are then granted the opportunity to have one night to use their influence to sway someone's Pledge.

When the Courting Ball was new, the Wardens would attend frequently, with hopes of stealing special individuals, most often those with unique Mythica, from their fellow Wardens. However, in the last several decades of the ball's history, it became increasingly rare for the Wardens to attend. In fact, most years none of them attended at all.

Only one Warden has attended in the last fifteen years, The Warden of Silence. He attended twice within a few years, but both of the Pledges he spoke to ended up Pledging to their resulting Court anyway. It had become so commonplace to Pledge to the Court that you received as a result of the Trial that there was little to no use trying to sway anyone's mind anymore. So instead of being Courted at the ball, this event had turned into a way to celebrate the Courts they intended to choose the following morning.

And say goodbye.

I had very little to celebrate, and I had even less to be excited about but attendance was required. So that is why I found myself standing in front of the gilded mirror, admiring myself in the floor-length emerald gown that hung from my shoulders and hugged my curves tightly. There was a time when I despised finding the right clothing to dress my larger body, but with Riley's assistance, I found the right style for me. Two thin straps held the garment up, and a long deep V in the front traveled down to just below my breasts, showing off more cleavage than I was used to. Flaring out just slightly at the waist, the skirt had a golden shimmer effect that glistened in the light as I shifted back and forth. The folds of the dress draped down the floor in a stunning cascade of viridescent wealth. It was more risqué of an outfit, showing a lot more skin, than I normally would choose, but Riley had insisted I looked "As hot as the fires of the Sunken Province Prison" and call it selfishness, or call it confidence, but I wanted Chandler's eyes on me and only me tonight. My life as an Uncourted began tomorrow and for one more night, I wanted to feel worthy of something special.

My long black hair fell down my back in large bouncy curls, and I even let Riley convince me to darken the lids of my eyes. Then I reached for my mask. The tradition of the Courting Ball being a Masquerade originally began so that if the Wardens did attend to sway a Pledges loyalty from their suited Court, they may do so with anonymity. Honorable in thought, but impractical in practice.

In a class of around fifty students who had grown up together in close quarters for the first twenty-five years of their lives, no mask would be able to hide their identities from each other. And I couldn't imagine that a measly swatch of embroidered fabric would dampen the prowess and stature of the Wardens. But despite their impractical purpose, they were still a requirement for the ball. Tradition is something that Verihdians tend to hold onto long after they should let go.

I lifted the black lace mask to my eyes and tied the silk ribbons behind my head. Analyzing myself in the mirror, two thoughts immediately came to mind. One, I have never felt more beautiful and two, I looked nothing like myself.

Good.

I didn't want to be me tonight. Not the Uncourted girl with nothing extraordinary about her. I wanted to be something else. Something better.

A knock against the door frame tore my gaze away from the confident stranger in the mirror. Chandler inched the door open and slid inside the room. He wore dark-colored breeches with a white shirt and black doublet. His dirty-blonde, normally shaggy hair was slicked back.

"You look very handsome tonight, Chandler." I placed my hand on my hip so that my hourglass shape was even more prominent and waited for him to comment on my attire for the ball. His eyes darted over to me, and then passed me to the mirror.

"Thank you. I knew I had to look my best tonight. Especially since one of them is coming." He strode into the room and stood next to me in the mirror, admiring himself in the reflection.

I had to clear my throat to swallow the string of curses that bubbled within me and cover the pathetic whimper that threatened to spill out from my lips.

"What do you mean by one of them?" I asked, moving away from the mirror, giving Chandler full use of it.

"There's a rumor that a Warden is attending." My heart skipped a beat. A Warden? This year? Why? And for whom? "I don't want to get my hopes up or anything, but I have shown skills that would be useful in multiple Courts. I can guarantee they stated as much in my assessment. That coupled with my Final Trial being such a success. The Warden may be coming to sway my allegiance." I managed not to roll my eyes at the conceited notion, but only barely. He might be right. His Mythica offered him a physical advantage over others. I could see The Court of Echoes wanting someone like that guarding their prison. If that were the case, then The Warden of Echoes would be leaving this evening rather disappointed. I'm positive nothing would deter Chandler's fixation on The Court of Shadows, maybe not even death.

"That would certainly be something, wouldn't it?" I advanced across the room towards my door. "Why don't we go then, wouldn't want to keep the Warden waiting."

Chandler turned to face me, the eagerness practically oozing from his pores, so thick I might have drowned in it.

"Yes, let's." He paused only briefly at the door to allow me a moment to slip my arm into his and then escorted me through the winding halls of The Institute to the Grand Ballroom.

Equally anxious Pledges walked arm in arm towards the event as well, dressed in bright colored gowns and handsome suits. No one but the current Pledge class is permitted to attend the Courting Ball, and yet each year we've watched as the entire Institute turned into a frenzy of preparations - the decor being hung, the dresses being made. We watched as the oldest class moved gracefully down the halls towards the event, longing for the moment to be ours. Even now, as Chandler and I traversed the halls, eager heads poked out of the rooms of the younger students, their eyes scanning us, admiring all of the glittering dresses, and handsome tunics.

I had once done the same. Craned my neck outside my door to catch just a glimpse of the beautiful women, the dashing escorts, and the handsome men as they ventured into the ballroom. But now, at this moment, I wished I could go back to being the person admiring from the sidelines. There I may have felt left out, I may have begged for time to move faster so that I too could participate, could feel as beautiful as those women did, but at least I had a future to look forward to. Or at least I thought I did. Now instead of floating across the stone floor with my head held high and my heart pounding with anticipation, each step felt as if my feet were encased in stone and it took every ounce of my strength to continue forward. I was suddenly thankful for the mask, hoping that it could hide some of the reservations that surely showed on my face. My shoulders were hunched over and I slumped against Chandler's solid frame as we arrived at the massive dark wooden doors to the Grand Ballroom, which opened wide to offer an invitation into the decadence that was just beyond its threshold.

The large circular ballroom lay directly in the center of the Institute, in the exact center of The Living Lands. If you were to stand on the Verihdian Institute Crest that was painted in bright white paint at the center of the dance floor, you would be the same distance away from every Court in Verihdia. Seven empty thrones of varying design and material sat on small platforms along the outer ring of the room, from dark golden blocks of impressive wealth for The Court of Silence to a deep black satin draped throne for the Warden of The Court of Passion. Each Court was represented by these thrones and as I stood there, I couldn't help but feel as if they were taunting me. Chandler encouraged me forward into the space, pushing past the entrance of the ballroom and into the last day of normalcy. The rest of the room was frenzied with activity. Dancing had already begun, and several of my classmates and some of our Instructors twirled with laughter around the open floor as the stringed symphony played a mysterious dark waltz that invoked a type of melancholic joy.

Everywhere I looked, my eyes were met with a new display of decadence. The food carts piled high with the delicacies of each Court that we had rarely been offered the privilege of indulging in here in The Living Lands. The rafters of the room had been strung with strands of Starlight that shimmered and danced, basking the entire room in an ethereal glow.

My eyes caught on Axel as he spun a young woman in a deep red gown by her hand. His blue eyes matched the ocean-colored mask he wore. A silver doublet graced his figure. He looked every bit the shining star I always knew he was and could be. He smiled brightly when he saw me. I bowed my head in his direction but made no move to approach him. It would have been selfish of me to dampen his excitement with my sour mood, so when Chandler made to whisk me away towards the other end of the ballroom, I let him. I scanned the crowds of my classmates, a sea of masks and smiles. The eager energies could be felt to my very core. There was no doubt in my mind that this event would end with many of them well into their cups and I would not be surprised if a significant amount of celebrations ended in a bed that was not their own.

Chandler stopped our walk just before the throne of The Court of Shadows. He admired it with a dark glint in his eyes. This throne defied all logic, and instead of a solid surface, it looked to be thick green smoke packed together into the form of a chair. I'd never seen anyone sit in it - of course not, only the Wardens were permitted on the platforms with the thrones and there hadn't been a Warden at one of these events in years - so I wasn't sure it was actually able to be sat on or if the Warden would just fall right through to the ground below if he tried. I stifled a laugh at that image playing in my head.

"Maybe one day I can be Warden of this Court." My gaze snapped to Chandler just in time to witness his face twist in the type of look a man only gets when he covets something. Something he knows he can't have.

It was a silly notion of course. The Wardens were immortal and had held dominion over their Courts since their inception a few centuries ago. They needed no successor or heir. I hoped for Chandler's sake he was able to extinguish the thought long before anyone important heard him. I knew it would not end well for him.

"You shouldn't say things like that, Chandler," I whispered against his arm.

"Of course not. Just a dream I had, that's all." My grip relaxed. "But wouldn't that be something?" I didn't dare respond. As an Uncourted, any sign of treachery was punishable by death without trial. I simply stood and watched Chandler as he leered at the smokey mass of the throne before him.

Out of the corner of my eye, I saw the familiar green robe of Lilith Hargrove cut through the crowd towards us. I tugged on Chandler's arm to alert him of her impending presence. He bowed his head as she approached us.

Lilith wore a white mask that covered her entire face from hairline to chin, but the judgment in her eyes as she looked at me would have been clue enough of her identity had her green cloak not given it away.

"Dean Hargrove," Chandler spoke confidently. "You look wonderful tonight."

He wasn't wrong. Beneath her green cloak, she wore a forest green silk suit with golden buttons. She bowed her head in thanks but offered no verbal response.

"Miss Cromwell?" She spoke it as a question, but the look of disdainful recognition in my eyes told me she knew well and truly who I was.

"Yes, Dean," I answered curtly. "Good evening to you."

Lilith studied me for a moment in silence. Chandler needed no other invitation to interject.

"I heard rumor of a Warden's appearance tonight." Lilith's eyes did not leave mine, and I found myself unable to look away. Perhaps it was pride, perhaps I did not want her to see my weakness, or perhaps she had paralyzed me to my very core with her icy stare.

"The Seven have been tasked with receiving a guest tonight, yes." She spoke carefully. She clearly wasn't allowed to tell us who it was, or perhaps she was but chose not to. Either way, the vague answer was just enough to make Chandler clap his hands in front of him as he laughed.

"That's excellent! What a historic moment for our Pledge class to be a part of." He smiled then, and his lips stretched from one ear to the other. It looked painful. Perhaps it was. Lilith's eyes finally left mine and turned to analyze Chandler.

I released the breath I unwittingly had been holding just as she spoke again. "A historic moment indeed." Something in the tone of her voice sent a chill down my spine. Maybe I could excuse myself for the evening. I made an appearance. My brother saw me, Dean Hargrove saw me. No one could challenge that I had not attended.

"Dean Hargrove, Chandler, if you'll excuse me, please have a good evening." I bowed my head slightly again before turning on my heel and moving through the crowd towards the refreshments table. If I was going to go to bed, I would at least indulge in some of the chocolate cakes from The Court of the Undying before I left.

It had to be a very special event for us to be served these delicacies. Growing up there were only two reasons they were ever brought to The Living Lands. The Courting Ball and the First Trial Festival. Seeing as I had never attended a Courting Ball before tonight, my only exposure to these delectable treats was the festival that occurred once a year, on the outskirts of The Living Lands near the veiled borders into each Court. A celebration of the very First Trial, the ones our Wardens completed to become who they were today. It was a lavish event that we as students were not only invited to but required to attend. People from each Court would cross over the veil into The Living Lands with carts of delicious foods, Court-made gifts and clothing, performances of music, spoken words, and art. It was customary to give those closest to you a gift from a Court that they do not belong to, or do not intend to belong to, as a way of truly celebrating the gift that is our Court system. It was an old folk tale that at midnight on the evening of the First Trial Festival, you could make one single wish to the Gods and it would be granted. The First Trial Festival was nearly a month and a half away, and it had been far too long since I had tasted these magnificent treats.

Before I could reach out and grab one of the mouth-watering delicacies, a comforting voice called my name behind me. I turned to see Oliver Throne approaching. He wore his white robe over dark pants and a navy blue shirt. A dark blue mask covered the left half of his face. He smiled brightly as he came to a stop in front of me.

"Lexa, you look beautiful tonight," he held out his hand for mine and as I slipped my hand into his grip, he kissed it and bowed slightly. I nearly laughed at the sight of someone bowing to me. As if I deserved that.

He stopped my hand and moved to grab a treat off the table next to me. He popped the pink cube from The Court of Talisman into his mouth and made a small noise of appreciation as he swallowed.

"I know as an Instructor, I'm not supposed to play any favorites with the Courts, but those Talisman sure do know how to make dessert." I reached for one as well, tossing it into my mouth as Oliver sucked on each finger to savor every last crumb.

"Oh…" I said, impressed. The cube melted swiftly after it touched my tongue, coating it in an intense burst of delectable sugar that lasted for a few moments.

"I apologize I've been so busy this past week. I wanted to ask about your Final Trial. How did it go?" My face fell, I hoped he couldn't see it behind the mask.

"Oh.. that. Right." Panic seized my heart. Oliver Throne had been an incredible mentor, and friend to me during my time at the Institute. The thought of disappointing him made me feel physically ill. Sweat beaded on my palms and my breathing came raggedly.

"Lexa, what's wrong," he asked, worry etched on his face.

"Nothing, I just.."

Do I tell him? Do I tell Oliver what my result is?

I was of two minds about it. On one hand, I trusted him completely and he often had just the right words to say to keep me calm and provide comfort when I needed it most. On the other hand, if I told him that my result was Uncourted and he saw how upset I was, that could offend him. I don't know the circumstances of how he came to be Uncourted. If he chose it freely, then he could see my misery as a slight. And the thought of offending one of the best people I know was nearly painful.

No, I couldn't tell him. I couldn't risk it.

"I'm just trying to decide if the result feels right. You know?" He nodded knowingly, his arms crossing in front of his chest.

"I understand that." He mused. "It's hard to see yourself in one of these Courts when you feel like you belong to all of them or none of them for that matter. Especially having never experienced them. Not really." I tried not to let my shock show on my face. I had never heard an Instructor speak so freely about the pitfalls of the Pledging process.

"Yeah, exactly. Everyone around me has such strong feelings about these

Courts. They know exactly where they belong. They feel so confident, but I don't know anything about them. I haven't seen them, I haven't felt them, experienced them. They're nothing but strange, foreign lands with secrets I will never uncover. I think that's why I never felt drawn to any of them." He exhaled through his nose sharply and nodded at that. "I want to belong somewhere, but how am I supposed to figure it out?"

"That's what the result is designed for," He said, clearly fishing for me to divulge my result to him.

"What if it's wrong?" I lowered my voice. I trusted Oliver not to turn me in for asking such a treasonous question.

"Do you think it was?" He looked at me with a type of empathy only someone who understood me could muster. I watched his weathered face twist into an expression of concern.

"I didn't say that."

But yes.

Oliver stood straight and popped another pink cube into his mouth as his eyes surveyed the ballroom. "I'm quite a bit older than you, so I like to think I have a bit of experience in this thing called life." I smiled softly at him as he continued. "So believe me when I say that the greatest lesson you'll ever learn is to be careful where you place your trust and fiercely trust the things you believe in." I felt his eyes studying me as I considered his words. "Follow your gut, kid. It will lead you where you belong."

Belong.

I lifted the mask off my face just enough to wipe the tear that had fallen before smoothing it back down on my face. Oliver simply stood, waiting for me to respond.

"Thank you, Instructor Thorne." He chuckled, the worry being washed from his face.

"If you call me anything but Oliver again, I will make it snow on you." He jokes, upturning his palm to show me the small flurry swirling there.

"Fine! Put that away!" I joked, pushing his hand aside. He joined my fit of laughter, letting his hand, and the snow building in it, fall to his side. As our laughter faded he placed a wrinkled hand on my shoulder.

"Enjoy the rest of your night, Lexa. You deserve it." Grabbing one last pink cube from the dessert table, he tossed it into his open mouth and sauntered away.

As I watched Oliver disappear into the crowd again, a set of arms wrapped around my waist from behind. I gasped, but ultimately relaxed into the hold when I heard Riley's laughter.

"Goddess, Riley, you just about stopped my heart. Is that what you want?" I turned to face my friend and offered them a genuine smile. Their short blue hair was styled up to a full point. They wore dark pants with knee-length pale justaucorps over a dark pink waistcoat. Their mask was fashioned from the same material as their waistcoat and was a bright colorful addition to their face. They looked quite handsome.

"You are easily the most attractive person in this room, Lexa. And I'm not saying that as your friend, I'm saying that entirely objectively." They scanned my body once and they made a humorous sound of admiration. I laughed with them.

"Sure." I joked, pushing their shoulder playfully. They stumbled off center and for a brief moment, I forgot. I forgot that tomorrow they would be long gone, settling into their new home while I was here.

"Sorry to interrupt." Chandler's voice cut in as he came up behind me.

"Chandler, you look nice tonight," Riley murmured half-heartedly.

"I know. Thank you." Riley almost rolled their eyes but managed to refrain as Chandler's arm draped across my back. He was beaming tonight, and I couldn't deny that he was a handsome man. I'd always thought so, in fact. When we had our first Court Traditions class, we were told to pair up with another classmate and prepare a presentation on one of the various events, histories, or traditions from our assigned Court. We were partnered together to present on The Court of the Undying.

I did most of the work, but I didn't mind, because for the first time I didn't just see a classmate, I saw a handsome young man, and I experienced something I never had before - I got butterflies.

Our attraction burned fast but simmered faster. Instead of the deep passionate connections that we witnessed growing between some of our other classmates, we had a comfortable understanding. We knew what the other wanted, we knew how to comfort each other. It was a beneficial arrangement for both of us emotionally and physically.

"Dance with me, Lexa" Before I could protest, Chandler had pulled me onto the dance floor amid the twirling skirts. Chandler's hand rested gently on my hip and I gripped his shoulder as he held me at a casual distance. I'd never claimed to be a good dancer, and despite Chandler's attempts to lead me across the floor in a winding display, I fumbled indelicately, stumbling over every turn. Chandler's laughter at my misfortune turned into aggravated grunts the longer it continued. "You are a terrifically terrible dancer," he joked in a frustrated tone, or at least I hope he said it in jest. Although, most jokes are rooted in truth, aren't they? I didn't say anything as we let the rhythm of the music direct us. My eyes focused on watching my feet, and my mind was flooded with my voice counting the steps in my head.

I was so caught up in my concentration that I didn't notice the door open. I didn't notice the dancers pause to turn in that direction. I didn't even notice the music come to an abrupt stop. It wasn't until I heard Chandler's sharp intake of breath and felt his grip tighten on my waist that I turned my gaze up to Chandler's face. He was staring, open-mouthed at the wide doors to the Grand Ballroom. His expression was one of pure, unadulterated shock. I knew there was only one thing that could cause this type of reaction. The visiting Warden must have arrived. But even as I thought it, something didn't add up. Chandler knew of the rumored visit, and yet the look on his face was not that of a person who has confirmed a rumor. Instead, an expression of wonder, of disbelief was etched on his pale handsome face.

Gasps and whispers filled the hall and I turned on my heel to face the dark wooden door to the ballroom. Suddenly all the air escaped from my lungs and I think I ceased breathing altogether. Standing there, shoulder to shoulder at the entrance to the room, looking out nonchalantly at the silent crowd that gaped at them, were all seven Wardens of Verihdia.

I couldn't entirely process the sight before me, not only had I never seen a Warden in person, but this was something out of Legends. It is as common knowledge as our names that The Wardens have not all been in the same room at once in decades, maybe longer. A few here and there, sure. Three, maybe four, but all seven? This moment, this unbelievable event would go down in our history books. It would live on, long after the students in this Pledge class die off to give way to the next generation. We were living history, right now.

And to think I almost went back to bed.

They didn't speak, instead, their eyes surveyed the crowd calmly. I'd only ever heard tales of their ethereal beauty, but hearing about it and witnessing it were entirely different experiences. I couldn't help but stare, and neither could the rest of my Pledge class. The Wardens were dressed in marvelously extravagant regalia, sporting their Court's color on the material of their wardrobe, or in the accents that adorned them. Their faces were hidden by masks that only added to their mysterious allure. Although I knew that even without the color of their attire, it would be impossible to misinterpret which Court they each belonged to. Or rather which Court belonged to them. I couldn't help but internally scoff at the person who thought these masks could ever promote anonymity or hide these Warden's natural and unmistakable beauty. Their intense and colorful eyes, stature, and demeanor alone were enough to set them apart from anyone else in this world. If they chose to speak to you, you would have no doubt in your mind who it was that was gracing you with their attention.

The silence was palpable, and it would seem nobody wanted to be the first to resume the festivities. We wouldn't, of course, until the Wardens allowed it. I didn't know what the protocol was for this specific situation. None of us did. I'd wager even The Seven were unsure of how to interact at this moment. Most of The Seven have only had their positions for a decade or two at the most, so this moment was just as new to them as it was to us. Part of that realization thrilled me, the prospect that even the most sovereign of people in The Living Lands had never encountered this before. We were all here together, a blank slate, attempting to make sense of this charged moment. If I didn't know any better, I would also wager that the Wardens themselves seemed to feel out of place, uncomfortable by the tight stances, the rigid posture, and the slight furrowing of brows. But I knew that was impossible. These Wardens never felt fear or discomfort. That is why they were given immortality by Buyhay, the Goddess of Life, and tasked with the honor of leading The Verihdian Courts. These calm and collected individuals could weather any storm without so much as a hair out of place. Or so I've heard. Until this moment, I had never actually seen one in person.

The Wardens' gazes shifted over the crowd again at a glacial pace. At that moment, it became abundantly clear, that they were looking for someone.

Of course, they are.

That's the whole purpose of the Courting Ball, they have all come here to sway a Pledge's loyalty. A sudden rush of excitement flooded my veins. Did they each have a different Pledge they hoped to speak to tonight? Or were they here for the same Pledge? Were we about to witness a Verihdia-wide pissing contest over one of our peers?

Who could it be?

Unlike my classmates, I managed to tear my eyes away from the imposing figures at the front of the room and joined them in scanning the faces of the people I grew up with. Who could they possibly be here for? Who could possibly be so important that it would warrant a visit from every single Warden in Verihdia? My eyes swept past Axel and I smiled briefly at his showmanship. He stood with shoulders back and head held high, his eyes dark with a look of determination and drive as if he was poised to say 'Go ahead, Warden, plead me your case.' Not that I didn't have trust in my brother's abilities, but I truly couldn't believe that all seven Wardens would come to this event for a Vacant, no matter how impressive my brother was. No, they had to be here for someone with Mythica. They had to.

My eyes darted to the man beside me. His shocked expression was now one of extreme pride. There was no doubt who he believed they were here for. As I was studying him, other classmates in the crowd turned their heads to look at him as well. One by one, slowly each pair of eyes landed on him. No doubt the Warden's gaze had landed on their intended target. I suddenly felt the weight of their attention, silently thanking the Gods that the weight was Chandler's to bear.

I didn't dare move. I didn't want to draw any of the attention Chandler was currently receiving away from him, even if I did feel the twinge deep inside the pit of my stomach that wished I could understand how it felt to feel that coveted, even for a moment. Instead, I stood in place at his side and watched his smile beam brightly in the direction of the Wardens.

He soaked in this moment like a flower yearning for the sunshine, taking every last drop of it to sustain himself. Then his smile faltered, slightly, slowly at first. I might not have even noticed had I not been studying his expression so closely. His eyebrows furrowed in confusion as his gaze darted for a moment across the front of the room as if he was reevaluating what he was seeing in the Wardens. His eyes turned to me, and there was a fire there that I didn't recognize, a type of anger that Chandler had never once directed towards me. Not even when I used my Mythica on him. It took all of my restraint not to cower. I knew that Chandler was a powerful and imposing man that could cause even the most secure person to flinch when he chose to - his Mythica offering him a distinct and unnerving shield of strength - I just so rarely witnessed it. I had only a moment to analyze his gaze before I felt the pressure of the attention burn into my skin. Burrow itself deep within me, clawing at me, begging for me to acknowledge it.

My own eyes scanned the crowd of classmates around us, and it was then that I saw that their focus was not intended for Chandler, but for me. There was no hiding the confusion painted on my face, even with the mask, as I cautiously turned my head to face the double doors and the line of visitors at the front of the ballroom.

There were the Wardens of all seven Courts of Verihdia, and they were all staring at me

FIVE

*T*hree more days.

I reminded myself again as the room around me bustled with obnoxious and excessive activity. The Forsaken Quarters, my home, lies in the heart of The Court of Shadows, and much to my dismay, every single year following The Pledging Ceremony, my space is bombarded with decorations and festivities of debauchery and mirth to celebrate the new additions to our Court. It had been years since I found any joy in the event. Originally, new additions to The Court of Shadows were a necessity - the only way our sliver of existence could grow to its full and impressive potential. However, in the many, many centuries since the inception of the Courts, mine has grown to meet and exceed its growth potential. I stopped caring about the new arrivals, I stopped courting Pledges. I didn't need to. My Court not only survived, but it also thrived. Gone were the days of struggle, gone were the days of fighting tooth and nail for a place at the table of Verihdia. Now I watched over a powerful Court, with no desire to change.

In three days, the Pledges will have arrived and we will have had our celebration and things can finally go back to normal. I ducked out of the way as two individuals carried a large table into the room. I rolled my eyes and bounded up the grand staircase towards my private living quarters. The entire top floor of The Forsaken Quarters belonged to me and me alone. Only one other person was allowed onto this floor without express permission.

I stormed up the obsidian stairs, ignoring the decorators' voices as they called to me with trivial nonsense. I couldn't care less how they decorated my home for their frivolous party, as long as it was entirely gone the morning after the event. Taking the stairs two at a time, I was able to avoid their prying questions and arrive at my private floor with ease.

Three more days.

My home is my own for the majority of the year. Save for the few council meetings and small events my advisors recommend I throw for the people of my Court every once in a while to make me seem 'accessible' and to boost 'morale'. Honestly, if I had my choice, I wouldn't see a damn person again for the rest of my existence. I would be perfectly content in living in solitude until Kamatayan decided to finally take me. After spending centuries dealing in secrets, half-truths, and coveting everything I never had, I've grown tired of social interaction entirely. Even the occasional nighttime visitations I receive have grown tiresome and menial. After all, I've seen and experienced in my life, nothing is surprising anymore. Nothing offers any distraction from the day-to-day desperation I'm destined to be trapped in.

I closed the door to my study behind me and sighed deeply when I noticed the familiar frame of my Dean sitting atop my desk. Lilith sat perched on the corner of the large mahogany table, she wore a dark green shirt that hung off her shoulders and perched dangerously low on her chest. Her legs were cloaked in a tight green fabric that hugged her perfectly. My Dean was a beautiful woman. She has been The Dean of Shadows for 10 years now. An honor she took willingly, as they all did. I never told her that the honor was not much of an honor at all, seeing as my previous Dean had died and needed replacing and she was the only graduate that year to produce a result in The Court of Shadows from her Final

Trial. An act of necessity, not honor. Had I been given a choice that year, I most definitely would have chosen someone with Mythica. I was the only Warden with a Vacant Dean. Which didn't bother me…until the other Wardens brought up their Mythica-wielding Deans. I am envious by nature, and my siblings knew just how to torture me, by implying that my Dean was not as good as theirs. However, Lilith had come into her own in the position and had willingly taken on the bulk of my duties, so I was thankful for that. She also made for a decent enough partner in bed for when I craved intimacy or a distraction.

Lilith slid off the desk seductively, leaning forward so that the top of her breasts were on full display for me. My length twitched slightly, less in anticipation and more out of habit.

"Do you have news for me, Lilith?" I asked coldly, indifferently. She either enjoyed that about me or was smart enough to keep it to herself if she didn't. She smiled darkly.

"I do, but I'd love to serve you in other ways before I share it with you, my Warden. I've missed you." Her eyes flicked down to the outline of my bulge behind the fabric of my trousers. I knew what she wanted to give me, and frankly, after the day I had, watching as decorators destroy my home, I could use the release. I moved to sit in the massive black leather chair behind my desk and unlaced my pants. She moved to stand in front of me and without breaking eye contact she slid down onto her knees between my legs.

"My Warden, would it please you for me to taste you?" Such a filthy mouth and it sounded so unnatural, forced even, coming from her harsh voice. I grunted in agreement because I didn't care to say anything else. She made quick work of pulling my growing erection from the confines of my trousers. Her cold fingers gripped my length and held me tightly. She ran her hand up and down slowly, teasing. Although, if growing my anticipation was her desired effect, she missed by a mile. Instead, her slow movements did nothing but instill in me an impatience that was growing with every torturous second she played the vixen.

"It's been too long since I've had you in my mouth, my Warden." She spoke quietly near my erection, her cold breath sent a shiver through my body, and she smiled as if she had elicited a positive reaction from me. I wouldn't correct her. I gripped her hair and pulled her head towards the tip of my impatient arousal. She groaned sensuously before opening her mouth for me and taking me into it.

She struggled against the size of me, taking only half of my length into her throat, her tongue awkwardly coating me. She moaned in pleasure and I closed my eyes, leaning my head back against the leather of the chair, letting my mind drift off into nothingness. Allowing the minimal pleasure Lilith was offering to drag me away from the monotony of my lonely existence.

Her warm mouth was not experienced in this act of sexual nature, although I found I preferred her company in my chambers to the many others because unlike them, Lilith never wanted anything from me. And that was worth it. My fingers tightened her hair in my fist, pushed her down onto my length, and thrust my hips into her mouth. I heard that delicious gagging sound and knew she had reached her capacity. The thought drove me forward. Her tongue wrestled me for space inside her throat. I felt the muscles tighten around me.

That will do.

I thrust into her open mouth twice more before I felt my release spill into her throat. She let out a pleased groan as if my release was the greatest thing to grace her tongue in weeks as I pulled myself from her. Her lips were slick with evidence of my arousal and my length was coated in her saliva, it shined in the candlelight. She wiped her mouth with the back of her hand before standing to sit on my desk again. This time she positioned herself delicately on the edge of the desk, resting one leg on each of the arms of my chair, spreading her legs for me. I could feel the heat pulsating from her center even from here.

So much for never wanting anything from me.

Although I have to admit, compared to secrets, power, or money... A little sexual reciprocation was not an unfair payment. She looked down at me through lash-shrouded eyes, her blonde hair messy from where my fist had held it tightly.

"Take these pants off," I ordered. If I was going to give the way she gave, I was going to get it over with. Her eyes smiled with anticipation and she shimmied out of her tight pants before returning to her spread position before me, this time entirely bare.

"Tell me what you came here to tell me while I pleasure you." Surprise flashed across her face. I wanted to return to my solitude and I was going to multi-task.

"Of course, my Warden." She whispered in hushed tones. I slid my chair closer to the desk on which she sat, I refused to sink to my knees for anyone, let alone someone beneath me in the hierarchy of my own Court. I leaned into her open legs as she took a deep, steadying breath of anticipation. My tongue flicked out to contact the swollen bundle of nerves at the apex of her thighs. She released a scream of feigned passion, entirely too dramatic and flashy as if she wanted to put on a show. My tongue returned to her center and licked desperately, which could be misconstrued as desperation to pleasure her, which was rather a desperation to know what it was she came here to tell me.

"Talk, Lilith," I growled against her sex before dipping my tongue inside of her. She arched her back and her sounds of pleasure filled the study, she spoke hoarsely in a voice that sounded more pained than sensual.

"We received the results of the Final Trial," she panted. I moved my tongue to circle the small bud and pushed a single finger inside her. She gasped. We received the Trial results every year and she never came to tell me about them in person. There was either a very good reason she was here now, or she was looking for an excuse to find her in this position now writhing beneath my touch. I slid a second finger into her in hopes of encouraging her to continue. She screamed.

"Keep talking," I ordered frustratingly.

"We.. uh, we have one student who… who… Oh, goddess. Yes, my Warden, dear goddess, yes." I withdrew my tongue from her apex and looked at her.

Her head had fallen back and she had gripped one of her breasts in her hand, squeezing it for added stimulation.

"Lilith, tell me why you are here. Now." I returned to her center and let my tongue run over the exposed bundle of nerves as I moved my fingers within her, thrusting at a devastatingly quick pace. She rocked against me forcefully in a lost cloud of ecstasy.

"Her results.. were… oh goddess, yes there, please don't stop," I growled again, anger boiling up inside of me. I released her swollen bud from my lips and withdrew my fingers completely from her. She whimpered.

"If you cannot multi-task, Lilith, then perhaps it is best if we do not continue this so you can tell me the information you have come to give me." My voice was low and threatening. Her head snapped up and her eyes met mine in a desperate fog.

"I'll tell you. Please continue, my Warden." I nodded once before sliding my three fingers back into her easily. She moaned at the stretch but took a careful breath before speaking again. My tongue found her clit again and I moved in rhythm with my fingers quickly and expertly, methodically.

"She received a strange result, one that I believe you should know about." This was unusual, it was not often that Lilith told me about individual results. More often, she would send me a parchment with the listed names of those who placed with The Court of Shadows and I would then skim the profiles of my new constituents before approving the list and then wait a year to repeat the process. My tongue darted across her slick center as my curiosity peaked.

"What was the result?" I asked quietly against her sex. I felt her body shake and her muscles constrict against my fingers. I knew she was nearing climax. "And hurry, if you're not finished with your story, I won't let you finish either." She whimpered under my touch.

"Her placement was…" her hands gripped the edge of the desk tightly, she was well aware that I did not want her to touch me. She struggled against the last part of her phrase. It could be the building climax, or the news itself, but either way, Lilith writhed under me.

"Now, Lilith, tell me now," I ordered.

"Forgotten!" She screamed. "She placed Forgotten!" She screamed as her release racked through her body.

I've been alive for centuries. I've been a Warden of this Court for almost as long - at this point, I thought nothing could surprise me. And yet, there I was. Surprised.

I sat back from Lilith, still panting on my desk, and gripped my head in my hands. "There must be a mistake." I spat. Lilith, recognizing the tone, quickly slipped off my desk and redressed. It was time to talk business.

"I thought so too, my Warden. I assure you, I have double-checked, triple-checked even. Her result was Forgotten, clear as day." Lilith stood in the corner of my study, her cheeks still flush from her release, but other than that, she was the picture of professionalism. I really appreciated that about her. There weren't strings attached with us. Lilith has only been my Dean for a short time. She wasn't alive when The Forgotten Court wasn't- well, forgotten. Not many were. Years tend to slip away when you have nothing to hold on to, the Wardens may be the only living beings alive who knew The Forgotten Court before.

And that's a good thing.

The entire Court was completely eradicated so long ago that it's been decades since I had allowed my mind to drift to the memories of its existence, its power, and its horrors. But that didn't stop it from infiltrating my nightmares. The only Court to have a Mythica so strong and manipulative that it affected even the Wardens. The reasoning behind the inception of these Courts was to establish order in Verihdia. Each Court has its own purpose in the structure of Verihdia and no one Court is more powerful than any other. But that wasn't exactly true. The Warden appointed to sit on the throne of The Forgotten Court was in every way, more powerful than the rest of us combined. I could tell. Even though that was exactly the thing the Gods were trying to avoid. The power in his little finger could topple Verihdia as we knew it, and it had the other Wardens, including myself, shaking in our boots. You'd be hard pressed to get any one of them to admit it though, especially Avalin of The Court of the Vanguard who couldn't admit someone was better than her if it meant life or death, but I could. I could admit it, and I was jealous. That Warden had the type of Mythica that wormed its way inside of your mind, took what it needed, and left you helpless to its invasion. I do not doubt that he could have single-handedly won if a war was waged. But that's not how we removed The Forgotten Court from existence. No. What we did was so much worse than that. Something I used to have nightmares about, something I refuse to ever do again. Nobody alive, apart from myself and the other Wardens knows what happened back then. I'm thankful for that.

I hadn't let myself be consumed by the thoughts of that era. It took nearly a century to stop myself from waking in the night covered in sweat with a guilty scream caught in my throat that never seemed to disappear. Eventually, I forced myself to forget The Forgotten Court. I should have known it was too good to be true. Here it was, back to haunt me.

"Does she know?" Lilith shook her head.

"We told her it meant she was destined to be Uncourted." I couldn't control the laugh that came from my throat.

Uncourted? Someone with a deep connection to the incredibly powerful Forgotten Court, Uncourted?

It was almost too ridiculous to imagine. Lilith cleared her throat and spoke clearly, "I figured that was better than to have rumors spread across the Institute." I nodded. She was right, of course. Not only has no student placed Forgotten since its demise, but The Forgotten Court is rarely spoken about at the Institute either. All but completely erased from our histories. The types of rumors that could have been spread would be inaccurate and probably destructive. It was good that this student didn't know.

"I'm assuming the other Deans are visiting their Wardens as we speak to tell them the very same?" Moving to the drink cart in the corner of the room, I poured myself two fingers of whiskey, watching the amber liquid swirl around the bottom of the glass. Lilith did not move from her spot.

"They are." She didn't say anything else as I took a long sip of my drink. The burning sensation warmed my chest, I tilted my head back and let the fire spread within me.

"Her file?" Lilith was beside me quickly, a small green folder in her hands. Opening it, I couldn't shake the anticipation that crawled up my spine. Glancing over the information contained within was like reading a forbidden book, something that felt dangerous, capable of toppling our delicate structure. Not much information was listed about her Mythica, but what was there was enough to send a shiver wracking through my body. She apparently could rip truths from others' mouths. To convince them to tell her their fears, their desires. According to this file, her Mythica caused some issues with other students.

I knew what I needed to do now, what everyone else would be doing now, and as much as I hated it, there was no way I was going to let another Warden take this from me, from my Court. I placed the empty glass back down on the bar before turning to Lilith.

"Prepare the carriage, I'm going to a ball."

Lysander

SIX

The Verihdian Institute. A charming little gothic building, cozy I suppose, but nothing compared to the majesty of my Forsaken Quarters. The walls of the school are stone and cold, covered by decorative memorabilia from past students and the accomplishments of those who have found success since Pledging to a Court and leaving this school behind. Famous Verihdian Gladiators, members elected to Parliament in The Court of Silence, individuals who've made important medical advancements, written important texts…the walls were littered with members from every single Court of Verihdia. Except for mine. What we do, we do in secret. If I were a prideful man, it might bother me that nobody here knew the extraordinary nature of the people in my Court, that people don't see the incredible things they've accomplished. But if I were a prideful man, I would not be the Warden of the Court that I was.

They led me to the receiving room for the Warden of The Court of Shadows, and the room was decorated as such. Draped in green tapestry and curtains, the floor covered in a deep forest rug, and the plaques and pictures on the wall showcased the hundreds of students who Pledged to The Court of Shadows. My Court. It was appropriate that my Court's pictures were hidden inside this room. Secrecy was our specialty.

Although I could tell that they attempted to clean this room recently, cobwebs still hid in the corners and dust seemed to linger in the air after being disturbed from its years of sitting idle. I'm not even sure how long it's been since I last attended the Courting Ball. At least a decade, maybe two. I hadn't needed to. That is no longer the case. Everything has changed this year. She changed everything. I hadn't seen my fellow Wardens yet, my family for all intents and purposes, but I knew they were here. I could feel them. The air seemed thick with electricity whenever we all came together. Which hasn't happened in… well I'm not sure that's happened since…

Everything's changing.

And all because of her.

Lexa Cromwell.

Her Final Compatibility Trial offered a Forgotten Court result. Twin brother, Axel Cromwell, Vacant, Final Trial offered a Court of the Vanguard result. I rolled my eyes at that. Avalin was going to use that to her advantage tonight. Of course she was.

I would.

I have spent the last three days studying every piece of literature in her file, reading all of her essays, examining every word, every thought. Trying to understand this girl whose existence could mean the downfall of us all. Her profile is rather in depth on everything except her Mythica. It is clear she has some, and there are accounts of her being able to discern fears and desires from others, but it's all rather vague. How could this Mythica qualify her for The Forgotten Court? That's unheard of, that's impossible - that's why we all want her.

I moved before the mirror and ran my palms over the dark velvet material of my suit in my signature color. I honestly hated the fabric, the heat of it all, but the last time I saw Rein Mithroar, Warden of The Court of Echoes, he wore a dark red velvet suit, and damn if he didn't look incredible. I had my own made the next day.

Sometimes my jealousy got the better of me. But that's what makes me such a formidable Warden. I am never content with what I have. I witness the strengths that others possess and see them, not as threats, but as something I can adopt, take, or steal. My Court isn't stuck grasping onto its archaic traditions because they are familiar or safe, we grow, we adapt. We get stronger. And all because I want what others have. Being in The Court of Shadows does tend to mean you favor jealousy, that you allow the green-eyed monster to dictate your emotions and actions. But it's not just that. What sets us apart from any other Court is that we understand that you cannot wait for power to come to you. If you want something, you have to make it happen. That is why I am here.

I want something that someone else has. I want Lexa Cromwell. And I'm going to take her.

A knock at my chamber door echoes through the room. When I crack it open a small framed man in dark black clothes bows his head. Nerves shake his body.

"Good Evening, Warden of Shadows. I am Cristo, and I am here to take you to the Observatory. The other Wardens are on their way as well." The tiny man, Cristo, did not make eye contact but instead kept his eyes trained on my shoes. It's been so long since I've been around an Uncourted individual that I had forgotten how nervous they were around us. I smiled briefly before leaning to the table near the door and retrieving my mask. My siblings could say what they wanted about the tradition of the masquerade, but I considered it an exceptional expectation. Not that anyone would have difficulty knowing who we were, but it added to the mystery of it. The tensions. You could be someone else behind a mask, or you could be entirely yourself. Either way, you were free.

Cristo bowed his head deeper before retreating down the hallway. I opted for a half-face black mask, the dark hue of the material was just a few shades darker than that of my own rich complexion. After securing the ties behind my head, I drew up the top half of my shoulder-length curled black hair into a small bun. Once the mask was secured to my face, I followed after him. Cristo walked with feverish speed as if he was trying to outrun me, not lead me to my destination. It amused me, and I found myself counting how many of his short and anxious steps equaled one single bound of my own gait.

Four.

I allowed myself the brief distraction from the task at hand, and it felt good to forget why I was here, to forget what I was meant to be doing this evening, and what the stakes were. But I did not have the luxury for long.

I felt them before I saw them. The Wardens of Verihdia.

My own Mythica manifested in such a way that I could sense other's powers, I could see and feel their Mythica as if it was a physical thing I could simply reach out and touch. But that wasn't the only facet of my powers, no, the part that truly pleased me was that with a single touch, I am granted the ability to copy a type of Mythica and use it as if it were my own for a very brief window of time. A Mythica fitting of the envious Warden if ever there was one. My mind flashed only briefly back to a time of my life I often tried to forget - when I was appointed to the throne of The Court of Shadows. The ritual, the ceremony... the trials. A shudder rippled through me.

Pushing that thought back into the corner of my mind it belonged in, I continued forward. At that very moment, the feeling of six very different, distinct, and powerful Mythicas were assaulting my senses. It was... overwhelming to say the least. I had to rub my temples to calm the idle pain that tickled the edges of my mind.

Cristo slowed his accelerated pace just before a set of ironclad double doors. The arch was decorated in a dark, vine-like filigree that promised to snake down around you if you made the brave choice to enter its domain.

Mental note: add vine filigree to my study door.

I must have made an audible sound of approval because Cristo turned to me before opening the doors. "I hope you are finding your return to our Institute satisfactory, Warden of Shadows." He bowed his head. I was growing tired of the incessant groveling already. Not that I didn't expect respect, demand it even, but I hated submission. I long for a good challenge. Unfortunately, people so rarely are brave enough to verbally spar with a Warden, knowing that any word of indignation could be their last.

"I am. Thank you, Cristo." He smiled lightly, the blanket of fear slipping from his expression. Good. I don't want him to be afraid of me. That's the secret to my position. When someone is afraid of me, they are not as willing to offer secrets or make a deal, and in my line of work that could make or break me.

"Do you enjoy your position here, Cristo?" His eyes widened in shock.

"Yes, very much, Warden." I could tell by the fond smile on his lips that he spoke the truth.

"In another life, I think I would have liked to have gone here," I said honestly, glancing up at the door in front of me. The Institute was built after my ascension to Warden, my siblings and I never had the luxury - or burden depending on which of them you ask - of attending.

"It's a great school," Cristo said, fondly. "It's an honor to continue my service in these halls."

I didn't recognize Cristo's name, so I knew that he wasn't a potential Pledge for The Court of Shadows.

"I think it's noble when people willingly choose Uncourted. Our world would not exist the way it does were it not for the people who work tirelessly to ensure that The Living Lands produce strong, educated people." It was a gamble, to assume that he willingly Pledge Uncourted, but one I was willing to take. His face lit up.

"Thank you, Warden. Not many see it that way." His body relaxed, the tension he had earlier melting away with every moment.

Good.

"That's a shame." He smiled and I knew our time was running short. I needed as much as he could give me. "Do you know why we're here today?"

Cristo shook his head, fidgeting with his fingers.

"We're here to Court one of your students. All of us, for the same one." Cristo's eyes widened. This information is something my siblings might argue as confidential, but everyone would know the reason for our visit the moment we walked into the ballroom. What's the harm of telling this man a little earlier, if it means I get something in return? "Do you know, Lexa Cromwell?" Cristo's face contorted as he thought. His lips pursed in concentration.

"I do. Lovely girl." He looked at me with bright eyes. "You're here for her?" I nodded. "Wow, she must be pretty special then."

You have no idea.

"I'm sure you've noticed, even reading about her Mythica was enough to raise an eyebrow. You were here, you witnessed it." I was pushing harder than I normally did when pulling for secrets. But my siblings were on the other side of this door and I knew I only had a few more moments before we were interrupted.

"Oh yeah, it's something out of nightmares." I saw Cristo shutter at that.

"You don't say?"

"She's better at controlling it now, but when she was younger she had several of her classmates cowering in fear." Her Mythica, from what I read, was capable of learning the fears and desires of others. As impressive as that is, it doesn't quite lead to 'cowering in fear'.

"Thank you, Cristo." He beamed proudly. And bowed slightly at the waist. "I suppose I shouldn't keep my siblings waiting any longer."

"Right this way." Cristo placed his hands on the iron doors and pushed. They opened to reveal an Observatory, a small circular room with an entirely glass ceiling. The dark stone of the walls and flooring was illuminated in moonlight, but the room was not the most impressive thing. No, it was the six daunting figures standing around a large, round stone table, that truly stood out. The Wardens, my family.

"About time you showed up, Lysander." Vander Midesues, The Warden of Silence, spoke first. The irony was not lost on me, but that was a common misconception about my brother's Court. They are not mute, but they do value discretion, especially when it matters most. His fiery red hair was tousled and hung in waves cropped just above his ears and an exuberant golden crown sat slightly askew atop his head. His frame was adorned in a black long-sleeve shirt that buttoned up the front and his trousers seemed to be made of actual golden thread. Considering his Mythica, the ability to turn items to gold, I wouldn't put it past him. His hands were covered in his signature black leather gloves. I am almost positive my brother has complete control over his Mythica, and would not accidentally cause something or someone to turn to gold, however I applauded the intimidation tactic.

I could see just the briefest glimpse of his Court Mark on his wrist jutting out beneath the top of his glove. Each of us had one, a slightly different marking that identified you uniquely as a member of your Court. Once a student Pledges, they are given the Mark as well. Cementing their place in Verihdia for the rest of their life. Vanders' Mark was simple, a round golden coin with a pair of lips and one single finger crossing them, like the way you would quiet a child. Whenever I see the Mark of The Court of Silence I can almost hear it echoing "shhhhh."

"I wouldn't be me if I didn't make an entrance, brother." I moved forward with my hand outstretched, he clasped my forearm in his hand and pulled me in for a quick embrace.

"It's been too long," He chuckled into my ear. "Come, our siblings were just about to start fighting."

"We were not." Rein spoke this time, his tone laced with all the disdain and disgust that I'd expect from The Warden of Echoes.

Most of the Wardens had looks that made them stand out, between our otherworldly beauty and the tell-tale shade to our eyes, but Rein was without a doubt the most exotic looking of us all. His skin once used to be pale pink, but somewhere along the way, either through Mythica or perhaps his affinity for standing too close to open flames, it had turned a light ashen grey with small cracks forming on the edges as if he might crumble into nothing but ash at any given moment. But one would not be so bold as to test that theory, for my brother was prone to violence and anger, and those who tested him often did not live to tell the tale. I hadn't seen it in years, but I knew his Court Mark was tattooed onto his back. A silhouette of a flame climbing from the base of his spine to lick the very edges of his hairline on his neck, and inside the darkened outline, several cracks of lightning. A raging storm inside a flame - I'd never heard of a better analogy for the individuals of The Court of Echoes. His red eyes glistened as he looked back to the table. "We are about to discuss the rules for this evening."

"Rules, rules, rules" My slender framed sibling spoke next. Korzich barely wore anything, their lower half draped in a silk skirt and they wore a sleeveless button-down silk blouse that they must have forgotten had buttons seeing as not a single one was closed. In fact, the only part of their body that was entirely covered was their face, and even the mask was made of lace and left very little to the imagination. Their chest was peppered with their Court Mark. While it was only required for a member of each Court to have a single Mark to signify your Pledge, The Court of Passion's Mark looked like someone with painted lips trailed sultry kisses all across their flesh. If it weren't for the small sprig of leaves that hung from the bottom corner of each set of painted lips and the thin diamond outline, I may have believed my sibling enjoyed some simple pleasures before attending this meeting. Which they very well could have, but at least the evidence of that wasn't staring at me from their naked chest. It did seem rather promiscuous for The Courting Ball, although I'm willing to bet this outfit was modest in comparison to the usual dress in The Court of Passion. Their long black hair had golden gems and threads braided into it and it cascaded down their back. They smiled at me before leaning forward onto the golden table, suggestively popping their hips. "You know how much I detest rules, siblings. They're no fun." They pouted and I had to force myself not to laugh.

"It is important though, Korzich, that we understand how to go about this event. We are clearly all here for the same purpose and it would be reckless of us not to acknowledge that." The slow, methodical drawl of my sibling Miya Moonshackle of The Court of the Undying is impossible not to recognize, even given the decades that have passed since I last spoke with them. The white lines of their tattoos against their black skin stood out even more drastically in the moonlight from the Observatory window above. Their cleanly shaven head was decorated in runes and their Court Mark of a sunburst design behind two outstretched hands. Their skin acted as a tapestry of important healing Mythica and rituals. It was their way of ensuring that they would never be caught without a way to help someone in need.

"Exactly. Thank you, Miya." Rein nodded his approval at our sibling. "It is no secret why we've all decided to gather at this Courting Ball."

The room suddenly quieted as the reason for our visit was brought back to the forefront of our attention. As if it ever truly left.

Lexa Cromwell.

"My suggestion is each Warden is allotted twenty minutes with Ms. Cromwell tonight in an attempt to sway her allegiances," Miya spoke again, but this time they were met with groans of disapproval.

"Twenty minutes is not enough time!" Vander exclaimed.

"That's barely even foreplay," added Korzich.

I remained quiet, as I normally did. I always learned more by watching than participating anyway. That was when my sister spoke up.

"Unless we wish to talk her ear off and exhaust her, twenty minutes is sufficient enough. If you are not confident in your ability to make a powerful impression in twenty minutes, then perhaps you are not the Warden deserving of her Pledge." Avalin always had a way of knocking our siblings down a peg while simultaneously hoisting herself up. She was a stunning female, at least to me. Her Mythica has the impressive ability to change her appearance to be pleasing to anyone who looks at her. Generally, Mythica does not work on the Wardens. I've tried. However, Avalin's Mythica is placed on herself, not on us, that's why we were able to see the illusion. To me, her hair is a deep red with soft eyes, slight curves, and a hidden smile. But to my siblings, she looks entirely different. Korzich once said it felt like they were looking in a mirror when they looked at her. I was not surprised in the least. Apparently, her Court Mark, two crossing daggers covered in climbing vines, shifts positions based on where the viewer thinks is the most appealing place for a tattoo. I have never been able to see her Court Mark, so it's safe to say my idea of attractive placement was not exactly appropriate.

"Twenty minutes it is then," Vander spoke again. My brother couldn't help but take charge in moments like this, seeing as his Court was often in charge of carrying out and enforcing the law in Verihdia. "What is on the table and what isn't?"

"Ohh, I love a good consent checklist." Korzichs mouth upturned in a sensual smile. "Lay it on me." My sister beside them rolled her eyes, Ivis Grey, The Warden of Talisman. Her plump frame was draped in an elegant pink dress that matched the irises of her eyes and hugged her curves as it fell delicately down to the floor. She pursed her lips and her dark brown skin tightened at the movement.

"Must everything you say be an innuendo, Korzich?" Ivis challenged.

"Don't tell me you're afraid of expressing your own lines and veils, sister?" They leaned closer to Ivis' ear, planting a kiss on the skin of her neck just above her Court mark, a symbol of a scroll wrapped in a sprig of evergreen, before continuing, "Is using innuendos a hard limit for you?" I smiled at Ivis' visible disgust at Korzich's jesting. So many years had passed since the seven of us were in a room together - I pushed away the memory of our last meeting that threatened to escape from its carefully crafted prison in my mind - and yet it truly felt like no time had passed at all. We seemed to slip right back into our roles so easily around each other, not so much the roles of Warden that we had to wear every day, but the role of family.

"Enough, Korzich." Rein spoke again. "You cannot promise anything physical, be it sexual, or monetary." Both Korzich and Vander frowned at that.

"You cannot use her brother as a selling point." Miya directed towards Avalin. She rolled her eyes but nodded. Not that it mattered too much, chances are rather high that Lexa's brother has told her where he placed and she was well and truly aware of which Court she should Pledge to be with him. That thought spiked a familiar green-eyed feeling deep inside my chest. Avalin had such an advantage over me right now, and I hated that.

"And no using her boy toy either, Lysander." I jolted my head in Korzich's direction. They taunted me with their eyes.

What are they talking about?

As if they could sense my confusion, Korzich smiled before hopping up onto the stone table. They crossed their legs, the silk of their skirt riding dangerously high up on their thigh. "Don't tell me I was the only one smart enough to ask who our darling Lexa was fucking?" A few cringed at Korzich's declaration, but I felt a burning bubbling inside of me.

How did I not think to ask about that? Why did Lilith not tell me?

I made a note to scold Lilith for withholding important information from me, just as Korzich spoke again. "Chandler Mills, in case you're wondering… placed Court of Shadows in his final trial."

"Yes, no using any of the people in her life as selling points," Vander confirmed, looking at me. The others around the stone table followed suit, waiting for me to confirm. I nodded.

This changes things.

Suddenly I felt more confident in my ability to sway Lexa Cromwell to Pledge my Court. I just have to hope this fling of hers is important enough to her to follow when given the choice. I couldn't speak about him, sure, but that didn't mean I couldn't use him to sway her.

"Only speak positively of your Court, don't spread rumors, or speak negatively of each other's Courts. No matter how badly you want to." Ivis added this one. Fitting, seeing as many of us deemed her Court boring and impractical. An entire Court dedicated to reading and documenting? It's easy to see why some of the other Wardens, who spent most of their time in gladiatorial arenas, dealing in secrets, in the throes of passion, or bringing about punishment, were quick to pass judgment on such a passive Court.

"Fine, agreed." Rein nodded. "Who goes first?"

"Me." Vander practically pulled his shoulder out of the socket by raising his hand in the air, claiming that first impression he loved so much. The others quickly chimed in, claiming their own slots in the lineup to meet and woo Lexa Cromwell. My silence earned a few questioning looks from my siblings until I spoke up, finally. "I want to go last."

"Of course you do." Avalin's eyes rolled again and she laughed to herself.

"So we have an order, and we have our rules," Vander spoke carefully, allowing plenty of time for others to interject. They didn't. "Anything else we need to add?" The room went quiet again. The Courting Ball was already in full swing downstairs, so we all knew that the moment we adjourned this meeting, the challenge would begin.

"Should we talk about why this happened? Why she received this result?" Miya broke the silence, asking the question that I'm positive each of us had spent the last three days wondering ourselves.

"I looked into her family, but there was no connection to The Forgotten Court." A few Wardens inhaled a sharp intake of breath as Rein muttered those words. I nodded to confirm Rein's story, I too had dug into her file. Trying to see if the connection to this Court was familial. It wasn't that I could tell. I thought back to what I saw in her parents file. Nothing outwardly suspicious, but definitely interesting.

"You all know as well as I do that familial ties are not always what suit you for a certain Court," Vander spoke quietly, ashamed almost. He was, of course, referring to his two sons, who both placed and Pledged to different Courts. You see, even the offspring of the Wardens were not exempt from the expectations of all children born in Verihdia. When Vander's first son, Elias, was born he was taken to the Institute to complete the training and Pledging process just as any other student. And just like any other student, he was not given any information as to the identity of his parents. And a few years later, Vander's second son, Kael, too joined the student body of the Verihdian Institute.

To keep it fair, Vander did his best to keep his visits to the Institute at a minimum. Until he received the results of Elias' Final Trial. Vander attended that year's Courting Ball and did everything he could, save for divulging his familial connection, to convince Elias to Pledge to The Court of Silence. It didn't work, however, and Vander had to watch the next day as his oldest son Pledged his body and soul to a Court that was not his birthright.

A few years later, Kael did the same.

I do not have a child, so I cannot truly sympathize with how it felt to watch as his two children chose a different Court, however, wanting something that someone else has? That is something I am all too familiar with. So I fully recognize the look that Vander tosses at Avalin and Korzich, the Wardens in charge of his sons.

"The Final Trial hasn't yielded a Forgotten Court result since the Court's demise," Ivis spoke. "We all know that the Final Trial does not only find the singular Court that each student is suited for, but rather a few that the student could fit nicely into." That information is solely for the Wardens and their Deans; however, the Trial only offers the singular Court to their students. "But as I'm sure you're all aware, Lexa's results did not show compatibility to a second or third Court." I did notice that, and it felt right. Someone who is so well suited for a Court like The Forgotten Court truly couldn't fit in anywhere else. But she would have to if she wanted to survive. "Traits best suited for this Court are widely contested and depending on who you ask, their stories may differ. And seeing as the only individuals who were alive to see to its downfall are in this room, I think we alone are best suited to determine what qualities this Ms. Cromwell possesses that make her a candidate for that Court beyond a shadow of a doubt."

Again a solemn silence settled over the room. None of us dared speak about the fact that plagued our minds.

Do we want Lexa Cromwell because she'd be a good fit for our Courts, or because she'd be too powerful an enemy?

This was the unasked question that hung tauntingly between us as we exited the Observatory quietly and headed towards the ballroom. I truly hated being the center of attention, so to say I was dreading walking into that room was an understatement. At least I had my siblings to stand at my sides, to share the spotlight of adoration and kiss-assery. I wasn't sure what I was expecting to see when we entered the room. Confused faces, sure. Eyes filled with wonder, I guess. This was the first time in the span of these students' lifetimes that all seven of the Wardens were present at the same time, so it's bound to be a shock. What I didn't expect was her.

I knew it was her the second we entered the space, her Mythica called out to me - practically screaming for attention. It sang out for me and I found myself entirely incapable of tearing my eyes away. Not that I would. As if it wanted to prove to me that it was far more powerful than my own. And I wasn't entirely sure it wasn't. Most of the time, Mythica was visible to me in a sort of colorful ombre hue, an array of bright colors that hung around the person who wielded it like a calm cloud.

Her Mythica was nothing like that. In fact, it was like nothing I had ever experienced before in my very long, very full life. It surrounded her in an almost black fog, it slowly leaked from her skin snaking around the people in her proximity in smokey tendrils that were reaching and prodding for entrance to their minds. It felt dark, volatile. Like at any given moment it could explode and combust everything in this entire chamber. A cool shiver ran down my spine. I did not scare easily, but something about the low boiling power hiding beneath her skin did just that - scared me. It was easy to pick her out in this crowd of dozens. But it was clear to me that she would still stand out in a crowd of millions.

The look of innocence on her face infuriated me, watching her companion with interest as if he was the one who my siblings and I had come here for.

Does she not understand how powerful she is?

As the heads in the room turned to follow my gaze, I knew my siblings had also discerned who we were here for. How could they not? Even without my gift, I would have known exactly who she was. Everything about her just screamed that she didn't belong here. Her dark black hair cascaded over her pale shoulders, her bright blue eyes visible even from here and her curves were hugged by a deep emerald green gown.

Good choice.

Finally, every single eye in the room was on her, and there it was again - that infuriating helpless look in her eye as she turned to face us at the front of the room. A dark emotion colored her face as she realized what was happening, and who we were looking at.

Her Mythica surged violently, swirling around her in a vicious cloud of darkness.

What else are you capable of, little storm?

Korzich smiled at the members of the band and spoke clearly, their voice echoing through the room. "Don't stop the party on our account. Play, play!" The music tentatively swelled back into a rhythm, but she didn't move. Her classmates began to sway mindlessly to the beat, their eyes darting between Lexa and us.

The storm of her power thrashed again as if it was feeling threatened. Why, I couldn't understand. Compared to the other Mythica that was present in this room, my siblings and I included, it was without a doubt one of the most powerful. That was a fact I was acutely, and unfortunately aware of.

The party had slowly begun to ramp back up as my siblings and I dispersed along the edges of the circular room, walking slowly, our eyes trained on Lexa and only Lexa. The students instinctively herded towards the center as if we were ravenous animals preparing to feast on our prey. Which isn't the worst analogy. If only they could see what I could see now in the dark cloud that surrounded Ms. Cromwell. She was not the prey, not by a longshot, and one day she was going to recognize that in herself, and I wanted to be her Warden when she did. My siblings had all come to a stop in front of their respective thrones, each designed with their Court in mind. I smiled at the structure of solidified smoke beneath me as I sunk onto its seat. A few students gasped, fully expecting me to fall through the cloudy mist. We sat still for a moment, perched on our thrones, while the students whispered. They had stopped watching Lexa now, but I didn't.

Her crystal eyes opened even wider as Vander stepped forward off of his golden pedestal and moved through the crowd as it parted for him. I didn't need to see her Mythica react to see that she was terrified.

I hope you're wide awake, little storm, it's about to be a long night.

SEVEN

*T*here was a time when I was younger when I felt ashamed about my size. Not because I was embarrassed about being bigger than the other girls in my class, but because being curvy meant I had curves - curves that I had no idea how to dress for or utilize. I was too busy being awkward to really appreciate the full-framed figure I was given. It was years before Riley convinced me that with the right size clothing and adding a slight sway to my walk, I could be desirable. Not that I necessarily wanted to, but it was encouraging to know that I could should I choose to. Riley convinced me to give it a try, to let my self-consciousness take a backseat to confidence for a change.

That was when Chandler noticed me. Really noticed me. And I started to fall in love with my curves, the way that I stood out in a crowd. I took up space beautifully and powerfully. I haven't felt the urge to hide my body or shrink in years. However, standing here, in the center of the ballroom, with every single pair of eyes scanning me, including the seven Wardens of Verihdia, I wanted nothing more than to take up less space. To completely disappear - but I couldn't do that. They were here, all of them.

This must be a mistake. They must think I'm someone else.

"Lexa…" my best friend's voice was quiet behind me, even though the music had begun swelling again and the party continued tentatively, I could tell that nobody wanted to be the first to take focus. I didn't dare turn to look at Riley, my own eyes were too busy watching as the Wardens stalked around the edge of the room like hawks watching their prey.

Me.

"Lexa, why are the Wardens looking at you?" Riley whispered again. I blinked rapidly in response. I couldn't answer because I didn't have one. There was no reason why all seven of the Verihdian Wardens were here at this Courting Ball, and even less of a reason why they all seemed to be interested in me. "Why is The Warden of Silence walking towards you?" The urgency in their voice wrapped around me, constricting my breathing. My breath caught in my throat and I felt my heart pumping wildly inside my chest, thrashing against my ribcage as if it was aiming to escape.

Me too, heart. Me too.

But escape was not an option. I was trapped, and Vander Midesues, the Warden of The Court of Silence, was standing in front of me. He towered over me and I had to crane my neck to offer him the same eye contact he was gracing me with. Golden eyes met mine from behind a golden mask that sat on his face and I felt my entire body tighten. I had to physically force myself to bow my head to him, but apparently speaking and moving at the same time was impossible at the moment because as much as I tried to greet the imposing figure before me, no words spilled from my mouth. I was beyond grateful when Chandler spoke up.

"Warden Of Silence, it's an honor to be in your presence tonight, sir." Chandler's tone was so calm, collected, and proud. I couldn't help but feel jealous of his ability to keep his cool at a time like this. Chandler has always had a very diplomatic air about him, he had this ability to command respect in even the most unmatched of power dynamics, and here he was again - being ever the gentleman to one of the most important people in all of Verihdia with the type of calmness one would have when speaking to a close friend.

Vander's eyes did not leave mine, and I almost flinched as Chandler's hand tightened around my fingers to an almost painful degree. No wonder he was suited for The Court of Shadows, I could almost taste the envy rolling off of his skin as this Warden gave every ounce of his attention to me, and me alone.

"Miss Cromwell," Vander's melodic voice chimed. "It is a pleasure to make your acquaintance, I am Vander Midesues." I nodded, with what I'm sure was a lopsided half-smile, probably completely unable to hide my shock that he thought he needed to introduce himself to me, but very thankful that my own mask was in place to conceal the blush that was creeping into my cheeks.

As if everybody in this room doesn't already know exactly who you are.

"Good evening, Warden." Ah! At last, my vocal cords cooperate. Although I would have preferred my normal voice to this hoarse and tense sound that came out of me. Vander smiled a bright, toothy grin.

"Please, call me Vander." The gasps from the people nearby who were pretending they weren't eavesdropping echoed in the room.

Yeah, not gonna do that.

"With all due respect, Warden. My training here at the Institute has taught me the importance of your title and I wouldn't want to offend you by stripping you of it, even in casual conversation." There she is. My voice returned with a confidence I definitely didn't have at the moment. Vander didn't answer for a few moments, his face staying completely devoid of emotions, impossible to read. And then he laughed. A deep throaty laugh, one that bounced off the walls and filled the space.

"Miss Cromwell, will you do me the honor of joining me for a dance?" My palms started sweating, my throat closed to an almost lethal degree and I'm pretty sure a slight breeze could knock me completely off my feet.

"Of.. of course, Warden," I managed to whisper. His eyes brightened as he held out his gloved hand for me. The knowledge of his particular power was widespread enough that I knew the reasoning behind his black gloves. Even with the layer of protection between his skin and mine, I couldn't help but feel my nerves skyrocket as I placed my hand in his. The pale hue of my skin looked positively simple compared to the golden sheen of his attire. In fact, everything about me seemed out of place next to this wealth-shrouded individual. He led me to an open section of the dance floor, which could have been anywhere considering how quickly my classmates darted out of his way as he took gallant steps around the room. He turned to face me, his left hand reaching for my waist and carefully pulling me into him until the fabric of our clothes brushed against each other. The music drifted into a bright waltz and suddenly, I was dancing with The Warden of Silence.

True to his namesake, we danced around for a few moments in silence as I adjusted to match his impressive gait. I had to actively remind myself not to look down at my feet. I was lucky I hadn't fallen already.

"So, Miss Cromwell. Tell me about yourself." He spoke again. My head was spinning, he had not yet informed me why he was here, dancing with me. I'm such a lackluster individual, my life story is only going to prove to him that he has got to have the wrong person. He did not mean to come here for me.

But he said my name, he has read my file. He knows who I am.

"Well, I, um... There's not much to tell truthfully, Warden. I spent most of my schooling here with my brother and my best friend. I wasn't top of my class, but I wasn't far behind either. I'm painfully average, I'm afraid."

And you have the wrong girl!

I wanted to scream, but Vander looked thoughtful as he pondered my words.

"That is where I must disagree with you, Miss Cromwell. You are anything but average." His eyes bore into mine as if he was trying to see into my very mind. Based on the intensity of his gaze, perhaps he could.

"I'm sorry?" He couldn't have just said that, right? This doesn't make any sense. I'm supposed to be Uncourted.

"Let me tell you about my Court, and why you should Pledge to it tomorrow."

His demeanor shifted slightly as he twirled me around, sending me spinning out, only to pull me back in gracefully. I couldn't respond. I only nodded.

"The Court of Silence, as you know, is home to the governing faction of Verihdia. My Court is responsible for keeping order among the Courts." I nod again, I knew this. We have been taught this, but none of that explains why Vander Midesues wants me to be a part of it. He continued, telling me about the inner workings of the government, explaining to me the monetary benefits of Pledging to him, but I could tell he was being careful as to not promise any wealth to me directly. I wondered if bribery was frowned upon at the Courting Ball. I listened intently, hearing this information in a new light this time, comprehending it not as a student who will be tested on this information tomorrow, but as a Pledge with a choice to make. A life-altering choice. A choice I had completely given up all chance of having after receiving my Uncourted result at the Final Trial. Vander spoke with such reverence of his Court, something he was very obviously convinced was the right choice for me. We had stopped dancing and moved to the edge of the dance floor when the small-framed figure of Miya Moonshackle approached from behind Vander.

"Time's up brother. It is my turn to speak with Miss Cromwell." Vander's golden eyes rolled in his head and he stepped back from me, removing himself from my personal space for the first time since he gripped my hand.

"Very well, sibling." He turned back to me. "I hope I was able to highlight the beauty of my Court, Miss Cromwell, I hope you truly do consider Pledging to me tomorrow, because," he leaned in, his mouth only inches from my ear, his hot breath washing over the skin on my neck, "you would look exquisite in gold." With a wink, he was gone. Once again, I was thankful for the mask that hid my embarrassment at the Warden's parting words. I didn't have the luxury of a moment to shake it off though because Miya Moonshackle, The Warden the Undying, stood in front of me, their stunning black skin was decorated with beautiful runes and script. Their periwinkle-colored were eyes hidden behind a small silver mask. I couldn't help but search the crowd for Riley to see their reaction. This figure before me was soon to be their Warden. Were they jealous of me, or were they upset with me for having Miya's attention here today? I caught a quick glimpse of Riley's bright and colorful hair amongst the crowd. Their face was shrouded in a dark mask but I could clearly make out their expression. Complete, and utter happiness. They met my eyes, and smiled brightly, flashing me two quick thumbs up and I could practically hear them telling me to listen carefully to every word this Warden was about to say to me.

So I did. I listened while Miya spoke of all the good their Court did for others, the types of innovations they brought to Verihdia and the lives they've saved over the centuries. I could see why Riley would belong in a place with this Warden. They were gentle, kind, and soft-spoken. They never once claimed their Court was better than others, in fact, they spoke quite highly of their partnerships with other Courts. Riley was going to love having Miya as a Warden. But could I?

When Miya left, Ivis Grey of The Court of Talisman was quick to replace them. She spent her time with me speaking bluntly about the types of knowledge and information only members of their Court were privy to, holding these deep dark secrets of the world above my head like a carrot taunting a small animal. However, I still listened intently as she described the daily tasks of her Court Members and moved about the refreshment tables, trying a small sliver of every dish offered. I frowned at the pink cube of sugar as she popped one into her mouth. Was it only an hour ago that life seemed so simple? Oliver's parting words echoed in my head.

Follow your gut, kid. It will lead you where you belong.

"Ivis, I believe it is my turn." I turned to the feminine voice and couldn't help the smile that crossed my face as I saw a stunning woman in front of me. Her thick red hair was short and cropped, tousled slightly at the top of her head. Her features were quite strong and chiseled, her body adorned with a dress that looked like it could double as warrior attire. I didn't doubt that it could. Her eyes were the same shade as Chandler's, exactly the same shade in fact. That odd detail threw me off for a moment and I didn't notice when Ivis Grey retreated to leave me alone with Avalin Earheart of The Court of the Vanguard.

"I'm sorry, Warden," I uttered, bowing my head, pulling my gaze from Chandler's eyes staring back at me.

"Not to worry, many people are often taken aback when first seeing me. Tell me, what do you see?" Avalin smiled and did a small twirl. I recognized then, that not only did Avalin carry Chandler's eyes, but her features here seemed to mirror his as well. Even the hairstyle was similar.

"I see my boyfriend... well he's not exactly my boyfriend per se, but we've been known to...what I mean to say is..." Avalin giggled before placing a hand on my shoulder. Her touch was cold against my exposed skin.

"You see what you're most attracted to when looking at me. I'm sure you've heard that in your studies." Of course I have, but I never expected this. Her entire frame, while still holding that unique feminine shape, was almost a carbon copy of Chandler.

I didn't realize I was so drawn to his looks.

A deeply melancholic feeling washed over me as I pondered that. If I am most attracted to Chandler, but I still feel very little attraction to him, what does that mean for the future of my romantic relationships, if there even is any future? I shake off that unpleasant thought and smile at Avalin.

"I've heard of your Mythica before, Warden. Hearing about it and seeing it in action are two entirely different experiences." She nods.

"That they are. So Miss Cromwell. I am Avalin Earheart of The Court of the Vanguard, as you already know. I am not only the winningest gladiator in my Court, but I am also one of the most powerful Wardens in Verihdia." My eyebrows raise at that.

I am well aware of the pride that often inhabits members of the Vanguard Court, however, it is a well-known fact that every Warden has Mythica of equal power. No one Warden is greater than another, no one Warden holds more power than another. It was designed that way, they were chosen for that exact purpose all those centuries ago.

"I know what you're thinking. That my Mythica isn't as powerful as the others. Well maybe not, but I don't see Mythica as the only factor in determining one's strength. In fact, strength is a lot more than the power you were given for free, it's the might you have inside that you had to work for, craft, foster, and develop. There is no Mythica stronger than a will of iron." While I didn't necessarily agree with her statement, it filled my heart with warmth. Axel had been self-conscious about being Vacant for as long as I could remember. I used to stay up late praying to the Gods for them to grant Axel even the smallest bit of power, something to make him feel comfortable in his own skin, something to keep him safe. I once, as a child, even asked the Gods at midnight on the evening of the First Trial Festival to split my power with him. I had more than I needed. But of course, that never happened. He got used to a life without Mythica and worked incredibly hard to prove his strength so it truly made me happy to know that he was going to a Court with a Warden who not only saw Vacant individuals as equally worthy but encouraged strength beyond Mythica.

"I can't tell you how elated I am to hear that, Warden. My brother Axel is suited for your Court and no doubt intends to Pledge to you tomorrow. He is Vacant, and I am glad to hear he will be in a place that sees that as a strength and not a weakness." A flash of something crossed her face as if she wanted to respond, but she only nodded before continuing to tell me about her conquests in the gladiatorial ring. A few minutes later the next Warden was upon me.

I hadn't even taken the time to look around the room for quite some time now. The students had clearly gotten more comfortable with the presence of the Wardens because they had begun dancing freely and enjoying their time. The Seven stood guard at the base of each of their Warden's thrones, ensuring that students did not feel bold enough to talk to them unless spoken to, and as far as I could tell, these Wardens were not interested in speaking to anyone but me.

"Lexa Cromwell." The Warden before me uttered my name as if speaking the word was the most sensual thing they could possibly do with their mouth, and considering their Court, I highly doubted that.

"Warden," I bowed my head. A slender finger caressed my chin and lifted it so I was once again staring at their face. They were gorgeous and wearing entirely too little. Their outfit left very little to the imagination.

"Lexa, I hope you know I believe foreplay is very, very important." I couldn't stop the incredulous gasp from escaping my mouth at their admission. "And I so do apologize for needing to get right to business with you, but seeing as I have limited time, I want to make every second count." Their voice was barely more than a whisper and I felt my entire body heat up. Not even my mask could hide this blush. Korzich Blunt was the Warden of the Court of Passion for a reason, a reason they explained in detail, with in-depth descriptions of multiple positions they've held in the Court, diplomatic…and otherwise. I think my mouth was going to be stuck in a permanent jaw-dropped position for the rest of my life. No one had ever spoken so freely and openly about sex with me before. Even the person I was having sex with.

"Have you found your mate yet, Lexa?" I wrinkled my nose and frowned deeply. It was common knowledge that true mated pairs were a gift from the Warden of The Court of Passion themself. Back when the Courts first were formed, Korzich fancied themselves a matchmaker and would gift mated pairs to just about every baby born in Verihdia. The bond of a mated pair is something so deep and powerful that when two halves of a pair find each other and complete their bond, they are forever linked, forever connected. Even in death. As the centuries went on, Korzich did not gift mated pairs as often, in fact, it's rather rare now. It's no secret that some of the original mated pairs created issues within the Pledging system. It was not uncommon for mated pairs to receive different results in their Final Trial but nearly every time they would completely disregard that and Pledge to the same Court as their mate. It's easy to see why The Court of Silence found this troublesome.

Let no single thing influence the Pledge.

Korzich was asked to stop creating mated pairs. And they have. I thought.

"I do not believe you have given me one, Warden," I spoke calmly, my mind briefly flashing to Chandler. One afternoon after the first time we had sex, we sat in his bed, my head on his chest listening to his beating heart, and I wished that he was my mate. I wanted it so badly, a connection like that. Someone who would love me no matter what happened, someone who would always know when I needed them. Someone who could see what I was feeling before even I could. However, there was no bond, no connection beyond the physical with us.

"Hmm," Korzich closed their eyes and took a deep sniff of the air around them. Their expression was colored with an unreadable emotion for the briefest of moments. Something almost like disbelief. But they composed themselves just as quickly and smiled at me with that bright, inviting smile. "That won't do." Their eyes scanned me quickly. "Well…What would you say if I told you, you could have one…right now."

I waited with bated breath for them to make good on their promise. Aside from finally meeting my parents, the only other thing I wanted as badly was a mate. Korzich simply watched me as my chest heaved with each nervous breath. "You look like you would enjoy that, like you would love to have someone who was made for you. Belonged to you. And you to them. Is that right, Lexa?"

Once again my traitorous vocal cords had gone on strike, so I nodded.

"Tell me, Lexa, do you enjoy being touched?" I swallowed hard, my throat was dry. Like I was parched, not for water, but the kind of desire Korzich spoke about. My body thirsted for it.

"I .. uh.."

"Don't be embarrassed. Tell me the truth." Korzich's hand began tracing lines up and down my exposed arms and my entire body broke out in goosebumps, i felt their Mythica seep into my skin, sending a wave of euphoria through my body. Their black eyes darkened even more as they took in my reaction. But they tossed their gaze quickly to something over my shoulder. I was too deeply entranced by their words to follow the look.

"Now tell me, do you like being touched?" Their voice lowered and I could feel their mint cool breath on my lips. It tasted like pure sin.

"Yes." I blurted in a whisper. It felt like someone had pulled the answer from my lips, like my own Mythica is capable of. But I knew the only force at work here was my own dormant desire.

"Good girl," they whispered.

Oh, my gods.

"Have you experienced many partners, Lexa?" Korzich asked, their breath tickling my throat.

I shook my head. "Only two, Warden." Their eyes widened as they took me in. I had only ever told Riley about my brief tryst with Anika Farley. It was fleeting and had no strings attached, but she was, without a doubt, a more attentive lover than Chandler. I was not surprised she Pledged to The Court of Passion two years ago.

"Did you enjoy them?" I thought back to both of my previous partners. While I found pleasure in the act with each of them, it always felt like we were just a tad out of sync.

"They were both pleasant." Korzoch's shocked expression nearly made me laugh.

"A woman like you deserves more than pleasant," they slowly circled me, until the heat of their chest was pressed against my back, their mouth close to my ear. "You deserve fire, and passion, and love. You deserve to embrace your own pleasure, Lexa." My eyes fell closed, and my head slightly lulled backwards, offering Korzich more of my exposed neck.

"Tell me where you like being touched, Lexa." I felt the heat pool between my legs in a rush of unbridled desire unlike any I had ever felt with Chandler.

"I...I like it when.."

"It is my turn, Korzich." My heart skipped two full beats before I was able to breathe again. Reins Mirthroar's voice behind me had me ready to jump out of my skin, the very skin that was heated and sensitive, begging for contact just moments ago.

Korzich smiled coyly over my shoulder at Rein and nodded, but before they sauntered away, they leaned into me again, their long hair brushing against the exposed skin of my chest, sending tingling sensations throughout my body.

Holy shit. Is that what it feels like to be turned on?

"Don't look too hard for your mate, Lexa. You might just make me jealous." And with that Korzich sauntered away, their hips swaying tantalizingly. The other students watched them with mixtures of curiosity and desire marking their expressions.

"I hope my sibling didn't make you uncomfortable. They have a way of doing that."

Oh right, Rein.

I turned around to face the large man behind me. His ashen pale face was cracked, and his eyes burned red beneath his mask.

"I apologize, Warden, for my reaction to your sibling's words." It was like I was completely entranced by their promise of lust

Maybe The Court of Passions wouldn't be so bad after all.

"No apologies needed. I just hope they did not cross a line with you. We are here to convince you to join our Court, not our beds." I choked on the breath I was taking and found myself in a coughing fit. Rein stood there, analyzing me.

"No, no of course not. They simply showed me how they often behave in that Court. I did not feel uncomfortable." I managed to respond, regaining some of my common sense and control over my own body.

"Good." Rein seemed angry. That wasn't out of character for The Court of Echoes, but it did throw me off. Every other Warden who had claimed my attention tonight seemed to be eager, excited even to explain to me the joys of their Court, but Rein here seemed positively furious that he had to spend his time here with me, convincing me to Pledge to him.

"I do not want to sell you on reasons to join my Court as I'm sure my siblings have." I agreed to his statement silently. "I want to tell you why you deserve to be in my Court, not why my Court deserves you." My eyes widened at this. Leave it to The Warden of Echoes to change the game.

"Miss Cromwell, you are probably wondering why we have all decided to come here tonight, after so many years of avoiding this very event. Why now, and why you. Right?"

Five other Wardens have now spent time with me, and not a single one of them has told me why they were so interested in me, why they all came here to Court me, and of course, I was curious, but it would have been improper to ask.

"Yes, I must agree, I am rather confused why you all have come here for me, considering my Final Trial result."

Uncourted.

That's what I am destined to be, so why are they all so keen on changing that?

"Your Mythica is powerful, is it not?" Rein spoke again in a tone of disinterest.

"Yes, it is. I try not to use it. I am still understanding the full scope of it." I answer truthfully. Something tells me the truth is important to Rein Mirthroar.

"I see. Well, Miss Cromwell. I do not want to sugarcoat it for you, but my Court is where the most destructive and vile people are sent because we have the capabilities of handling them. Of making the tough choices, of implementing punishments." I took a breath. The prison. He's talking about the prison. Where the people who have done the most wrong are sent to live out their lives in dark cells at the top of a mountain. From what I've read, it is a dark, vicious place. A place forged with nightmares. The only reason they are allowed to cross the veil into The Court of Echoes is because the Court Mark is branded into their skin as a punishment. A one-way ticket to Sunken Province. A chill crawls down my spine as I think about it. Each cell is specifically designed to be the perfect brand of torture for the criminal that will inhabit it. Like a fingerprint, no two punishments are quite the same. I know those individuals are horrible people who have committed unthinkable acts, but it still turns my stomach to think about the things that occur within those stone walls.

"I want you and your Mythica on my team, Miss Cromwell. Your brand of power could assist in proper interrogation and punishment of the guilty." My stomach dropped. Rein wants me to steal the truth from their lips, to rip their confessions of guilt right out of them. Find their fears so that they can exploit them. A pit formed in my stomach, and bile rose in my throat. Of course he thinks I fit perfectly in his castle of torture. I'm immediately thrown back to the beach, the two men on their knees at my feet, their lives in my hands. A feeling that reminds me a lot of disgust overtakes my senses and I have to fight everything inside me to not tell Rein Mirthroar right then and there that I would rather die than be used as a weapon.

"Thank you for being honest about your expectations for my Mythica were I to Pledge your Court, Warden." That's all I can manage because it's the truth. I'm glad he told me because now I know that I could never subject myself to that.

"I have several more minutes with you, but I believe you and I understand each other well enough already, so I will not take up any more of your time unnecessarily." With a slight bow of his head, he returned to his throne of iron and flame. My entire body fought the urge to convulse as the residual feelings of dread Rein had invoked washed over me. Anger flooded my senses and before I knew it, I actually growled under my breath.

Calm down.

In. Out. In. Out. Deep breaths were the only thing keeping me sane when Lilith made her way to me.

"My Warden is requesting your presence," she said, slowly scanning my face, something like judgment was hidden behind her full facial mask.

"That's unexpected," I huffed back, my tone laced with sarcasm. Lilith was not amused by my attempt at humor. I waited for her to continue, I glanced over her shoulder at the shadow-shrouded figure behind her on the dark, gravity-defying throne. His eyes burned into me, and I felt entirely exposed, like he could see into my very essence. He watched me carefully, like he was seeing something in me that nobody else could. His dark bronze face was framed by shoulder-length, obsidian hair, hanging in loose ringlets. He sat back on his throne of shadows, casually relaxed, leaning onto the palm of one of his hands. His legs were spread, one gracefully slung over the armrest of the throne as if to prove his own nonchalance. Emerald eyes bore into me from behind a small, black mask. I watched him with interest for a few moments, but he made no move to stand. If he was planning on joining me here on the dancefloor like his siblings, he showed no sign of it.

"Is he coming?" I asked Lilith, although my gaze never left The Warden of Shadows. Something about his stare had me completely enraptured. He looked at me like he was someone who knew me - like he was someone who knew everything about me, even my darkest and deepest secrets. Maybe he did… I'm not sure I could have looked away if I wanted to.

"My Warden is requesting that you join him on his platform," Lilith uttered, saying the only phrase that could have broken the spell that this Warden's gaze had on me. I turned to look at her face, she was clearly not amused with being tasked to deliver this information to me. My stomach dropped and I felt the muscles in my neck tense as I focused on her declaration. It is punishable by life in the Sunken Province Prison to touch one of the Warden's thrones in this room. They aren't even cleaned by the Institute's staff, the only people permitted even close to them are The Seven. To even think about stepping foot on the platform made me feel physically sick.

"I can't. I'm not allowed." Lilith rolled her eyes.

"Clearly that rule can be overruled by the Warden himself. Now, please, go, and do not keep him waiting any longer." Lilith issued the demand and then disappeared into the crowd. Obviously, she wasn't going to be escorting me. Something felt wrong, she wouldn't do this to set me up, would she?

Is she jealous of me for occupying all of the Warden's attention tonight?

A large part of me knew she would never actively try to sabotage me. Not in such a public and permanent way. However, the small voice in the back of my head was screaming that this is exactly the type of behavior I could expect from a member of The Court of Shadows. I had to go up there, no matter how terrified I was. Dread settled on me like a blanket, sweat began beading on my forehead as I struggled to calm myself. My breathing became ragged, and the weight of the entire night began to fall over me like a darkness I wasn't sure I'd ever be able to recover from. My heart pounded, my vision blurred, and I felt my Mythica inside me raging.

This is what dying feels like.

Then my eyes found him again.

He watched me with a knowing, burning stare, but instead of feeling exposed, this time, this stare grounded me. I could have sworn I saw him take a deep, exaggerated breath, beckoning me to do the same. I did. We stood there for a moment, our eyes locked in an intense connection, breathing together. Soon I started to feel my heart rate return to normal, and the voice in my head had silenced. I watched the corner of his mouth raise in an almost taunting smirk and he curled his index finger in the air three times - asking me to join him. No, not asking. Demanding me to join him.

The students in the ballroom had been doing a pretty abysmal job of pretending they weren't watching my every move tonight with the various Wardens, but at least they were trying to put on a show. At The Warden of Shadows' gesture, however, the room fell silent again save for the soft drone of the music. Shocked gasps and looks of disbelief were shared as I made my way across the dance floor towards his platform, his throne...him.

The sea of students parted, watching each step with ravenous eyes as I walked past them on my journey to where no student had gone before. I might have fallen apart if it weren't for his gaze, still locking me into place, still begging me to breathe. All I could focus on was his eyes, the emerald-green orbs held me captive, so bright and welcoming, brighter than a sea of green grass in a meadow, brighter than the most precious jewels, I knew then that I'd never be able to see this shade and think of anything other than his gaze ever again.

Before I could register it, or over analyze it, I was stepping onto his platform, coming to a stop a foot from The Warden of Shadows and his throne.

"I thought you were going to pass out for a moment. Glad to see you made it here in one piece." His voice was exactly what I pictured when looking at him, it was deep and dark as if each word he said was casting another shadow over me. It felt consuming, overwhelming, like his voice had the power to completely envelop me. But it had a mischievous tone to it too, lively, devilish. Intoxicating.

"I'm not quite sure we should celebrate yet, there's still time," I retorted, and he laughed. The kind of deep throaty laugh that lit up his face as his brown skin crinkled around his eyes.

"Then perhaps I should prepare myself to catch you," he playfully responded, and my heart jumped. He stood then, rising to his full height above me. This man before me had to be the tallest of the Wardens, or if he wasn't, he certainly held himself like it. The shadows trapped within the throne behind him swirled in fury as if they were feeling the effects of his absence. With the kind of presence this man held, I completely understand. "Lysander Bladespell, Miss Cromwell."

"So, let me guess. You saw the chance to be the only Warden who allowed me onto your platform and you simply had to break just about every rule you could by bringing me here." I couldn't quite tell behind the mask, but if I had to, I'd bet that his eyebrow raised in surprise. Maybe it's the way he was looking at me, or my place of power here on the Wardens platform, or maybe it's the fact that I've spent all night listening to the most important individuals in all of Verihdia tell me they want me to Pledge to their Courts, but I felt confident. I felt important. I felt wanted. Best, and probably most dangerous, of all, I felt invincible.

That reason is why I said what I said next. "Isn't that right, Lysander?" The dark expression that crossed his face was unreadable, and if I wasn't positive I'd fall if I tried to run, I would have made a mad dash out of there and away from his glare.

Ok, too much confidence, Lexa. Tone it down. Tone it way down.

He leered then for a few moments in silence. He was studying me, watching my every movement, keeping a close watch on the rise and fall of my shoulders. I stood my ground despite my ever-growing desire to get out of there. It must have been minutes that we stood in silence. I didn't even notice that the party had begun again behind us, students returning to their hushed conversations. I couldn't notice anything else but him. So when I heard a familiar voice from just in front of The Warden of Shadow's platform, I nearly jumped out of my skin.

"My Warden, I apologize for the intrusion. I noticed that my girlfriend did not have a refreshment and I wanted to oblige." Chandler stood his ground at the base of the platform, his golden hair and pale complexion a stark contrast to the Warden's dark skin and features. I couldn't believe my eyes. I knew Chandler was bold, reckless even, but to actually approach a Warden without permission was a little reckless, even for him.

Wait, did he say girlfriend?

I turned my gaze back to Lysander who had not yet acknowledged Chandler's presence, instead, his eyes were still fixed on me. Well not me, but the air around me.

Weird.

I decided not to let Chandler stand here any longer, because at any moment Lysander could see this intrusion as an act of violence or disrespect and enact any number of cruel punishments. "Thank you, Chandler," I said, gripping the stem of the champagne flute in my hands. Chandler smiled like the charming man he was, but he did not look at me. Why would he, when his future Warden was mere feet away from him? Once I held the refreshment in my hand, I expected Chandler to have the good sense to walk away. That was expecting too much, apparently.

"It is a great honor that you have graced us with your presence at this event tonight. I look forward to Pledging to your great Court tomorrow morning, my Warden." I felt like my tongue was about to fall out of my mouth from how far my jaw had dropped. Not only was it completely taboo to address any Warden that wasn't yours as 'My Warden', but it was entirely inappropriate to speak to a Warden without being spoken to. Chandler was going to get himself killed, right here in front of me. When I looked back over my shoulder at Lysander, I half expected him to call for the guards in the room to take Chandler away to a place where I'd never see him again. At the very least, I expected anger, or disgust to be painted on his face - but still, he was watching me.

"Thank you for bringing Miss Cromwell her drink, you may leave us now." Lysander's calm voice was eerie, devoid of the playful nature he had just moments ago with me.

This is The Warden of Shadows.

A strange sensation that felt almost like warmth spread over me when I thought about that. He wasn't putting on the mask of Warden with me. I appreciated that. This Warden wasn't playing around anymore, his 'thank you' rang as a warning. One that I hoped Chandler would recognize and heed.

He didn't.

"Until tomorrow, my Warden." He bowed and I tensed. "Lexa." He nodded to me, still not letting his eyes fully meet mine, and then he left. I watched him strut confidently back through the crowd of shocked students. I never knew Chandler was capable of breaking such important rules so casually. His dedication to The Court of Shadows never made much sense to me, but now I could see it clear as day.

"You're noticing it too, I assume?" Lysander spoke from behind me. His voice was closer than before, so close I could feel his breath on the back of my ear. A chill climbed down my spine. I knew that if I turned towards him now there would be mere inches between us, so I stayed put.

"Noticing what?" I almost whispered.

"That he was jealous," he taunted, his voice so low that it sent vibrations through my body. "That he was envious of you being here, with me." It was closer now, his whispered words being spoken directly into my ear, I felt the stubble that decorated his chin graze against my ear, and I tensed, every nerve in my body was on fire. I could tell myself that these were residual feelings from my previous conversation with Korzich, but I'd be lying. This reaction was entirely because of him. Because of Lysander.

"Then he is well suited for your Court, Warden." He sighed then, his breath dancing on my neck from his close proximity behind me. I could feel the heat of his frame pressing up against my back. It took every ounce of willpower and common sense I could muster not to lean into the warmth he promised to provide.

Damn you, Korzich, getting me all hot and bothered.

"I'm not here to discuss your boyfriend's place in my Court." He pulled away and I immediately felt emptier without his presence. I remembered the throne reacting similarly and instantly felt flushed and embarrassed. When I regained control over my body, I turned to face him once again. His eyes were alight with a fierceness that had the complete and total ability to swallow me whole.

"Then I'm all ears." I thanked the Gods that I was able to channel some of the confidence I had felt so drunk on earlier.

For a moment, the entirety of the Ball drifted away and there was nothing but our gazes locked on each other. Then his eyes slipped, and a strange expression crossed his face. Following his eye line, I saw my mentor, my friend, Oliver watching the two of us from across the space. He wasn't watching with curiosity like so many others in this room but rather his eyebrows furrowed and his head tilted, watching the man next to me with a studious gaze. By the time I returned my attention to the Warden, he had peeled his eyes from Oliver and was trained solely on me again.

"Miss Cromwell, have you ever wanted something that someone else possessed?" I tore my eyes from him and surveyed my classmates in the room. Classmates that have known so clearly and confidently where they belonged and what they wanted to do with their lives.

Only every single day.

"I have," I answered. He nodded, as if impressed, or pleased by my honesty.

"Have you ever done something about it?" His voice hardened, letting the facade of the Warden that he showed to Chandler seep in.

"What do you mean?"

"I mean…" He took a menacing step forward until he was once again in my personal space, but this time I was facing him and there was no reprieve from his imposing shadow as it began to envelop me. His fingers grazed my arm and my flesh erupted in a warm fluttering feeling. I heard the unspoken question, the silent pull for information echo in my bones.

Have you ever reached out to take what you wanted? Regardless of who it might hurt?

Then I felt it. A tendril of wretched and vicious Mythica wrapped around my mind. Slowly, almost imperceivable at first, as if it was attempting to hide in the contours of my memories, but then it took hold. Sinking into my very essence, biting down on my soul, while simultaneously caressing the edges of my consciousness. This Mythica was not hostile, but it was relentless, determined. It dug deeper into me, beckoning for the truth to reveal itself - no, not the truth… my guilt. I stopped breathing altogether. While this was the first time I had ever experienced this pull, it was most definitely not the first time I had come in contact with this Mythica.

Because this nightmarish and sadistic Mythica was mine.

I felt the pull as my Mythica reached the information it was after, the tidbit of knowledge it wanted to rip from my lips, and as hard as I tried, I could not combat the brutal intrusion. Tears blurred my vision as I fought against the admission as I spoke it involuntarily. Each word branded my throat like red-hot fire as they were wrenched from the deepest recesses of my guilty conscience.

"Axel fell very ill a few years back," I started, the salty tears streaming down my face touched my lips. "They were not sure he was going to make it, so they were going to grant him early access to the information about our parents." The words fell from me like lava pouring from an eruption, doing as much damage as well. "They asked me if it would be ok with me if he was given the information…" I did everything I could to stop the next words from exploding from my traitorous mouth. Clawing at my throat did no good, and The Warden of Shadows only watched me struggle with mild interest. " I said…"

Please. No. Don't make me say it.

"I said…" I choked out. Fighting sobs that wracked my entire body.

What did you say? Lysander pushed silently. My Mythica dug deeper into the guilt it had grasped and yanked harder. The pain was unimaginable.

No wonder Rein thinks I'd be best suited for his Court.

The vision overtook my senses, erasing the Courting Ball entirely. Shadows encroached on me, darkening my mind until there was nothing but the infirmary wing, a dying Axel, and me.

Axel coughed a wet vicious cough. One that wracked his entire body. I moved to his side quickly.

"Hey, here drink some water, ok?" I held out the cup of cool liquid for him. He nodded weakly before attempting to lift his hand, unsuccessfully.

"I..can't…" He whispered between labored breaths.

The Lost Sickness is what they had called it in part because any record of how to heal it had been long since lost, and because nearly every person who developed it was…

"I've got you." I placed the edge of the cup on his cracked lips and lifted it, pouring some of the water into his mouth. He swallowed slowly, painfully. His head fell back onto

the pillow and his eyes drifted closed.

It had been two months since the sickness took hold of him. Two months of worry, pain…goodbyes. But I wasn't ready to say goodbye. Not to him.

Having a sibling is one thing, but a twin… a twin is a part of you. A half of you that can never truly be filled, or replaced. Tears streamed down my cheek as I sat at his bedside, his hand folded in mine watching as he slept.

"Lexa," Oliver Thorne's comforting voice called from behind me. I turned to see my favorite instructor standing in the doorway to the infirmary. He watched Axel carefully, his blue eyes filled with sadness.

"Instructor Thorne," I said, wiping tears away with the back of my hand.

"May I speak with you for a moment?" He gestured for me to join him near the doorway. Reluctantly, with a kiss on Axel's forehead, I made my way across the room to him.

"How is he today?"

Worse.

The answer was always worse. Each day, another part of him slipped away. I knew if we did not get a miracle that one day, far too soon, Axel himself would be the thing that slipped away.

"We're holding out hope." It's what I said after every healer's unsuccessful visit, after each diagnostic test that showed nothing. It's all I could say, though every day it was getting closer and closer to a lie.

"The Seven have been discussing your brother's illness. The threat of it." I nodded. "They have agreed to give him his golden envelope now. So that he can know the truth about his parents before he…" Oliver trailed off, his sorrowful eyes filling with tears.

"They what?" The words spilled from me in a hushed shout.

"I convinced them it would be the right thing to do." The right thing to do. I nearly scoffed. "As long as you agree, he will be given the information."

"Will I also receive it?" I asked, eagerly. It's no secret how badly I wanted to know about my parents. Oliver placed a hand on my shoulder and shook his head.

"No. I'm sorry, Lexa. You will make it to the Pledge." He turned to Axel, tears falling down his cheeks. "He will not."

Oliver stood, his eyes locked on Axel in a tortured gaze. He truly cared for his students. Apparently, he cared so much he convinced The Seven to do the unthinkable. They were going to break their rules and give Axel his envelope early? But not me. An evil, dark cloud of an emotion that I had never fully felt before filled me. Something sinister took root, spreading like wildfire through my veins.

"They can't." I spat out before I could stop myself.

Oliver's eyes snapped back to me. A question burning behind them.

"What do you mean?" Oliver's face was twisted into an expression of confusion. Of disappointment.

"I don't…" I struggled to say the words, but the look that Oliver was giving me told me that he knew exactly what it was I wanted to say.

"You don't consent…" He whispered, incredulously. And then it fell over me. Guilt. Burning, white-hot guilt.

I shook my head because I couldn't say it.

Oliver's tears continued to fall, his eyes darting between me and the shell of my brother.

"I urge you to reconsider, Lexa." His judgment was clear on his face. He thought I was a monster.

I was.

"I can't…" Oliver's tears fell quicker then, nodding slowly to himself as if he was giving me time to change my mind, to do the right thing.

I couldn't.

"Ok," was all he said before he left.

Leaving me alone with my brother, and my guilt.

The infirmary evaporated into smoke as the scene was pulled away. As the shadows cleared, I found myself back at the Courting Ball.

Silence.

The party continued behind me as if nothing had happened. As if my entire soul hadn't just been torn to shreds, my worst confession out in the open. At first, I felt shame, guilt. I hadn't thought of that selfish moment for so long. Not since Axel got better. My admission hung over me like a dark cloud.

Then I looked at him. Lysander Bladespell, the Warden of The Court of Shadows. The vile man who had just forced me to relive that moment and all I could feel was rage. A strange emotion colored his expression, but he managed to compose himself just in time for me to release the wrath that was building inside of me.

"What did you do to me?" I practically growled at him. All formalities were out the window. "How did you do that!" I had to force myself not to scream at him the way I truly wanted to, unleash every ounce of this fury on this pathetic excuse for a Warden standing before me.

"Nothing that you haven't done to others," Lysander responded in a smug, relaxed tone. He moved to sit back on his throne, slinging one leg over an armrest, the picture of indifference. I wanted to kill him.

"That was my Mythica." I spat at him.

"It was. And oh my, what powerful Mythica it was." He smiled at that, fondly reminiscing about wielding my power.

"How dare you." I was seething, and I think Lysander could tell because despite his nonchalant body language, his gaze locked on mine again, silently begging me to breathe.

Not this time.

"How dare you steal my Mythica and use it against me? How dare you steal my secrets that were not willingly given and how dare you call yourself an honorable Warden then act in such a vile manner?" Luckily for me, I was able to keep just enough wits about me that I kept my voice lowered, slinging these insults at him in a violent whisper. I moved closer to him so that I towered over his place on the throne until my own shadow eclipsed his. I don't know what I was expecting from The Warden of Shadows, but for him to sit there, accepting my onslaught of accusations calmly, while watching the air around me with interest - that was infuriating.

"No wonder your Court is known for its envious nature." I spat. Lysander's eyes left the space around my head and met mine again. His head cocked questioningly. "Why wouldn't they be envious of other Courts, when their own Warden has to resort to stealing someone else's Mythica to be worthy of anything?" As the words fell from my lips I heard them, really heard them. I had just antagonized one of the Wardens of Verihdia. The blood drained from my face, leaving me lightheaded. My vision, the same glare that was steadfast and trained on the Warden before, blurred. And all of a sudden, the room was spinning and I was falling.

EIGHT

$\mathcal{A}$sh and venom.

That's what her Mythica felt like as it was coursing through my veins. The second I reached out with my own Mythica to grip onto hers, it fought back like a poisonous snake protecting itself. It took every ounce of my own power to grip onto hers and wield it as my own. In all my years on this plane of existence, not once had I ever had such difficulty wielding someone else's power. Well, perhaps once before.

It burned. Flaming through my blood until I was convinced that at any moment I would catch on fire, completely engulfed in a blazing inferno of Lexa Cromwell. I was able to recognize the very second she realized what I had done to her. What I had stolen from her and what I had forced out of her. I had to return to my seat on the throne to keep from losing my own balance when her Mythica was expelled from my body, I could feel the absence of it like a crater in my soul.

Her playful banter was quickly replaced with venom-laced threats.

At first, I told myself I wasn't going to wield her power. I tried to convince myself all night as I watched her that I didn't need to have a taste of that storm, and didn't need to feel the energy in my own skin. But as the night continued, when I saw the way her storm raged above her when her jealous boyfriend made his way over to us, I found myself drawn more and more to the tumultuous, ravenous cloud of Mythica above her. It was a type of power I had never felt before in my life. I couldn't help myself.

I needed to feel her.

I had no idea how painful it would be. But I can't say that if I did know, I wouldn't have done it anyway. As she so gracefully pointed out in a flurry of insults, I was the Warden of Shadows, envious to a fault. Even after experiencing the excruciating burn of her Mythica, I know I would do it again. Just for a taste of that strength she wields.

That is what I'm pondering as she towers over me, her spiteful words aimed directly at me. I can't focus on her crystal-blue eyes, instead, I watch as the cloud of shadowed Mythica around her explodes out at an almost lethal capacity, and in that moment something is abundantly clear.

If Lexa Cromwell ever truly discovered how powerful she is, no one in this world could stop her.

Then she's falling.

In a flash, I move to her and cradle her frame in my arms. As her eyes close and her limbs go weak, the angry cloud of Mythica calms to a quiet, threatening degree. If my siblings weren't watching me already, they were now. Students nearby had quieted again, gasping at the sight before them.

The Warden of Shadows, cradling Lexa Cromwell in his arms.

I'd probably stare like that too if I were them. I pulled her close to me, letting her head rest against my chest as I descended the platform and exited the ballroom.

I felt it then, the strongest scent of envy I had come across in quite some time. I didn't have to turn my head to know that it was radiating off of Chandler, the blonde kiss-ass. What I couldn't tell though was if he was jealous of me for being the one to care for Lexa at this time, or jealous of her for having my undivided attention. Based on his earlier shameless interaction in order to be in my proximity, pathetically begging for my gaze to drift to him, I was going to guess the latter. I knew I was going to have to keep a close eye on that particular Pledge.

"Brother, what happened?" Miya was on my heels as I exited the ballroom and started down the corridor to the Observatory where I had met with the Wardens earlier this evening.

"There may have been some unforeseen ramifications as a result of using my ability." With a disapproving tsk, Miya reached over to grip Lexa's hand as we continued down the hall.

"Oh Gods, Lysander, she's practically depleted. What were you thinking?"

I was thinking I couldn't survive one more moment without experiencing her Mythica for myself.

"Will she be ok?" Despite the worry that was settling in the pit of my stomach, my tone was even - I had centuries of practice controlling my emotions to thank for that. Miya kept pace with me but moved their hands across Lexa's pale face. The space between their brows crinkled.

"Yeah, she will be fine. But you sure did a number on her. Guess we don't have to worry about her choosing your Court tomorrow." They laughed softly and my heart constricted. The idea of this power belonging to anyone else but me was almost too much for me to bear. Now that I've tasted it, I'm not sure I'd ever be satiated without it. My mind began swirling with plans, ideas, and loopholes as Miya and I burst into the Observatory. I sauntered to the table and gently placed Lexa down on its surface just as my siblings entered the room.

"What just happened?" I couldn't help but roll my eyes at Rein's tone.

So touchy.

"She's fine. Miya checked her out." I tossed over my shoulder, I didn't want to tear my eyes from the peaceful woman in front of me. Her features were soft, and her raven-colored hair spilled over her shoulders and onto the cool, stone table below her.

"I have to hand it to you, Brother," Korzich's sensual tone teased from the entrance to the room. "If you had told me that one of us would have Miss Cromwell fainting for them by the end of the night, I would not have bet on you."

"Korzich, enough." I forced through gritted teeth.

"You tried your little trick on her, didn't you?" Vander spoke now. Not lifting my eyes from Lexa, I nodded, ignoring the sting at his likening my Mythica to a 'little trick'. "Even without your particular affinity for recognizing Mythica, I could tell she is immensely powerful. How did it feel?" I couldn't help but feel the residual pain from her Mythica shudder through my body, mixing with the complete euphoria of experiencing that kind of power.

I could lie. Keep the truth of her capabilities to myself. No doubt they all recognized the strength within her as I had, but none of them were capable of truly feeling Mythica the way I could. I could tell them that she fainted because she was too weak to have her power ripped away by me. I could tell them that. But they would know I was lying. She fainted, not because I drained her, but because she reached an overwhelming boiling point, almost too strong for her form to contain.

"It was unlike anything I've ever felt before." It was almost a whisper. A confession that we all felt weighed on us. Several silent minutes passed before Avalin spoke.

"What are we going to do about this?" She asked. This was exactly the avenue of conversation I needed. But I knew it was important to play my cards just right here.

"Tomorrow she makes her choice at the Pledging Ceremony and we have to honor that choice." Ivis chimes in. She must feel confident her meeting with Miss Cromwell went well. I, however, felt no such confidence. I had a plan. I knew how to correct the wrong that occurred at my hands here tonight, but if I suggested it too eagerly, my siblings would know I was only attempting to keep my own Court in the game. This situation was delicate and it required a delicate touch. It had to seem like their idea. It was time to play the part of the Warden of Shadows.

"Perhaps we can each have a little more time with her?" Korzich this time. They did a poor job of hiding the desperation in their tone, a desperation we all were feeling. Not for sins of the flesh as Korzich often lusted for, no, they desired what we all did. The security that Lexa Cromwell would offer us.

I know my siblings well. And while I wouldn't necessarily call us allies, I do trust them. I do not fear a rebellion, or a takeover, not the way I did when The Forgotten Court existed. But that doesn't mean we all didn't understand the importance of being the strongest Court. Not that we are expecting to need to defend ourselves against our siblings, but I think I speak for us all when I say we want the ability to, should the situation call for it.

Whichever one of us Lexa Cromwell Pledged to would take the place as the most powerful Court in all of Verihdia. There was no question about it.

Just as I opened my mouth to put my plan into action, a soft moan sounded from the sleeping frame on the table in front of me. I watched as her chest rose and fell quicker, and her eyes opened slowly, adjusting to her new surroundings.

At first, she was anxiously glancing around, then her eyes landed on me and the vicious detestation returned to color her ocean-blue eyes.

There she is.

And now it was time to put my plan into action.

Don't worry, Lexa Cromwell - this is far from over.

NINE

Two thoughts crossed my mind at almost the same time. First, 'where am I, and what happened?' The other, and arguably more potent of the two, 'I want to kill Lysander Bladespell.' I'm not sure when I was transported to the Observatory, but there I was, the glass pane ceiling above showcasing thousands of stars decorating the inky black sky. The last time I was in this room, I received news that I was destined to be Uncourted for the rest of my life, and now seven pairs of eyes watched me carefully as I dragged myself to an upright position on the table. Those eyes didn't belong to just anybody. The Wardens of Verihdia were here, and they were Courting me. My future looked a lot different right now than it had a few hours ago, but still no less uncertain. My head felt heavy like I would need a full day of rest to recover from whatever Lysander thought he had the right to do to me.

With my Mythica.

Just as my blood began to boil again and my eyes met his, someone spoke.

"Miss Cromwell, how are you feeling?" Miya Moonshackle squeezed their way between Lysander and myself, blocking off my line of sight, and as soon as I could no longer see his face, my anger started to fade. I turned to look at Miya, they had removed their mask and were slowly running their hands in front of my face. No doubt trying to see what happened to me. I wonder if they could discern what Lysander did, what he stole from me.

I felt sick all over again. Not only had The Warden of Shadows used my own Mythica against me, but he had forcibly dragged my most shameful secret from my lips. One that I had fully intended on carrying with me to my grave.

"I'm feeling ok, thank you, Warden, for your concern." I twisted from my perch, my dress bunching up my leg as I moved, and saw the other five Wardens standing quietly around the round table. They watched me closely, waiting to gauge my reaction to this, no doubt. "I can see that I have inconvenienced you, I deeply apologize, please allow me to take my leave."

"No." One word and I was frozen to my spot. A small flash of desire built in my core, despite the pure loathing I thought had replaced any instance of attraction. Lysander moved from behind Miya and his eyes found mine again.

"Tomorrow is the Pledging ceremony, and I think it's only fair that we give you a few minutes to ask any questions you might have to help you make your decision." I wanted to mock him, I wanted to slap the indifference from his face.

Does he not understand what he just did to me? Does he not care?

The next thought solidified before I had a chance to stop it.

I hate Lysander Bladespell.

But he was right. I did want to ask questions. I had so many. At the beginning of the evening, I expected to have one drink, dance with Chandler, then make my way back to my room to have yet another nightmare and worry about my soon-to-be Uncourted reality. But now? Surrounded by all seven of the Wardens of Verihdia, I had options. I had a chance for a future, and I had no idea why. Despite my repulsion to this Warden, it was actually pretty thoughtful of him to offer me this chance to get some clarity.

"On second thought, I'm sure you've already made up your mind. We wouldn't want to tire you out before tomorrow." He tacked on with a flippant wave of his hand. I resisted the urge to punch him. Barely.

"Wait!" I spat. "I do have questions. Questions I didn't know if I was allowed to ask before. Truthfully, I'm nowhere near ready to make a decision like this." I could have sworn I saw a quick smirk spread across Lysander's face, but it was gone before I could blink.

"I thought I was going to be Uncourted just a few hours ago. This is… a lot to take in." I continued when nobody responded.

"I'm not sure how much we could help you with a few questions, Miss Cromwell. You have to make a choice tomorrow morning." Mr. Whiplash himself spoke up again. This time appealing to his fellow Wardens. "She heard your pitches. She knows what would await her in each Court. The type of life she would lead."

"No, I don't!" I almost screamed. The Warden of the Vanguard stepped forward, her face still resembling Chandler, although I did have to admit that even since the last time I was in her presence in the ballroom, something seemed almost darker about her appearance. I couldn't quite put my finger on it.

"We cannot expect her to make this decision in one day." She spoke clearly, making eye contact with each of her siblings.

"The Pledging ceremony is tomorrow, Avalin," Vander called from his spot across the table. He slowly removed his golden mask, and for the first time, I saw his bare face. He was incredibly handsome, I couldn't deny that. And those golden eyes were entrancing. I think I'd be content to stare at them forever.

"I think Avalin is right. I think we can all agree that Miss Cromwell's decision tomorrow is very important for the future of Verihdia." Ivis Grey responded, casually.

What?

How was that possible? How did my choice of Court have that kind of weight? None of this made any sense.

"No one is denying that, sister," Vander retorted.

"Maybe she needs more time?" Miya suggested meekly from their position in front of me. My gaze bounced from Warden to Warden as they spoke about my future, my decision. Any more of this and my neck was going to be sore for weeks.

"Maybe she needs to truly understand what each Court can offer before we ask her to Pledge," Korzich cooed before winking at me.

"How do you propose we do that? We can't just escort her from Court to Court and let her see how life is?" Lysander spoke again, tossing his hands up in a dramatic fashion as if this entire conversation was beneath him.

Smug bastard.

"Yes. That is exactly what we should do." When Rein spoke, the room fell quiet. No quick retort, no more verbal sparring.

"Rein, you can't be serious?" Lysander spoke clearly and directly, his gaze searing into The Warden of Echoes. They remained there for a moment that seemed to drag in uncomfortable tension.

"I've never been more serious in my life, brother." Rein finished and before Lysander could respond, Vander spoke again.

"I think it's a good idea. We can't possibly ask Miss Cromwell to make this choice without proper time to absorb the information and the benefits." Vander made careful eye contact with the other Wardens around the table, making a familiar connection with each of them.

"She can't just walk around the Courts unchaperoned." Lysander spat. This time he looked directly at me, an expression of what I can only determine as disgust crossing his face. I restrained the impulse to slap him. The fact that he was a Warden of Verihdia was the only thing that spared him.

"So she gets a guide." Ivis chimed in. My head turned again, my neck already sore from the game of catch they were playing with my attention.

"One of our Deans?" Korzich offered.

"They cannot travel into Courts other than their own. There are no people who are permitted to travel to them all," Miya responded calmly.

"Wardens are permitted to travel across Courts," Vander spoke, and silence fell over the room.

"You cannot suggest that one of us be given all that extra time with her?" Avalin's face tightened in frustration.

"That would clearly give an unfair advantage to whoever her guide was." Ivis placed her hands on the stone table in front of her and leaned into the hold.

"Ivis is right. As of now, we each have the opportunity to have Miss Cromwell Pledge to our Court. Equally." Lysander spoke from behind me, and I couldn't suppress my scoff. Lysander lifted an eyebrow in question. Or challenge. Either way, it spurred me to respond the way I did.

"If you think I would ever Pledge to The Court of Shadows after what you did tonight, then you are not as wise as I have been told." I didn't expect Lysander to react, he seemed so in control of his emotions, but what I didn't expect was a flash of approval in his eyes. So quick, I might have imagined it.

"Surely, I still have a chance, even the smallest of odds?" He leaned forward, his green eyes narrowing as if he was trying to read my mind. He didn't need to read my mind to know exactly what I was feeling, because I was going to tell him.

"Not if you were the last Court in Verihdia." I spat. He tilted his head slightly and gathered his bottom lip between his teeth in a shrug.

"Well if that's the case, Miss Cromwell, I think we have our guide," Vander spoke again and this time when I turned to look at him, my entire body shuddered.

Wait. What did I just do?

"Brother, this is insanity," Lysander spoke, his eyes tearing away from me leaving me feeling hollow.

"You heard Miss Cromwell, you are the only Warden whom we clearly do not need to worry about receiving the extra time with our Pledge." Vander finished and the other Wardens around the table nodded their approval silently. My eyes flashed back to analyze Lysander's reaction, and somewhere deep in my bones, I couldn't shake the feeling that I just walked right into his expertly laid trap.

"So what? I have to spend a week with him while he chauffeurs me around Verihdia?" They didn't answer. I was really starting to come around to the prospect of being Uncourted.

"That would not be sufficient time to truly learn and understand the intricate details of each Court, don't you agree, siblings? Travel time alone would take days." Gone was the Vander who charmed and enticed me earlier, this Vander was the picture of authority, a true leader. The Warden of Silence.

"What do you suggest then?" Miya spoke quietly, their eyes drifting towards me as if to check that I was still breathing. I'm not sure I was.

"One month." Rein. If I was breathing before, I definitely wasn't now. "One month at each Court. That will give her plenty of time to not only observe the day-to-day life but to participate." That sent shivers down my spine, the thought of Rein asking me to torture prisoners as a way to participate almost had my stomach lurching.

I wanted someone to object. An entire month at each Court? That's six whole months if they exclude The Court of Shadows, which wouldn't surprise me, seeing as I have made my intentions with that Court abundantly clear. Half of an entire year. They must really, truly want me in their Courts. I still don't understand why.

"One month it is." Vander nodded as he spoke, as if he was overseeing some delicate proceeding. Which I guess he was. "Let's discuss an order."

"She has to come to visit me first," Korzich spoke then, their eyes dancing with excitement. "My Court holds our annual Endless Nights event a short while after the new Pledges arrive. I'd very much like for Lexa to experience that." My throat tightened. We had heard about this Festival in our studies. It is a full week-long event full of frivolity, debauchery, and lust. Never, in my entire schooling did I think I would attend such a thing.

"Ok, The Court of Passion will have the first leg of the tour, does anyone else wish to align their tour month with an event in their Court?" Vander continued in his commanding authoritarian tone. The Wardens chimed in mentioning their Courts biggest events, balls, festivals, tournaments. All vying for a prime spot on the Lexa Cromwell tour of Verihdia. Some of the most important and well-known traditions and events in all of Verihdia were being casually listed off as if they were a course schedule.

When all was said and done, the next six months of my life were completely accounted for, filled with extravagant parties and exhilarating events. I was almost envious of myself. I could only imagine how the others would feel. Vander, ever the diplomat, wrote our little tour schedule down on a piece of parchment and passed it around the table. The Wardens took turns signing their names with dark, black ink, sealing my fate with every stroke of the quill.

Out of the corner of my vision, I saw Lysander roll his green eyes.

"Fine." He laughed. "But she spends the first week with me at my Court. I cannot be expected to miss my own Pledging Ceremony celebrations, and I'm sure you all will be too busy with your own events to receive her so soon afterwards. This way you have time to prepare for her arrival."

"Fine, a week in The Court of Shadows before she begins her tour," Vander declared, making sure the addition was included in writing on the piece of parchment before sliding it to Lysander for his signature, which he added halfheartedly.

"Don't I get a say in this?" Before I could stop myself, the words fell out. Not that I didn't mean them, but even if I was being Courted by these Wardens, I didn't feel like I had any right to ask things of them.

"You've said plenty, Miss Cromwell." Lysander flippantly said, shaking his head as if my concern was of little consequence to him. I was not going to survive six whole months with him as my guide. There was no doubt I would try to kill him by then.

"Do you not wish to see the Courts before you make a decision?" Miya asked, calmly, kindly, their eyes soft and welcoming, as if they were truly ready to hear my concerns.

"That's not it, I just… an entire month feels like such a long time." I trailed off as the realization hit me. Most individuals in Verihdia have only ever seen The Living Lands and the Court that they Pledge to. No one is permitted to travel to a Court they do not belong to, ever, under any circumstances. Yet here I was being offered the chance of a lifetime. The adventure I used to dream of. A chance to not only visit every single Court in Verihdia but to actually participate in their customs and traditions, to truly see what it means to live as a Pledge of these Courts. This is a dream come true, one I'm positive Chandler would kill for. So why did I feel so overwhelmed?

Because you're not worth it.

Most of the time, I tried to block out the little voice in my head that talked down to me, the one that made me feel inferior, but this time it was right. I was inferior. I had no right to be here, there was no reason these Wardens were fighting over me so passionately that they were willing to break laws that have been in place for as long as our Courts have existed just to have the chance to woo me.

"I don't understand. Why me?" It was a whisper. I know they heard me because I could feel the tension in the room thicken and electricity buzz between their loaded, shared glances.

"Allow me," Lysander smirked, but I felt too dejected in this moment to stoke the fire of anger he lit inside me. "Lexa, I believe you're smart enough to have put together that your Final Compatibility Trial result was not actually Uncourted, yes?"

No.

I had thought about it, sure, but actually settled on it? Absolutely not. "But Lilith said…" Lilith wouldn't have lied to me, right? She is a Dean of this school and must be honest with her students, right?

"Lilith needed to keep the truth from you until my siblings and I had the opportunity to speak about your result." A rare flash of seriousness crossed his face as he glanced around at his siblings. I wanted to look at the others with him, to see what he was searching for in the other Wardens' expressions, but I couldn't tear my eyes away from the frustrating man in front of me. He must have gotten the encouragement he was after though because his eyes returned to mine and he said the words I never in my entire existence thought I would hear.

"Your result is that you are best suited for The Forgotten Court, Lexa."

TEN

$\mathcal{N}$one of us wanted to tell her the truth, that much was clear, but my plan was already in motion, and if I was going to sway her to choose my Court over the next six months, I needed to show her that I was someone who would be honest with her, even when it was difficult. That's how I would play this. Her eyes widened, and her Mythica swirled in a panic above her. It was astonishing really, the way her pale skin flushed bright pink, contrasting deliciously against her low-cut green evening gown, as this cloud of dark, powerful divination swirled above her in a possessive, threatening way.

It didn't take a mind reader to see how this knowledge affected her. I expected her to ask questions, to essentially fall to pieces, but she sat there, calmly, and nodded. If I wasn't able to see the storm cloud of Mythica raging above her, I might have believed the facade.

"I'm sure you have questions, and luckily we have six months for me to answer as many as I can." I really attempted to stay impartial, to keep any tone that could be construed as comforting out of my voice. But seeing her, watching her face fall, her Mythica reacting defensively, I'm sure I didn't do a very good job of hiding how much her pain was actually affecting me.

Not that I care, but I need her to trust me for this plan to work.

My plan. I had to fight a smile as I watched Lexa unknowingly play her part so beautifully. I was banking on her anger, her fury. I needed her to say those things. I needed her to announce how little of a chance I had.

I'd prove her wrong.

We were going to spend six months traipsing across Verihdia. Spending all that time with my siblings wasn't ideal, but it was such a short amount of time in the grand scheme of things. And it was in pursuit of something I desperately wanted, something I deserved. Six months was worth it. Lilith could handle things in The Court of Shadows while I'm gone. Besides, it's not like I've been very hands-on in the inner workings of my Court lately anyway. The work has gotten stale, stagnant, and predictable. I've found it hard to devote any time or energy to do the same old things, day in and day out. This task was exactly what I needed to shake things up. This challenge. I couldn't remember the last time I felt this inspired, this excited.

"Questions. Yes," was all she said, and I knew we were done for the evening.

"Alright, I think it's time to call it a night." Vander clapped his hands together, sending an echo around the circular room.

"I'll escort you back to your room, Miss Cromwell." I extended my arm to assist her in dismounting from the stone table, but she shook her head and slid off the surface on her own. I caught a quick glance of her pale thigh as the material of her dress bunched up when her feet touched the floor. I didn't look away as any proper gentlemen would in this scenario. Instead, I found myself analyzing the creamy white skin of her thigh, pulling my bottom lip between my teeth instinctively.

A quick, burning glance from her told me she had witnessed my mild transgression. I winked at her as she scoffed.

Come on, fight back.

"I have lived in the Institute for my entire life. I do not need an escort to my room."

Good girl.

With our rivalry solidly in place, I threw my hands up in defeat and stepped back from her, allowing her all the space she needed to flee the room, but she didn't. Instead, her gaze traveled back to Vander, something dark crossed her expression.

"What about my parents? Do I still get my envelope tomorrow even if I do not Pledge?"

I inhaled sharply at her question. I, like my siblings, had already looked into her parents, to try and see the connection, the reason behind her result. We already possessed the information she wanted to know so desperately.

Although I think I alone knew truly how desperate she was to have that knowledge. I had her Mythica to thank for that.

"Miss Cromwell," Vander started. I knew what he was going to say. Even though I disagreed, this was not the time to advocate for her. I needed my siblings to believe I truly had no chance of Lexa Pledging to me. "You understand that we do not give that information to Pledges because it could influence their choice." She nodded. "I hate to be insensitive here, Miss Cromwell, but if you learn about your parents' Court tomorrow, can you truly tell us you would not be swayed in your decision?" She was quiet for a long moment, no doubt trying to find a way to convince us that her choice would not be affected by the information. But we all knew that wasn't true. I knew that wasn't true.

"No. I cannot tell you that." She whispered defeated, her eyes filling with a sheen of tears.

"I'm sorry, Lexa. We cannot give you the information about your parents until you make your Pledge." Vander's voice softened. He wasn't sorry, the entire practice of removing the children from their families at birth was of his own design. Although, maybe after experiencing the unknown and accidental betrayal of his sons, he had come to see the true pitfalls of this system.

Lexa attempted to speak again, but her breath caught in her throat. She sighed deeply and tilted her head to the ground, hiding her eyes. She tried to speak again.

"And my brother? Will he get to know?" Realization hit me. After the truth I unwillingly stole from her mind, I understood the pain behind her whispered words.

"He will know the truth after his Pledge tomorrow," Vander spoke clearly and deliberately. Lexa's deep and frustrated sigh cut through the silence. "Unless." Her head shot up, her eyes locking on Vander. "Unless you do not wish for him to find out without you. It is within my power to withhold that information from him until it can be given to you both."

Once again, Lexa Cromwell found herself at the center of a difficult choice. Her brother was once again being offered the chance to know the truth about their family, but only if Lexa approved. I watched her carefully, as I think all my siblings did. A decision like this was incredibly telling. How someone resolved a dilemma of this nature often gave a glimpse into a person's true colors. This type of situation is exactly the kind of thing one might find in the Final Compatibility Trial. My siblings and I all held our breath, watching with anxious anticipation to see what Miss Cromwell's true colors would be.

Her Mythica danced above her in a swirling pattern creating a funnel of smoke above her head. Indecision, I decided.

She opened her mouth to speak, but shut it again, clearly reevaluating her choice.

"Will he know I made this choice?" There it was, I had to fight the urge to smile. She was going to make the same choice, I knew it. But she needed reassurance first.

"Of course not," Vander replied, and she nodded repeatedly, up and down, up and down.

"I want him to wait." It was a whisper, a quiet confession. Her head slumped low until her eyes were fixed on the floor. Her Mythica was constricting with guilt, I'm sure. Vander nodded, and my siblings glanced around at each other, analyzing this new information. But this wasn't new to me.

I didn't care what part I had to play at that moment, I didn't care that she was currently fighting the war within herself.

Her envious side was showing.

And I'd make A Court of Shadows member out of her yet.

ELEVEN

The walk back to my dorm was quiet. I'm sure the party in the ballroom had ended and by now my fellow Pledges were tucked into their beds, warm and safe, excitedly dreaming about the ceremony tomorrow where the rest of their lives would begin.

I, however, was none of those things. Warm, safe… excited. I was guilty. I cursed myself as my bare feet slid across the stone floor of the Institute's hallways. My heels were hanging by their straps from my index finger, bouncing against my thigh with every slow, torturous step.

I'm a traitor.

The wind howling outside the windows seemed to scream its disapproval with me.

I'd done it again. I'd made a selfish, horrible choice. A choice that affected the person I loved most in this world and why? Because I couldn't stand the thought of Axel knowing about our parents for six whole months, while I traveled around Verihdia just as clueless about my family's origins as before. I knew that made me a horrible person. I felt it with each lonely step.

Six whole months. For six months, I will be paraded around the Courts of

Verihdia. For six months, I will be introduced to the customs and traditions of the Courts. For six months, I will force Axel to wait to receive his birthright. The truth about his family. Our family. The truth he was promised twice now. And yet, twice I kept it from him. And the worst part is, he won't even know I was the one to make this choice.

I hate myself.

My thoughts were so consumed with utter disappointment in myself that I didn't notice the crowd of people buzzing outside my room until they were already surrounding me.

"What did they say?"

"What did it feel like?"

"What did they promise you?

"Who are you going to choose?"

"What was your Final Trial Result?"

"Why did they come for you?"

The onslaught of questions left me very little space to answer, or breathe. The bodies of my classmates crowded me, pushing in, as if getting close to me meant they could get closer to the Wardens themselves. People I've known my entire life, people who've regarded me as an acquaintance and nothing more, were here groveling at my feet as if I was in some sort of position of power as if I was a Warden myself. I felt my face flush, and no doubt the others could see the pink tint to my skin, but they didn't care. Their questions continued to barrage me. My eyes darted across the crowd, searching for the faces I needed to see at this moment. The faces of comfort. I needed to see Riley.

I scanned the crowd for their colorful hair, silently begging for some sort of reprieve from the vicious attention, and my eyes landed on him. Axel. My twin. My family. My biggest regret. I forced down the guilt that threatened to overtake me and reached my hand out to him. He pushed through the crowd seamlessly, showcasing his raw strength.

"Get out of here. It's been a long night, and we all have a big day tomorrow." When the crowd did not disperse, he slid his thumb and index finger into his mouth and let out an ear piercing whistle. He was so good at that, it was a skill I never learned. Our classmates' voices quieted to a low murmur as Axel reached me, embracing me fully in his muscular arms, and gently led me back towards my door through the mass of bodies blocking the way.

Axel didn't release me until I was safely inside my room and the door was shut tightly behind us. I must have started to cry because Axel's comforting touch reached my cheek as he wiped away tears that slid down my face.

"Are you ok?"

My heart constricted. My brother, my best friend. I had just experienced a once-in-a-lifetime event, I was the only one with an inside scoop, real information. But instead of asking me about that, instead of bombarding me with questions like my classmates did - he asked me if I was ok. He truly is the best brother a girl could ever ask for. And it only reminded me that I was the worst sister in all of Verihdia.

"I don't know. I really don't know." Despite the nagging voice telling me I didn't deserve his comfort, I craved it. So I collapsed into his arms and sobbed as he held me. We stood there for a while before I heard the start of a commotion outside of the wooden barrier. Clearly, my classmates hadn't gotten the hint to leave yet.

"Out of my way, I swear to the Gods. Best friend and fuck buddy coming through." I cringed at Riley's flippant and crude description of Chandler. There was some sort of mumbling argument that spurred them on. "Oh! You think you're her best friend? Tell me, what's her middle name?" Quiet. "That's what I thought, now get out of here you weird, gossip-hungry vultures!" Axel smiled down at me before stepping away, leaving me to stand on my own two feet again, which I did - mostly, and he opened the door. Riley and Chandler slid in, still in their party attire, still slinging insults at the crowd outside the room until the door was shut once again. Riley wasted no time coming up to me and embracing me in their arms. I was much more composed now than I had been only minutes ago, but I'm sure the remnants of my breakdown were still present on my face. As if Riley could hear my thoughts, they used their thumbs to carefully wipe under my eyes, removing dripping kohl from the darkened waterline around my eyes.

"Ok, when you're ready to talk about it, we're here." Riley smiled at me before moving to sit on the bench near the window.

My gaze shifted to Chandler and I could feel his jealousy from here. His resentful eyes scanned my face slowly.

"Why are you crying?" He asked. Simple. Plain. No edge of concern.

"I guess I just got a little overwhelmed. I'm ok now," I responded, moving to sit on the edge of my bed, dropping the heels in my hand to the floor near the end table. I crawled up into the center of my bed carefully, as to not rip my dress, and sat with my legs crossed in front of me. I dragged a pillow from behind me onto my lap and hugged it tightly to my chest. I knew I had a lot of explaining to do, so I needed a little shield of comfort.

Axel sat down on the other end of my bed, within arm's reach of me. His face still twisted into a mask of concern, but I could see a hint of confusion and anticipation as well. He was the only one who knew my Trial result, well the one I was told at least. So he must be just as confused as I was, why all seven Wardens of Verihdia came to Court an individual who was destined to be Uncourted. Chandler moved slowly around the perimeter of the room, watching me carefully, before sinking down onto the ground with his back against the wall.

"Ok," I sighed. Let's get this over with. "I'm ready to answer your questions."

Chandler, Riley, and Axel exchanged a silent glance before retraining their gazes on me. Riley spoke first. "What did they say to you?" Their unbridled excitement and wonder were truly childlike and innocent and it made me smile as I began to answer them.

"They each spent their time telling me about the pros of their Courts. All the positive things they have going for them and why they think I'd be happy there. Honestly, they just reiterated things I already knew from our studies, but I guess it really did feel more real coming from them." Riley nodded as they took that in.

"What was Avalin like?" Axel practically shouted. He, like Chandler, was jealous that I was permitted a close encounter with his soon-to-be Warden. But unlike Chandler, Axel didn't disturb our meeting under the guise of care just for a chance to be close to them.

"She was so interesting, strong, and powerful. A no-nonsense kind of girl." He smiled. "You're going to love it there."

"What did she look like to you?" Riley asked. "We were having debates on the dance floor. It was so weird to be looking at the same thing as someone else and still see something completely different." I nodded. It was strange to see Avalin's Mythica up close and personal.

"She, well... She looked like Chandler to me." I shyly glanced at the stoic form on the floor across the room. His eyes softened ever so slightly before his eyebrows furrowed again.

"Gross." Riley made a gagging motion and Axel joined them in laughing. I gripped one of my other pillows from the bed and tossed it at Axel, falling into a fit of laughter myself. It felt good to laugh, like I was suddenly lighter and the pressure of the evening slipped away, slowly.

"Why do they want you?" Chandler's deep voice cut through our laughter. Axel turned towards him with a frustrated and challenging look on his face.

"Gods, man, really?" Axel shook his head at Chandler who simply shrugged, but never removed his gaze from me.

"You're both thinking the same thing too. Why am I the bad guy for asking it?" Chandler's slow, deliberate words sunk into me. Neither Axel nor Riley corrected him though. Of course they were curious. As far as Axel knew, I was destined to be Uncourted for the rest of my life. Exceptionally unexceptional.

Riley and Chandler had no idea what my Final Trial results were, but they never expected this. Of course they didn't. This is unreasonable. Unheard of. Impossible.

Except it's not. It's possible and it's happening to me right now. I felt my heart rate pick up slightly, I prayed they couldn't tell how hard it pounded, or how I had to force each breath.

Moment of truth, Lexa.

I pondered for a moment about what it would be like if I told them what I knew now about my real Final Trial result. Would they be interested? Afraid? Would they see me differently? Would they tell the others?

I was almost certain Axel and Riley wouldn't tell a soul if I asked, no matter how badly they wished they could. Chandler, however, I was much less certain about. Not that I didn't trust him, but I understood him. That was part of why we comforted each other so well. We understood each other. And something this big, this world-shattering - I'm not positive he'd be able to keep it to himself and I'm not positive I'd ever ask him to.

So that is why I decided to keep that information to myself.

"My Final Trial Result was unique," I spoke slowly, cautiously, taking care to choose each word. I saw Axel out of the corner of my eye down at the end of my bed, his eyebrows furrowed together, pure confusion painting his features. I mean, sure, we had never heard of anybody being given the Uncourted result after their Final Trial, but surely that's not 'All seven Wardens are trying to win your allegiance' unique.

"And what was your result, Lexa?" Chandler pushed. His tone came out more as an interrogation than a friendly chat. I understood that too though. He's destined for The Court of Shadows after all. They deal in secrets.

A cold shiver traveled down my spine at the thought of that Court, and that Warden. Lysander Bladespell.

That Mythica stealing, no good son of a-

Warden. He was a Warden of Verihdia. And no matter how completely and relentlessly furious I was with him, that would not change the fact that he held the highest position of power in this world, and I was set to spend the next half a year at his side. I needed to control my impulses. No matter how badly I wanted to strike that smug look off his stupid, sarcastic face, I could be executed for such action, and I was not about to die before I even had the chance to live.

I looked up at Chandler, he was searching my face, watching me carefully as I spoke. I decided then to protect my little secret. Secrets were currency, and I didn't doubt Chandler's ability to use them to his benefit somehow. Truthfully, something about that didn't sit right with me, so that's why I said, "Uncourted. My Final Trial told me I was best suited to be Uncourted." Riley gasped, and Axel hung his head. But Chandler, I could instantly tell from the look on his face that he didn't believe a single word of it. But he didn't say anything. He just watched me as if he was trying to discern the truth. He always reprimanded the use of my Mythica, but something about the look on his face now told me that given the chance, he would use it right now, on me.

Just like that self-centered, good for nothing ass-

Stop. No more bashing a literal Warden. Not even mentally.

"Lexa, are you serious? Uncourted?" Riley asked, their voice filled with pity. "So like you don't match with any of them?" Their eyes widened as a thought crossed their mind. "Or do you match with all of them equally?" I nodded. That seemed a good enough excuse. "Why didn't you tell us?" Probably because your voice is filled with pity.

"I didn't want to ruin your good news. You had all gotten the result you hoped for, and I was so proud and happy for you. I really was. So I kept it to myself." Tears formed in Riley's eyes but they blinked them away quickly.

"I hate you for lying to me and keeping such a terrible thing to yourself. But I am so lucky to have a friend who would do something like that." They smiled at me, and I felt warmth spread through my chest and my body, easing the tension I didn't realize was being held in my muscles. If one comforting look from my best friend could do that, I can't wait to see what incredible things they'll accomplish in The Court of the Undying. And I literally will have the chance to see it. With my own eyes. All three of them. I have been given the incredible opportunity to visit each Court before making a Pledge. Something that no single person in the entirety of Verihdia has ever been offered.

"You're going to be a great healer, Riley. I can't wait to witness it." Their eyes widened and their eyebrows raised in a questioning surprise.

"You're going to choose Undying!" They claimed, jumping from their seated position at the window seat.

I probably should have worded that differently.

"No. Well, maybe... I'm not sure." Riley's expression fell. Hesitancy colored their face.

"Wait, I'm confused," Riley exclaimed, plopping back down on the cushioned window seat.

"Me too, how do you not know where you're going to Pledge? You have to decide by tomorrow." Axel's voice hardened. I couldn't tell if it was worry, or something else.

"Actually, I don't." I started carefully. They watched me, silently. "They are extending my deadline, I do not have to Pledge anywhere tomorrow." That's the easy part of what I have to say. These people mean the world to me and I love them dearly, but that doesn't mean I'm not concerned with how they'll react to the news that I not only am being fought over by all seven Wardens of Verihdia, but they all want me so badly that they've thrown out the rule book and offered me a once in a lifetime opportunity. Something that has never occurred, and probably never will again.

"So you have an extra week or something?" Axel asked, his usually melodic and joyful tone was serious.

"Six months." Riley choked on the breath they were taking and coughed violently.

"Six. Months?!" They forced out between coughs.

"Yeah. They want to make sure I have plenty of time to decide. It's apparently a really important decision." I still cannot believe the words that are coming out of my mouth and that this is my life.

"They did all this for an Uncourted?" Chandler snapped out the title, his teeth clenched and his breath coming out in short angry huffs. I could taste the envy in the air around him like I could taste the incoming rain in the damp sky. Consuming, present, and threatening.

"Chandler," Axel warned.

"Don't give me that, Axel, she's being cryptic, and I want to know what is so special about Lexa Cromwell. Why did all seven of the Verihdian Wardens come here? Why are they extending her Pledging deadline? Why her?!" Chandler's brown eyes were wild with fury, with jealousy. Gone was the pseudo-composure he had minutes ago.

"Chandler, calm down." Riley chimed in, their gaze narrowing on him. How Riley felt about Chandler has never been a secret, so the disdain they channeled in his direction now was not uncommon.

"Tell me, Lexa, tell me why you?" Chandler stared at me, unwavering. I wasn't in love with Chandler, but I did love him. I loved the companionship, the comfort. And if you had asked me yesterday if I thought he also loved me, I would have said yes. Without a doubt. But something about the way he was looking at me now, with complete and utter disdain, disbelief, and hatred painted on his face, told me he felt many complex emotions regarding me, but love was most definitely not one of them.

"They are giving me one month in each Court, one month to see their customs, experience their traditions. Then I will be asked to choose." It was so quiet in my room that I could have heard a whisper in the wind.

"Wow." Riley was the first to break the silence. Axel's eyes did not leave my face and Chandler's entire body tensed, his fist clenching to a probably painful degree.

"Wait, you said 'each' Court? But only six months?" Riley probed.

"Yeah, I am most definitely certain that I will never choose The Court of Shadows," I spoke this part directly to Chandler. Maybe it was to comfort him that he and he alone would be in that Court out of this group, or maybe it was to declare that I could never be the type of person that fits in with those people.

Again, the room was thick with silence. Riley mindlessly picked at their nails, Axel rubbed the back of his neck, and Chandler continued to stare at me.

"Good for you, Lexa. I hope you enjoy your tour of Verihdia." Chandler stood and left the room. In the blink of an eye, he was gone.

"Don't mind him, he's Court of Shadows for a reason. I mean, I'm not even the envious type and I'd be lying if I didn't say that I'm pretty damn jealous too, " Riley admitted, averting their gaze as if they were ashamed of their own confession. "Look at it like this, you're making history here, Lexa. Kids at the Verihdian Institute will read about you for centuries. The girl all the Courts wanted so badly that they broke every rule they ever made to get her." I knew they weren't upset with me, but something about their melancholic tone sent a shooting pain directly through my chest.

"I didn't ask for this." It was a whisper and the most honest thing I've ever uttered in my entire life.

"I know." Axel slid forward on the bed until he was able to wrap his arms around me. Within a few moments, I felt Riley's warmth embrace me from the side. I'd been here before, safe in the hold of the two most important people in my life, but it felt different, tainted. I sat there, in quiet fear, with the bleak but indisputable knowledge that the life that I had grown to love would never be the same.

TWELVE

*A*s far as first impressions go, I've done worse.

But I've also definitely done better. With a frustrated grunt, I ripped off the velvet jacket and tossed it onto the chair in the corner of my temporary chambers. It's been only twenty minutes since our meeting concluded, since it was settled that Lexa Cromwell would be coming with me back to my home, The Forsaken Quarters in The Court of Shadows. Four hours ago, I would have scoffed at such a ridiculous plan, to escort an Uncourted Pledge around all seven of the Courts. Devoting half a year to this endeavor is not only unheard of, it's absolutely absurd. But Lexa Cromwell has something I want - her Mythica. And if I cannot wield it, I am going to have it in my Court at my disposal. This plan is how I will accomplish that.

She played her part so perfectly, without even knowing it. Her anger was exactly what I needed from her. However, I'd be lying if a dark, vicious part of me wasn't burning with fury at her declaration.

'Not if you were the last Court in Verihdia' she had said. No, she didn't say it, she spat it, with a venom-laced tongue. Of course, it is exactly what I had wanted her to say, but who did she think she was, sending such ire towards a Warden of

Verihdia? Her displeasure was the perfect opening for me to solidify my place as her escort, but it's also the very thing I'm going to need to overcome in these next few months to convince her to Pledge herself to me. To The Court of Shadows.

I slid the dark green trousers down my legs, stepping out of them without bothering to pick them up. I'd get it in the morning. I moved to the large bed that sat atop a green, wrought-iron bed frame. Sometimes I hated the notion that because of my Court, I only liked the color green. As if every other color caused me physical harm to see. Or Gods forbid, wear.

I enjoyed other colors too, although I couldn't admit that. Blue, for example. Calming, peaceful. Vibrant like it holds secrets. I slid under the satin sheets and pulled them to my chin thinking of the blue of Lexa's eyes. So full of fury when she regarded me. Filled with disdain and judgment.

I had a lot of work to do if I was going to recover from the residual effects of my first impression with Miss Cromwell. I did not intend to cause her pain or discomfort. Most of the time when I utilize my own ability, they cannot even tell that I had borrowed their Mythica. Generally, I simply copy the Mythica and go about my merry way. But pulling her Mythica, borrowing that magic from her, was not like creating a copy, but instead felt like I was truly ripping pieces of her own Mythica away. It was not my plan to hurt her. I didn't intend for that. In fact, it took all of my willpower to keep the surprise and worry from my expression as she fainted. Nobody's ever reacted like that before. Seeing her limp in my arms, eyes closed, I felt a twinge of an emotion I hadn't had the displeasure of experiencing in quite some time.

Guilt.

I tossed the satin sheets off my body, leaving my frame exposed, lying on the mattress. I don't feel guilty. Ever. I take what I want, damn the consequences. So why is it that this young, infuriating Pledge fainted and all of a sudden, I have this pit in my stomach keeping me from taking a full breath?

She hated me now, rightfully so. But that would not be the case for long. I had a goal, and when I have a goal, nothing can stop me from achieving it. Guilty or not, I wanted Lexa Cromwell and her Mythica to myself.

Tomorrow is the Pledging Ceremony and the first day of my adventure with Lexa Cromwell. I had a lot of ground to cover, now I just needed to decide on an approach. Just as I was beginning to think of how I could go about achieving this goal, the door to my chamber swung open. In strutted my Dean, Lilith. She had changed from the dark pantsuit she wore at the ball and now wore a simple, green nightdress.

"What do you want, Lilith?" I bit. I was in absolutely no mood for her brand of distraction.

She held my gaze and closed the door behind her, locking herself into the chamber with me. I rolled my eyes. "Not now, Lilith." She did not step closer, but also made no move to exit.

"You seem tense, my Warden. I could help you relax?" I pushed up on my arms until I was seated with my back rested against the iron headboard. With the blanket kicked down by my feet, the only thing that covered my body at the moment was my undergarments. I couldn't help but feel slightly exposed, not that she hasn't seen all of me intimately before, but something about being outside the contained environment of my quarters back home made it feel less casual. If a sexual affair transcends Court Boundaries, then it means something. And this relationship certainly does not mean anything.

"I'm not interested tonight, Lilith." I pulled one of my knees up to my chest and leaned my arms casually on it, trying to lace in as much disdain and annoyance that I could muster.

"How about a debrief then?"

So we've established she's not leaving.

My eyes rolled as I motioned to the chair in the corner of the room. She moved to it slowly and sunk into it, the leather creaked under her weight.

"You put on quite the spectacle tonight, didn't you?" Her accusatory tone was impossible to miss. So that's how this conversation will be going.

"Certainly left an impression," I murmured. She sighed. I watched as she crossed her legs, the hem of her nightdress climbing higher on her thigh, but I didn't dare give her the satisfaction of seeing the movement draw my eye. Instead, I focused on her white hair and how it seemed blinding in the moonlight that seeped through the small crack in the green wool curtains.

"I heard about the arrangement," she almost whispered, laced with contempt. Lilith clearly thought the pageantry of our showboating was embarrassing, but she was smart enough not to say a word.

"Yes, I was going to send for you in the morning, but seeing as you're here now," I did not hide my annoyance, "I need you to leave first thing tomorrow for the Forsaken Quarters and prepare Miss Cromwell's chambers. She will be with us for a week."

Her eyes widened. "But the Pledging ceremony is tomorrow, my Warden. I am to receive them. Someone needs to accept their Pledge." She spoke through clenched teeth.

"Well, it's a good thing I am here then," I bit back. Her mouth opened as she prepared to retort, but thought better of it.

Smart.

"Yes, my Warden." Defeated. She gave in so easily. Pity. I watched her in silence for a moment, waiting to see if she would excuse herself. She did not. Instead, she sat, content, in my leather armchair and watched me.

"Can I help you with anything else, Lilith?" Her brows furrowed together, and she went to speak, but lowered her head and sighed instead. "Spit it out," I demanded.

"I went to Miss Cromwell's room earlier," my blood boiled. If my siblings found out my Dean was snooping around her, they would have questions. Questions I wouldn't be able to answer.

"Who gave you the authority to do so?" I sat up straighter in my bed, one of my legs hanging off the edge so my foot sat on the floor, ready to jump up at any given moment.

"My Warden, it is within my rights and duties as a Dean of this Institute to check on my students. Especially those who recently fell ill." She spoke hurriedly, defensively. I sighed. She was right, of course, but I still couldn't let anything risk my one, very fragile chance here.

"I understand your line of thinking, Lilith." She visibly relaxed. "But do not make any decisions regarding Lexa Cromwell without my express permission ever again. Is that understood?" Her face twisted in shock, but after a moment she nodded.

"Good," I said, leaning back into the headboard. "Now tell me, what did you say when you visited her?" I was curious, of course. This situation with Miss Cromwell was delicate, one wayward unplanned word from Lilith, and she could ruin the small chance I might still have.

"I did not end up seeing her," I exhaled a breath of relief. "She had company." My ears perked up at this. What was Miss Cromwell doing having company after fainting, after such a long and drawn-out event? Perhaps it was her brother?

"Company?" I prompted her.

She nodded once, "Chandler Mills, you may recognize the name…" A deep heat burned in my stomach…anger.

"The gentleman who gave himself the permission to approach my platform and speak to me." Lilith tensed, no doubt out of fear of retribution. She was supposed to be watching my platform so that very thing would not happen after all.

"And Miss Cromwell's boyfriend." She finished. I felt the familiar bloom of envy crest in my chest. "He left looking rather flustered." I understood the implication behind her words. They were together.

Suddenly, any guilt I was harboring for my actions and how they affected her earlier dissipated. Instead, biting jealousy took its place. Not jealousy that she spent her evening with a man in her bed, but jealousy that she was able to incapacitate me with thoughts of my own wrongdoings and misconduct. That she made me question my own sinfulness, only to turn around and indulge in sins of her own. With her saddened crystal eyes and shaky unstable breaths, she fooled me. I am not often fooled.

"On second thought, Lilith. I would like your company in this bed tonight." Her eyes snapped to mine, wide in question.

"My Warden...?"

"Do you want to ride me tonight or not?" I asked, slowly slipping down my undergarments, giving Lilith an eyeful of my growing erection.

It wasn't Lilith's presence or even thoughts of the infuriating Pledge that spurned this desperate need inside me. It was the envy. If Lexa Cromwell could release her tension tonight, guilt-free, then I would too.

Lilith was up and across the room in an instant, climbing onto the bed and throwing one of her legs over my hips until she was comfortably straddling me. I instantly felt the heat from her core rubbing on my sensitive appendage. It seemed the nightdress was all the clothing she wore.

I shimmied underneath her until my back was flush against the headboard and she was hovering above my length, now achingly hard. She swirled her hips sensually, making only the briefest of contact with my tip.

I grew tired of her games. Gripping her hips, I pulled her down onto me, spearing her. She cried out as I filled her. Her head fell back and her mouth opened in panting breaths as she sat still, adjusting to the thick intrusion.

Then she moved, slowly at first, up and down at a glacial pace. A growl escaped my mouth. Misunderstanding, Lilith smiled and continued her slow performance.

"Enough playing around, Lilith. Ride me." I almost growled between clenched teeth. Gripping her waist, I took charge of her pace, forcing her to move at the speed I needed. She whimpered beneath my touch, slinging curses as her breasts bounced invitingly. My mouth found the swollen peak through her nightdress. She moaned as my tongue moistened the fabric and played with the hardening flesh beneath. Biting down slightly on the bud between my teeth, she screamed. Her hands clawed at my bare shoulders. My lips moved from her breast to her exposed throat, possessively nibbling and licking the soft flesh there.

"Tell me, Lilith. Did Chandler look half as content as you are right now? Was he satisfied?" With my hands still gripping her hips, I bounced her quicker, chasing the kind of high I only truly get from coveting. Her head snapped up and her eyes met mine. I knew what she was thinking, that I was jealous of this Chandler being with Miss Cromwell. But that wasn't it. I wasn't thinking about how her curves would fill my palms so much better than Lilith's small frame. I wasn't thinking about the soft moaning sound she uttered when she woke up after fainting. I wasn't thinking about how I wished it was her blue eyes looking down at me as Lilith rode me. I wasn't thinking about that at all.

If Lexa gets to have mind-blowing, guilt-erasing sex tonight, then so do I.

"Tell me, Lilith." I thrust into her harder, and her breath caught in her throat.

"No, no he wasn't… he wasn't.." She let out a scream as she climaxed. I pushed further into her, spurred on by her words, knowing the sex I'm giving Lilith right now is better than whatever pathetic attempt at passion Chandler was able to give Lexa. I'm willing to bet she has no idea how good it can be.

With that thought in my head, I came. Hard.

After a satisfied Lilith left my chambers, I cleaned up and returned to bed.

I was done feeling guilty about what I did tonight. And now I knew exactly how I was going to win Lexa Cromwell.

THIRTEEN

It seemed like every person in The Living Lands was here. Just outside the walls of the Verihdian Institute sat a large outdoor colosseum. Nowhere near the size of the legendary Chaos Colosseum in the heart of The Court of the Vanguard, but impressive nonetheless. The sand-covered floor, usually barren, now housed fifty-six chairs, one for each Pledge in my class, and a large raised platform. A massive canvas map of Verihdia hung at the back of the stage, slightly blowing in the wind. This map was familiar. It was what we studied as children, analyzed as young adults, and stressed over as soon-to-be Pledges. Throughout our entire residency at The Verihdian Institute, this map was there. Taunting us with the possibilities for the future. For the last few years, all I was able to feel when I looked at this simple rendering of Verihdia was panic and fear. Knowing I had no clue which Court I belonged to, knowing I didn't feel connected to any of them. Now what I saw when I looked at this map were the seven Wardens who were so keen on convincing me to Pledge to them. Now instead of seeing seven Courts and knowing I didn't belong, I saw seven Courts and knew that I could.

Life changes so fast.

Every year, the Pledging Ceremony stage was set to accommodate seven large, throne-like chairs, equally spanned across the front of the stage. This is where The Seven sat and watched as the Pledges made their life-altering choices.

The Seven were authorized to accept or deny any Pledge request, but that so rarely happened, it almost seemed like a tall tale made up to scare the students of the Institute.

But this year, instead of the seven thrones, there were fourteen. I don't know why it surprised me that the Wardens would stay for the Ceremony, but it did. Especially since we already made the deal that meant I would not be Pledging today. I expected them to be long gone by now. All except Lysander of course. My escort. My fists clenched at my side at the mere thought of him.

I so rarely held grudges, but I'd also so rarely been violated in the way he subjected me to. My own Mythica was ripped from me by his selfish, envious hands and I refused to allow him the chance to repeat his offense ever again.

Shaking off the anger that was building in my veins, I focused again on my surroundings.

The climbing stone seats were filled by the younger Pledge classes, Instructors from the Institute, and what seemed like thousands of citizens from all across The Living Lands. All come to witness the most exciting day in every young person's life. Sitting among them in the audience these past years, I never really thought about the Uncourted individuals who sat next to us. It didn't cross my mind to wonder why they were here, still in The Living Lands instead of happily Pledged to one of the Courts. But now, sitting here at the precipice of the biggest event in the lives of my classmates, that was all I could think of. Will all my classmates be accepted? Will any of them be rejected today? Will any of them choose Uncourted? Questions clouded my mind, I didn't realize I had missed something Riley had said until they waved their hand in front of my face.

"Hello? Are you still with us on this plane of existence?" Riley's playful tone was undercut by a twinge of nerves. Their colorful hair was pulled back to a bun at the back of their head, and they wore the same white silk robe from the Final Trial that all Pledges were required to wear at the Ceremony, the crest of the Verihdian Institute boldly on display.

"Yeah, sorry. I just… thought today would look different, you know?" Riley nodded in understanding. At the end of the day today, Riley would, barring any issues, be making their way to The Court of the Undying. And I would be preparing to travel to The Court of Shadows to begin my tour of Verihdia.

"Well snap out of it!" Their voice was playful, but stern. "Since you aren't Pledging today and therefore have no reason to freak out," they started.

"I'm still freaking out, but continue." They chuckled briefly before returning to their thought.

"I need you to be calm while I panic, ok?" The corners of my lips upturned as I took in my best friend. I had been trying so hard to forget the reality of today. That after this ceremony my best friend, my brother, and anyone else I care about will be gone.

The only thing holding me together at this moment is that I will be able to see them again when I am in their respective Courts on this tour. That's what I have, that's what I hold on to.

"You have nothing to be worried about, Riley. You were born for The Court of the Undying. You were made for it." They sighed, letting my words sink in.

"I've never wanted something so much in my entire life, Lexa. I want to help people, I want to be at the forefront of medical innovation. I want to use what I have to save lives." Their eyes misted over as they spoke. I couldn't help the budding pride I felt for my friend.

"That right there is why you have nothing to be afraid of. They would never turn away someone as passionate as you are about what their Court does." They nodded and offered a small smile that didn't quite reach their eyes. I jumped as a hand clapped me on the shoulder. I turned quickly, half ready to slap whoever it was behind me, but my eyes welled with tears as I saw the face of my brother. I sunk into his frame, hugging him. His skin looked quite tan against the bright white robe. Mine, however, almost matched the pale fabric. I should have spent more time outside. Axel always offered, asking me to join him out at the colosseum playing games with his friends. I should have gone. Those were hours I would never get back. Hours I will not get to spend with my twin ever again.

"Hey Lexa, don't cry. Come on. It's a happy day." Easy for him to say. He was headed to the Court of his dreams. I couldn't bring myself to tell him how much I'd miss him and ruin his bright mood.

"I'm ok, just so excited for you both." Axel squeezed tighter, his arms wrapping me in a temporary blanket of comfort.

"Come on, let's find our seats." Riley grabbed my hand and led me towards the fifty-six chairs in the center of the arena. Suddenly, the panic set in. I wasn't Pledging today, would it be inappropriate for me to sit with the other Pledges? Should I have even worn the Pledging gown today? What do I do when they stand and make their way to the stage? Do I just sit here?

I was spiraling into a deep ocean of worry, the only thing holding me to this existence was my best friend's hand in mine.

"Miss Cromwell, where do you think you're going?" My muscles tightened at the silky timber of the voice that called from behind me. I knew who I would find standing there. I was positive his irritating voice would be etched in my memory for the rest of my life. His stupid, playful, sarcastic, taunting voice. A voice that was attached to the only person in Verihdia who I can confidently and without guilt say I despised. Had it only been last night that I heard it for the first time? Seems like I've hated him for a lifetime.

I couldn't help but roll my eyes at his words. 'Where do I think I'm going?' Something about that felt loaded. Like he wasn't just asking about where I'm going at this moment, but rather asking me about where I think my future leads. It only made me hate him more.

I turned slowly to face him, to snap back with a quick retort or scathing remark, but when my eyes met his, I forgot how to speak. He wore a dark forest green long-sleeve shirt, buttoned up the middle. The sleeves were rolled haphazardly to just below his elbows, and the first few buttons on the shirt were undone, revealing the top of his rich and chiseled chest. His dark black pants were tight against the skin of his legs, giving me a fairly accurate outline of the muscles that rippled underneath the fabric.

But it wasn't his outfit that drew my eyes, it was his face. Seeing The Warden of Shadows without a mask was more paralyzing than I anticipated. Like the small silk fabric that covered the top half of his features last night diluted his stature somehow. Leveling the playing field.

I guess the masks do serve a purpose.

"Warden," Axel interjected. I silently thanked Buyhay for my brother's presence while I attempted to gather the strength of my ire towards him in order to speak. "We were just going to our seats with the other Pledges." Ever the diplomat, my brother spoke clearly, directly, and if he was nervous to be speaking to a Warden of Verihdia, he did not let it show. Lysander's eyes examined my brother carefully, a blank expression etched on his face.

"You must be Axel." My brother smiled one of his bright, toothy smiles that lit up his entire face. I guess nonchalance only goes so far when you're being recognized by a Warden.

"I am, it's an honor to meet you, Warden." Axel bowed his head slightly before returning to his upright position.

"Likewise, Mr. Cromwell." If I didn't know my brother any better, I would have expected him to faint. "Now, Miss Cromwell... I believe I asked you that question. You are capable of speaking for yourself, are you not?" My fingernails dug into my palms as all sense of awe and admiration was washed away by his arrogance.

"Yes, I am. I just chose not to respond." Axel and Riley went completely still, the blood draining from their shocked faces. Yesterday, I would have never

163

said anything like that to another person, let alone a Warden of Verihdia. But yesterday changed a lot of things, and Lysander should get used to it.

It might be a fairly foolish and naive notion, but I figure if the other six Wardens want me alive, then perhaps I am offered a bit of immunity when it comes to any thoughts of retaliation from the Warden in front of me.

We remained there, in a standoff, for a few excruciating moments. His eyes were scanning my face, looking for a sign of weakness or regret. I would not give him the satisfaction of finding either.

"You're not Pledging today Lexa, or need I remind you of our little arrangement?" He crossed his arms in front of him, leaning his chin on his thumb and index finger, his lips curling up into a teasing smirk.

"I figured I could sit with my classmates today to support them," he watched me carefully. "Warden." I spat. Speaking the honorific as if it was the vilest thing to ever grace my tongue.

I felt Riley's hand tighten on mine, in a warning. I could practically hear them screaming 'Gods, what are you thinking?' I quickly squeezed back, trying to convey to them that I'm not afraid, and they shouldn't be either.

"You figured wrong. You will be sitting up there." He gestured casually with the finger that was just supporting his chin. I followed the direction with my gaze and instantly regretted it. Lysander had pointed directly at the stage, in front of everyone, with all the Wardens and The Seven. "With me." He finished.

"You can't be serious? I can't sit up there." The look on his face told me he was indeed serious.

"Come now, Lexa. The Ceremony is beginning soon, and you wouldn't want to be the reason it's postponed, would you? The reason that all these people have to keep waiting?" His eyebrows lowered over his taunting eyes as he cocked his head to the side.

Bastard.

A flash of the guilty truth he ripped from me only last night sparked between us. He knew what he was doing. It was a challenge. And I wasn't about to let him win. I tossed my eyes towards Axel. He still stood with his mouth agape, completely frozen at my inexcusable actions. For a moment, I let myself wonder about what he would think if he knew what I'd done. Even the smallest thought of that had my eyes welling with unshed tears. I couldn't risk that. I could never let him know.

"Lead the way," I issued through clenched teeth back at Lysander. With a quick squeeze of Riley's hand and a brief hug from Axel, I followed after The Warden of Shadows as he led me to the front of the stage.

"How dare you allude to my guilt in front of my brother?" I spat in a venomous whisper once we had cleared the fifty-six chairs and were nearing the stage.

"I did no such thing, Miss Cromwell," he tossed back, a devilish smirk painted on his face.

"You must understand that what you stole from me needs to stay a secret." I wasn't about to beg the man I hated to keep this secret for me, but I wasn't above being a little threatening.

"What secret is that, Miss Cromwell?" He abruptly turned, until he was facing me. His face was mere inches from mine. We stood just a few feet from the front of the stage, in clear view of the other Pledges, as well as every single person who had come to attend the Ceremony today.

"Are you always this awful to individuals you wish to Court?" His green eyes glistened brightly, and his dark black hair seemed to shine with an almost blue hue under the warm sun.

"Are you saying there's still a chance of me Courting you?" He drew his bottom lip between his teeth and smiled at me. The contrast of his bright white teeth against his bronzed skin was stark.

"Absolutely not," I answered almost too quickly. He let out a quiet chuckle, one that moved his shoulders ever so slightly.

"Then I have no reason to be anything other than myself around you, right?" His head tilted and his eyebrows raised at his rhetorical question. I only scoffed and moved past him to the stairs of the stage. I heard his laugh behind me but didn't dare turn to face him as I made my way onto the platform.

When I reached the top, I saw the Deans begin their ascent up the stairs from the back of the stage, and they slowly took their places at the chairs. Stoically and ceremoniously, and it only made me feel even more out of place. Unwillingly, I looked back to Lysander, silently wishing for some guidance.

He ignored my look and walked towards the only empty platform. It seemed Lilith Hargrove, the Dean of Shadows had not arrived yet. I followed quickly behind, shuffling awkwardly across the stage.

He led me directly to the two empty chairs where I would have expected Lilith to be and he plopped down in the larger chair that sat behind the other. I stood uncomfortably next to him, waiting for him to issue instructions, or to tell me where he needed me to sit. But he just sat there, watching me with his playful, green eyes. He was going to make me ask. I wanted to strangle him, but I quickly squashed that thought. My potential and entirely theoretical immunity will only cover me so far.

"Where should I sit?" I asked, careful not to let my anger influence my tone, seeing as the Deans of the other Courts were not far away and I can't imagine they'd be thrilled with my general lack of decorum around this Warden. They'd spent quite some time in our lessons teaching exactly how to act when in the presence of a Warden.

"Well, I'm going to assume you'd prefer not to sit on my lap?" His mischievous eyes darkened in provocation. I could not control my scoff. He laughed fully, his entire form shaking from the movement. "Sit in the open chair, Lexa." He pointed to the open space in front of him.

"But this chair is reserved for the Dean? For Miss Hargrove." He rolled his eyes.

"If she were here then she would sit there. But clearly," he gestured to the stage and the other Deans comfortably in their places. "She is not here. Now sit." I wanted nothing more than to fight back, but the sound of a fanfare distracted me. I turned to the back of the stage where the Wardens of Verihdia were ascending the staircase and arriving majestically on the platform.

The Wardens did not usually attend the Pledging Ceremony, and by the audible gasp and wave of shocked sounds that crashed over the audience, I could tell that the citizens of The Living Lands, and even the younger Pledge classes, did not expect this to occur today. After a brief moment of awe, the younger students erupted into applause. I scanned the mass of Uncourted individuals who had come to witness the event. They did not applaud the way the students did. Instead, they sat calmly, watching with quiet interest. The air in the arena had changed. Even I could admit that. This was a once-in-a-lifetime event, and they were living it. I know what that feels like. My entire Pledge class does. I'd been so lost in my anger for the Warden seated in front of me, and my own insecurities, that I hadn't really let myself think about the implications of this historic event I was firmly at the center of.

I quickly scrambled to sit in Lilith's chair as the other Wardens fanned out to their respective platforms. Vander cast a suspicious glance over at me, then to Lysander, and out of the corner of my eye, I saw the Warden behind me shrug nonchalantly.

I swear if he made me sit up here and I didn't even need to, I'm gonna rip his fuc....

"Welcome Pledges. Welcome students of the Verihdian Institute and welcome to the citizens of The Living Lands." Vander spoke from a standing position in front of his throne. His voice echoed through the colosseum, sending an almost electric thrill through the crowd.

Not only were the Wardens here at the ceremony, but they were facilitating it as well? Talk about history in the making.

"I am Vander Midesues, Warden of The Court of Silence," The students applauded for a moment until Vander raised his hand to silence them. Again, the

Uncourted individuals did not show appreciation towards the Wardens. Perhaps more of them were rejected than I remember. I tried not to overthink it. "Thank you all for coming today to witness the most recent class of the Verihdian Institute take their Pledges."

I looked out over the sea of students draped in white gowns to find Riley and Axel. They had chosen seats next to each other and I could see them exchanging excited glances from here. I wished I could be down there with them. I exhaled an angry huff through my nose, tossing an indignant look over my shoulder at the Warden who insisted on embarrassing me.

He sat casually on his chair, his eyes watching me. I couldn't read his expression, no doubt he was enjoying watching me squirm with discomfort.

"Before we begin, we have a small prepared statement." Vander's gaze drifted towards me.

No. Gods no, please.

"As you can see, one of our Pledges is not seated with the rest of her classmates, and instead finds herself here with us." The crowd murmured in whispered speculations and I felt the blush creep into my face, burning hot. "Miss Lexa Cromwell was visited by the Wardens of all seven Courts last night."

A collective gasp of shock erupted from the arena. All but my fellow classmates, who had already witnessed this spectacle last night, were learning this information for the first time. Maybe it's because the entirety of The Living Lands was here, or that every single Pledge class at the institute filled the stands, but I suddenly felt completely exposed. Like each pair of eyes could see right through me, seeing me for the fraud that I knew I was.

Vander's hand raised in the air again, and the incredulous exclamations from the crowd died down until the entire arena was blanketed in an eerie quiet. "Due to the unprecedented situation, we have agreed on an unprecedented solution. Miss Cromwell will not make her Pledge today with her Classmates and instead will spend one month in each Court, then she will make her Pledge." The spectators erupted again into a frenzied cacophony. I wanted to sink into the ground beneath me and never emerge.

I could practically hear their confusion. 'Why her?' "What makes her so special?' Things I've asked myself a thousand times since the moment the Wardens appeared last night at the Courting Ball.

Kamatayan, just take me now. Put me out of my misery.

"But we are not here to celebrate that. We are here to celebrate the fifty-five students who will make their lifelong Pledges today." Tentative applause began to slowly overtake the curious whispers. I wanted to sink into the chair and completely disappear.

Vander nodded to his Dean before taking his seat. Keegan Morsoe then stood and moved to the front of the stage to proceed with the Pledging Ceremony.

"Thank you, my Warden. And thank you all for being here on what is sure to be remembered as a historic Pledging Ceremony. Please join me in reciting the Pledge of the Gods."

Every last person in the arena, Warden, Pledge, student, and spectator alike, lifted their chins to the sky and repeated the Pledge of the Gods, a short Pledge that was traditionally recited at the start of any large gathering or event to give thanks and ask for guidance from the Gods of Verihdia.

Keegan began the Pledge, and the chorus of voices, thousands of them, joined in. My breathing was ragged as I added my own timid contribution. "May the darkness of Madiliam shroud me when I fear for what lies beyond. May the light of Banyad guide me when I am too weak to continue. May Buyhay's gift of life bring me courage when I am afraid and unsure. May Kamatayan's gift of death bring me peace when it is time." I, like many other citizens of Verihdia, found a warm comfort in this Pledge, in the existence of our Gods. A thought solidified as I watched the Wardens speak this Pledge. These seven people have actually met the Gods, they were gifted immortality by their very own hands. My chest tightened at the realization. I'd felt their presence, their influence, of course I have, but meeting them? That was unheard of. There have been many nights when I would lie alone in the darkness of my room asking Banyad, the Goddess of Light, to illuminate my fears only for the moon to suddenly shine its luminescence through my window. Or days when I wanted nothing more than to disappear with myself and my overwhelming feelings, begging The God of Darkness to veil me from the prying eyes and tormenting whispers. I wished Madiliam could cloak me now.

As our chins lowered, Keegan continued his introduction to the Ceremony.

He spoke directly to the Pledges then, explaining the process as if they hadn't watched this very event unfold every single year throughout their entire schooling. One at a time, the Pledges would make their way to the stage, and then move to stand before the Dean, and Warden, of the Court of their choice. If they are accepted, they receive their Court Mark and are ushered back to their seat. If they are not, they are escorted into the stands to sit with the other Uncourted members of The Living Lands. It's very rare for someone to Pledge Uncourted right from the start, but not entirely unheard of. Those who aimed to be an instructor at the Institute for example. As Keegan spoke, I looked around the arena at the thousands of faces that were not younger students of the Institute. Thousands of them. How have I never thought about it before? Either more people Pledged Uncourted or more people were rejected than I remember. I tried to rack my brain for the memories of Pledging Ceremonies past. There were always a few... but never enough to fill the thousands of faces here today.

That doesn't make sense.

I always loved watching this event every year. Viewing it from a distance felt so magical. But sitting here, as close to the action as I could get, I couldn't help but feel true and honest fear. See things more clearly from this perspective.

My best friend and my brother were about to make their Pledges and for the first time, it hit me that it was possible their Pledge could be rejected. They could be denied entry to their chosen Court and forced to live as an Uncourted individual for the rest of their lives. I tried to take calming breaths, but they came to me in quick, ragged spurts. I couldn't seem to take in a full lungful of air.

"Relax, little storm, you're going to explode." I felt Lysander's breath on the back of my neck as he leaned forward to speak to me in a teasing tone. One part of me, and arguably the more dominant part, wanted to slap him for entering my personal space. The other part welcomed the distraction from the event about to begin.

I'm not sure if it was his words that calmed me or my desire to prove him wrong, but a wave of calm did wash over me, just in time for me to realize Keegan had taken his seat again and the first student was beginning to ascend the steps at the front of the stage.

I recognized my classmate, Violet Graves, as she arrived on the stage platform. I was never very close with her, but I knew she had an early connection with The Court of Talisman, so it didn't surprise me when she quickly made her way to stand before Ivis and Vitrola, the Warden and Dean of that Court. She bowed her head and spoke the Pledge. The very same Pledge every student of the Verihdian Institute has memorized from the very beginning of their schooling.

"I, Violet Graves, having completed my training at the Verihdian Institute, now humbly Pledge my allegiance, loyalty, and life to The Court of Talisman." Vitrola did not turn to look at Ivis, it was clear they had already discussed their potential Pledges and did not need to confirm their plan, instead, she nodded once, deeply. The flood of relief on Violet's face was easy to see, even from my side of the stage. Applause erupted from our classmates, and the stands.

Vitrola stood to greet Violet with a handshake, gripping her forearm. Then came my favorite part. "Where would you like to bear your Court Mark?" Vitrola asked, retrieving the Mark Patch from her robes. Violet held out her arm, turning it over and pulling the sleeve of her robe up to expose the inside of her bicep. Vitrola nodded and placed the Mark Patch on the unblemished flesh there. She laid her palm on the thin fabric, whispering a quick incantation. Violet winced as the Mythica used to bind the ink to her skin took effect, but the pain in her expression only lasted a moment. Once Vitrola removed the Patch, there in its place was the Mark of The Court of Talisman. A scroll wrapped with a small sprig from a pine tree. Violet beamed, and I couldn't help myself from smiling with her. Her entire life had been building to this moment, and now she was where she belonged.

My smile remained in place for the next several classmates who ascended to the stage. Damion Winfield, accepted into The Court of the Vanguard. He was a good friend of Axel's. I sent a silent thanks to Buyhay that should my brother's Pledge be accepted, at least he would be with a friend.

Gia Farshout, accepted into The Court of Silence. Not a shock at all if you knew her. She couldn't help but fall into leadership roles in everything she did. Gia in The Court of Silence made as much sense as Riley in The Court of the Undying.

Callum Andras, The Court of Echoes.

Bea Shallot, The Court of the Undying.

Laine Vidner, The Court of Passion.

One by one my classmates came, Pledged, and received their Mark, and the more people who were accepted the more nervous I became about the fate of my best friend and my twin. I watched as the line before them dwindled, my heart constricting tighter and tighter with every accepted Pledge.

Then my best friend stood, smoothing the front of their white gown before eagerly making their way to the stage. I might have forgotten how to breathe. What if they aren't accepted? What happens to them?

I tried fruitlessly to take deep breaths, but again my lungs refused to fill and they burned with painful torture.

"Little storm…" Lysander's silky voice behind me stopped my ragged breaths altogether. I couldn't find the air if I wanted to.

Why does he keep calling me that?

"You're spiraling." He said matter of factly, his whispered tone dark and gravelly in my ear.

"I am not." I forced out breathlessly, sparking a cough from my dry and pained throat.

"Your friend and brother will be accepted," he said as casually as if he was talking to me about the weather. I don't trust him as far as I can throw him, which is not far at all, but something in his words did have a calming effect.

"How do you know?" I didn't turn to look at him. Instead, I faced straight forward, watching my best friend climb the stairs.

"No Warden would risk turning them away in fear of pissing you off," he spoke flippantly, but his whisper had an edge of taunting to it.

I couldn't imagine a Warden of Verihdia would care at all what my feelings were about whether a Pledge was accepted or not, but something in Lysander's words rang true to me. They were going to incredible lengths to make me feel comfortable and welcome with the prospect of joining their Court, and by now they have probably discerned that simply housing one of the two most important people in my life would give them a definite advantage.

Not that I could particularly see myself in the gladiatorial arena of The Court of the Vanguard, and I never showed much prowess in any healing rituals. But it was an enticing thought, to be able to be near them.

A small tug in my heart sent a cloud of sadness through me. Before last night, I think I'd be just as concerned about Chandler's Pledging today, but after how he reacted last night, and the whole 'I'd rather die than Pledge to The Court of Shadows' thing, it was weird knowing Chandler Mills might be out of my life for good after today.

Riley had moved to stand in front of Miya Moonshackle and Vance Darkwing. Riley had developed a close bond with Vance, a strong mentor-mentee relationship. It was clear from a young age they belonged in The Court of the Undying and Vance quickly took them under their wing. My anxieties melted a little more when I saw Vance's beaming smile as Riley approached them.

My friend smiled back, the only indication of any nerves they felt was their fingers dancing awkwardly together as if they could not remain still. They cleared their throat and spoke, confidence radiating from them.

"I, Riley Wynn, having completed my training at the Verihdian Institute, now humbly Pledge my allegiance, loyalty, and life to The Court of the Undying."

I didn't even have time to worry before Vance nodded enthusiastically.

My hands clapped together in overjoyed applause. Riley tossed a quick smile in my direction before slowly sliding the robe down their arm, turning to expose their shoulder to Vance.

Riley and I once spent an entire afternoon with craft supplies, painting horrific replicas of Court Marks on various places on our bodies to decide the best placement for when the time came. I had Riley paint a few different marks on me, seeing as I had not made any connection yet, but I drew the Undying Mark over and over and over. I couldn't help but feel overwhelming pride in my best friend.

They took their Mark in stride, their face not twisting in pain at all even as the Mythica bound the ink to their skin. They raised their fists in the air in a joyful expression before heading to return to their seat.

My joy was short-lived though, as I watched my brother move towards the stage. Panic seized me, my heart pounded so violently I was certain it would burst right out of my chest.

"Breathe, little storm. Breathe." Lysander leaned forward until his lips were nearly touching the base of my ear, his cool breath tickled the skin there as his whisper sent goosebumps erupting across my skin.

How does he know what I'm feeling?

Another trick of his, I'm sure. I shouldn't let him get to me, I concluded. But I did force myself to take deep, calming breaths. Because I wanted to, not because he told me to.

Lysander had leaned back, but I could still feel the shadow of his presence enveloping me, sending sparks of fury through me.

Axel took proud, confident strides across the stage towards Avalin and Salazar Fortwright, his strong frame noticeable even under the ill-fitting Pledging gown. I continued my attempt at breathing, but it got more difficult the closer he got to them. But this time, I was able to directly identify the source of the anxiety.

If Axel was rejected today, he would not receive the information about our parents, and he never had to know that I asked to have it kept from him.

The moment the thought crossed my mind, I felt sick to my stomach. Shame bloomed inside my chest, spreading out until I was sure everyone could see me for the terrible person I was.

"Hey," Lysander's voice returned, not having nearly the same effect it did only minutes ago. No, my shame was much too powerful now. "Where did you go just now?" His tone was deceivingly comforting, lacking his usual jesting. How did he seem to be so attuned to my every emotion? I'd be furious if my guilt wasn't currently eating me alive.

I could say a million things. He's one of the only people alive who knows my deepest shame, so I could tell him what vile thoughts crossed my mind just now. But I refuse to allow this man into my mind again, with Mythica or without.

"I'm fine," I said quietly as Axel came to a stop in front of the Dean and Warden of The Court of the Vanguard. I held my breath, and out of the corner of my eye, I noticed a few of the other Wardens studying my reaction carefully.

"I, Axel Cromwell, having completed my training at the Verihdian Institute, now humbly Pledge my allegiance, loyalty, and life to The Court of the Vanguard." His head was held high, and his shoulders rolled back in pride. He didn't look the least bit nervous. He looked like he was already accepted and this was a mere formality. Gods, what I'd give for a drop of that confidence.

Salazar then reacted in a way no other Dean had during the entire ceremony. He turned over his shoulder to glance at Avalin. My heart sank. In anticipation, in worry… in hope? I banished that thought quickly and focused on what was occurring across the stage. The confidence in Axel's eyes faltered, almost imperceptibly, if I were not his sister, I probably would not have even noticed. But I did. Suddenly the distance between us felt immeasurable. I wanted to go to him. To comfort him, to hold him in this moment of uncertainty. But a stronger part of myself knew I didn't deserve to be his comfort in public, while simultaneously being his torment in private.

Then Avalin stood. A gasp erupted from the crowd. I was still holding my breath. I couldn't help but acknowledge that the Avalin here before me today looked differently than the Avalin I had met last night. With slightly longer hair and darker features. I tried not to think about what that meant for my relationship with Chandler. She made her way around Salazar to stand just a mere foot from my brother. Time ceased to exist to me, you could have told me an hour had passed, or perhaps a millisecond, and I would not have been able to correct you either way. There was only my brother and this Warden.

Her handsome features remained stoic as she took him in, letting her gaze move up and down his form.

And only then, as my lungs burned and begged for oxygen, as the crowd's shocked gasps turned to nervous whispers, did she nod.

The crowd cheered, and a smile bigger than any I'd ever seen appeared on my twin's face.

Finally, I breathed.

Axel lifted his right arm for Avalin, who had extended her hand out for him. Their arms locked in a powerful clasp, a handshake of welcome, of pride. Avalin reached back and Salazar handed her the Court Mark. I couldn't believe my eyes. My brother was here, being branded for the Court of his dreams, by his Warden herself.

This was incredibly rare. I could only imagine the pride he must be feeling at this moment as he extended his left arm, flipping it so the pale underside was exposed to Avalin. She placed the Patch just below his elbow and instead of pain on his face as she sent a wave of Mythica through the Patch onto his skin, he laughed a bright, full, joyful laugh.

Avalin glanced over to me, obviously trying to gauge my reaction to the incredible display of honor she had bestowed on my brother. She was hoping to invoke a feeling of pride, a feeling I often felt when my twin accomplished something great.

Instead, I was jealous.

My best friend and my twin both made their Pledges today to Courts they truly belonged to and were accepted. They get to start their lives. They get to move on. But not me. Never me.

The familiar green cloud of envy enveloped me until I couldn't continue to watch the spectacle before me. I turned my head away from my brother and his Warden and focused my gaze out into the crowd before me.

The shadows were back then, not mine, Lysander's. I felt his presence flood the space behind me, electrifying the very air between us. "Jealous, are we?" His breath was cool on my neck as he spoke to me. A deep understanding in his tone. Of course he knows. I bet he can smell it or something. I looked out at the crowd to see if anyone was witnessing this take place, but nobody seemed to be paying attention to me at the moment. No one except The Warden of Shadows that is.

"Not at all." I bit back, refusing to turn my gaze back to him.

"You cannot lie to me, Miss Cromwell." My muscles tensed as he purred my name. "I know envy when I see it." He had me. He knew exactly what I was feeling, and that spurred my anger even more.

"You don't know anything about me." It wasn't true, of course. He had read my file, he probably knew more about me than many of my classmates did, but I wasn't going to admit to that unfortunate reality.

"I know more than you'd think," he breathed, his lips nearly grazing my earlobe as he taunted me. "You know, you'd fit right in at The Court of Shadows."

My fists balled tightly on my lap, the fabric of my white gown wrinkling under the motion.

"I will never Pledge to your Court." I wanted so badly to look at him, to let him see the fire in my eyes. However, I also wanted to keep my decorum. To remain stoic. That resolve was wavering with every passing second his taunting lips were near my skin.

"You mean to tell me there isn't even a chance? None at all?" He whispered, clearly attempting to come across as tantalizing, but it only stoked the fire.

"None. I wouldn't join your Court if it was the last one in Verihdia." I tried not to let myself be embarrassed by my infantile retort. Lysander chuckled, his deep-chested laugh vibrating through my skin from his close distance. I inhaled a sharp breath at the sensation.

"I don't think that's true, little storm." His lips grazed the skin just below my ear and I felt as if I had been electrocuted. My eyes fell closed and I tried to contain my building fury.

"Stop calling me that." My voice came out breathless. Traitorous little thing.

"Tell me I still have a chance," he pleaded, his voice low and full of challenge. I was a few seconds away from dropping my carefully crafted facade and striking the man behind me with all the ire that had been building since the moment he stole my Mythica from me.

"I wouldn't want to lie to you." I was thankful that the confidence had returned to my voice. Now, it almost sounded like I was completely unaffected by his presence. Even if it were untrue, I was thankful for the perception. That's what I needed.

"Hmmm," he mused and slowly backed away. I suddenly felt a flood of relief at his absence. But it only lasted a moment, as his lips encroached closer to my other ear, his silken voice lowering to a darkened promise and he whispered. "Oh look, your boyfriend is on his way up now... I wonder which Court he will Pledge." My entire body tensed, Chandler was indeed making his way up the stairs towards us, his eyes locked on mine, an expression of resentment etched on his face. I couldn't imagine what he might be thinking, seeing Lysander so close to me, whispering in my ear. I eagerly wanted to correct his assumption. Not that I owed him anything, but I didn't want to hurt him. I never wanted that.

"You know, I have the power to say no." My blood froze, and my whole body suddenly felt cold. His taunting promise sliced through me like a red-hot blade cutting through thin fabric. "It would only take one word and your little friend would be Uncourted." He whispered the words in a venomous promise. "I wouldn't even need to explain myself. I could just …say…no." His lips once again grazed my earlobe, but this time it set my blood on fire, boiling with complete disgust at this manipulative, vile creature behind me.

"You wouldn't dare." I challenged him, but I wasn't so sure. This is exactly the type of behavior I had come to expect from this Warden. I wouldn't put it past him to ruin someone's entire life to prove a point.

"Are you willing to bet?" His chilling dare snaked its way around my throat, constricting my already thin airway, as Chandler took the last few steps onto the stage in one gliding bound.

"You are vile." I felt his lips upturn into a smile against my skin.

"Just admit the truth and I'll accept him." The truth?! What did this man expect me to say?

"What truth?" I whispered, forcing as much of my bottled fury into my tone as I could muster. Which unfortunately wasn't much. Not when the heat from my anger was building low in my core, forcing me to press my legs together for some relief.

"Tell me my Court still has a chance." I rolled my eyes and scoffed out loud, watching Chandler take large strides across the stage towards us.

"There is no chance."

"It feels natural doesn't it?" I felt as if my entire body erupted in goosebumps as his lips touched the sensitive skin on my exposed neck. "Being envious. It's as easy as breathing for you, isn't it?" His cool breath sent shivers over the patch of skin that was being held captive by his mouth. My muscles tightened in response.

He wasn't wrong, and I hated that. In fact, I often found myself feeling envious of those around me. Especially as the Final Trials and the Pledging Ceremony approached. More and more frequently, I had found myself feeling the bitter sting that came with wanting something I wasn't able to have. The thought that I might truly belong in The Court of Shadows was not a new one, that possibility did cross my mind, several times. But now the notion caused physical and primal disgust to bloom in the pit of my stomach.

"Better hurry, he's almost here." He warned. And once again, for the second time in so many days, I was faced with a terrible choice.

"I despise you," I growled. The vibrations that accompanied his mocking snicker echoed through my malleable body. A dark fire burned low in my chest threatening to consume us both.

"What'll it be?" He asked just as Chandler came to a stop in front of us. He eyed the proximity between the two of us, and a spiteful and accusatory look darkened his features.

"I, Chandler Mills, having completed my training at the Verihdian Institute, now humbly Pledge my allegiance, loyalty, and life to The Court of Shadows." He tore his eyes from me and instead watched the foreboding figure that sat behind me like a puppeteer expertly demonstrating his mastery over his puppet.

Lysander lowered his voice even more and whispered once again, taking his time with each word, drawing the syllables out as if to squeeze every last bit of time he could from this powerful showcase of his own dominance. "What'll it be, little storm? Tell me I still have a chance."

Chandler waited, watching the exchange between us with quiet ferocity.

I quickly turned my head towards him for the first time so Chandler was not able to read my lips and found my face inches from his and I spat, "Yes, ok? Yes, your Court still has a chance!" My vicious whisper reached his ears, and his face lit up with a victorious grin. He wasted no time before turning his eyes towards Chandler and nodding. The crowd cheered and Chandler's eyes softened, a smile spreading across his face. He turned to the spectators and offered them a large victorious gesture, he was met with roaring applause.

"Good choice." Lysander's lips grazed my ear with a featherlight touch before he stood, releasing me from his immediate hold. I suddenly felt lighter, like a weight had lifted. At least I tried to convince myself it was lightness that I was feeling and not emptiness. Because if I were feeling empty, that would have meant I enjoyed the closeness of his lips, the feel of his body behind mine, and I most definitely did not.

He moved around me, grabbing the patch for his Court Mark from his pocket. Chandler beamed at being the second individual today to receive his Mark directly from the Warden of his Court. He probably didn't care that it was only because Lilith was not present to do it herself. I'm positive that detail would be left out of any future retellings of this story.

Chandler slowly opened his robe and unbuttoned the white shirt he was wearing beneath to reveal the untainted ivory skin of his chest. He pointed to the open space just above his heart, and I watched as Lysander delicately placed the Patch and muttered a few short words. Chandler's eyes closed only for a second at the intrusion of the Mythica. When Lysander stepped back, there on the once bare skin, was a swirling pattern of green lines, weaving together like a perfectly choreographed dance and climbing up his chest like a cloud of smoke. He was officially, and forever more, a member of The Court of Shadows.

I didn't smile at him when his eyes found mine again as he buttoned his shirt, and neither did he. Instead, he clenched his fists - slightly, barely perceptible- but I noticed. Then he was gone, descending the stairs to the applause of the other Pledges.

Lysander returned to his seat behind me, still close, but miles away compared to our connected positions just moments ago. "You must think you are so clever, but you are nothing more than a manipulative scoundrel," I spoke without turning to look at him, so I did not lose my already wavering confidence. My voice was low, but I knew he could hear me.

"That's Warden Manipulative Scoundrel to you," he teased, an edge of probing to his voice as if he was looking for a fight.

Well, hold on tight, Lysander, because I aim to destroy.

"Are you sure you're Warden of the correct Court? With an ego the size of yours, I would assume you'd find that you are a much better fit in The Court of the Vanguard." I toss the vicious words at him and then hold my breath. Not only had I just insulted a Warden of Verihdia, but I had just committed the number one faux pas. Questioning, even in jest, someone's loyalty or compatibility to their chosen Court is one of the most abhorrent things a person could do. And I just did it. To a Warden, no less.

He was quiet, no quick-witted response, no fatal verbal blows, just silence. Three more Pledges had come and gone, and I struggled to control my rapidly beating heart. I didn't allow myself to look back over my shoulder at him, to study his reactions. To see how my words affected him. No matter how deeply the want ran, I stayed put. Out of fear, probably. But I guess the steadfastness could also double as sticking to my assessment. I didn't want him to think I was second-guessing my insult, even if a small part of me was. It was so incredibly clear which Court this Warden belonged to, and which Court belonged to him. To suggest anything otherwise was not only a slight but astoundingly incorrect.

Ten more Pledges came and made their choices, receiving their Court Marks, and I tried to focus on the Ceremony instead of the potentially volatile man sitting behind me with the power and right to kill me where I sit and send me to Kamatayan for my blatant disregard of Court decorum.

We neared the end of the Ceremony and despite the anxiety taking up most of my attention span, I couldn't help but realize that so far, not a single Pledge had been rejected and none of my classmates had willingly Pledged Uncourted either.

I looked out among the faces in the crowd again, the weight of this unanswered question resting heavily on my mind.

Where did you all come from?

The Ceremony ended with a fanfare, and the Pledges jumped up in a flood of excitement, embraces, and decadent celebration. Music sounded from somewhere in the colosseum, as the audience feverishly applauded the recent Pledges.

The Wardens and their Deans stood, exiting carefully off the back of the stage, and only then did I look to Lysander. He had remained seated, casually, his chin propped on his hand, his hooded, emerald eyes bore into me with a quiet, restrained vexation.

The arena had begun to empty, the rather unbelievable mass of citizens from The Living Lands made their way back to their modest Uncourted lives, and the younger Pledge classes filed back down the long walkway to the Institute to await their own chance to make their Pledge. My classmates' celebration was dwindling and they began to break off into small groups, running around to each other, offering their eager and heartfelt congratulations before taking off towards the Institute to prepare for their move to their new homes.

As the rows and rows of spectators emptied, Lysander and I sat with eyes locked in silent challenge. I lost track of time as he stared at me with his knowing eyes. If he was going to kill me for my transgression, I guess I could be thankful he was choosing to wait for us to be alone so no one else had to witness my demise.

There were perhaps only thirty people left in the entire colosseum when he leaned forward from his relaxed position, placing both elbows on his knees. His unbuttoned shirt gaped slightly away from his skin, offering a slight glimpse of the toned chest beneath.

"Pack your belongings. You venture to The Court of Shadows tonight." And then he stood, breaking the intense eye contact we had held for what seemed like hours. Once the spell of his gaze was broken, I felt my mouth fall open, shocked at the utter nonchalance he was exhibiting. Had what I said not affected him? Or had it affected him so much that all pretense of playful banter was long gone? I wasn't sure which option I would have preferred. He turned to exit the stage after his siblings but stopped and turned back to me. "Oh, and Miss Cromwell," he said, a wicked smile gracing his face as he leaned forward until his face was mere inches from mine. He was so close I could see the pulsing of his own heart in the vein on his neck. "Game on."

And then he was gone.

I don't know how long it took me to finally regain my composure enough to leave the stage and begin my trek back to the Institute.

Game on, he had said. I didn't know many things, but I did not know that whatever this was between us was most certainly not a game. But if that is how he intended to do this... play a game with me. I, sure as the sun in the sky, was going to win.

FOURTEEN

he ceremony ended six hours ago, and all of a sudden, my entire life was packed into two small cases. Including all of my favorite scarves, dresses, and shirts. I could vividly recall the pivotal moments when I wore them all. Events in the grey blouse. Tests in the green skirt. The sweater I wore the first time I met Riley, outside on the lawn. I had been studying when this fiery individual with bright red hair plopped down next to me and started a conversation as if we had known each other for years. To their testament, it had felt like that. It was so easy to speak to them. I never had that kind of effortless connection with anyone before, not even Axel. I loved my brother, of course, but by nature of siblings, we were destined to butt heads on nearly everything. But not with Riley, we had developed our own language. Completely in sync. I'm not sure I would ever find that sort of ease with anyone ever again. I don't think I would ever be capable of expressing how deeply and completely I would miss that.

The door to my room burst open, and in strutted Riley, their hair now a much more cool-toned color than it had been when we first met. Their joy was palpable the moment they entered and the second I saw the golden envelope in their hands, I knew why. I smiled at my best friend, despite the budding resentment in the pit of my stomach. I knew what this envelope contained. Riley was about to learn about their parents.

"Have you opened it yet?" I asked, doing my best to feign excitement. It must have succeeded because they beamed brightly, shaking their head.

"Not yet, I was going to, but I think I needed to do it with someone… Just in case." The subtle meaning behind their words was clear. There was a huge possibility today that many of the recent Pledges would learn their parents were not members of the Court they had just Pledged and chances are slim they'd ever meet them. They could of course all come to The Living Lands for a visit, but except for the First Trial Festival, there was very little reason for a Courted individual to ever come back here. The unfortunate truth is if your parents are members of a different Court, you are lucky to see them once a year. While that option was pretty dreadful, it was preferable to the alternative of discovering one, or both of your parents are no longer alive.

That particular fear had kept me up late at night, haunting my dreams. I couldn't begin to describe the millions of ways my spirit would break if I received that outcome.

"I'm here," I said, reaching out to squeeze Riley's arm. They nodded, their hazel eyes brimming with a glossy sheen. Only the contents of the envelope could tell if these tears would be of joy or heartbreak.

"Alright, here I go." Taking a deep, steadying breath, Riley opened the golden parcel in their hands, slowly, carefully, as if any bad information could jump out and bite them. I held my breath. I may have been filled with unquenchable jealousy that I was not holding my own envelope in my hands right now, but that does not mean I was not also filled with a hope for my best friend that was so deep and so strong. I needed them to get exactly what they wanted. So I knew that it was possible.

And I hoped one day I'd get the same.

Pulling the contents out of the envelope, they closed their eyes briefly before opening them to scan the page. I watched their eyes carefully, prepared to hug my friend in whatever capacity they needed.

"Ms. Loanne Wynn and Ms. Gia Wynn," they smiled at the feel of their mother's names on their lips. I could see the delight begin to bloom in their chest as their eyes scanned down. "The Court of the Undying." They squealed, almost dropping the paper in their celebratory jump. I laughed with them, smiling a true smile of happiness for my friend. They steadied themselves, letting their excitement slowly simmer as they read the next part of the page, arguably the most terrifying section of all. "Status…" they started and again my heart constricted. "Alive!" They screamed, and I couldn't help it. I did too. Whatever jealousy I felt moments ago was gone. If anyone deserved this type of news, it was my best friend. I threw my arms around their neck and held them as they sobbed tears of relief, of joy.

"I'm so happy for you, Riley." And I meant it.

"Thank you, oh Gods." They took a step back, trying to compose themselves. "I'm sorry, Lexa. I know that must have been hard for you."

"Don't. Don't apologize for sharing this moment with me. I am honored I got to be here with you." They smiled, and I returned it, whole heartedly.

"I love you, Lex." They hugged me again with so much force it almost knocked me off balance. We stumbled together, laughing as the door to my room opened again.

"I guess you got good news then," My brother's voice from the doorway erased the feeling of bliss that was permeating through me. I stepped back from Riley carefully and turned to look at him. But I didn't need to. I could feel it. The disappointment, the pain. I knew why he felt that way. It was my fault after all.

"Axel, hey! Yeah, I did. My parents are in The Court of the Undying." They beamed, and Axel, despite his best effort, wasn't able to dispel the melancholic look on his face.

"Congratulations, Riley!" He rushed forward to embrace Riley, his face alight with a smile that never reached his eyes. "I'm so happy for you."

Riley pulled back from the hug, still soaring with happiness, and looked at my twin in his blue eyes.

"Um…" they cast a glance over their shoulder at me. "Did you… Uh, are you allowed to talk about it?" Treading carefully, Riley hinted at his envelope. The one I knew he didn't receive.

"I'm not allowed to tell Lexa" Axel replied and my eyebrows furrowed. He certainly seemed content. Had he actually received the information? No, of course not, the Wardens made me a promise. They wouldn't go back on that. Right?

But then I was hit with an unsettling thought. Why did I trust the Wardens at all? It's not like I knew them. And it's pretty commonly known that these Wardens are only out for themselves and their Courts. And as of right now, I am neither of those. They want me for their Courts so desperately they are willing to make some serious concessions. But does that mean they would actually alter another one of their precious rules, simply because I asked?

Had I forgotten so easily who I was? Lexa Cromwell, a nobody from The Verihdian Institute. Not someone the most powerful people in all of Verihdia would bend for.

"Don't worry, Axel. I've come to terms with it." He nodded, an unreadable expression on his face. Which was saying a lot considering I usually could read my brother like a book, with ease. But this guarded person before me looked unrecognizable, had the divide already begun?

"My caravan is heading out soon, I just wanted to say goodbye." Riley and Axel embraced once more before Riley turned to me. Throwing their arms around my neck, tightening until there was only us.

"I'm going to miss you so much, Lex." They whispered into my ear, their voice cracking under the weight of our goodbye.

"Thank you for being my friend. You are a part of me, Riley. You always will be." The tears flowed then, and we stood there locked in our sorrowful embrace.

"Ok, I have to go meet Vitrola. We're leaving in an hour." They pulled back, their beautiful eyes puffy with tears.

"Enjoy every moment of your new life, Riley. You deserve it." I squeezed their hands in mine. They opened their mouth in an attempt to speak, but nothing came out but a subtle sob. So instead, they nodded to me, their eyes expressing everything I was feeling. With one last squeeze of my hand, they turned and left. I managed to contain the breakdown that threatened to overcome me, solely because I knew what came next.

I had to say goodbye to my twin.

Axel's facade broke the moment my eyes met his. He rushed forward gathering me in his arms and together we cried.

Saying goodbye to Riley was difficult, but saying goodbye to Axel was near unbearable. I felt a white-hot blaze raging in my heart, threatening to envelop me and never let me go.

"Promise me one thing, Lexa." I had never heard my brother sound so lost, so broken.

"Anything," I promised.

"Don't choose my Court just because you miss me. Choose the Court you belong to, ok?" His words sunk in, and for the first time, I realized I had the choice to be with him again. Forever. I could easily Pledge there just to reunite what little family I had. But he was right. I might have him, but if I don't truly belong there I would be miserable, and Gods forbid, even start to resent him. I couldn't let that happen. And he knew it.

"I promise." I couldn't see his face as we embraced, but I felt him nod, his arms tightening on me.

"Try to see me when you're in the Vanguard Court, ok?" Now it was my turn to wordlessly nod. If I spoke I was afraid I would never recover.

"I love you," was all he said. And I was lost. Lost to grief, lost to fear. The sobs wracked my body as the loss I had been futilely preparing for for weeks swallowed me whole.

I held my brother in my arms, for the last time as Verihdian Institute students. Siblings were rare at the Institute, unless you were born in the same year they typically did not inform the students of their own flesh and blood walking the same halls. 'Let no single thing influence the Pledge.' I couldn't imagine getting an envelope after Pledging only to realize that part of your family has been down the hall from you for your entire life. And yet, they still kept it hidden. I have no doubt they would have tried to hide it from us too, had we not been mirror images of each other. It would have been impossible to keep us in the dark. Unlike the very few other sibling pairs we've seen throughout the years, we did not fight, not really. We did not bicker beyond playful banter, we did not fight or hold grudges for more than a few hours, and in every way there was…we were best friends. I knew one day we would leave, that our family would cease to exist in the form we'd come to know. But knowing it, and experiencing it could not have been more different.

"'I love you' isn't enough," I said. And he tightened his hold before slowly backing away. His blue eyes, a mirror of mine, glistened with tears.

"You're right. It's not enough," he spoke, clearly trying to regain a small amount of composure, but failing. "You are my soul, Lex."

"And you're mine." With one last squeeze of my hands, he turned and left.

The moment the door closed behind him, the loneliness descended on me like a blanket. Half of my heart just left through the door, and I wasn't sure anything could fill its void. Throughout our entire time here, I had felt this connection, this tether between us. No matter where we went here in The Living Lands, I knew he wouldn't be too far. But as he moved away from my room, away from me, I felt the tether between us strain, crack. I hoped to the Gods it would never break. I was not sure I'd be able to survive that. I thought back to the life I had here at the Institute with fondness, sending a prayer to Banyad to keep my memories bright and vibrant, to never let them fade. He's been gone just a minute, and already I feared I would forget the sound of his voice. The exact shade of his eyes.

I didn't have time to mourn the life I had experienced here, the caravan to The Court of Shadows was scheduled to leave soon, and I was expected to spend an entire week there. From my class, only four students Pledged to The Court of Shadows. So I would be traveling with them.

I tried not to think about one specific Pledge who would be on this trip with me as I grabbed my two cases and made for the exit.

The feeling of leaving my bedroom after twenty-five years paled in comparison to the stabbing pain deep at the center of the empty spot in my heart where Axel belonged.

All the recent Pledges were expected to meet their Deans outside the Institute. The Court of Shadows Pledges were given instructions to gather outside the greenhouse, so I began the trek down the halls of my school one last time. Chances were high I would never set foot in this building again. I would never need to.

"Don't tell me you were about to leave without saying goodbye." The tears I was precariously holding back began to fall instantly at Oliver's voice. Dropping my bags to the ground, I turned and sprinted towards my favorite instructor. He embraced me tightly, a gentle hand caressing the back of my head as I sobbed into his shoulder. "Hey now, don't cry." The tears slowed and I wiped away their remnants with the back of my hand.

"Sorry," I said through muffled sobs. My composure was coming back to me in waves. Oliver simply watched me with comforting eyes as I put the pieces of myself back together. His eyes glistened with remnants of recent tears.

"Don't apologize to me, Lexa. Not for this." His head tilted down so he could catch my eyes. "We haven't had a chance to talk since…well since you became the most coveted person in all of Verihdia." He said the phrase as if it was not an accomplishment, but rather a burden. That comforted me in a way I didn't know I needed to be comforted. "What are you thinking?"

I took a deep breath, my heart slowly returning to a normal pace. "I think there must be a mistake and there's no way I deserve this kind of attention." Oliver nodded, listening intently. "It feels like I've been given this incredible opportunity, and I didn't earn it." He sighed, placing a hand on my shoulder.

"Let's get one thing abundantly clear, Lexa." He spoke with an authoritative tone. "You deserve everything this life has to offer and then some. Do not ever settle for less, and do not ever doubt you are worth every ounce of trouble these Wardens are going through for you." His wrinkled hands clasped over mine and I felt a single tear escape my already red eyes.

"I'm going to miss you, Oliver." He pulled me in for a hug, holding me firmly in place for a few comforting moments. I felt him inhale, preparing to speak.

"Did you know your brother did not get his golden envelope today?" Guilt gripped my heart, squeezing to the point of pain. Axel had been so vague about it earlier, that I wasn't sure if the Wardens had respected my wishes. Hearing they did, and Axel was denied his birthright because of me had me feeling like I do in my nightmares. Hopeless, lost… already dead.

I nodded because I couldn't say the words aloud. The deep sigh Oliver released told me he understood. He knew I had done it again.

"I hate myself." It was true. I did. I couldn't believe that I had once again been so selfish, so horrible to my own flesh and blood. I watched his face closely, as he struggled to find the right words.

"I'm trying to understand," he said carefully. I knew what he wanted to say. He couldn't say anything I hadn't already said to myself hundreds of times.

"There's nothing to understand, Oliver. I'm a selfish person who would rather make my brother suffer than let him know about our parents without me." He nodded again, absorbing the truth I willingly gave.

"It's not just your brother who's suffering from this choice." Oliver never shied away from telling me exactly what I needed to hear, even when it wasn't the most pleasant. But these words hit me with a force I had never experienced before. He's right. Of course he's right.

"I know." Weak. Guilty. Painful.

Oliver closed his eyes and took a deep, steadying breath before pulling me back in for another embrace.

"Axel will forgive you." I wasn't so sure, but it felt nice to hear. "But you need to forgive yourself too, Lexa." His grip tightened around me. I sat in that moment for as long as I could. Here was someone who knew my worst guilt, and still saw the good in me. One day, I hoped I'd see what he saw.

"Alright, enough of this." He said, pulling away to look at me again. "Tell me about your tour." I spent the next few minutes recounting the events in the Observatory, how The Warden of Shadows would be my guide, and the six-month tour planned for me. Oliver listened with interest, his eyes widening slightly with every new facet of information.

When I had finished, he was running his hands through his dark, peppered hair.

"You never told me what your Final Trial result was." He said finally, after a few silent moments.

"I wasn't sure how to tell anyone." He smiled, faintly.

"You're not going to tell me now either, are you?" I trusted Oliver explicitly, but there was a distinct difference between trusting someone to offer advice and trusting them enough to tell you you belong in a Court that doesn't even exist anymore. My posture slumped.

"I can't." He nodded.

"When you're out seeing all of Verihdia, please don't forget that Uncourted is an option. And just know you'd have at least one friend here if that's what you choose." He smiled then, a large toothy smile that lit up his face.

"I'll keep that in mind, Oliver. Thank you. For helping to shape me into the person I am." His breath hitched and an unreadable expression crossed his face as he gripped my hand again.

"You made it easy." He sighed, the impending goodbye cresting like a wave about to crash.

"I don't want to say goodbye anymore today." I didn't recognize my own voice. It was desperate, angry.

"Then don't say it." He hugged me once more before pulling away, his blue eyes glistening in the afternoon sun that poured in through the windows. With a nod, and a deep breath, he turned and left.

I watched him walk away for a few painful moments before retrieving my bags and continuing my final walk through the Verihdian Institute.

With every step, I focused on the beautiful building around me, trying to memorize its scent, the sounds that echoed as I walked, and the small intricate detailing on the ceilings.

I was tired of saying goodbye. So instead of thinking of this last walk through these halls as a goodbye, I tried to reframe my thoughts to regard this as a celebration. A celebration of all the things I learned while I was here. All the people who have irrevocably changed my life. A celebration of becoming who I am today. Each step was a name echoing in my heart.

Step. Riley. Step. Axel. Step. Oliver. Step...Chandler.

I arrived at the massive, green-tinted glass doors that led to the greenhouse too quickly. I was almost tempted to turn around and take the walk once more, but a voice behind me stopped me in my tracks.

"Lexa." Cold, distant, emotionless. Chandler. I turned to face him.

"Chandler." He scanned me. "Congratulations on your Pledge. I'm really happy for you." It was true, despite how he had acted in the last twenty-four hours, I did care for him. And I did want what he thought was best for himself. Even if that meant The Court of Shadows.

"Thank you." He pushed forward, opening the glass doors and entering the greenhouse. A tall glass room, filled to the brim with exotic plant life from each of the seven Courts was spread out before us. We had several classes in this space growing up. It was important, they said, that we spent time around the natural flora of the Courts because then we would know if we showed any signs of allergy or discomfort around their native plants. It would be 'unfortunate' if we Pledged to a Court only to find out we could drop dead at the first large breeze that jostled the pollen from their trees.

Beyond The Court of the Undying, each Court was equipped to handle minor injuries and ailments, having been introduced to medical innovations and rituals developed in the Undying Court, but a severe allergic response was something even the most skilled healers from outside the Undying Court couldn't handle. And by the time you traveled across borders to an Undying healer, you'd be gone.

Luckily, my immune system had not fallen victim to any of the exotic pollen, although maybe if it had, it could have made my decision easier. Chandler pushed forward past the potted plants with bright colored flowers spilling over the edges, not stopping to look at the bright blue stacked petals from The Court of the Undying or the deep palm leaves from The Court of Passion. I tried to keep pace with him, but it was clear he had no intention of continuing our conversation. It pained me that this was how our relationship would end. I did not love Chandler in any way resembling romance, but I did love his friendship. His companionship, his comfort. I loved the way he made me feel, most of the time. I didn't want to ignore all of that because of some stupid jealousy.

"Chandler," I called after him. He slowed his pace but did not turn. "Chandler," I said again, a little more forceful this time. He came to a stop next to the trees with bright golden leaves, a staple of The Court of Silence. He didn't turn to face me, however, but I would take it. "I don't want this to be how we leave us." It was almost a whisper but I knew he heard me.

He turned slowly, still holding his bags in his hands. His brown eyes were full of a tormented emotion.

"I hate that they want you." He spoke quietly, confessing. I held my breath. I did not have to use my Mythica here, but I knew he was being honest with me. That much I could tell.

"I know," was all I could say. Of course he did. He probably wasn't alone in feeling it either. I couldn't imagine I'd feel any different were the roles reversed. Hadn't I felt that twinge of envy when I thought it was him the Wardens were staring at?

"I hate that I'm mad at you." He confessed again. This felt raw, real. My heart jumped in my chest, longing to embrace him. Comfort him in the way I knew he needed. The way we so often did for each other.

"I know."

His bags dropped to the ground and he rushed forward, a type of fierceness in his eyes I recognized. He needed to be reassured. He needed to be wanted.

I could do that. Because as much as I tried to avoid the sinking feeling in my chest, Chandler was a lifeline in an open expanse of water, and I was going to hold on.

He kissed me, his lips crashing into mine forcefully, eagerly. I kissed him back, thankful I was able to have this goodbye.

His mouth was selfish, taking what it needed from me, but I was more than willing to oblige. If for no other reason than to finish my time with Chandler, the way we spent it. Giving each other exactly what we needed.

He held me to his body and I sunk into his hold. This was the last time. I couldn't say I'd miss the physical aspect of our relationship, but rather the emotional connection. As I kissed him, I didn't think about how his lips felt, or feel a building desire deep in my abdomen. Instead, I tried to memorize how good it felt to have someone want to kiss me. Even if it was for selfish reasons.

"Am I interrupting?" I pulled back from Chandler as the dark, familiar voice called from the exit to the greenhouse. I felt my face flush as my eyes met Lysander's. He was leaning on the door frame, framed by the tinted glass, the light pouring through the colored panes illuminated him in a verdant hue, perfect of course. He was still wearing his outfit from the Ceremony, but his dark black hair was now hanging loose around his face, down to just below his ears. He didn't look as imposing when his hair was down, I noticed. It seemed to soften his features, give him a boyish charm that negated the bastard vibes he so expertly gave off.

"My Warden," Chandler spoke, bowing his head in Lysander's direction. "Forgive us, we were simply saying goodbye." He smiled at me then, and I felt a weight lift from my soul. I didn't want to admit it, but I knew it would have hurt me deeply to leave without the chance to have this moment with him.

"You are saying goodbye, even though you're traveling to the same Court?" Chandler's eyes snapped back to me, a question painted in them.

"I thought you said you were not going to Pledge to Shadows?" He asked, an accusatory tone slipping through.

"I'm spending a short time in The Court of Shadows before my tour begins," I explained to Chandler.

"Why?" He asked, fiercely.

"Because I am her guide, and I am expected to be in my Court for the receiving festivities," Lysander answered casually. I cast my gaze over to him in a silent plea.

"Her guide? For her tour?" Chandler's voice raised ever so slightly, but I could tell he was very nearly approaching a boiling point.

"Yes, the whole thing. We're going to be spending quite some time together, aren't we Miss Cromwell?" He smirked, his green eyes glistening.

I hate you.

Chandler tensed beside me, I felt the anger radiating off of him in a warm haze, his Mythica pulsating through the muscles under his skin. For a moment, I was frightened of his reaction. He wouldn't let his emotions get the better of him here, in front of his Warden… would he? "What an exciting opportunity." He spat through clenched teeth. He wasn't fooling anyone, but Lysander responded with a jovial nod.

"Isn't it?" He beamed at me, relishing at the moment he not only ruined but poisoned.

"I should go to our meeting place." Chandler strode away from me, slowing only slightly to pick up his bags, and continued towards the exit Lysander currently blocked. The Warden turned to allow Chandler all the space he needed to storm out of the greenhouse, then turned back to face me with a dark smile on his face.

"Do you enjoy ruining important moments for me?" I snapped. My feet were glued to my spot.

Lysander took a step, letting the glass door close us inside. His eyes remained on me. "Was that important? From where I stood, it seemed like you were desperate for someone to save you." I saw red. Rushing forward until I was only a few feet from him, I dropped my bags at my feet so that I could extend my right pointer finger towards his smug face.

"Not that I expect you to understand this, but I have people in my life that I care about. People I want to give a proper goodbye to. People I might never see again because of you." His smile faltered.

"Because of me, huh?" He questioned, his fingers reaching out to caress a dark green flower beside me. Four large, emerald petals drooped into an almost upside-down angel. A dark black center bled onto the petals, creating the effect of paint spreading with water. The official flower of The Court of Shadows. It was a beautiful bloom, I'd always thought so. But watching his rough hands caress the yearning petals, I felt sorry for it. To be touched by such a selfish creature would truly be a shame.

"Excuse me, I need to meet my caravan." I stooped to grab my bags when Lysander beat me to it, grabbing them up in his hands effortlessly. "What are you doing?" I whispered so I wouldn't scream.

"You are not traveling with that caravan," he said matter of factly. It made me sick.

"What are you talking about? Am I not to spend the first week in your Court?" I had watched the Wardens sign their little schedule. I knew my life was painstakingly planned for the next six months and one week, and I knew where it started.

"Yes, but I am your guide. So you're traveling with me." I tried not to let my shock show on my face. "Besides, the caravan will consist of some Pledge training. You aren't allowed to participate in that yet." *Yet.* I rolled my eyes at his clearly intentional choice of words.

"Who is leading it? I assumed you had to" I asked, knowing that Lilith was not in The Living Lands right now.

"I have another trusted member of my Court leading the caravan. Don't worry, little storm, they will be well taken care of. As will you." His eyes darkened.

"When do we leave?" I asked, ignoring the way his gaze made my heart rate quicken.

"Now," and then he turned on his heel and exited the greenhouse with my bags in his hands. I turned my gaze to the ceiling of the greenhouse, where a muted sunlight was seeping through and said a silent prayer.

Banyad, please keep my heart pure so I do not commit a crime of anger against this Warden.

I hope she heard me. For both our sakes.

FIFTEEN

$\mathscr{I}$ was supposed to lead the caravan. After sending Lilith off, I had to scramble to find a replacement. I didn't think about it when I asked her to go ahead to The Forsaken Quarters and prepare a room for Miss Cromwell, something that could have easily been completed upon our arrival. Maybe I just didn't want Lilith at the Pledging Ceremony, maybe I wanted her seat empty for Miss Cromwell. But she was supposed to lead my new Pledges and begin their training. I'd always found that the nearly two days of travel that it took to get to The Forsaken Quarters was better utilized by preparing the recent members of my Court for life in the Shadows.

But foolishly, I sent away their instructor. Luckily for me, Salvador Louden, a well-trusted and respected member of my Court, had made the journey to the Ceremony to watch his son take the Pledge today. And luckily for him, his son Pledged to The Court of Shadows. Salvador jumped at the chance to lead my caravan back to the Forsaken Quarters and give his son, and the three other new members, the first introduction to their new home.

That way I had Miss Lexa Cromwell's attention all to myself, and I could give her every bit of mine. Undivided. I had made an important bit of progress by getting her to admit my Court still had a chance but it would be imprudent of me to think that was enough.

She had not said a word to me since we exited the greenhouse. Not even when I offered a hand to help her step up into the green and gold painted carriage. Or when I asked if she needed anything before our journey began. She simply gripped the handle to the door and pulled it closed, locking herself inside the small box of comfort provided by the enclosed wagon. I admit, I much prefer her venomous tongue to her cold silence. I held the reins to the dark black horse in my hands, appreciating the feel of the air caressing my skin as we traveled away from the Institute and towards the veil. Lexa was seated only a few feet behind me inside the carriage, while I rested in the driver's box, but the distance felt much more vast. I could see her out of the corner of my eye through the small window just behind me, staring out the side of the transport at The Living Lands. She watched it with such intent that I found my gaze trailing in the same direction if only to catch a glimpse of what had her so enraptured.

"We are nearing the veil." I tossed over my shoulder at her, keeping her in my periphery. She simply nodded. That moment in the greenhouse with whatever his name is must have meant a lot more to her than it seemed. I had meant it when I said that it looked like she needed saving.

When I entered the humid glass enclosure, I did not expect to find her lips seared to his, especially not after how he looked at her at the Pledging Ceremony, with such a deep loathing. How could someone look at her like that one minute, then capture her in a kiss the next? How could she let them? She looked overwhelmed like his large body was foreign in her arms. His mouth covered hers in a possessive manner, and while she did not pull away, she did not sink into it. She did not submit. Her Mythica practically aimed to push him off of her. Dark tendrils gripped at his shoulders, begging to rip him away. It was difficult to witness. So I put a stop to it.

I was lost in my mind when a small gasp tore me from my thoughts. I turned just enough to get an eyeful of the woman in the carriage behind me, mouth slightly agape, and ocean eyes wide. Her Mythica danced around her head in a convivial manner, as if it was welcoming an old friend. She had slid forward on the velvet-padded interior seats, her head nearly sticking out through the window by my driver's box to get a good look at the view that was stretching out in front of us.

The shimmering wall of Mythica was impressive. Even though I'd ventured through it hundreds of times, I had not yet become desensitized to its beauty. The surface of it danced with glittering diamonds in the sunlight, offering the same kind of blanket of fluid jewels one would find in the ocean. The veil had a bright white and silver hue, swirling like a storm, cloudy like moonstone. It stretched up into the sky, towering hundreds of feet over the small homes that dotted the area. And it expanded as far to the left and the right as I could see. I knew the veils to each Court met each other at their edges so that the entirety of The Living Lands was surrounded by these veils. I shuddered thinking about the veil that remained standing today despite the eradication of the Court that lay beyond it. As far as anyone knew, the seven Wardens were the only people alive that could travel through that veil. But we never did. There was nothing left there. And I did not need the visual reminder of what we did that night. The forest was created that evening. With Mythica dropped seeds into the ground, we planted a wooded shroud to cover our misdeeds.

My teeth had begun to grind together so I rubbed my jaw and turned to look at Lexa again, taking in her expression of wonder with a smile. We neared the veil and her blue eyes glistened with the reflection of the shining wall. I suddenly felt the urge to force her to Pledge to me right then and there. Take her arm and place the Mark of my Court on her smooth, pale skin, and claim her. I shook off the effects of my veil, the Mythica heightened my already envious thoughts the closer we got.

"Have you ever seen the veil before?" I asked. It was possible she never attended The First Trial festivals, unlikely, but possible.

"Yes, I've seen them." She looked out past me to the wall of Mythica. "It just sort of takes your breath away every time, ya know?" I did know. The corner of my lips turned up. It brought a sort of warmth to my chest that Lexa experienced things so deeply. It was something I was growing to admire about her. She was quiet for a moment, as if she was wrestling with herself. "Do you know which Court my parents are in?" I inhaled slowly.

"I've read your envelope, yes." She leaned forward, her sweet scent flooding my nostrils.

"Tell me," she demanded. I nearly laughed. I turned just enough to catch the determined look on her face.

"You know why I can't do that." She groaned.

"I don't care about the stupid rules, Lysander. I want to know. I deserve to know." Her eyes burned. I recognized the effects of my veil immediately. Her voice raised. "The other students found out today. I've done the same classes, the same tests, I did everything I was supposed to." Envy was a beautiful color on her. A hand went to her mouth, covering it. She sighed. "I'm sorry, I... I don't know where that came from." Her voice was meek, embarrassed.

"Don't ever apologize to me for coveting something," I responded, quickly. "The closer you are to the veil the stronger its influence." She nodded, her eyes scanning the shimmering wall ahead of us.

"Grab my hand," I said, offering my arm through the small carriage window. She leaned back, disgust coloring her face.

"Absolutely not." She bit back, and I had to hide my excitement at the return of her baneful banter.

"It is not for my own pleasure, Miss Cromwell. You do not bear the Mark of this Court and will be unable to cross the barrier without my assistance." I saw the disbelief cross her eyes as she glanced between my hand and my face. "Take my hand, or be left behind, Miss Cromwell." She threw a worried glance towards the veil we approached before reluctantly offering her hand to me. Her skin was as smooth as I remember it from last night at the ball and my very brief encounter with it during the Ceremony. I held it in my grasp and leaned forward, using my free hand to steer it into the Mythica.

As our carriage slipped past the threshold of the veil, I felt her hand tighten around mine. I squeezed back, offering every ounce of reassurance I could muster. If she was going to Pledge to me, I was going to need to show her that she was safe with me.

Venturing through the veil to The Court of Shadows brought with it a powerful, dangerous sensation. No matter how many times I made this trip, I was never quite prepared for the wave of emotions that threatened to engulf me. As if the Mythica that shrouded my Court was asking for penance in return for allowing passage, it often asked for a memory. A dark one, an envious one. The veil wanted to know why you deserved to pass through.

Being who I was, I had no shortage of memories to offer in payment, but it was usually one memory this veil called to. The same face, with wide dead eyes looking up at me. I let the image fall away. I wondered only briefly if I should have warned Lexa of this particular feature. She no doubt had plenty of material to pull from. In the last day, she had already shown me several key markers of a person suited for my Court.

Still, the Mythica took a toll, even on me. I hoped she wasn't too affected. We had several veils to cross in the next six months, after all. And each one had its price.

When we arrived on the other side of the veil, my body immediately relaxed, all the tension it had been carrying from the moment I arrived in The Living Lands yesterday morning slowly slipped away. The first noticeable difference in our surroundings were the colors. Where The Living Lands was in a constant state of green, lush grass, and full trees, The Court of Shadows was dotted in vibrant fall coloring. The trees were dotted with colorful red, yellow, and brown leaves, stuck in an eternal state of transition. The grass itself seemed more vibrant. And the air nipped at me with a cool wind that seemed prepared to dive to lower depths, but never would.

Home.

Lexa pulled her hand away from me to wrap her arms around herself. She had never lived outside the entirely boring temperament of The Living Lands. And while her eyes and senses danced with happiness at the colorful sight, I couldn't help but notice her body struggling to adapt to the new environment. Her Mythica wrapped around her, attempting to offer warmth. It continued to surprise me just how alive her Mythica felt. In others, their power was more like a shadow that hovered around them, but rarely did I see power this animated, this alive. I wondered, if her magic was this lively, did it remember me wielding it? If so, would it be vengeful? Would it welcome me back?

"There is a cloak for you in that chest," I said, pointing to the floor of the carriage. She scowled at me, but ultimately moved to retrieve the dark green cloak and slung it around her shoulders. Immediately color returned to her face.

Her eyes darted around at the landscapes that stretched out in front of us with wonder, excitement, and admiration. I felt a sense of joy in my Court.

I wish I could see it through your eyes.

But watching her experience my home was a riveting alternative.

We continued in silence for a few hours, I watched her carefully out of the corner of my eye, smiling at her small gasps and squeals of joy as she absorbed each hill, each river, and each small town, bustling with energy and excitement.

The citizens of my Court knew me well, they smiled and offered welcoming waves as we advanced along the road. The sun began to descend through the sky, giving way to the vast and bright stars. I loved the night sky in the Court of Shadows. Bias as I might be, I truly believed it was unparalleled. We did not have storms or winter clouds to hide their beauty, we did not have unbearable heat that made it impossible to enjoy stargazing, we simply had the sky. Full of stunning silver stars, glistening with a pureness one could never find on the ground. Corrupt and tainted as it is.

As we approached the next village, I pulled our carriage to the side, stopping in front of a large wooden building. Two stories, with a golden awning. The words "The Nightly Stray," painted in green, were displayed proudly.

This was not our most visited inn on this journey, but that inn was occupied by the other Pledges currently on their caravan back to the Forsaken Quarters.

I told myself I did not want Lexa to accidentally overhear any confidential training conversations by putting them in the same location, but a certain blonde male's smug face crossed my mind and I couldn't help but acknowledge that he possibly had something to do with my choice as well.

"Why are we stopping?" Lexa asked timidly, her eyes scanning the building through the carriage window. I hopped down off the driver's box, stretching my sore back for the first time since we left the Institute.

"We still have about a day's travel left, we need to rest." A short man with rosy cheeks rushed forward to greet me.

"My Warden," he bowed his head. I nodded to acknowledge him. "Please allow me to escort your horse to our stables for the night."

"That would be much appreciated, thank you…" I drew out the word, waiting for him to offer his name.

"Michael, sir," I smiled at him.

"Michael. Please see to it that she is well-rested and prepared for the next leg of our journey in the morning." The man lowered his head to me again.

"It would be my pleasure." He got to work, releasing my horse from her harness and leading her around the back of the inn. I gripped the door handle of the carriage, preparing to open it when I caught a glimpse of Lexa climbing out of the coach from the other side. A deep chuckle rumbled through my chest. She circled the wagon and came to a stop near me, waiting expectantly. I saw the fear and uncertainty in her eyes, but she did not falter.

A powerful little storm.

I tilted my head and gestured for her to lead the way through the wooden doors. She rushed forward, entering the inn with a smirk plastered on her face. I followed, suppressing my smile unsuccessfully.

The inside of the inn was more quaint than the usual stop on this journey, but sometimes I enjoyed that about this place. Where the other location had a large lobby with a winding staircase and a stunning crystal chandelier hovering above it all, this place had low ceilings, light wooden stairs, and a much more charming air to it. I'd wager a bet that given the choice, Lexa would choose this inn. I know my brother, Vander, and others like him, and Lexa just didn't seem to fit the bill.

I approached the small desk and the slender woman flitting about behind it. Without looking she called over her shoulder, "Welcome to The Nightly Stray, I'll be right back with you!" She moved with purpose, filing papers and organizing what seemed like a logistical mess behind the counter. I took this moment to study Lexa, even after a full day of travel, she seemed fresh-faced and pristine. She held the green cloak tight around her body. It fit her well. When I left for the Verihdian Institute, I didn't plan on returning with a guest. At least not personally. So I did not actually have a cloak prepared for her. Instead, when I noticed the chill wracking her full frame, I pointed her in the direction of my own cloak. The dark emerald fabric was thick and warm and draped across her body to hang just above the floor. The mantle was trimmed in golden braided markings, not too different from the braided pattern in the Mark of The Court of Shadows. The lustrous yellow clasp at her neck depicted the predatory bird, skua, with wings outstretched.

She stood stoically, analyzing the small lobby space with an unreadable expression on her face. What I wouldn't give to know what she was thinking.

"Sorry about that, how can I…" The young woman behind the counter turned and I could see the exact moment the blood drained from her face as she recognized me. "My Warden… I am… I am so deeply sorry to have made you wait. Please forgive me." She babbled anxiously. I raised a hand in the air and her mouth closed instantly. I saw Lexa's judgemental gaze wash over me. I did not look at her.

"No apologies necessary. I will need two rooms, please." The young woman hurriedly nodded, and Lexa's eyebrows rose in surprise. Whether it was at my dismissal of the young woman's apologies or my use of the word please, I couldn't tell.

That's it. See that there's more to me.

"Oh.. um.." the woman began, her brown eyes beginning to well with anxious tears. "I'm so sorry, my Warden, we only have one room left," I smirked, exhaling a quick laugh through my nose. It wasn't an unappealing notion, but I knew Lexa was not going to take this lightly. "I can knock on the doors, sir, I'll find you another room. I'm sure someone would be willing to give up their accommodations for the night for you." She rambled and I once again raised a hand, shaking my head.

"No need. One room will do." I felt the burning gaze of Lexa's blue eyes searing into my temple but I refused to look at her. I didn't dare let her see how the prospect of sharing such close quarters with her had affected me.

"Here's your key, my Warden." She slid the small silver key across the counter and I smiled at her as I gripped it between my fingers.

"Come, Miss Cromwell. We should get our rest." I moved then, making my way down the hall towards the door with the same number etched into the key with Lexa hot on my heels.

I felt her ramping up to say something, so I quickly opened the door and rushed inside. I did not hate her fiery disposition, but I also refused to allow anyone else to hear her speak to me in that manner. I had a reputation to uphold of course.

The moment the door closed behind me and I surveyed the space, I knew what she would say.

"One bed?!" There it was. "If you think I am going to share a bed with you, then you are completely deranged, Warden or not." She spat. Her eyes were wild.

"Calm down, little storm, I am rather tired and we have another long day ahead of us." I tossed myself onto the bed, feeling my weight sink into the mattress. It wasn't the firmest or the softest mattress I'd ever felt, but with how exhausted I was, it would do just fine. I patted the open space next to me with a taunting grin on my face.

"This is unacceptable." I sat up, this wasn't going to be easy.

"What do you wish me to do, Miss Cromwell? Let the clerk displace someone from their room in the middle of the night?" This softened her features, slightly. But the Mythica around her still thrashed violently, allowing me a more honest look at her emotions.

"I will not share a bed with you." She responded forcefully. I tilted my head and analyzed her. She stood with arms crossed in front of her chest, pushing her breasts together and up. I forced my eyes away from them.

"The floor looks like it's clean," I retorted, turning in the bed until my back was to her. It may have been a tactic to rile her up, but I couldn't deny that I was also incredibly drained from the Ceremony and the hours of travel.

"You are a horrible man." I waved her off with one hand, nestling into the pillow underneath my head. My eyes were already growing heavy. I heard her open the door, and I quickly turned towards her.

"Where do you think you're going?" I asked, lacing my tone with all the 'Warden' power I could muster at the moment. She spun to face me, her dark black hair bouncing with the movement, sending stray strands across her forehead.

"To sleep in the carriage." I rolled my eyes. This woman.

"No, you're not," was all I said. I was already tired of this diatribe.

"Yes, I am. I'd say goodnight, but I wouldn't mean it." She pushed through the open door and disappeared out into the hallway. I had half a mind to go out there and drag her back in here but a larger part of my mind reminded me that I needed her to trust me. If that meant respecting her wishes to sleep outside in a carriage at night in the frigid air instead of in a bed with me, then I would honor that. No matter how ridiculous it was, or how furious it made me.

Little storm. You will be the downfall of us all.

Sixteen

If only rage could keep me warm.

I certainly had enough of it at the moment. I was laying, huddled underneath the thick cloak Lysander offered me, in the back of a carriage with open windows. The cold air nipped at my skin, biting into me with taunting lashes. If this temperature was considered mildly cool, I was already dreading my adventure into the eternal winter of The Court of Talisman.

Here I was, teeth chattering and body aching while that monster of a man probably slept soundly, enveloped in the warmth the quilted comforter offered. The bed had looked so inviting until he threw his massive frame onto it, removing any desire to climb in. Was this stubborn and prideful? Maybe. Did I regret it? I would have to reassess in the morning. Was I going to admit any of that to him? Absolutely not.

I curled my body tighter, pulling the cloak as far around me as it would go, trying to put a cloth barrier between my skin and the cold material of the carriage seat. This was not how I expected this day to end. Cold and alone. Had it only been this morning that I woke up in my own bedroom after one of my nightly drownings? Strange that now, blanketed in the frigid cold, I was starting to miss the warm comfort of my nightmare. I sent a silent prayer to Buyhay that my dream tonight does not disturb anyone.

This was his fault, I tried to tell myself, but even as I thought it, logic threatened to smooth my fury. He had asked for two rooms, I heard it with my own ears. And instead of authorizing the ousting of a paying customer in the middle of the night, he accepted the room they had. Which, I admit, was more honor than I thought he was capable of. For the briefest of moments, I thought I was seeing a different side to this Warden. That maybe there was more to him than the selfish, Mythica-stealing jackass I had come to know. But that all fell to ruin the moment he suggested I sleep on the floor.

There were several reasons why sharing a room with Lysander Bladespell would bring nothing but disaster. One, he was a Warden and there had to be a law against this kind of fraternization with a Pledge. Two, I was not particularly happy with the prospect of Lysander witnessing my nightmares. While I had grown comfortable and familiar with them, I could not ask the same from someone else. That was the main reason why I never allowed Chandler to stay the night in my room. Although, he never asked to.

And third, and probably most unfortunate. If I were to share a bed with Lysander, chances are high that one of us would have strangled the other by morning.

No, I couldn't share a room with him. Ever.

"I hate him," I whispered through chattering teeth. I attempted to focus on that anger, that deep resentment, hoping it would be enough to warm my blood enough for me to sleep.

I drifted off to the comforting thoughts of Lysander Bladespell in mortal danger.

I was jostled awake by a slight rocking of the carriage sometime later. My eyes drifted open, groggy and unfocused. The night sky was still blanketing the world outside the cold comfort of the wagon.

A quiet rustling sound from just outside the door caused me to still.

It's just an animal, Lexa. Calm down.

I pulled the cloak higher above my head, hoping the creature would lose interest without venturing through the open windows. The sounds continued. Slow, methodical steps. Light, but heavier than I could confidently attribute to a small animal. I heard the sound of something slide against the outer wall of the carriage, in a sickening wet hiss. Then I heard it, low, almost unperceivable, a deep guttural clearing of a throat. My heart rate raised to an unnatural speed as I willed my breathing to slow and my body to remain still. Someone was standing just outside of this carriage.

I was pretty confident the visitor had not noticed my presence because if they had, I was not sure I would be safe here. Suddenly I found myself regretting not sleeping on the floor of the room. I would have been just as uncomfortable as I was here, but at least I would be safe.

Safe with Lysander. I would have scoffed at that notion, had I not been nearly paralyzed with fear.

I listened to the figure outside as they continued whatever it was they were doing to our carriage. Not stealing, I determined. If they were after riches or material possessions, they could easily slip their hand through the window and grab the ornate cloak that looked like it was carelessly bundled on the seat.

My heart rate slowed the longer they stayed and the longer they didn't look inside. It would be foolish to let my guard down, I knew that but suddenly the warmth I had been begging for all night had enveloped me, in part because I had the cloak completely concealing my head, and because my shallow anxious breaths were expelling warm air quicker than it could dissipate. I wasn't going to be able to remain under this cloak for much longer without overheating.

Slowly, with every ounce of caution that I could muster, I slid the thick cloak from above my head, angling my chin slightly, just enough to inhale the icy breeze. I moved at a glacial pace, knowing that whoever was just outside the carriage would be able to hear my movements the way I was able to hear theirs.

Slow. Slow. Carefully.

The fresh air washed over my lips as they reached the slight opening. It felt like a cool pool of water on a warm day, refreshing, necessary. I got greedy. Moving the hand that held the cloak back further to give me just a slightly bigger opening, I was too late to stop the golden clasp from sliding with the movement, filling the air with the smallest metal-on-metal grinding sound. One that, at any other point in the day, would be completely ignorable. But here, in the utter silence of the night, with a person standing mere feet away, sounded like the world was coming crashing down.

Suddenly the sounds outside the carriage halted. I held my breath, ignoring my protesting lungs. I couldn't move.

It was silent for a while. Maybe the figure got scared and left. I could only hope, but I didn't dare move just yet.

The cold air sliced into me as the cloak was ripped from my body. I let out a scream, but it was muffled under the hand that closed over my mouth in a tight seal. My arms and legs thrashed against their hold, but they were strong, stronger than I was. I looked up at the face of my assailant and saw nothing but a dark mask hiding their features. The hollow, white mesh covering their eyes made it seem like this figure could see into the very depths of my soul. Their entire torso was in the carriage now, leaning through the window. Their other hand made quick work of gathering my swinging arm and keeping it from hitting them. I screamed again, with no real success.

Is this how it ends?

I used my feet to push against the door to the carriage on the opposite side. If I could just get out I might be able to outrun them. I was fairly quick on my feet, and Lysander was only just inside the inn. I needed to get to him. He could help me.

The attacker gripped my face, hard, covering my nose with the palm of their hand. My already burning lungs cried in pain, begging for oxygen that would not come. A familiar sensation flooded my body. But instead of dreaming, I was wide awake - and instead of drowning, I was being suffocated.

I thrashed at them with my free hand, digging my nails into their arm, hoping I was able to cause even the slightest of pain through their long sleeves. My feet fought against the other door, and my body convulsed from the lack of oxygen. The edges of my vision blurred and darkness began creeping in, threatening to overcome me. I bucked wildly, but this figure's hold was steadfast. I was slowly losing strength, fog obscured my mind.

The darkness beckoned to me. Reaching a hand out as if to say, 'welcome home.'

And then the hand was gone, oxygen flooded back into my lungs, and they drank it up with eager, selfish breaths. I coughed, attempting to regain control of my weak body. Slowly, my world returned to focus, and that was when I heard it.

Sitting up quickly, I spotted two figures engaged in a violent match of strength. Locked in a deadly embrace, they struggled against each other. One of the figures was clearly the masked man who had attacked me, the other was none other than The Warden of Shadows himself.

Lysander moved with a skill I had never witnessed before. His movements seemed so fluid and lethal that if I cared at all about the figure in front of him, I might have pitied him. I didn't.

The masked man sank to the ground and kicked out a leg, an impressive move that would have knocked any good fighter to their backs. But Lysander was better than good. He was a Warden. Dodging the swing of the man's legs, Lysander kicked his foot out, making direct contact with the figure's chest, sending him toppling back to the ground. He rolled over his shoulder, his legs propelling him backward, landing on his feet. He crouched, readying his next attack with less confidence than he had before.

Lysander wore only a pair of low-sitting trousers, it was easy to see his massive muscles ripple with exertion as he swung a fist at the masked man. He landed the blow and the man stumbled back, cradling his face.

Behind the mask, I saw a soft glow of light, spilling out through the white mesh that covered his eyes.

Mythica.

"Lysander!" I screamed, wanting to warn him. But of course, he already knew. He barely dodged out of the way before a bright burst of electric energy shot out from behind the mask and seared the ground where Lysander had just stood. He rolled over his shoulder to return to a standing position and I saw him smile a deep, wicked smile. It sent a flutter to the very depths of my stomach.

A moment later, Lysander's eyes began glowing. The man in the mask's entire body tensed as he recognized what the Warden was doing. He was using his Mythica against him. My assailant knew he had very little time before his own electric energy would be his downfall. I saw it in the way his shoulders flexed.

The figure turned his gaze towards me for the briefest of moments before breaking into a dead sprint away from us. For a moment, I feared Lysander would run after him, leaving me alone, and based on the tension in his muscles and his deep growl, I could tell he had to restrain himself from doing just that.

Within a few moments, the man became nothing but a dot on the horizon in the light from the stars. Lysander watched him, and I watched Lysander. The charged energy in his eyes dissipated, reverting to his beautiful emerald green. His chest rose and fell with heavy breaths, his skin glistening with a thin sheen of sweat. His physique was not only impressive, but it also seemed God-like. The definition of his muscles was carved of stone, like the statues in the hall of art back at the Institute. Without a shirt, I was able to see his Court Mark. The swirling pattern climbed up his spine from the base to just between his shoulder blades. It seemed to embrace his tense back as he watched after the assailant.

I wasn't able to speak. Although, I don't know what I would say if I could.

After a few more tense moments of silence, Lysander turned to me. His green eyes were full of something dark and vicious as he surveyed me.

"Are you hurt?" He asked from his position. He didn't move closer. And after what just happened, I appreciated that. Was I hurt? My lungs still stung from the deprivation, and my wrist was sore from where he held it down. But other than that, I was fine. I was lucky.

"I'll be ok," I answered, my voice was meek, quiet. I hated how weak I sounded.

"Tell me the truth, little storm." His expression softened and I took a deep, steadying breath.

"Just a little shaken, but I'm ok. I promise." He nodded, continuously, his head dropping down to look at the ground. I didn't know what else to say. I knew I should thank him, but something about that felt wrong. He saved me from an attacker tonight, but he himself assaulted me yesterday with my own Mythica. Was I able to look past that right now? I coughed as the last breath sent a searing pain through my chest. Yes, I think I could look past it just this once.

"Thank you, Warden," I whispered the words, but I knew he heard me. His eyes lifted to mine again, his eyebrows furrowing in what looked like pain. "Are you hurt?" Without thinking, I rushed from the carriage and arrived at his side. He seemed taller. I felt his body heat radiating off of him against the chill of The Court of Shadows' night air.

"Don't worry about me." He watched me intently, his hand rising to grip my arm, but he stopped before he made contact, hovering an inch above my goosebump-covered flesh. I felt a wave of panic course through me. Not that I felt he would hurt me at this moment, but someone had. He must have recognized the fear in my eyes because he slowly lowered his hand to his side. His gaze searched my face, scanning for injuries, or a sign of a breakdown.

I took a deep breath and prayed that he found neither.

His eyes bore into mine, and we stood there for some time, just watching each other. His breathing had returned to normal, and I could see the rise and fall of his toned chest slow to a steady pace. There was something in his expression I didn't recognize from him. Was it regret? Worry? Guilt? There was one way to know for sure, but I forced the thought from my head the moment it entered. He may have been bold enough to use my Mythica on me, but I was not quite as foolish to do the same to him. It wouldn't work anyway. So I wouldn't search for answers with my mind, but that didn't stop me from watching him closely, analyzing his gaze. His eyes flicked briefly to something over my shoulder and I saw his entire demeanor shift from a warm expression of concern to a cold mask of terror. I hadn't seen this emotion in the Warden before. But I knew it well. Panic. Fear.

He kept his eyes trained on something over my shoulder, the color draining from his face. Following his gaze, I saw what it was that terrified him, although I had no idea why.

Painted on the side of the emerald carriage with bright white paint was a symbol. A raven's silhouette, the stem of a large petaled flower in its mouth hanging towards the ground. I couldn't recognize the species of flower, I didn't believe I knew it, although it was hard to tell from a rough painting. It seemed harmless enough.

At least I knew what the man was doing now. But what did it mean? I'd never seen anything like this before. Nor had I seen a flower that looked quite like that.

"Lysander, what is it? What is that symbol?" I asked, my voice hoarse from my muffled screams. He didn't answer me. He scanned the vandalization with a level of fervor that seemed almost methodical.

"Why did that man paint this on your carriage?" I asked, knowing he would not respond, but needing to fill the ominous silence.

"Come inside, we need to rest." His voice was restrained and even, but no matter how hard he tried to keep his composure, I noticed the cracks. This painted image, whatever it meant, truly troubled him to his very foundation. Something I never expected was possible. I wanted the safety of a room right now, more than anything. Even now, I could still feel the phantom of a gloved hand across my mouth. I darted my tongue out to wet my suddenly dehydrated lips. But by being in the same room as him, would I just be trading one monster for another?

"I can't stay in the same room as you," his head snapped towards me, emerald eyes blazing with madness.

"You were just attacked," he said as if he wasn't sure I knew what had occurred. I scoffed. The fear that had its debilitating grip on my body just moments ago began to slip away, replaced with indignation.

"I am well aware of that, thank you." His hands ran through his unkempt black hair as he released a sigh of frustration.

"You'd rather sleep out here after what just happened than spend the night in a room with me?" He spoke with such complete confusion, his tone laced with accusations. As if he thought I was the most ridiculous person in Verihdia. Ridiculous, no. Stubborn, absolutely.

"He's gone. I'll be fine." Even as I said the words, I knew I didn't mean them. But I was not about to admit defeat.

"Madillam save me," he exhaled, his head falling back as his eyes rolled in his head. He was not happy with me. "You are so incredibly frustrating, do you know that? Why would you willingly put yourself at risk? Just to what, prove a point?" He asked, his voice rising slightly with each frustrated word. "Well, consider it proven. I get it. Congratulations. Now, can we please go inside?" His nostrils flared and I knew I was seeing a different side to this Warden. He had asked something of me, he was nearly begging. I'd be willing to bet he did not often do this. For anyone.

"Lysander, I'm not sharing a bed with you tonight. Or any night." It didn't matter to me if I was terrified. It didn't matter that he had saved me. It didn't matter that I had wished for him to come to my rescue. This man in front of me had done something so incredibly horrible to me. He had stolen something from me. Something personal, heart-wrenching, terrible. He'd caused me more pain in the last twenty-four hours than anyone had in my entire life. And being in a room with him meant he would learn yet another secret about me. My nightmares.

I was already set to spend the next six months by his side, I would have very little space from his manipulations and games. I knew that soon enough he'd hear my screams in the night and put together the truth of my nightly drownings. I had no control over that fact. But tonight, this was something within my autonomy. I could say no. I did not have to compromise.

"Please respect that," I added. Not that I wanted to beg him, but that I needed him to see what this meant to me. He closed his eyes and inhaled a long breath, he did not speak for a few moments. I simply watched the way his throat moved as he swallowed.

His head lowered quickly and his eyes popped open to look at me. There was something there, deeper than anger, but full of what I had hoped was understanding. Retrieving the key from the trousers hung low on his waist, he held it out for me. I reached for it tentatively. It dropped into my open palm, the metal warm against my cold flesh. I didn't realize how cold I still was, and would be again once the adrenaline wore off. I suddenly became very aware of my lack of cloak. The man had pulled it off of me, where did it go?

"Take the room," Lysander said in a flat voice before stalking off in the dark, cold night.

I wanted to ask him where he would be staying, I wanted to go after him to thank him for the room. But I didn't do either of those things. Pride maybe, residual anger. I retreated to the carriage to retrieve the cloak, now crumbled on the ground next to a discarded receptacle of white paint, and one of my cases. With one last look at the mysterious symbol, I made my way inside the inn.

The desk was unoccupied and quiet. I moved quickly to the room, shutting and locking the door behind me. Finally allowing myself to breathe.

I moved slowly across the room, tossing my case and the cloak onto the bed, to pull the blinds tightly closed. Checking the lock on the window three times before I made my way to the large bed. It was disheveled and slept in and suddenly guilt crawled up my throat, threatening to consume me. I forced it away from my mind and settled into the very center of the mattress, pulling the comforter up to my chin.

It was still warm from Lysander's body heat. His scent was so strong under these covers. I inhaled deeply. It smelled like a fire, pleasant, fragrant, like the sweet smell of burnt ash. The kind of scent that so easily reminded me of cozy nights around a fireplace, with friends and a good book. How could someone so dreadful have such a calm, comforting scent? That was the last thing I remember thinking before my eyes fluttered closed and the sweet escape of sleep took me.

SEVENTEEN

The warm amber glow of the morning sun caressed my face and beckoned me to wake. I didn't remember a time I had slept as soundly as I just did. Surprising, after an attack such as that, to get a full night's rest. But something about this bed was just so inviting and calming that when I slipped into unconsciousness, I stayed there. I sat up quickly as the realization hit me.

I had slept soundly, deeply…

I didn't have a nightmare.

There were few constants in my life. Axel. Riley. And nightmares. I could always count on them. But for the first time since I was a young girl, I slept without my nightly visit to the depth of the ocean. For the first time in nearly two decades, I didn't drown. My heart raced as this new information sunk in, filling me with a sense of worry, dread…of happiness.

You don't realize how much of a toll dying every night takes until there's a night you survive.

My body felt lighter, and calmer. I didn't know how much time I had left before we had to leave for our last leg of the trip, but after the long journey yesterday and the events of last night, I simply couldn't resist a bath. I ventured into the washroom to start filling the tub. Within a few minutes, the entire room was humid and thick with the steam of the warm water. After double checking that the bathroom door was closed and locked, I disrobed and stepped into the large clawfoot tub.

I sunk until the water covered every inch of my body save for my face, basking in the way the warmth and weight enveloped me. Every ounce of residual tension simply melted away with each lap of the water against my skin.

Last night, I displaced Lysander from his room. Shirtless. He didn't even come back in for his case. Did he have another shirt somewhere? Would he be shirtless when next I saw him?

The image of him, muscles straining as he fought off the mysterious masked figure, replayed in my mind. His usually stunning emerald eyes brimming with a stolen Mythica. I let my head rest against the edge of the tub, closing my eyes. I needed to shake last night from my mind, all of it. The feel of the man pinning me down, the mysterious symbol that seemed to terrify Lysander, and the way his chiseled chest looked illuminated by the starlight. The way his scent enveloped me and drifted me off to a night of sleep devoid of nightmares.

"Ugh!" I sunk into the water, completely submerging myself. I refused to believe that I found that vulgar man attractive. It must be some sort of stress-induced dependence. Not that I was his captive in any way, but I was still stuck with him, despite my wishes. I did not find myself drawn to him, my mind was simply reacting to witnessing him come to my rescue. That had to be it.

So why do I feel so guilty about kicking him out?

I held my breath, willing the fluid to wash away the guilt that was a bigger threat to drown me than the water that enveloped me. I felt my Mythica bubbling under the surface of my skin, dancing through me with newfound energy, almost like it could taste my own sinfulness and was growing stronger because of it.

Beneath the water, I let the weight sink me lower to the floor of the tub. Testing the capacity of my already sore lungs. I did this often, more often than

NIKKI ROBB

I liked to admit. After having dreams of drowning every night, you'd think I would have grown afraid of the water, but it did the opposite, in fact. It made me curious. I would sink under the water to try and regain that control. Because unlike in my dreams, when I went underwater I knew there was a surface.

Then an eerie feeling washed over me, like there was another presence in this water, drifting beneath me. My eyes snapped open, and instead of the clawfoot tub around me and the inn's ceiling above me, I was floating in an endless ocean, the saltwater burning my eyes and I forced them to stay open. Darkness spread in every direction, and panic seized my heart. Looking up, I saw no surface, I saw no light. I pushed through the water, up…up…up. The last bit of my oxygen was wavering.

No, no, NO!

I wanted to scream. I wished I could. But I needed to save what little bit of life-saving air I had left. Frantically, my hands spliced through the water. But no matter how hard I swam, I made no progress. Had I been on land, tears would have been pouring from my stinging eyes. This was not like any dream I'd ever had before. It felt so real, so vivid. Trapped inside a waking nightmare.

I was going to die here.

Buyhay, save me.

Goosebumps erupted on my flesh as the eerie feeling returned. I was not alone in this water. Slowing my thrashing movements instinctively, I stilled. Floating in the nothingness of this calm sea. I felt my vision blur as I began to lose my battle against my lungs which begged me to take a breath.

Something moved beneath me, slowly, traveling through the shadows. Between the pitch-black void that extended in every direction and my nearly blacked-out vision, I wasn't able to get a look. My skin crawled, and I felt every muscle in my body scream in unison, for air, for escape, for safety.

For Lysander.

But he wasn't here. I didn't even know where *here* was. My body convulsed, and I lost what little restraint I had against inhaling a lungful of this salty elixir.

223

Precious oxygen was replaced with water and I coughed, choking on the intrusion. There was not a doubt in my mind that this was not a nightmare. My dreams had never felt like this. Had never hurt like this.

I thrashed, kicked, and screamed... fighting. And just as my body's convulsions slowed, my vision darkened, and I felt the cool touch of Kamatayan's embrace, I could barely make out the thick, long tentacle that reached for me from the darkness.

Then I sat up, coughing violently to expel the water from my lungs. Large puddles formed on the floor as I jumped from the clawfoot tub. I looked around at the inn's washroom. Just the way it had been only minutes ago, unaltered, and yet at the same time, everything had changed. I rushed to the vanity, and placed one hand on either side of the basin, leaning forward to analyze my reflection in the mirror.

Water from my long black hair dripped steadily into the basin, and droplets ran down my pale skin, painting each curve. My shoulders rose and fell unevenly as I struggled to regain control of my breathing.

Was that one of my nightmares? It certainly made sense to call it that. Despite how vivid it was, and how painful it felt. It couldn't have been real, right? But as I darted my tongue out to wet my lips, the taste of saltwater sent a shiver down my spine.

Wrapping my body in the grey towel, I rushed out of the washroom quickly, still panting, leaving soaking wet footprints in my wake. I didn't care about that though, I just needed out of that room and away from that tub.

I heard the handle of the door to the room turn and I nearly dropped my towel in shock. A scream caught in my throat as I turned to see The Warden of Shadows strut into the room. He had donned new clothing and looked as put together as he had yesterday. Wearing a dark green button-down, the first two buttons remained unfastened. His black hair was pulled back and loosely gathered in a bun at the nape of his neck, with a few wispy curls framing his face. He held something in a cloth wrap in one of his hands.

"Get out!" I screamed at him, clutching my towel tighter to my chest with one hand and pulling it lower down my legs with the other. Thank the Gods it was long enough to cover all of my curves. He didn't stop. He continued into the room, closing the door behind him. "Get out of here! I'm not dressed!" I snapped again. The forceful tone pained my aching throat, but I refused to show weakness.

"It is nothing I have not seen before, Miss Cromwell." He said, crossing the room to his bag that sat untouched on the floor near the bed. Anger rose in my chest.

"Do you seriously have such little regard for what anyone else in this world wants?" He turned to look at me, a fire behind his emerald eyes. He took cautious steps forward, I backed away until the backs of my knees came into contact with the edge of the bed. He did not stop. "Stop," I said in a warning tone. But again, he didn't listen. He was inches from me within seconds, towering over me. His fiery scent enveloped me again, it was so much more powerful coming directly from him than it was on his pillow last night. His eyes dropped to the towel in my hands and traveled down the length of my body. Scanning me.

I wanted to push him back, to yell at him, but his gaze held me still. Frozen in place by the intensity with which he studied me.

He raised a hand, slowly, his fingers making contact with the wrist of my hand that was holding the hem of my towel. For the second time this morning, goosebumps spread across my exposed flesh. Suddenly the air felt so warm. He lifted his hand then, grazing my arm on its way up towards my neck. "What's wrong?" He asked, his eyes scanning my features and clearly finding something there that concerned him. I very nearly told him about the incident in the tub but thought better of it. Finally, my senses came back to me. I shoved him back, my palms making contact with his unyielding chest.

"Do not touch me!" I cried out. He dared to roll his eyes at me. As if he thought I was kidding.

"Will you relax for one single moment, little storm?" His humorous tone was laced with an edge of seriousness. It was enough to cause me to pause. I let my arms cross in front of me tightly, ignoring the urge to push him back again.

He nodded his head slightly in appreciation of my submission. It took most of my willpower to keep my limbs from lashing out again, while his hand continued its way up my bare arms.

When his palm reached my shoulder, he pushed down with minimal force, but enough to clearly indicate what he wanted from me. Without breaking eye contact, I lowered myself onto the edge of the bed, hoping the venom in my eyes was enough to let him know that I was only sitting here because I chose to, and not because it is what he wanted of me. I rested my weight on the edge of the mattress, careful to keep a tight grip on the towel that covered me. I looked up at him, and he watched me from his standing position for a moment, a small smile playing on his lips.

Then he began to sink onto his knees before me. I swallowed hard, banishing the panic that was building in my chest.

I hate this man. I hate everything about him. I hate the way he speaks to me. I hate his entitlement. I hate his Mythica. I hate that he forced me to tell him my guilt. I hate that my body was begging for him to touch me.

He set the bundle from his hands on the ground next to him. I couldn't see what was in it from my position, nor could I possibly tear my eyes away from him at this moment.

"I want you to stay very still," he whispered. His voice was dark, with a rasp, and I fought to keep my wits about me. But that willpower was waning with every slow breath he took. His eyes left mine only for a moment, so he could look at the bundle at his side. My heart began to pound, and I felt my clouded mind clear in the absence of his gaze.

"What do you think you're doing?" I made a move to stand, but his hands quickly found my bare knees, holding me to the bed. His rich brown skin stood out against the pale backdrop of my thighs. I watched as his thumb moved ever so slightly, back and forth, leaving a trail of goosebumps in its wake on my skin. The room was quiet, all I could hear were my heavy breaths and my beating heart in my ears.

"Sit still for me, little storm." His emerald eyes, shrouded with an emotion I couldn't recognize, pleaded with me.

"Fine." I bit back, hoping it came off more confident than I was currently feeling. The corner of his mouth lifted in a quiet smirk. I watched his face. His facial hair had come in more since I first saw him at the Courting Ball. The black hairs dotted his brown skin. I had to admit, it framed his face well. I could still clearly see his defined jawline beneath the stubble, and I suddenly found myself wondering if it felt as sharp as it looked.

Shoving that thought completely out of my mind, I focused back on his hands, which were now gripping something from the bundle he had placed. Then they were on me. I jumped at the sensation, and he shot a brief warning glance at me. His hand gripped my ankle and lifted it from the floor, just a foot or so, but enough that I struggled to keep my towel in place. The rough fabric that wrapped around me slid up, riding higher on my thigh exposing more of me, inch by inch. My breath caught in my throat as I fought to keep my thighs pressed together.

His fingers wrapped around my ankle as his eyes locked on me. I couldn't look away. I was mesmerized by his gaze, as I was the night of the ball. It made me feel safe, it made me feel calm. It felt like a lifeline. Before he ruined everything.

But that sense of calm washed over me again now, and I studied him, carefully, as his hand trailed up my calf towards my knee. I felt him slide something onto my leg, but I didn't tear my eyes from him. Leather, I decided, because of the cool and smooth material that grazed my skin.

His eyes didn't leave mine as he pushed the leather strap higher, higher, cresting above the knee. A small gasp escaped from my mouth involuntarily. His face softened, the smirk giving way to a slightly parted mouth, he could see how he was affecting me. However, I didn't feel regret or shame. Against my better judgment, I wanted him to see what he did to me.

He moved the strap up my thigh, his fingers delicately brushing my skin that nearly burst into flames under his touch. He stopped then, halfway up my thigh, just below the base of the towel that I suddenly wished wasn't there, and without looking down, began to tighten the strap. His head lowered, and I watched with bated breath. Opening his mouth slightly, he took the end of the leather strap in between his teeth, pulling it taught. It bit into my skin slightly, not to the point of pain, but just enough for me to part my lips, a strained moan escaping me. He fastened the buckle and lifted his head again.

He was so close to the center of my arousal and I was utterly disgusted by the fact that I wasn't disgusted at all. In fact, at this moment, for some unknown reason, I wanted him there.

"Lysander." It was a plea, a whisper. Breathy and lustful. I didn't recognize the sound of my own voice. His tongue darted out to wet his lips, and his gaze trailed down my face to watch my lips. Lips that were begging for him to touch me. His hands left my thigh then, and I nearly whimpered at the absence. Silently, I cursed my weak constitution. But his eyes never left mine, and mine never left his.

He grabbed something from the floor and quickly his hands returned to my thigh. I felt something cold, metallic almost, touch my skin, and I wanted to look but I couldn't seem to drag my gaze from the man who was on his knees before me.

He glanced around me, watching the sky around my head again as he often did. I would have asked him why he did that if I wasn't completely and utterly under his spell. I knew right then that I'd give this man anything he asked for. And I so desperately wanted him to ask.

"Now, perhaps the next time you're a stubborn little girl, you will at least be able to defend yourself." He stood, rushed towards the door, and then he was gone. My mouth hung agape, my breathing still coming raggedly as I stared at the door he closed behind him.

The connection that was growing so steadily between us was severed, and I finally regained control of my limbs. I felt every muscle in my body relax, only to tighten again with anger.

How could I be so foolish?!

I stood, frustration guiding me, and locked the door, moving a chair to rest under the door handle. Once I was positive I'd have no other unexpected visitors, I tossed off my towel and moved across the room to grab my dress for the day. But as the towel slid to the floor, my eyes caught on the new addition to my leg. A dark black leather strap encircled my mid-thigh, comfortably staying in place as if it was meant to wrap around my leg. Resting gently in the holster was a small dagger, poised to attack.

I reached down to retrieve it, taking it in my hands. It was lighter than it looked, a dark obsidian metal blade, six inches long, glistened with small flecks of starlight. As I rotated it in my hands, it seemed to shimmer with the intensity of the constellations and the depth of the night sky. It was breathtaking.

The blade was fixed on an emerald hilt, a twisted and braided design climbing from the blade like a tower of green smoke, similarly to the Mark of this Court. A single word was carved into the obsidian near the spine of the blade.

'Vahlach'

I scanned my memory, trying to find any mention of this name, but came up short. If this meant something, I didn't know what it was.

I slid the dagger back into the holster on my thigh, shivering slightly as the metal grazed my skin, or maybe I shivered at the memory of Lysander's hands doing the same just moments ago.

Was it a thoughtful gift, or a slight because he thought I couldn't protect myself? I scoffed out loud in the quiet room. Of course, it was a slight. Lysander didn't have a generous bone in his stupid chiseled body.

I dressed quickly, throwing on a long blue tunic dress and fastening a small corset belt around my waist. I felt my usual ire towards the insufferable Warden returning tenfold and carefully made sure my mask of disdain was firmly in place. Once I was sure there would be no repeats of this morning, offering just a quick stolen glance at the dark washroom, I left the room. The gifted dagger from the Warden of the Court of Shadows was still firmly in place against my thigh.

EIGHTEEN

*T*he next several hours of the journey to The Forsaken Quarters were quiet. Lysander had not said a word to me after helping me into the back of the wagon. The carriage had been cleaned, and I noticed that all traces of the mysterious symbol from last night were gone. A shiver coursed through me as the memory resurfaced. The rough hand closed over my mouth, the way his fingers restrained my wrist so easily. I hated how weak I felt. How pathetic my attempt to escape was. Maybe I should have taken Axel up on his offer to train me. Maybe then I wouldn't have needed saving.

I foolishly looked at the Warden who sat casually on the driver's box of the carriage. His eyes were completely devoid of any passion I thought I might have seen there previously. In fact, his eyes avoided me altogether, as if he couldn't be bothered to glance in my direction. Like my mere presence meant nothing to him. Shame shrouded me, burning a hole through my trusting heart. Had I really been so daft as to think perhaps there was more to this man than the Warden who would do anything within his power to get what he wanted, no matter who he hurt in the process? He was simply doing what he did best, manipulating me. I felt a quiet rage bubbling just under the surface.

I swore a silent oath to never let him under my skin again. As much as I'd prefer to never speak to him, or see his face again, that simply wasn't a possibility. The better part of the next year of my life would be spent by his side, and the least he could do is make it bearable. And if he wasn't going to be the one to bridge the gap, I would.

"Where did you sleep last night?" I asked towards the window at the front of the carriage. I could see the back of his head and most of his shoulders through the small opening. I watched him carefully.

Without turning, he spoke over his shoulder, "You don't need to concern yourself with that." I rolled my eyes.

"You know, for someone who wants me to choose his Court, you are certainly not very forthcoming." I joked. Although I had promised to give his Court a fair chance, it was fairly obvious that I could never devote my life to a place where Lysander Bladespell ruled. I think he knew that too.

"For someone whose life I saved last night, you're not acting very gracious." He snapped back, but there was a slightly playful edge to it. I leaned forward on the padded bench until I was a foot from the window.

"I said thank you, last night."

"Yes, well. Words and actions speak very different languages, Miss Cromwell. Wouldn't you agree?" His head still didn't turn to look back at me, and I couldn't help but feel annoyed by that. We hadn't seen another carriage on this road in over an hour. It's not like he desperately needed to watch the road ahead. Just then, his head drifted slightly, one side to the other, scanning the area, and it hit me. Of course, he wouldn't take his eyes off the surrounding area, that man got away last night, and he could come back any second.

It was obvious that the man didn't intend to use violence. His lack of any weapon was evidence enough of that. He simply planned to send a message. But my presence caused a problem, I became a loose end. I shuddered to think about what might have happened to me had Lysander not awoken and come to my rescue. I was suddenly no longer annoyed that his eyes remained trained on the horizon.

Words and actions speak very different languages.

I thought back to this morning in my room, the hold his gaze had on me, the gentle way he touched my skin. The way his mouth was so close to...

And then the way he disregarded that, calling me nothing more than a stubborn child and storming off. His words and actions could not have been more in opposition.

Was he trying to tell me something?

"I guess so." I agreed. "However, I've found that when words and actions are speaking different languages, misunderstandings can occur. People can get hurt."

His head began another scan of the area, but I saw his shoulders tense at that. We were in dangerous territory, and I remembered my vow to make this experience as painless as I could. That meant avoiding treacherous topics.

"Yes, they could."

I leaned back against the back of my seat then - watching him, watching the world.

"So, the other Pledges are getting introduced to the cultures of The Court of Shadows right now on their caravan, are they not?" This seemed like a safe enough avenue of conversation. Plus, if I had to speak to him, learning about his Court would be a good use of the time.

"They are."

"Well then, tell me about your Court, Warden." His head tilted to the side, and I so wished I was able to see his face. What was he thinking? Was he annoyed at my persistent talking, or did he relish the chance to speak highly of his home to me?

"What do you wish to know?" My eyes rolled again, involuntarily.

"What's worth knowing?" I teased, and to my surprise, he chuckled. His shoulders shook with the action.

"Everything is worth something to someone." I took a moment to let that sink in. He wasn't wrong, I suppose. One person could detest a book, while at the same time it could be considered a favorite to someone else. It was a good way to look at life. Everything has worth. Everything matters to somebody. No matter how lost, broken, lonely, or weak…everything is worthy. Everyone is worthy.

Even me.

It must have been a while since I responded because he spoke again. "How about I tell you what I love about my Court?" It was an impressive offer. He was not planning to reiterate some carefully concocted pitch designed to cater to a variety of needs and wants, but rather truly open up and let me see what mattered to him.

I wondered how many people in all of Verihdia had ever had this type of chance with a Warden before.

"I'd like that," I answered truthfully.

"The best thing about my Court is the weather," he began. I looked out the side windows at the lush landscape of colorful leaves and thriving crops. The sun was shining down, casting a vibrant blanket of light and warmth as far as my eyes could see. It was stunning, that much was easy to admit. And while I found the nighttime temperature undesirable, I could concede that at the moment, midday with the sun shining, it was quite pleasant. "And you can't beat the views." This time as he scanned the horizon, I saw him visibly relax. He wasn't keeping watch with this sweep of his eyes across the landscape, he was enjoying the sight.

"It is rather beautiful," I confessed, watching the world move past us in a blur of color.

"Each year, we hold a harvest festival. I normally despise big, lavish, and gaudy functions, but that's one I have yet to tire of." The longer he spoke, the more his voice filled with a jovial tone, with excitement.

"Stop the carriage," I said authoritatively. Suddenly, Lysander was on edge again, his eyes rapidly surveying our surroundings for the threat he thought I had witnessed. "No, there's nothing out there. We're ok." His shoulders slumped but he didn't stop the carriage. "I can't hear anything from back here."

"I'll talk louder," he said, demonstrating with his now strained vocal cords.

"You're not going to stop?"

"I would prefer not to be a sitting duck out here," he spoke again with his painful-sounding attempt at amplifying his voice.

"And you call me stubborn," I said under my breath as I began to move, pushing my torso through the small window at the front of the carriage.

"What in Gods' names are you doing?" Lysander asked, struggling to maintain control of the reins as I clumsily toppled onto the driver's box next to him. It was an awkward, inelegant display of my lack of athleticism. My legs pushed against the frame of the carriage in an attempt to sit upright, but I fumbled, spilling myself onto Lysander's lap. My head rested on his ridiculously muscular thigh. I felt my face flush a deep crimson as I rushed to right myself. Once I was seated, comfortably in the seat next to him, I smoothed my blue tunic dress in silence. "I could have stopped, you know." His joking tone sliced right through my discomfort. My hand lashed out, smacking his bicep.

"You are vile!" I spat, but I couldn't control the laughter that juddered my body. He, too, had devolved into a fit of hysterics.

"Ok, now that I can hear you…tell me more." I didn't miss the smirk that lit up his face as he resumed.

And that continued for what seemed like hours, and yet the time moved so quickly. It was only just after midday, and the sun was still brightly radiating in the sky. He told me we would arrive at his castle late afternoon, with only a few hours to unwind before the Welcome Ball. I knew I should rest if I was expected to attend this event, but I simply didn't want our conversation to end.

He went from describing the harvest festival to talking about the cuisine, and my mouth watered at some of the things he spoke of. Then he spoke about his home, the Forsaken Quarters. He described it in such detail, that I was sure I was so familiar with the layout that I wouldn't need a map once we arrived. He spoke with such pride, such love, it was impossible not to smile.

Maybe The Court of Shadows isn't so bad.

But I quickly pushed the thought down and buried it. I couldn't have the Court without the Warden, and I wouldn't do that.

"I know a common assumption about us is that we are all thieves, liars, and spies." I didn't correct him, because he was right. "And while perhaps that rumor is founded in some modicum of truth, our Court is so much more than that." I wasn't sure I heard him right at first, but he had said it, clear as day. Our Court. Every Warden I had the honor of speaking with previously, including Lysander, had referred to their Courts as "my". With a sort of tight claim of ownership, like they alone possessed it. But as Lysander spoke, his words filled with wonder and pure admiration for the Court over which he presided, he referred to it as "our" Court. A Court he shared with every member who Pledged to the Shadows. Who knew such a small word could have such a large impac?

"I do not doubt that." And honestly, I didn't. He turned his head towards me, making direct eye contact for the first time since we entered the carriage, and my breath caught in my throat as he flashed me the most dazzling smile I had ever seen. His face was light and seemed almost younger as if the simple pleasure of speaking about his Court shaved years of worry and stress off him.

Before I could stop myself, I smiled back.

"So why deal in secrets?" His tongue ran along the front of his teeth as he thought.

"Have you ever kept a secret for so long that you felt as if you might explode?" My mind drifted to my nightmares. Axel was the only person alive who knew the truth about them. Sometimes the weight of that secret felt unbearable. I nodded.

"We deal in secrets because sometimes people just need to tell someone. They just need to let it out." He rubbed the back of his neck with his hand, mindlessly. "So we listen."

"So you let people vent their secrets to you, out of the kindness of your heart?" I joke sarcastically. He laughed. "Who are you and what did you do with The Warden of Shadows?"

"We listen when no one else can." I nodded, understanding. "It doesn't hurt if I'm the only one in the world to know the secret, either." His eyes glistened with a mischievous light.

"Ah, there you are." I chuckled and watched him readjust his grip on the reins. "Can I ask you something?" The last thing I wanted to do was ruin this small blissful moment, but the Warden had the answers I needed and he was in a good enough mood that maybe, just maybe, he'd give me some.

"You do not need to ask permission, little storm," he spoke through a slight laugh. I tried to memorize the good spirits he was in, knowing that after I asked my question, it could change drastically.

"Why do you think I got the result I did at the Final Trial?" He didn't tense the way I expected him to, but instead, he went calmly still - if he was still breathing I couldn't tell.

"I was wondering when you'd ask about that," he responded after a while. I didn't interject. I simply waited for him to tell me what he knew. "What do you know of The Forgotten Court?" He asked, his voice lowering to a frightening degree as he uttered the name.

"Very little. Only that it existed, and now it doesn't." He nodded as if thankful so little was known.

"They were once very powerful people, led by a very powerful Warden." I studied his face as he talked, his eyes were trained on the horizon, but now instead of watchful and attentive, they were glazed and vacant. "You likely received that result because you are also incredibly powerful, Lexa."

It didn't make sense. Of course, I had Mythica, and when I was younger it was hard to control, but that didn't make me powerful. That didn't make me more special than anyone else. "A lot of people have Mythica," I whispered. He sighed.

"No one has Mythica like you, little storm." His gaze once again flicked up to watch the space around my head. "Trust me, I've felt it."

I rolled my eyes, remembering the hate I have for the man next to me and why.

"Yes, I distinctly remember that." I bit at him. He lifted his hands in a mock surrender with a smile. We continued in a melancholic silence for a little while before he spoke again.

"What is it like…your Mythica?" His tone was earnest, genuine interest lacing every word.

"Don't you already know?" I tried to usher it as a joke, but the very real and very strong anger that still burned inside of me managed to seep through. He lowered his chin slightly, and I swear I saw regret dance behind his eyes. I sighed before continuing. "It used to be debilitating," I confessed. "Some of my Mythica is harmless enough. Getting to the root of someone's fears and desires is a violation of privacy, sure, but that's not the part that scares me. It's the guilt." I shoved the memories that threatened to return back down to the corner of my mind where I kept the reality of those first few years under lock and key. "I didn't know how to stop it. So every conversation, every question I asked…I would end up stealing their secrets. And never on purpose." I added, directed at him with an ounce of spite. "My favorite instructor helped me learn to control it before I ruined every single relationship in my life." I played with my fingers in my lap, avoiding his eyes, his hands tightened slightly on the reins. "Knowing what someone is afraid of, or what someone wants, that's fine. That's easy enough to help. But knowing their guilt. Being a fly on the wall for the worst moments of their lives and not being able to do a damn thing about it…it's unbearable." His knuckles paled from the intensity of his grip.

"For what it's worth, I apologize for what I did at the Courting Ball." I risked a glance in his direction and found him staring at me. His emerald eyes were filled with truth. I didn't need to use Mythica to feel the guilt.

"Why did you do it?" I didn't mask my frustration. I wanted him to see every ounce of it.

"I'm the Warden of Envy. The jealous Warden. The Covetor." He spoke each vicious label aloud as if he was forcing them to fit. "It's what I do." If I didn't know any better, I would have thought he seemed almost sad.

"But, is it who you are?" He scoffed, raising an incredulous eyebrow.

"I am what I covet. That's what makes me such a formidable Warden. I'm never satisfied. I always need more." A deep rasp flooded his voice, making him seem almost vicious. "I can never settle."

"That sounds lonely." I don't know why I said it. Especially when he was in this state. But each word he spoke was like a brick being placed in the wall he was building to keep everyone at arm's length. I recognized it well. I had my own.

I expected him to explode, to snap back at me with the same venom I tended to speak to him with.

But instead, he sighed, looking back at the horizon in quiet contemplation.

"Well, my well-earned solitude will be ruined for the next six months thanks to you." He joked, but the playful edge I had come to appreciate in his banter was not present.

My eyes rolled involuntarily. "I believe this entire tour was your ridiculous plan, thank you very much. Perhaps I should be the one scolding you"

"I don't know what you're talking about. And you scold me quite often, or have you forgotten? Should I start keeping score?" He tried to fight the smile that played on his lips, unsuccessfully.

"You're not as slick as you think. Your whole manipulation was rather obvious." I was pretty certain I had fallen directly into his expertly laid trap the night of the ball, but I couldn't help but second guess myself.

Then he laughed and I knew my instinct was correct.

"Manipulation, maybe. Obvious? Decidedly not. My siblings never would have gone along with it if they knew it was my own little trick." He smiled brightly as if remembering his successful trap. "Have you considered that it was only obvious to you because you belong in The Court of Shadows?"

No, I hadn't.

It made sense though. I couldn't believe a Warden would willingly agree to this plan if they knew about Lysander's true intentions. And yet, I saw it so clearly. Once again, I found myself, unwillingly, considering a life in The Court of Shadows.

Shaking my head, I pushed away the thought. I can't Pledge to this Court. Or this Warden.

"But that's not where I belong, is it?" My voice was quiet. Weak. "Because the one place that I do belong doesn't exist anymore." I let it sink in. It was nice to understand why I never felt like I fit in with any of the other Courts, but knowing that the reason was that I don't belong anywhere anymore was…difficult.

"The Final Trial tells you where you would be best suited based on Mythica, aptitude, problem-solving…But it doesn't know where you belong, little storm. Only you know that."

"Can I ask something else?" He shot me a look as if to remind me of his earlier statement. "What does the symbol mean?" He sat back, resting against the wall of the carriage, and inhaled a long, slow breath. I didn't have to specify what I meant. He knew.

"Nothing you need to concern yourself with." My hands closed into fists at my side. I had been attacked by a man who painted this symbol on a Warden's carriage, and it was none of my concern?

"That's bullshit and you know it." I spat. "I deserve to know after what happened to me last night, don't you think?"

"I think you should have slept inside the room last night in the first place." There was nothing playful about the way he retorted. I scoffed.

"A gentleman would have let me have the room in the first place," I said, mocking him, but my fury was slowly replacing all the warm feelings that had begun to surface during our conversation. He frustratingly ran a hand through his hair, pulling a few strands free from their tie at the back of his head. Then he turned to face me. I didn't realize how close he was, having inched his body near mine, our legs entirely flushed against each other. His eyes met mine with the same fire I saw in the inn this morning. His burning sweet smell invaded my nostrils. An unrelenting heat pooled in my core, blending with my anger to form a volatile mixture.

"When have I ever claimed to be a gentleman?" His voice was dangerously low, a whispered challenge.

"Tell me then," I whispered back. A challenge of my own.

"No," he said, leaning towards me.

I knew if I backed down now, I wouldn't have this chance again. So instead, I leaned closer, quickly, until my face was inches from his, my lips nearly grazing his. My hands made quick work of my skirts, gripping the emerald hilt of the dagger against my thigh. I pointed it directly at his throat without breaking eye contact. His eyes widened in shock, but he did not retreat.

"Threatening a Warden, huh?" he taunted quietly, his voice barely audible. "Are you brave or are you reckless?" I held my ground. We both knew I would not use this dagger against him, but I couldn't deny the building tension in my core that pulsed with wild excitement at the sight of my blade against his strained neck.

There was a flash of movement, too quick for me to comprehend. Then I felt the cool metal against my own throat. Lysander had disarmed me and trained my - his - weapon back at me. He had dropped the reins and snaked his free hand around the back of my neck to hold me in place. I nearly growled in frustration.

"If you want to hurt me, you need to try harder than that, little storm," he whispered, his breath warm on my face. We sat there, his hand keeping me immobilized, my gifted dagger biting into the skin along my elongated neck. Our shoulders heaved in unison with ragged breaths.

The heat between my legs grew to an almost painful degree, I pressed my thighs together to find a fragment of relief.

And then he sat back, removing the blade from my throat, but kept his eyes trained on me. I took a shaky breath.

"We'll have to work on your reflexes." He said, nonchalantly, as if the palpable tension between us had been entirely one-sided. He held out the dagger, offering me the emerald hilt. I gripped it and slid it back into the holster, quickly tossing my dress down to cover my exposed thigh.

Embarrassed, I crossed my arms in front of me and watched the landscape pass by in silence.

"It's… the Mark," Lysander spoke quietly, I had to strain to hear him over the sound of our carriage bouncing on uneven gravel. "The Mark of The Forgotten Court." I couldn't contain the gasp that escaped my lips. I didn't even know there was a Mark for that Court.

"Who knows about it?" I asked with teeth chattering, and not from the chilly air.

"The Wardens." He started, pausing to swallow the lump forming in his throat.

"And?" The man who attacked me last night was not a Warden. I knew that, and so did Lysander. He wore a mask and we've already proven that a simple piece of fabric was not enough to dampen the prowess of a Warden.

"Nobody in The Court of Shadows should know about that Mark, other than me." There it was, the fear. The same fear I saw in his gaze last night. He didn't know who did this. But now, someone here in this Court not only knew about the Mark's existence but was terrorizing Lysander with it. No, not Lysander… me. They were terrorizing me. It couldn't be a coincidence. I received a Forgotten Court result, and now the Mark of the very same Court was showing up around me. Someone was trying to make a statement. And they were willing to go to dangerous lengths to do it.

My wrist throbbed slightly at the reminder of the man's determination.

"Am I in danger?" I couldn't stop the quivering of my lip. Lysander turned to me, a fierceness burning in his eyes.

"While you are with me, nobody will lay a hand on you." I believed every word.

"And when I'm not with you?"

He pondered that, his tongue darting out to wet his lips. "Then I'll ensure you can protect yourself." His eyes darted down to the thigh where my dagger sat idle against my skin.

I had more answers. But even more questions. Who was that man? How did he know of the Mark of The Forgotten Court? And why was he terrorizing the Warden?

"Tell me more about the Forsaken Quarters." He knew I was changing the subject to avoid facing my current reality. But luckily for me, he allowed it. He began telling me about his home, detailing some of his favorite 'hiding spots'. The tension from the previous conversation melted away, leaving only a man full of unconditional love and pride for his home and his people.

He spoke nonstop for another hour, and I gladly listened to every word. Thankful for the distraction and the man who was giving it.

"Thank you," he said, turning away from me to face the road ahead of us again. It was low, almost imperceptible but filled with truth and honesty. I followed his gaze, noticing that ahead a few miles in the distance, a town had begun to spring up along the horizon.

"For what?" I asked almost under my breath. But I knew he heard me. The only sounds were the impact of our horse's hooves on the pavement and my beating heart.

"For listening."

I didn't speak again. I didn't have to. We had reached a sort of quiet understanding. One I didn't dare question. One that gave me hope for the next six months and one week of my life.

The landscape on either side of the carriage shifted, the wide open expanse of trees and fields giving way to small stone buildings with colorful awnings. The path beneath us became rockier, I couldn't help but crane my neck for a better view. The pavement was gone, and in its place, a road made entirely of dark black bricks with white mortar. The bricks glistened in the sunlight, not unlike the blade of the dagger that was neatly holstered against my bare thigh.

The streets bustled with activity, people rushed from their shops to wave to the Warden, who to my surprise, waved back. Music filled the area, spilling from restaurants and taverns that made up this vibrant town center. The smell of apple cider and caramel reached my nostrils and my mouth nearly watered at the intensity of it.

Lysander steered our carriage down the busy path, taking time to call out to people on the street, wishing them well, asking how they had been doing lately. It was baffling how much these people seemed to adore him.

I heard a rush of water and leaned over Lysander to get a better look. I didn't notice whether or not he reacted to that, because I was far too enamored by the two-story tall fountain that took up the majority of a town square. The pool of the fountain was at least fifty feet wide, filled with stunning crystal blue water. The first layer of the fountain showed a grouping of statues, seemingly depicting people of all ages standing with arms above their heads, holding up a platform. Together. Sitting on the platform was a large marble carving of the skua, the bird most often associated with The Court of Shadows. Its head was upturned towards the sky and water spouted triumphantly from its beak.

Lively storefronts, boutiques, blacksmiths, confectioneries, and more lined the square, their doors all wide open and teeming with patrons. Busking musicians were stationed around the open space, and people would stop, listen, and tip them as their songs played on. The sounds were jovial, expressive, and beautiful.

I didn't know where to look. Everything was so vibrant, colorful, and alive. It was nothing like The Court of Shadows that I had imagined.

This was the town of Everwatch, the small village that sat at the base of the

Forsaken Quarters. I had read about it back at the Institute, but it was obvious the words on the page did not do justice to the sheer beauty of this place. Being here felt like a warm embrace from a loved one or being cuddled up with a good book. Safe. It felt safe.

Lysander continued through the town square, people smiling at him at every turn. As we continued through town, I felt a nervous energy spilling from him. What did he have to be nervous about?

I could find out…

The moment the thought came to me, I felt ashamed. It was impossible to use my Mythica on the Warden. But even if it were, I would never try. Threatening him with a dagger to his throat was one thing. But attempting to use Mythica was another thing entirely.

We continued away from the town square, and I instantly felt a surge of disappointment. I would make a point to ask Lysander if we could visit again soon. I was here to see what this Court had to offer, after all.

But those plans would have to wait, because cresting over the horizon, nestled high atop a hill, sitting pristine among hundreds of vibrant multi-hued trees… was the Forsaken Quarters.

It sat tall, overlooking the town of Everwatch, not in a looming judgemental way, but rather in a welcoming, protective nature. Again, I felt safe. Something I never thought I would feel while in this Court. Lysander kept our carriage steady as we began our ascent up the winding path that led to the heart of the castle-like structure. Six massive, round towers rose above all, each linked to the others with small open parapet walks that spanned between the keeps. The towers were connected by a lower, narrow bailey made of dark green stone that stood out against the reds and yellows of the trees around it. We crossed a small footbridge that led to a much larger, and more extravagant, drawbridge made of dark black wood. It lowered as we approached, and I looked up at the sound of guards shouting orders from the guardhouse and battlements just beyond the row of machicolations.

This castle was in every way more extravagant than the Verihdian Institute, which is still quite impressive in size and structure. I had to actively refrain from releasing squeals of appreciation as we ventured across the bridge and into the walls of the fortress. I could feel Lysander's appreciative gaze on me.

The view of this beautiful castle was even more impressive from this side. Flanking towers stood tall, casting powerful shadows on us as we continued deeper into the heart of The Court of Shadows.

Lysander turned his head, a mischievous smile playing on his lips. "Welcome to my home. Welcome to the Forsaken Quarters."

NINETEEN

There's something so incredibly satisfying about returning home after a long journey. Even when my home is overrun with decorators, entertainers, and my staff rushing about preparing for the influx of people that would intrude this evening. I normally despise this event, frivolous as it is. However, thinking about how Lexa's face lit up as we made our way through Everwatch, I think I will enjoy tonight's festivities - if only to see how she enjoys it.

The thought gives me pause. Lexa Cromwell is in every way a beautiful woman, that is something I can easily and freely admit. However, I am aiming to covet her loyalty, not her body...not her heart. And I needed to remember that.

As soon as we arrived, I had one of my staff escort her to her prepared room to relax. I had originally intended on taking her on a tour of the castle, but after the events of this morning, I'd be lying if I said I didn't need some distance from her.

I had planned on leaving the dagger on the bed for her to equip on her own, but the moment I stepped into that room and saw her standing there, in nothing but a towel with her dark wet hair dripping droplets across her creamy pale skin...I lost all sense of reason. I had this overwhelming urge to touch her.

To feel her. It was consuming, I'm not sure I would have been able to stop myself. Before I knew what was happening, I was on my knees for her.

I had never done that before.

Her Mythica swirled around us in that small room like a massive storm, but instead of pushing me back, as I had seen it do to Chandler, it embraced me. Beckoned me towards her and sent me to my knees. The dark tendrils of her power wrapped around my hands and led them up her calves. It guided me like possessive hands pressing down on my shoulders, telling me exactly where I belonged. On my knees for her. Its clutch was not gentle or careful, but rather demanding and lustful. The room nearly exploded with it, and I very nearly let it devour me. That was precisely why I had to pull away.

Then she threatened me with the very same dagger. Her Mythica shrouded us, completely devouring us in her darkness. A darkness that was not frightening, but welcoming. Offering cover so I could do exactly what I wanted to with her, should I choose to. It took every ounce of self-control I could muster to pull away from the challenge in her eyes and the intoxicating pull of her Mythica.

I've witnessed an individual's power ebb and flow with powerful emotions before, but never to this capacity. It was just another painful reminder that her Mythica, if properly wielded, could bring ruination to everything and everyone it touched. Which is exactly why I would not give in to any momentary lustful urges and devastate my Court's chance to woo Miss Cromwell.

I closed my eyes and tried to banish the image of her smooth, bare leg; the way her blue eyes watched me as her towel inched higher and higher….the way her skin smelled faintly of salt.

A knock on the door startled me, bringing me back from the dangerous edge I had been perched on.

"My Warden," Lilith spoke calmly as she entered. Her eyes didn't reach mine. She was Vacant, so the air around her was as empty as it had been before she entered. It used to annoy me that my Dean lacked Mythica, but it did offer me a bit of palate cleanser oftentimes. After large events with dozens of Mythica-wielding individuals, it used to overwhelm me, and while I have learned to adapt and control it, it still wasn't the most pleasant of experiences. I grew to appreciate the silence surrounding Lilith Hargrove.

But after the intensity of my little storm, Lilith's presence felt more like a burden than a reprieve. I silently prayed to Buyhay to keep me from developing an addiction to Miss Cromwell - an addiction that was already well underway, it seemed.

"Lilith, thank you for preparing Miss Cromwell's quarters. I trust you had no issues?" I moved from my desk to the bar cart near the corner to pour myself a drink of a warm amber liquid.

Lilith stepped forward into the room and took a seat in one of the leather armchairs that faced my desk.

"No problems, my Warden, she should be…very comfortable." I didn't miss the indignation in her tone. But I didn't care to address it.

I took several deep swallows of the drink as I made my way back to my large desk.

"Did you need something, Lilith?" It had been several moments since she spoke, and she knows how much I dislike being stuck in uncomfortable silence.

I thought back to the carriage ride, after our conversation where I told Lexa all about The Court of Shadows. We had been silent then, too. But it was anything but uncomfortable, in fact, it felt warm and understanding. Like we didn't have to speak another word to communicate. I hadn't felt that before. It was pleasant.

This was not.

"I was just coming to collect your speech for the ball tonight." Lilith had acted as my representative at this Welcome Ball for years, I couldn't be bothered to attend. She would collect and deliver my speech to the new Pledges herself. This year was different though.

"Not necessary. I will be attending tonight."

Her eyes widened in shock. "Pardon me?" I rolled my eyes. Must I repeat myself to this woman constantly?

"I am attending the ball tonight, you do not need to be my representative. You can simply attend and enjoy yourself." Her mouth hung open.

"I don't understand…" again my eyes rolled, and I sat on the edge of my desk facing her.

"Miss Cromwell is here to experience our Court, and because of my plan, she has significantly less time to see all it has to offer than she will with my other siblings. Do you think I would trust just anybody to show her The Court of Shadows?" Lilith's head shook quickly, her eyes widening. "I will be attending the ball tonight, with Lexa Cromwell on my arm."

"Understood." She spoke quietly, a familiar twinge of envy lacing her tone. Her eyes were trained on the floor.

"Wait here," I didn't stick around long enough to see if she heeded my order, but I knew she did. I shuffled through the side door and into my bedroom. My feet sank into the plush carpet as I passed the king-sized mattress that sat atop a large four-poster black frame with black chiffon hanging from each poster, delicately draped. I longed to jump into its comfort, especially after my unexpected lodgings last night in the hay next to my horse. Luckily for me, the stable hand found me early and offered me his home and an outfit for me. I left a hefty monetary gift for his troubles. I ran my hand over the tightened muscles of my neck, remembering the uncomfortable position. I made my way across the room, tossing one last glance to my bed.

Soon.

I stepped through the double doors and into the massive closet. Sliding my own wardrobe out of the way, I stopped when I found it.

My mother's gown.

She passed away nearly two centuries ago, and this dress could have been nothing but ash at this point if it weren't for the Mythica that kept it well preserved. I slid open the bag it was in, and tears instantly formed in my eyes. The ball gown was a white mesh material that clung tightly to the wearer's torso and was decorated with black lace applique clustered tightly around the waist and wrists and thinned out around the bosom, and shoulders. The skirt was a matching white tulle and the black appliques continued down into the folds of the skirt, offering an ombre effect.

No matter how many years sped by, I would remember the way my mother looked in this gown the night I was named Warden.

Not many textbooks mention the way the world was before the Courts existed before the Wardens were gifted immortality by Buyhay and tasked with leading their people. It was a dark world at that point, with no order, no rhyme or reason. My siblings remember. We witnessed it, and if they are anything like me, they will never be able to forget it.

Despite how bleak Verihdia had been, my mother was always a beacon of light, love, and warmth. She wanted what was best for me, she wanted me to succeed in my new position. And she would have loved to see her gown on a woman as powerful and as stunning as Lexa Cromwell. I gripped the dress in my hands and carefully handled it, sliding it back into its garment bag.

Pulling the hanger off the rack, I returned back to my office to find Lilith still in the chair.

"Have this sent to Miss Cromwell for tonight. And send a seamstress to ensure it fits." Lilith's eyebrows furrowed.

"What is that?" She asked, angling her head towards the garment bag I rested on the empty chair next to her.

"It is a dress, Lilith." She scoffed.

"I know that. But where did you get it?" She asked, unable to hide her jealousy. I smirked, scribbling a short note on a piece of parchment.

"It's been in my family since long before you existed. Now, are you going to be able to take this dress to Miss Cromwell, or should I get someone else to do it?" Her eyes darkened with unsaid insults, but she lowered her head in submission. "Good. See to it that she gets this soon." I folded the parchment once and handed it to Lilith, who took it hesitantly. "Be sure this is placed with the dress. And do not read it."

Lilith stood, but instead of reaching for the garment like I had expected her to, she stepped forward towards me.

"You had a long journey, my Warden. Would you like me to help you relieve some stress?" She glanced up at me through her dark eyelashes, and I felt absolutely nothing. No spark of want or desire, no pity, no excitement. Her sultry expression was superficial compared to the pure desperate need that was painted on Lexa's face in that room. The way her eyes burned when she held the dagger to my throat. I'm not sure I've ever seen that look on anyone's face before, and I don't know if I ever would again.

"Not necessary, Lilith. Please get this taken care of, and send for the Captain of the Guard. I have security measures I'd like to discuss for tonight." She left the room with the gown and a stunned expression on her face.

An hour later, my Captain, Gregorio, arrived and I had him painstakingly run over every security measure in place for tonight. I couldn't be too careful, especially after Lexa was attacked last night.

I was jolted awake by the vibrations of her Mythica. The storm that was a constant addition to the air around her had spread, thrashing wildly. It had reached a point of critical mass, and it called for me.

I was grabbing her assailant by the throat and throwing him off her before I even knew I was awake. I couldn't believe how careless I had been, letting her sleep outside in the carriage, just to spite her? To challenge her? Because I liked the way her Mythica thrashed when she was angry with me?

I let her sleep outside. I allowed this attacker the perfect opportunity to get to her. It was my fault. The guilt ate at me. I couldn't even speak to her this morning, in fear that she would detest me even more so than before, and

I would have deserved it. I put her in harm's way. I was the reason he even laid a single finger on her.

I had only felt this intensity of guilt twice before in my long life. I waved off that thought and finished my brief with the Captain.

I told him everything that had happened, save for the symbol that was painted on the side of our carriage. A shiver ran through me, an icy hand grabbing hold of my heart and squeezing.

I hadn't seen that symbol in damn near a century. I never thought I'd see it again. That was the plan after all.

I don't know what it meant. Was it my own guilt coming back to haunt me? Was it my past finally catching up and demanding penance? Or were we actually in danger here?

I resolved to speak to my siblings about it when I visited their Courts with Lexa and hope that nothing else occurred in the meantime. But for now, I needed a bath and a drink if I was expected to make it through this evening relatively unscathed.

Twenty

My room was almost bigger than the entire Observatory back at the Institute. There were dark stone walls, draped in magnificent tapestries, a massive four-poster bed, a large washroom with an in-ground tub that could easily fit three or four people - not that I would- and a bay window with a small bench. I knew I would be spending every ounce of my free time in that window right there, overlooking the beautiful forest that surrounded the Forsaken Quarters. If I pressed my face right up against the glass and looked to my left, I could almost see Everwatch.

My heart fluttered when I thought about that town. It was quaint, homey, and inviting. All things I never expected to be attributed to The Court of Shadows. I couldn't wait to return and explore the charming shops and busy streets.

But that was for another day.

Soon.

As I was escorted here, I saw very little of the inside of the Quarters. Plus, people were moving about like mad to prepare for their celebration tonight, so it was difficult to truly take in my surroundings when everything was a blur of movement and excitement.

Lysander didn't stress that I stayed put in my rooms, so determinedly, I set foot out into the hallway. I glanced in either direction several times, in an attempt to memorize the walls, the decor, and the landmarks. I wanted to ensure that I could find my way back, I would prefer not to get lost. Then I began my journey. The floor that I had been led to was rather quiet, but as I ventured down long corridors filled with portraits and trophies, and memories, the closer I got to the main staircase and the louder the bustling became.

I reached the landing of the massive staircase, it was nearly fifty feet wide, made of that similar dark black material that left almost a silver outline as my feet danced across it. There was another floor above me, the stairs led straight up, but I could not see the doors or corridors from my current position. I could go up and work my way down? But the sound of orders being barked and heeded drew my attention.

I'll start at the bottom.

I traveled down the stairs one at a time, appreciating the view as I continued. Each landing was another floor to the massive castle, and from my vantage point on the stairs, I could see each floor wrap around the open area, an atrium, with black railings trailed along the edge of the corridors. Plants and flowers hung from the walls and the pillars on each floor, reminding me of the greenhouse back in Verihdia. But on a much larger, and more impressive scale. Just above us was a massive glass ceiling with a swirled pattern of green glass, the Court Mark. The afternoon sun breaking through the ceiling cast a bright natural light, mixed with a green hue from the Mark.

As I neared the base of the stairs, the sounds grew louder. Following the hordes of people, I left the atrium and arrived at the Grand Ballroom. It was in a state of disarray, but I could still acknowledge its beauty. Floor-to-ceiling windows framed the walls, casting an amber glow on the room and the people in it. The ceiling seemed to be made of the same material as the stairs, and the dagger that still hugged my thigh. I made a mental note to ask Lysander about their obsession with the dark obsidian starlight.

Rather than a large single chandelier, like the ballroom in the Institute, there were strands of glittering jewels strung across the ceiling, meeting in the middle and spanning out towards the walls in a delicate draping pattern.

There was a head table, with several seats behind it, one slightly larger than the rest, but not as boastful as I would have expected. And just beyond the open dance floor, tables and booths for the buffet, food already being set.

People moved quickly across the space, putting final touches on the decor of faux foliage and glittering jewels that dotted the space.

I don't know how long I watched them, but eventually, I forced myself to move. If I wanted to see more of my home for the next week before the event this evening, I needed to be quick. Retreating out the large doors back into the atrium, I let my feet guide me. I did not have a plan or a path, I simply moved through the halls, admiring the decor, the way everything seemed so…alive.

At least an hour had passed before I began my ascent up towards my floor again. I had barely explored the bottom three floors before my legs grew tired and begged for a reprieve. And as much as I was dreading it, I could use a bath before the ball tonight.

What if it happens again?

I shoved away the memory of what had occurred only this morning. It had to be one of my nightmares. I just fell asleep in the tub. It wasn't real. There was no other explanation.

The faint salty taste on my lips returned and a shiver ran through my body.

I continued up the steps, but just then, a figure from just above, traveling along the corridors on the floor below mine caught my eye.

Chandler Mills.

My heart constricted. We had shared a moment in the greenhouse before being disrupted by Lysander, but something still felt off. The kiss was eager, punishing almost, it felt like he still hadn't forgiven me. Not that I had done anything that needed to be forgiven. At least not to him.

He was getting closer to the stairs. If I continued at this pace, I would run directly into him. I wasn't prepared for that. So instead I ran, hiking up the skirts of my tunic dress and taking the obsidian stairs two at a time. Focusing on keeping my footsteps light and quiet, I barely noticed when I had reached the landing. Allowing myself just a moment to look over my shoulder, I saw Chandler, arriving at the landing below me, his head turning. I moved faster. I burst through the nearest door and shut it behind me in a huff. I leaned my back against the wood and caught my breath.

There was a small chance he didn't see me, unlikely, but the possibility was what I chose to latch onto. Once my heart rate slowed, I glanced around the room before me. It looked a lot like my chambers, but it wasn't. It was larger, more lived in.

I had just begun to piece together where I might have accidentally ended up when a door within the room opened. Steam rolled out of the bathing chambers from another luxurious bathing tub, like the one I had in my room. And emerging from the tendrils of humid air, was The Warden of Shadows himself. His chest was bare again, a sight I was becoming uncomfortably familiar with, and a towel was hung haphazardly low on his hips. I forced my eyes to look at the ceiling.

"My apologies, Warden. I had no idea these were your quarters." I stumbled on the words, keeping my eyes trained above me. I had seen a playful side to Lysander recently, but I would be foolish to forget who I was dealing with here. This man before me was a Warden of Verihdia. And this Warden could see my intrusion as treasonous, and sentence me to death, or prison. I tensed, waiting for him to unleash his wrath.

Instead, I heard him chuckle.

"We really have to stop meeting like this." His tone was nothing like I had expected. Suddenly, I could breathe. I didn't lower my head, however, as I fumbled behind my back for the door handle.

"Lexa, you don't have to stare at the ceiling. I am decent enough."

Perhaps it was the fact that I wasn't looking at him, or the relief I felt that he wasn't angry, but something emboldened me enough to say, "I'm not sure decent is the word I would use to describe you," I teased, but instantly regretted it. Was I trying to get myself killed? Or did I simply enjoy antagonizing one of the most powerful people in the world? How far was too far with our banter? When would it stop being playful?

"You know, I don't normally tolerate people speaking to me like that." Slowly, I let my chin fall, my gaze training on him. He was standing near his bed, looking down at the outfit that was laid out on top of the silk sheets. "Once again, I find myself wondering if you're simply brave," he turned his head over his shoulder to look at me, his virescent eyes freezing me to my spot. "Or very, very reckless."

I didn't answer. I just watched as he turned back to the clothing in front of him, running his fingers over the material with a sort of sensual care.

"So which one are you, little storm?" He faced me completely now and took long bounding steps towards me. "Brave," he said as he reached me, standing less than a foot away and pinning me up against the wooden door. His recently cleansed yet still fiery scent invaded my nostrils. "Or reckless?" He whispered the word like it was a challenge.

Challenge accepted.

Placing the palms of my hands on his chest, trying not to analyze how firm it felt, I shoved him back. He was too quick to stumble, but his face did show that he was surprised.

"Reckless it is then." He smirked.

"If you think that you can convince me to Pledge to your Court by attempting to appeal to me sexually… then you insult me." His smirk deepened and his eyes lit with humor. I couldn't tell if I was lying or not.

He tilted his head quickly, his eyebrows rising in response. He did not take a step forward but did lean until he was once again in my personal space. "Little storm, correct me if I'm wrong…but you are the one who just entered my private quarters without an invitation, correct?" He was right of course. It was my fault I was here right now. There's no way he could have manipulated this. Right?

"You flatter yourself, Warden. If I had known where this door led, I would have avoided it with the same fervor that you avoid taking responsibility for your actions." His smirk remained plastered on his face, but the playful light in his eyes had been extinguished. Something I said melted his spirited facade, giving way to a quiet, rumbling fury.

"No, Miss Cromwell...you are the one who flatters yourself if you believe that someone of my stature and position could ever be interested in someone like you," He bit back, his eyes wild. My anger gave way to a sharp stab of pain.

"Every time I think there might be more to you than the selfish bastard I met at the Courting Ball, you prove to me that I have never been more wrong." We were not engaged in playful banter anymore, no this was true and honest detestation. Facades were gone, and gloves were off.

"And you think you've been so benevolent in your own life?" He said, his face darkening with a predatory tint. "Maybe we should ask Axel to share his thoughts on the subject? Oh wait, that's right, he can't. Because twice now you were selfish, and twice now you have lied about it." My heart stopped, and blood boiled beneath the surface of my skin, lighting me on fire. "You and I are one and the same."

"The Covetor, calling *me* selfish? That's a laugh." He flinched at the vindictive title but stood his ground, his lip curling up to reveal bared teeth.

"The difference, Miss Cromwell," He spat my name as if it disgusted him. "Is that I have never once pretended to be something I'm not." The muscles in his arms flexed as he tightened his fist at his side.

"Haven't you? I was once told that The Court of Shadows only deals in secrets that are freely given. That there was more to this Court than the rumors." I was careful to enunciate each word, despite my growing rage. "But perhaps that, like everything else you've said, is nothing but a lie."

I didn't wait to hear his response, I gripped the handle and stormed out of the room. My pace didn't slow until I made my way down to the next level and arrived safely behind the door to my quarters. I latched it on the off chance that he had planned to follow me.

Anger surged through me as I paced across the room. How quick he was to remind me that he knew my darkest shame and had no reservations when it came to using it against me. Gods, to think I had started to forgive him, to even… like him. I'm not daft, I know there could never be anything between the two of us, but I cannot have been the only one to feel pulse racing and heat pooling in that room. Or on the carriage. Or was I? He's trying to get me to Pledge to his Court. Feigning attraction is certainly one way to accomplish that, I just hate that my body fell for it. I took angry, loathing steps across the room, murmuring obscenities under my breath.

A bag placed on my bed grabbed my attention. I closed my eyes, rolled my shoulders, and attempted to breathe out the fury that was coursing through my veins before moving to the bed.

It was a garment bag. I slid open the closure to reveal the breathtaking dress inside. My fingers absentmindedly ran across the fabric. Just beside the dress, delicately placed on the sheets, was a folded piece of parchment. Gripping it in my hands, I unfolded it.

Little storm,

Tonight, we will welcome the new Pledges to The Court of Shadows. A tradition that frankly, I have tired of over the years. But I would be lying if I didn't admit that the prospect of welcoming you to our Court, however temporarily, thrills me. Please accept this gift, and believe me when I say that for the first time in a long time, I truly do look forward to tonight.

With care,

The Warden of Shadows

My heart raced as I read the words again, and again. Folding and refolding the page as if this next time, it might read something different. How could he show such care and honor one moment and accost me with such disdain the next?

I sat down on the bed, his letter in my hand, his dagger on my thigh, and for the second time in as many days - I felt guilty.

As much as I despised the thought of apologizing to him, I felt my heart tighten, and guilt spread like venom through my body. I needed to speak to him. To thank him for the dress at the very least.

Resolved, I made my way out of my quarters. I made it barely three steps outside my room before I ran into a solid frame. I nearly toppled back, but the figure's arms encircled my waist and held me steady. I moved to lift my head, expecting to see Lysander, but instead, I was met with a familiar pair of brown eyes.

"Chandler!" He watched me as I fought to regain my composure. "I'm sorry, I didn't see you there."

He surveyed me silently for a few torturously quiet moments while I fidgeted with the sleeves of my dress.

"Did you notice me on the stairs earlier?" He knew the answer already, of course, he did. The accusation in the subtext of his question was as clear as the discomfort I was currently feeling.

"I wasn't avoiding you," I blurted out, and Chandler raised an eyebrow in challenge. "Ok, I was. But not because I didn't want to see you." That part was true at least. My fear of seeing him had nothing to do with my feelings and everything to do with how I thought it would make him feel to see me here… in his Court.

"Then why did you run?" His eyes softened and he moved to lean against my door frame. He towered over me, casting a shadow of shame over me.

"It's the first day in your new Court. I didn't want to bother you," I whispered. He scanned my face.

"You don't bother me, Lexa." He lifted his finger to my cheek, letting it graze gently against the skin there.

"Are you happy, Chandler?" I looked up at him, studying his brown eyes. He smiled, softly.

"I am," he answered in a whisper. I nodded, and the hand that was caressing my cheek drifted lower until it gripped my shoulder.

"Good. That's all I've ever wanted for you." It was true. He had always brought such comfort to me, I wanted nothing more than to see him succeed, happy.

His hands trailed the space between my shoulder and my earlobe softly. "You're here for how long again?"

"One week." He moved closer now until his lips were only a few inches from mine. It was clear what he wanted from the burning look in his eyes.

"One week," He replied, leaning in again, his lips nearly grazing mine. "We better make it count then." And his mouth claimed mine. It felt different, foreign. Like the lips that were claiming me now, were not the same lips I had spent the better part of the last several years kissing. I sunk into the kiss, the comfort, as I have many times before, but for some reason, it didn't blanket me the way I was used to.

Chandler had a gift for making me forget my pain, even for a moment, and after my tense encounter with Lysander, that is exactly what I needed. Chandler's hands eagerly grabbed at my dress, lifting it. I was acutely aware of our entirely too public position, but I craved his comfort so desperately that I ignored the warnings going off in my mind. His hand snaked up my thigh to my center. He growled against my mouth at the wetness that he found there. I wasn't sure if it was from Chandler's touch or my encounter with Lysander earlier. I didn't want to think about that. Chandler slid a finger through my folds roughly, spearing me. I cried out, but it was captured by his mouth. My hands slid down his chest until I found his hardened length straining against his trousers. He moaned against my skin.

"You want to touch me, don't you?" He uttered between kisses. I nodded my agreement, dipping my hand beneath the band of his pants to find his erection waiting for me. He let out a guttural groan as my fingers enclosed around him.

His fingers at my core stopped moving, and I couldn't help but whimper at the loss of friction where I needed it. I became acutely aware that we were out in the open hallway.

"Where's your bed?" Chandler whispered against my lips, his words filled with promise. I felt my heart rate quicken. Keeping one hand firmly on Chandler's length, I used my free hand to open my door for him. His fingers disappeared from my core and he moved towards the door quickly, his large shadow finally releasing me from its hold, revealing a figure standing behind him in the hall.

"What are you doing here?" I spat, my voice filled with more fury than I had intended. My body flushed, burning with embarrassment. I pulled my dress down and removed my hand from Chandler's shaft. Lysander stood with his hands tucked into the front pockets of his trousers, a blue button-down now hiding his chest. His jeweled eyes burned. My entire body was on fire, knowing that he had just witnessed Chandler's mouth and fingers claim me.

Chandler turned around at my outburst and saw his Warden standing there, his eyes brightened in a way they never had when he looked at me. He quickly tucked himself away as he spoke, "My Warden, good afternoon. I trust your journey was comfortable?" I ran my fingers through my unkempt hair, trying to smooth out all evidence of the arousal I was just experiencing. How was Chandler able to address him so casually and collected right now? The Warden of Shadows just saw his erection…with my fingers around it. I nearly passed out.

"Miss Cromwell, a word." I didn't need to look at Chandler's face to know how Lysander's blatant disregard affected him.

"My Warden, I also would like to thank you for your…" Chandler began confidently, ignoring the slight.

"Miss Cromwell. A word. Now." Lysander's voice cut through the hallway like a knife, effectively silencing Chandler. I turned my head slightly towards the man in my room, a silent apology painted on my face. Lysander was mad at me, and he was taking it out on Chandler. I expected Chandler to walk away, to leave down the hallway to his own rooms, to forget the promise our bodies had made to each other just moments ago, but instead he leaned forward, planting a kiss directly on my parted lips.

I pulled back quickly, my eyes darting to Lysander who watched with an unchanged expression.

"I'll be here when you're done." He disappeared inside my room, closing the door behind him. I watched the wooden door for a moment, trying to collect my thoughts. I had just planned on apologizing to him moments before Chandler showed up, but the way he just reacted was appalling, making me forget why I ever planned to apologize to this man in the first place.

"How dare you speak to me like that? And how dare you treat a member of your Court in such a manner?" I rushed forward, an accusatory finger pointing at his chest. I was seeing red.

"Exactly, Miss Cromwell, *my* Court," he responded calmly, but I could feel the tension building just below the surface. "I can speak to whomever I'd like, however I'd like to." He too took a step forward, until my outstretched finger made contact with his firm chest. I didn't pull it back. I wasn't going to back down.

"Why are you here? I think you said plenty before." His eyebrows furrowed and he pushed forward again. I was forced to take a step back, but I kept my finger firmly planted against his chest.

"So a fight with me got you so riled up, you needed to find your little fuck buddy to relieve some tension huh?" His voice was low and taunting, a sensual edge creeping in.

"If anything, Chandler had to work harder to turn me on after what you said." I spat back, hoping the lie was convincing. He didn't react harshly to the words. Instead, he smirked, a vicious, taunting, self-righteous smirk. My hand moved to smack it off his face before I knew what I was doing. But before my palm could make contact with his face, his hand caught my wrist, encircling it tightly. He held me there, paralyzed.

I had just tried to strike a Warden of Verihdia. No matter how lenient he had been with my insubordination thus far, letting me actually threaten him with a weapon, I knew this was a line that even I, in my unique position, could not cross. Not for a second time. My heart sank to the pit of my stomach and the blood drained from my face. I watched him carefully. Was he going to kill me? He'd have every right to.

He held me close by my arm, his eyes burning into mine. I braced for the inevitable. I had gone too far, I had let my anger toward this man cloud everything I'd ever learned. I expected him to drag me away to a dungeon, or perhaps to send me right back to The Living Lands to live my life as an Uncourted. But instead, he smiled.

"Not many people fight back against a Warden and live to tell the tale." A cold shiver ran down my back. His breath tickled my skin.

"Will I?" I asked, breathlessly, almost too quiet to hear.

"Will you what, little storm?" His gaze bore into mine, coaxing the truth out of me. If I didn't know any better, I might have guessed he had stolen my Mythica again.

"Will I live to tell the tale?" His eyes trailed down my face, stopping briefly at my lips before traveling down to my hand still firmly in his hold. We stood there in silence for a while - him watching my hand, me watching him. His thumb began to idly rub circles on my wrist, and I'm positive he felt my heart rate quicken. Then he lowered his hand, and mine along with his until it rested at my side. His eyes left mine to flash over my shoulder at my door.

"He will never be enough for you." He spoke it, not as a statement, but as a promise. And with such a conviction that for a moment, I believed him.

Then I remembered who he was, and what he had done, and I felt my backbone slide firmly back into place. Mustering whatever confidence I still had, I leaned forward bringing my lips to his ear the way he had at the Pledging Ceremony. I felt him stiffen beside me in surprise, as my lips grazed the stubbled skin. "Neither would you."

I turned on my heel, leaving Lysander and my unushered apology behind me, and disappeared into my chamber. I allowed myself only a moment to regain composure, before scanning the room for Chandler. At first glance, he was nowhere to be found. I moved to the washroom, carefully glancing in to see if he had ventured in there. On the other side of the washroom was another door that led to the hallway around the corner from where my confrontation with Lysander had been. It was slightly ajar. I made my way to the door, careful not to spend too long looking at the tub to avoid thinking about my experience in the inn this morning. Outside the door, there was another hallway, and initially, I saw no sign of Chandler. A crumpled piece of parchment caught my attention, kneeling to grip it. I noticed as I went to stand upright again that from this spot in the hall, I could easily see the part of the hallway where Lysander and I were just a few moments ago. I thanked Madillam that he had already left.

Turning my attention back to the parchment in my hand, I carefully unfolded it, smoothing out the crumpled edges. A gasp caught in my throat. In my palms was the note that Lysander wrote to me, the one that accompanied the dress. And this confirmed that not only had Chandler read it, but he was positioned perfectly to have witnessed my tense, and charged interaction with Lysander.

I rushed back into my chamber, closing and locking the bathroom door tightly before padding across the dark floor to my bed. I quickly gave the dress a once over, ensuring Chandler had not harmed it in a fit of anger. A sigh of relief escaped me when I saw that the gorgeous garment was untouched.

Slumping down onto the mattress beside the dress, I felt my eyes begin to water as a feeling that was becoming increasingly familiar washed over me, enveloping me entirely.

Guilt.

TWENTY-ONE

*S*he looked stunning, as I knew she would. I wished I could bottle whatever emotion had hit me the instant she arrived in the ballroom wearing my mother's gown so that I could return to the electricity of this moment. She was a vision of beauty, of grace - of a simpler time.

I had been out of line earlier when she barged into my chambers. Not that I haven't felt a sort of dangerous attraction to her, because I clearly had. The pull of her Mythica nearly consumed me. But I was right when I said I could not be interested in her. I couldn't. It would be improper, foolish…reckless. I needed Lexa Cromwell to choose to Pledge to my Court and pursuing any of these feelings with her jeopardized that. No, I couldn't be interested in her, but I also didn't need to be such a brute about it. I certainly didn't need to bring up her brother. The look on her face as she ran from my room haunted me as I dressed. I told myself that it was better if she despised me if her Mythica stopped trying to envelop me every time we were within arms reach of each other. That I might be able to resist giving in to the growing desire that was burning inside of me if she wanted nothing to do with me.

I left my chambers and headed for her room, just a floor down, convinced that I was simply going to apologize for what I said and leave. She could hate me all she wanted, but I wanted her to know that I hadn't meant what I said in the way she thought, that I understood why she did what she did, and her brother would too. Because truth was, I did understand. I might be the only person in all of Verihdia to truly understand why she did what she did. But as I took each step closer, my plan was shifting. By the time my feet hit the landing, I resolved to tell her that I did feel something for her, something I couldn't exactly explain and wouldn't try to and that pursuing it would be a mistake. Lexa Cromwell did not deserve to feel inadequate, and I wanted to take back everything I had ever said that may have led her to believe that.

Then I saw her with him. Chandler. It took every ounce of my willpower to not grab him by the collar and toss him over the railing, down to the first floor below. Instead, I watched as his mouth claimed her greedily and his self-serving hands inched up her leg to her center, sliding into her heat. I couldn't help but imagine what the sensation felt like. Her fingers were so delicate, closed around his length, it was impossible not to picture those fingers wrapped around me, dragging out every last bit of passion. I felt myself harden at the sight of her. I knew I shouldn't watch, but I couldn't take my eyes off of her. So I stayed and watched...and pictured myself in Chandler's place. His selfish hands weren't there for anyone's pleasure but his own. She wasn't asking him for pleasure, she was asking for a distraction. I should know. I do the very same.

It was her Mythica that gave me the most pause. Instead of aiming to push him off as it had in the greenhouse back at the Institute, it hovered limply around her, completely devoid of the life I had grown to expect from it. She seemed so numb. Submissive. I felt physically ill thinking about her retreating into her room to submit to him.

She deserved better than Chandler, but better wasn't me. It could never be me.

I felt Lilith's eyes studying me from her seat next to mine at the head table, but I avoided her gaze. Instead, I watched Lexa. Her Mythica swirling around her head, alive and free. I didn't realize how much I missed that sight until it was gone. She moved around the room like she was fearless. A far cry from the shy woman who was cowering on the arm of her blonde brute of a boyfriend at the Courting Ball.

I stood then, and the room quieted. All eyes were on me. But there was only one icy blue gaze that sent a jolt of heat directly to my groin. I adjusted my stance to relieve some of the tension.

"Good evening," I said, my voice carrying easily through the ballroom. "You all are well aware of our reason for gathering tonight. Please join me in welcoming our newest Pledges." The room erupted in cheers as they celebrated their new peers. "This Court, these people…We are a tenacious group." I smiled fondly, remembering another person's tenacity. My little storm.

No. Not mine. Never mine.

I rocked back on my heels once and continued, "It is because of this that we survive." Another small smattering of applause rose from the crowd. "There are many people out there who consider us liars, cheats…people who say we are never satisfied, or unable to take responsibility for the things we do to get what we want." I don't have to look for her to feel her gaze sharpen on me. "To them I say, everybody casts a shadow, so why condemn those who choose to embrace it?" I scanned the crowd, taking in the faces of my people. People I've recently drifted away from. Suddenly, I regretted every second that I did not give these people every ounce of the attention they deserved. "Welcome, new Pledges, to The Court of Shadows. Welcome home."

Thunderous applause and jovial celebrations erupted as the music and festivities resumed. I sunk into my throne, making a vow to never miss this event again.

As much as I tried to avoid searching the crowd for her, I couldn't. She was a siren, and I was her willing victim. I knew this level of attraction was dangerous. I couldn't pursue this, no matter how desperately every fiber of my being longed to embrace her. To show her how she deserves to be worshiped. A feat that Chandler would never be able to accomplish.

Speak of the wretch and he shall appear.

Parting through the crowd, the massive blonde male made a beeline directly for my table. There was a distinct difference between confidence and cocksureness. And Mr. Mills was tipping dangerously towards the latter. I tore my unwilling eyes away from the woman at the back of the room and stared down at this man as he approached, brazenly climbing the stairs to the head table. I loathed him, and not because he shared a bed with Lexa Cromwell only three hours ago - although that certainly didn't help his case - but because he clearly had no idea how fortunate he was to have her.

"Chandler, you were not invited to approach the Warden," Lilith stood and leaned her hands on the table in front of her. He simply bowed his head but did not flick his eyes away from me. Lilith was not usually so informal with students, I worked hard to keep my suspicions from showing on my face.

"My Warden, apologies." His tone, however, told me he was not sorry at all.

"You are making this a habit. Should I be concerned?" I feigned disinterest, playing with my fork between my fingers. The image of his lips crushing against Lexa's in a fit of territorial marking sprung back to me, and I couldn't contain the spark of jealousy that lit deep within my chest. And if I had learned anything about my newest Pledge, it was that he couldn't stand being ignored. It was exactly why he fits well in my Court, and exactly what I would use to get under his skin.

"You need only worry if you do not wish to see such a proactive member of your Court." I had to fight against the impulse to roll my eyes. Any reaction would be too much of a reaction for him. He would not get both Lexa's attention and mine.

After a brief moment of silence, I addressed him again, barely letting my gaze rake over him. "Do you need something, Mr. Wills?" It's an age-old tactic, the incorrect name, but it works well against members of my Court and that of The Court of the Vanguard. Prideful, envious creatures.

I watched his face contort in restrained anger out of the corner of my eye, smiling internally.

"Just to formally introduce myself, and to offer my loyalty and service." I sighed deeply, closing my eyes to avoid showing him just how obnoxious I found him. "As you've noticed, twice now I am quite close with Miss Cromwell." My eyes snapped to him involuntarily. He smiled at the attention before continuing. "My deep connection with her is one that I believe could work in our favor." His words dripped with sticky sweet intimidation. I didn't miss his choice of words. 'Our favor.' As if he too understood her importance to this Court, and was willing to exploit her feelings to secure her loyalty.

A few days ago, I thought the very same thing, that utilizing her connection with this man might be beneficial, but now it made me feel sick to even picture it. I took a deep breath, mentally crafting my response before speaking.

"Consider yourself introduced. Now, if you'll excuse me. I have a beautiful woman to dance with." I stood then to leave, and I did not miss the shocked expression on his face or the hopeful one painted on Lilith's. Not that I attended these regularly, but she should be smart enough to know that I was not referring to her.

"Of course, my Warden. Please do not hesitate to call on me. I intend to prove myself invaluable to you." He called after me. His tone scratched my mind like the sound of metal scraping against itself.

I ignored him and moved across the ballroom, attempting to regain control over my rapidly beating heart. Citizens from Everwatch and other towns from all across The Court of Shadows danced and exclaimed with joy and delight. I couldn't help but smile at their infectious elation, despite the burning envy that clung to my every move. I approached her then, close enough to hear her and to admire the loose curls that hung down her back but not yet close enough for her to have noticed my presence.

"Do you often attend these parties?" She spoke to an elderly man who was dressed in a fine red suit. In fact, most of the people who attended this ball were in some variation of reds, oranges, and greens. Matching the foliage of the trees outside, as well as the decor scattered around the ballroom.

"Whenever I can, these parties are the highlight of my year… Every year. And as you can see, I've been here quite a while." He laughed, with a frail edge to it.

Robert Sanderson.

I recognized him immediately. His soft features may have wrinkled and aged, but his soulful eyes remained the same as they were on his first day in our Court. I took another step forward, prepared to cut in.

"Are you happy here?" She asked and my feet stilled. Neither she, nor Robert had noticed me nearby, so I waited patiently for his answer.

"It is where I belong," he responded with a twinkle in his eye. I smiled.

"Yes, but are you happy?" Lexa spoke with such attentive affection that I nearly felt compelled to answer her question, and not in the way her Mythica rips the truth from others, but because she crafted a conversation in which one could feel safe. My heart constricted.

"I am, truly," Robert responded, his wrinkled face twisting into a smile.

"And you enjoy living under your Warden's rule?" My eyebrow rose in surprise at how bold she was to ask that in such a public place, without even glancing around to see who might be listening in.

Robert smiled brighter. "He's not as closed off as he seems at first. And he cares for us more than most of us recognize." He held Lexa's hand clasped in between his and nodded to her. "I'm lucky to have a Warden like him. We all are."

Right then, I decided to turn on my heel and walk away, leaving the ballroom and the beautiful, infuriating woman behind me as I traveled up the steps towards my private chambers.

I had been going about this all wrong. I wasn't trying to sell *myself* to Lexa Cromwell, I was trying to sell our Court. And it might just do a better job of that without me interfering.

TWENTY-TWO

I didn't have a nightmare for three nights. Three blissful nights. I was more rested than I had ever been in my life. And despite attempting to postpone my inevitable bath, there was no repeat of the waking nightmare I had that morning in the inn. I couldn't help but wonder why now, after so many years, the nightmares had chosen to release their vicious clutch on my subconscious, but I was grateful for the reprieve. I wouldn't admit that a part of me felt slightly empty in their absence, because that would be absurd.

I also hadn't seen Lysander since the night of the Welcome Ball. I didn't know how I felt about that, and I hated that I didn't know. It should be abundantly clear. It should be so incredibly obvious. But it wasn't. Nothing was when it came to him. The last words we spoke to each other were positively vile and after his gift of the gorgeous dress, I couldn't help but feel a stinging pain in my chest every time I let myself think about it.

I truly enjoyed my time at the ball, even though I hated to admit it. My throat tightened when I first arrived in the ballroom and felt his eyes on me, seeming to burn me from the inside out. I ignored it for a few moments, attempting to focus on why I was there in the first place. To determine if I belonged in this Court. By the time I thought to look for him again, he was gone.

And I hadn't seen him since. The next day, I spent most of the daylight hours in the Forsaken Quarters' library, picking out a few titles I thought sounded interesting. Specifically searching for anything that might have information on The Forgotten Court.

The Forgotten Court was not taught at the Institute in any real capacity, in fact, it was barely more than an old folktale used to scare other school children. The veil of Mythica that led to its border had long since been blocked off by a dense forest. To be completely honest, I didn't even believe it had ever been real - until he said those words.

But of course, just like in the Institute, there were no titles that mentioned the mysterious eighth Court. It took me all day to comb through piles and piles of books only to completely come up short.

I thought briefly about asking Lysander about it again, probing for more than the small bits of information he shared on our carriage ride. But that idea was quickly quashed because I decided that I would rather remain in the dark than be the first to break this silence.

Damn pride.

In the evening, Lysander had sent a female guard, Joanne, to my chamber to teach me basic defensive and offensive maneuvers both with and without a weapon. My body was tired and my muscles were positively screaming, but after our lesson, I felt a wave of calm power wash over me, and I suddenly felt safer.

The following day, I explored more of the Forsaken Quarters I did not get a chance to see on my first excursion. I spent a good amount of time in the kitchens meeting the lovely cook, Clementine, and sampling her entire dessert menu. Not long after my indulgent meal, Joanna visited me again, running me through drills, and scenarios. I was not a natural by any means, but she had told me I was learning quickly. Which was good, since I had only a few days left in this Court.

Last night, I sent word to the Captain of the Guard that I wished to travel into Everwatch today. So the moment the sun peeked through the curtains, I was up and slipping into a long lilac chiffon off-the-shoulder dress, ignoring the dull ache in my over-worked muscles. I hadn't worn Lysander's dagger for two days, opting to use one of Joanne's extra daggers during training, and it sat idly on the bedside table. I didn't want to adorn it again as if using it meant I was admitting some sort of defeat - admitting that I forgave him - but the memory of how helpless I had felt in that carriage slipped back into my mind. With a sigh, I slid the holster into place and tightened it before exiting my chamber.

I rushed down the steps and out the front doors, making my way to the stables where the Captain's note told me to meet my escort for the day. A giddy excitement was building inside of me as I approached the stables and saw a small open-air cart already hitched to a gorgeous black horse, but all that exhilaration slipped away the moment I saw who was sitting atop it.

"What are you doing here?" Lysander turned his head in my direction. There was no playful smirk or glittering eyes. He simply looked at me, like one would regard a stranger.

"I was informed that you wanted to visit the town today. I am your guide, so I will be escorting you." He spoke nonchalantly, devoid of emotion. I didn't like this side of him. I almost preferred it when he was angry with me.

"I would have been fine with a different escort," I said, standing my ground outside the cart. "You must have better things to do." I didn't hide the accusation in my tone.

You are the one who flatters yourself if you believe that someone of my stature and position could ever be interested in someone like you.

His words had replayed in my mind in a near-constant loop for the last three nights. I couldn't have been so easily convinced that there was a sort of budding heat between us if there hadn't been. Right? Of course, I never wanted there to be anything between us, but it was there. I felt it. Or at least I thought

I had. And I thought he had too.

"Please get in the cart, Miss Cromwell." He said, reaching down to grip the reins in his hands.

"I do not want to spend the day with you." I meant it, but the harshness with which I stated it was enough to make me flinch.

"I will escort you and remain nearby should you need me. But you can explore Everwatch on your own." The offer was a good one, I didn't want my hand held like a child. This way I could see what I wanted, on my own terms. I couldn't help but notice he seemed dejected. I nearly asked him what was wrong, but instead, I silently climbed into the cart beside him.

The moment he was sure I was seated, the cart lurched forward as our horse reacted to Lysander's command. We made it across the drawbridge and began to descend the hill silently. I took this moment of quiet to study him. He was wearing a black vest with silver decorative trim, belted over a white long-sleeve button-down. His muted black pants were tucked into tall black boots. It was casual, while still clearly setting him apart. His dark hair was pulled back into a low loose bun.

He had hit a nerve with the whole 'Axel' thing. Even in my anger, however, I could admit he wasn't wrong. I was selfish. I had done exactly what he accused me of. And he wasn't the only one who aimed low in our argument. I called him The Covetor. A slur for all intents and purposes. A vile title given to him by people who I'd argue had never actually met him. I have. I knew him. And yes, while there was truth to the rumors - there was more. I'd seen it.

I wanted to thank him for the dress and apologize for the fight. But I couldn't bring myself to say a word. Stubborn. Prideful.

I was still formulating what I might say if I was brave - or reckless as he calls me - enough to say anything at all when we arrived in Everwatch. He pulled our cart off the path and slipped off the carriage with ease, his boots hitting the cobblestone streets with a loud thud. He was around to my side in a moment, offering me his arm without meeting my gaze. I reluctantly allowed him to help me down, but the moment my feet hit the stone, he moved to tend to the horse. It didn't escape me that he hadn't looked at me directly, not once.

Why do I want him to?

"I will be back in the cart at sundown to take you home. If you need anything before then, I won't be too far." And then he was gone, disappearing into one of the storefronts. I didn't miss his choice of words.

To take you home.

Home.

I watched after him, a strange emptiness forming in the pit of my stomach. Had I gone too far this time? How was it that my words did more damage than my dagger against his throat? But then again, how is it that his indifference now is causing me more pain than when he stole my Mythica?

I didn't have to worry about that, or how strangely Lysander was acting today because I was in Everwatch. Any thoughts of the Warden or how his detachment was making me feel would have to wait.

The energy was palpable, overflowing with a vitality I'm not sure I've ever experienced before. There was a sort of ease to it. Nobody here had to worry about where they belonged, because they were already here. I would have envied them if I wasn't enjoying taking a stroll through their world so much.

I spent the better half of the day visiting the shops, sampling the cuisine, and watching the people mill about town. I got lost for nearly an hour in the two-story bookshop, skimming through titles. Eventually, after much deliberation, I decided to purchase a small blue book with a cloth cover, the silver script etched onto the material read '*A Night Among the Shadows*'. It was an extensive guide about The Court of Shadows and specifically the traditions, festivals, and events. I read the passage about the harvest festival twice, remembering the fondness in Lysander's eyes when he told me about it on our carriage ride. He was so relaxed, so calm. He wasn't trying to manipulate me, or anyone. It wasn't part of some large scheme. He was just…happy.

Why had he been avoiding me? Was it not his mission to get me to fall in love with his Court? Not that his Court needed his help. Looking out among the bustling streets, the eager people milling about, unhurried and unburdened, it hit me that I could picture a life in this Court. I knew I could be happy here.

It was a slow realization, over several days, but it was true. The Court of Shadows was a stunning place full of warmth and life. I could admit that, despite my usual vehement distaste for its Warden.

Of course.

That had to be why he was steering clear of me. I've made my loathing quite clear, he must have known the best chance for me to fall in love with his Court was if he wasn't there. That sent a stab of guilt directly to my heart.

Lysander Bladespell was a manipulative, vulgar, frustrating man.

He was also a great Warden, according to every single person I spoke to. They didn't respond out of obligation, as if their praises of him were expected or rehearsed, but instead, they told tales of heartfelt and genuine interactions with the man they called Warden. I had begun seeing Lysander through different eyes these past few days. It makes perfect sense why he chose to distance himself from me.

That doesn't mean I particularly enjoyed it.

It was mid-afternoon when I made my way to sit near the large fountain. The rushing water provided a calming wall of sound in the backdrop of lively conversations. I found a spot near the ledge of the pool and sat down, feeling the mist from the fountain caress the back of my bare arms. Kids ran through the town square, chasing after each other with joyful laughs ringing, and carts of sweet treats were wheeled around and offered to the other individuals who sat at tables and benches spread out across the open area. It reminded me of the few times I attended the First Trial Festival at the veils but even that paled in comparison to the unfiltered joy these people had.

In a silent comfort, I leaned my head back, arching towards the descending sun, feeling the warmth spread across my face.

"Lexa."

My eyes snapped open to see the source of the distorted-sounding voice. Nobody was looking in my direction or looking around for the voice. Had they heard it too? The people in the square continued, but no one acknowledged me.

"Lexa."

My head spun around again, only to be met with the sight of more unbothered individuals. None of them looked my way. My heart rate quickened. I didn't recognize the voice, and nobody here should know my name.

"I need you, Lexa." The hollow sound sent a shockwave through my body. The voice, a whispered symphony of echoes, was coming from behind me. I turned quickly, expecting to find someone in the water of the fountain behind me, I saw nothing but the crystal blue pool, rippling with waves.

I adjusted so I was settled on my knees, looking down into the water. I watched as each word rippled across the surface as if the water itself was speaking to me. *"Help me, Lexa."*

"What do you need from me?" I knew what this must look like to those in the square, a grown woman kneeling over the ledge of the fountain nearly face to face with the surface speaking to it as if it could hear me - but I didn't care.

"Help me."

Before I could stop myself, my hand was drifting towards the cool water. Mist sprayed across my exposed skin, dampening the flyaway hairs on my forehead. Tiny vibrations on the surface grew stronger and wider until my reflection looked distorted and corrupted.

"Who are you?" I asked, completely disregarding the world around me. I didn't know what others would think or if they could see how the water reacted to me, but I couldn't help but lean into the tether readying itself to drag me to the very depths.

"FIND ME." The water splashed violently, I shielded my eyes and glanced around to see if anyone else was witnessing this display. I looked away for a

moment - only for a moment. Then something thick and powerful wrapped around my throat and pulled. My scream was instantly muffled by the water that filled my lungs as I was pulled deeper and deeper.

I thrashed against the hold around my neck as it constricted. Dragging me lower. My eyes adjusted slowly, faded blackness threatening to overtake my vision, distorting the image, and stealing me from safety. Once again, I found myself deep in an ominous and perilous ocean. Dark, empty waters stretched out in every direction around me, a never-ending, limitless expanse. The salt was so thick I felt it clog my nostrils, and assault my mouth, begging to be let into the only part of me still untouched by the restless sea.

Wicked desperation filled my chest as the burning in my lungs grew wild. Each jolt of my body against my restraint was another bit of my precious breath slipping away, making room for the onslaught of salted liquid, ready to consume me.

My hands viciously clawed against the clutch at my throat. It tightened as I struggled, and my already depleted supply of oxygen was vanishing to dangerous levels. The vine-like object was holding me, dragging me lower, deeper. A massive shadowed figure moved in the water below. I could not get a glimpse of it, nor could I escape it.

The panic hit me just as the living restraint tightened around my neck again, painfully. The pain washed over me in a blanket, acting as a warning of what I already knew to be true. If I did not get out of here soon…I would never breathe again.

I struggled against the firm imprisonment, flailing my arms widely in an attempt to claw my way to the surface. I fought, pressing my lips together with every ounce of strength I had, but that strength was waning by the second. It was barely a gap, my lips parted ever so slightly, but it was invitation enough for the hungry water to slip inside, filling my lungs with its salted promise of death. My body convulsed in pain, panic, and fear just as my vision nearly faded entirely, painting the world in a somber farewell.

I wasn't ready to give up, I refused to die here. Remembering my brief lessons with Joanna, I readied myself to fight back. My shaking hands pushed aside my skirts and found the dagger at my thigh. Pulling it free from its holster, I sliced aimlessly at the hold near my throat, missing. My limbs weakened with every slash.

I felt exhaustion threaten to overtake me, taunting me like a cruel villain. Weak. Lonely. Lost. Dead.

Not. Yet.

Beneath my core, thrumming with a lethal fury, my Mythica surged, expelling the liquid that had managed to work its way into my body. My mouth fell open in a silent scream and my power erupted through me, sending vibrations through the water, giving me a final taste of life. The black cloud of my Mythica floated in the water around me as if to tell me that I had limited time, but it had bought me what it could. Just enough.

With newfound strength, I turned the dagger, placing the edge of the blade on the writhing restraint around my neck, and I sliced. Sliding the blade deep into the flesh of my captor, spilling dark black blood into the water.

The hold on my neck loosened, just as a scream, inhuman and tortured, echoed through the water. My hands instinctively covered my ears from the bloodthirsty sound. It sent a tremor through my very soul.

I didn't have time to look down to catch a glimpse at my attacker, nor could I see beyond the black blood that was clouding the area, obscuring the already unilluminated waters. I didn't dare waste what precious energy I had left. Instead, I swam. Weak, fighting against my body's need to breathe. I pushed, higher, higher, towards the surface that didn't seem to exist. But I couldn't give up. I couldn't stop.

My lungs ignited, and every last bit of strength my Mythica granted me faded away.

I took a breath. The surface was nowhere in sight, and I knew then, beyond a shadow of a doubt, that I was about to die. Water flooded my lungs, my body convulsed as the ominous dark cloud of death began to overtake me.

I gripped the dagger in my hands, pulling it to my chest. Begging my subconscious mind not to drop it. Do not let it be lost.

Buyhay, I'm not finished yet.

This is how all my nightmares end. With darkness and death. But unlike my nightmares…when it was over, I wasn't going to wake up.

And then it was dark. And I was gone.

A strong pair of arms encircled my waist and I could faintly acknowledge the sensation of being pulled upwards.

I coughed, expelling water from my lungs, my back resting on solid ground beneath me. I vaguely heard the sound of shouting and felt warm arms surround me and lift me from the ground. Light blurred my vision, and I struggled to stay awake. Fear was still coursing through my veins. I thrashed against the arms that tried to hold me. I did not want to be held still again.

"Lexa, it's me. I'm here. You're ok. I've got you." His voice was strained, pained almost. But the moment I recognized who it was that held me now, the fear drifted away, replaced by a sort of comfort I didn't know I could feel in his presence.

Once again, he had saved me and made me feel safe. With that realization, knowing I was protected in the arms of Lysander Bladespell, I drifted off - but unlike before, this time I knew I could come back.

TWENTY-THREE

$\mathcal{I}$ noticed something was wrong the moment she turned to face the fountain. I had been keeping an eye on her from a distance all day, enjoying the view of her and experiencing all The Court of Shadows has to offer. It was intoxicating - her joy. I knew then this tour across Verihdia with her would not be the chore I had been expecting. Not if I got to witness her experiencing things.

She looked almost entranced by the pool, and while I could agree the crystal blue water did look particularly beautiful with the reflection of the fall trees in it, it did not seem like the type of sight to elicit such a response. I moved closer, standing just across the town square now, and watched her. Her hand drifted towards the surface like she was afraid she might break it if she used too much force. Then her eyes drifted upwards, only for a moment and she was falling headfirst into the pool.

My immediate concern was her head. The fountain was not very deep, a few feet at most. But the closer I got, I realized there was more to be concerned about. I rushed forward, carefully weaving my way through the people in the square. A few people had noticed her slip into the pool but were paying it little to no mind. It wasn't uncommon for someone to take a midday dip. In fact, some of the kids running through the square trailed drips of water behind them from their excursion into the fountain. It was common, but the way she fell in, almost like she was pulled, that was not common.

The crowded square seemed to stretch on as I moved through. She didn't surface. If she hit her head or passed out… she could drown. All of a sudden, I was running.

"Out of my way!" I cried out as my feet pounded the pavement. Lexa had garnered an audience at this point. Her body was thrashing under the surface, sending waves of water over the ledge of the fountain. A few people angrily cursed as their clothes were dampened. Then I saw the light glinting off the metallic object. Lexa had gripped her dagger and was wielding it blindly. The people watching on began to murmur in fear, a few people running in the opposite direction. "Everyone, clear the square. Now!" My voice boomed out across the square, reaching every corner of the busy area, and as the crowd that had gathered saw who the voice belonged to, they quickly dispersed.

I reached the edge of the pool and nearly cried out at the sight. Lexa, was unmoving and weak, convulsing underwater as she drowned. I dove in feet first. The water came up to my waist and I ran through it until I reached her. My arms circled her and pulled her to my chest. She was shaking, her entire body fighting against the intrusion of water.

Setting her on the ledge of the pool, I felt my heart quicken, tensing every muscle in my body as I worked, pounding on her chest to expel the water. My vision blurred with burning tears. Her Mythica was nothing more than a shadow around her. Still, empty, inanimate.

"Come on, Lexa!" My hands once again found her chest, forcing the water out. "Come on…" I screamed. My lips found hers without a second thought, forcing my air into her lungs. Again begging her to accept the life I was offering her. "Breathe, Lexa, please." My shoulders stung from the force I was exerting against her chest. "Buyhay, send her back! Send her back right now!" My lips covered hers again, pleading for her to accept my oxygen. Begging her to breathe.

She sat up quickly, coughing up a lungful of liquid. My breath came shakily then, a sob of relief wracking through me. I held her against my chest, swaying slightly as she continued to cough up the remaining water. She was alive. Although, the lifeless cloud around her was still unmoving.

My tongue darted out to lick my lips and my body stilled as the bitter taste invaded my mouth. I leaned down, burying my nose in her soaking wet hair. I took a deep sniff.

Saltwater.

I held her tighter. Confusion and fear began to overtake any instance of logic. I needed to get her away from here. While my citizens had dispersed from the immediate area, some prying eyes were watching. My fingers found the hilt of her dagger that had landed just beside her on the ledge. Carefully, I slid it back into its rightful place against her thigh. I didn't have time to analyze the overwhelming gratification that filled me knowing she still wore it. Even after everything I had said to her. About her. I slipped my arms beneath her knees and stood. Water dripped off me as I stepped out of the fountain.

She was nearly unconscious, her eyes fluttering somewhere between open and closed. I pulled her close to me so I could feel the rise and fall of her breathing against my chest. Proof she was still here. Still breathing. Still alive.

Her body went rigid, tensing as she felt my arms tighten around her. She fought back. Violently bucking, trying to get free of the hold I had on her.

There you are, little storm.

My lips curved into a smile at the beautiful, powerful woman in my arms. Her Mythica raged to life around her in a cloud of unrelenting force.

"Lexa, it's me. I'm here. You're ok. I've got you." It was a promise. One I intended to keep for as long as she would let me.

She relaxed into my hold, her head resting comfortably against my chest as I moved quickly through the town square towards our carriage. Anxious eyes watched me from storefront windows and behind corners. I knew I would need to make a statement about what just occurred. As soon as I understood it myself. But that couldn't happen now, I did not have time to quell their fears.

Climbing onto the carriage, with Lexa firmly in my lap, was not the easiest task. Logically, I could have laid her beside me on the bench. It was wide enough for both of us. But I couldn't seem to set her down. Not yet. With one arm firmly around her and the other gripping the reins, I rushed us back to the Forsaken Quarters.

With the sensation of her skin against mine, I was intimately aware of each steady breath. It was the only thing holding me together, keeping me from going back to that water and eviscerating whatever it was that did this to her.

What did this to her?

It didn't make any sense. There wasn't anything in the fountain with her. At least nothing I could see.

Saltwater.

I hugged her tighter and urged my horse on faster. The trip to the Quarters had never felt so long.

The moment we arrived safely at the castle, I steered the carriage directly to the door. Hopping off the bench with Lexa in my arms, I met eyes with one of my guards. Without slowing my stride, I called to him, "See to it that my horse is stabled, and send a healer to my quarters."

I heard him muffle "Yes, sir," under his breath - clearly still processing what it was he was seeing. I turned over my shoulder to him once more.

"I trust you to be discreet." I saw him nod furiously out of the corner of my eye before I burst through the front doors.

Luckily, the atrium was empty. I thanked Madillam for his gift of this particular shroud of darkness. I did not have the energy or time to devote to explaining why I was soaking wet and carrying an unconscious woman to my chambers.

I shuddered to think of the rumors. I picked up my pace, taking the steps to the tallest floor two at a time. By some miracle, we made it unseen. Kicking open the door, I rushed her forward, through my office, and into my bedroom. Laying her on the silk sheets carefully, my eyes stung with the threat of tears again. She looked so peaceful like she was sleeping. If I didn't know any better, I might have believed that.

Tracing my finger along the side of her cheek, I studied her closely for the first time. Scanning her face for any injuries. Her porcelain skin was dry, rough - how I would expect someone who was nearly drowned in salt water to feel.

"How is that possible?" I whispered, my hand continuing its trail along her skin. She shifted at my touch, a soft moan escaping her dehydrated lips, tilting her head into my touch, exposing her throat.

And I nearly lost every ounce of control I had left.

There, around her neck was the faint beginnings of a bruise encircling her throat in a thick coil. My vision blurred with a sort of vicious fury I knew I could not contain. The very blood in my veins threatened to boil over, exploding my wrath across this entire Court. The anger in my heart at this moment was enough to put even Rein to shame, I'd wager. I would hunt whatever did this to her, I would travel to the very ends of the world. I would visit every body of water in Verihdia if it meant I could prevent this from ever happening again. I would end the world for her.

"Lysander…" Her weak, fragile voice worked its way into my mind, dragging me back from the depths I had begun to descend to. The anger that clouded my eyes cleared and suddenly it was her, only her, that held me to this world. Her hand reached out, and I grabbed it instantly. Clasping it between mine tightly and firmly, the feeling of her hand in mine rendered me completely and utterly helpless.

It hit me then, like a truth I had so blindly been ignoring. I would go to incredible, impossible lengths for this woman. I still need Lexa Cromwell to Pledge to my Court, that much has remained true. But there is so much more at stake now. I need her, not for her power, not because she would make a formidable enemy - although she would - but because for a moment, I got a taste of what it might be like to live without her, and there is nothing I wouldn't do to avoid ever experiencing that again.

TWENTY-FOUR

The first overwhelming realization was that my throat hurt. Inside and out. It was parched, and rough, like the surface of a stone was grinding against my skin with every painful swallow. A burning sensation accompanied each torturous attempt. On the exterior, my skin felt like it had been stretched taut and my muscles flayed. Exposed, raw, agonizing.

The second realization came in the form of a warm hand encircling mine.

Lysander.

He had saved me. In more ways than one. Glimpses of memories flooded back to me, his arms lifting me, his words echoing in my head, soothing me. He had given me the dagger that allowed me to free myself, and he had pulled me to safety. A comforting warmth bloomed in my chest. A type of security I had never felt before blanketed me.

The dagger.

Panic seized my heart, constricting it as the terrible thought crossed my mind. Please tell me I didn't lose it. Sitting up quickly, I felt the weight of my body for the first time, begging to drag me down. A groan escaped my raw throat.

"Careful there." His voice warned gently. My eyes opened to see the inside of a room I had been in before, only briefly. Lysander's personal quarters. I felt the silk sheets, cold against my palms. My damp hair clung to my bare shoulders. Looking down, my body was draped in a sleeveless tunic, fitting snugly against my curves. But there, just below the hem of the tunic, and strapped to my thigh was my dagger. The relief washed over me in an instant. My hand ran over the dark green hilt, tracing its swirled design with a touch of genuine gratitude for the fine weaponry. Without it, there's no doubt in my mind I would not be breathing right now.

I felt Lysander shift in his seat next to the bed, and finally, I turned to look at him. His green eyes were framed by dark circles against his bronzed skin, the stubble on his chin slightly more pronounced and thick, and his chin-length obsidian hair was disheveled and untamed with unconquered curls springing loose. A far cry from the put-together - nary a hair out of place - Warden I had come to know. Something told me there were even more sides to this man than I had originally believed. Sides I might actually like. I gripped his hand tighter.

"You…" I tried to speak, but the pain in my throat nearly sent me tumbling back onto the mattress. "You…" I cleared my throat just as Lysander handed me a glass of water. Ignoring the initial flinch at the sight of the liquid, I took it and greedily swallowed it down. The cool water was refreshing, and cleansing. I instantly felt the burn in my throat subside to a dull ache.

"Don't strain yourself, Lexa." His hands moved then to place pillows behind my back, allowing me to sit comfortably. I didn't understand the loss I felt as he retracted his hand from mine.

"You saved… my life," It was barely more than a whisper. Pain spread across my neck, and down into my chest, but the urge to speak to him outweighed the discomfort.

His eyes met mine. An emotion I didn't recognize painted on his too-tired face.

"Thank…you." It was such a simple phrase, two minuscule words that in no way could encompass the immense gratitude and deep appreciation that overwhelmed me. But even though I knew he deserved more than that, I had to say them. He leaned forward, his forearms resting on the mattress next to my exposed thigh. His fingertips accidentally brushed against the skin above the leather strap, sending a jolt directly to my core. He must have misinterpreted my sharp intake of breath because he quickly curled his fingers in, leaning back again.

"I shouldn't have…" he said sadly, his chin lowering to his chest and avoiding my eyes.

This man sitting here was not The Warden of Shadows. This wasn't even Lysander Bladespell, charismatic, cocky, and challenging. No, this man, with his limbs draped on the silk sheets and his head hung low in shame, or fear… this was Lysander - just Lysander.

Before I let myself think about it, I slid over on the bed until there was a wide enough space for him. He watched me with questioning eyes, but I didn't have the answer. I didn't understand why I was doing this either. Why I needed this. I patted the open space with my hand, and after a long, torturous moment of stillness, clearly processing and analyzing the invitation I had offered him, he stood. Slowly, he leaned down onto the mattress, and it groaned with the addition of his weight. He moved at a glacial pace, it was rather obvious he was giving me plenty of time to object, to change my mind. Frankly, I was waiting for that too.

I wasn't going to.

He slid into the bed, laying on his side, his head propped up by his hand, and he watched me. There was such a distance between us, even now. Especially now. I watched him as he watched me. Neither of us was willing to break the spell our gazes had cast on each other by speaking or moving. But I needed him closer, I needed the safety that, surprisingly, he offered me.

Maneuvering slowly, still wrestling with the aches in my muscles from the lessons and the attack, I slid down on the silk sheets until I too was horizontal. His eyes burned into mine until I broke the contact and turned my back to him, inching backward. Slowly. Carefully. Stopping only when my back met with the firm warmth of his chest. He was still and rigid, I could practically feel him preparing to run away.

The tense wall of muscle behind me remained steadfast, even as I arched my back into him. Did I imagine every instance of compassion? Was I taking this too far? Maybe. Did I care about any of that right now? Not one bit. I needed to feel safe, and as confusing as it is, the place I felt the safest at the moment was in his arms.

The arms he was currently avoiding wrapping around me. I curled into myself, hugging my chest, the soreness around my throat spiking with the movement. I hissed as the pain traveled down my body. Still, he did not embrace me. He laid stiff against my back, afraid to touch me.

"Please…" The broken plea was ushered and I instantly felt him relax behind me, sinking into the mattress. His arm snaked around my waist and pulled me tighter against him. His palm spread across my abdomen and lit a fire in my blood, sending a shockwave of electric energy to every nerve in my entire body. He pulled me closer until it was impossible to tell where he stopped and I began, his warmth enveloping me in a blanket of security.

"Did you.." I started, the comfort of his embrace spurring me to ignore the pain in my throat. "Did you… see what happened?"

"I did." He said, his breath tickling the back of my neck. "But I know that what happened to you was more than I could see." His muscles tightened at that, the hand on my abdomen closing into a fist. I pressed my back into him harder. I felt his fist relax against me. His fingers trailed up my abdomen, grazing lightly against the tunic that adorned my body. Lifting them slightly until he was touching my exposed collar bone, just below the tender bruise on my neck. I winced, and his movement stilled instantly. My hand caught his and urged him to continue. His hand resumed its journey up my throat, tracing a feather-light touch along the reminder of my experience. I took slow, steady breaths, ignoring the pooling heat at my core. "Will you.." He started. His voice was shaking, breaking. With anger or fear, I couldn't tell. "Will you tell me what did this to you?"

I swallowed, straining against the red hot pain, and nodded. "Something.. grabbed me." His fingers continued their gentle exploration of the bruised skin. "It felt like a rope…but it was…alive." I felt him go still behind me again. "I was in…an ocean. I couldn't get out." The words came easier now, physically at least. "It called to me..said my name… it told me to find it." My voice was not above a whisper, but I knew he could hear me, his heart rate quickened as I continued.

"It was going to kill me." His fingers moved then to my cheek to wipe away the tears I didn't even realize had begun to fall. "If I didn't have this dagger…I'd be dead." His arms tightened around me. "I know it sounds impossible."

"I believe you." And that was all it took for the sobs to overtake me. He held me there for what felt like several minutes while I sobbed away the stress, the exhaustion, the fear. All the while completely engulfed in the arms of the man I despised.

Or at least used to.

It seemed he was determined to make me resent him, only to have the pleasure of convincing me to forgive him. And I was forgiving him. Each stroke of his gentle touch on my bruised flesh was an apology I was more than willing to accept.

As my sobs quieted and my tears ran dry, I felt him behind me, his hand had taken to running idle circles against my bare thigh.

"I'm sorry, "I whispered. His hand ceased its movement for a brief second before continuing to graze my skin.

"Never apologize to me for how you feel, Lexa." He spoke into my ear, it was a command. But one I felt like obeying instead of challenging.

"It's not just that I need to… apologize for." The more I used my throat, the less it stung, each word bringing a new relief to the burn.

"No, you don't," I rolled my eyes. I wondered if he could tell.

"Do not tell me…what I don't need to do…" his body trembled behind me with a deep vibration as he laughed.

"You still have your challenging personality, I see." He mused, his lips brushing against my uncovered shoulder. My flesh erupted in goosebumps and I closed my eyes in an attempt to regain my composure.

"I'm sorry…for what I said. For all the…horrible things I've said." My mind flashed back to the vicious and vile things I had thrown at him. My verbal attacks, while they didn't seem to affect him much, were out of line and I could see that now. I shuddered to think of how reckless I was to have drawn this dagger on him. Reckless and childish. "I was angry…I let it cloud my judgment." And then, the truth even I was afraid to admit spilled from my wavering lips. "I ruined everything." My brother, Chandler, my Final Trial, him. I ruin everything I touch.

He didn't answer for a while, his hand just continued trailing cool touches across my skin. My heart rate quickened and my aching center throbbed at each sensual pass. But then his hand was gone, and the pathetic whimper that escaped my lips was shameful enough to make my entire face flush a deep red. His fingers found my chin, gently urging my face to turn, to look at him. He moved with a compassionate touch, allowing me to twist my neck at the pace I was most comfortable with but unrelenting enough to know he expected me to face him.

The strain against the tender muscles was painful, but the look in his eyes as my head turned to him was enough to wash it all away.

"I love it," he breathed almost too quiet for me to hear as if he was speaking to himself rather than to me. His fingers trailed a chilling and comforting touch across the bruise that now darkened around my throat. The pain I felt from the injury was instantly overshadowed by the flood of want that washed over me, sending a pool of warmth and desire directly to my center at the apex of my thighs.

"Love what?" I asked, my traitorous voice sultry and unrestrained. The skin underneath his fingers was nearly burning at the contact. The fire ignited low in my core, and a strange emotion blossomed in my chest. Had it always been there? Had I been so blind all this time? His eyes traveled torturously slow from my lips to my eyes. The desire behind the green of his irises was easy to recognize, and I was positive he was witnessing a similar look within my own gaze.

"The way you ruin me." And his lips crashed into mine. Forceful enough for me to feel his desire that was climbing to unbelievable heights, as mine was, but tender enough to not cause my injured neck any pain. He claimed my mouth with his as if he was struggling for air and his only chance of survival was to breathe me in. I would gladly allow him every last drop.

His tongue danced with mine and I felt his length press hard against me from behind. I tensed beneath him, and I felt him begin to pull away. My hand snaked around his neck and pulled his mouth back down to mine, grinding into his growing excitement.

He groaned against my mouth as he twitched behind me. I suddenly needed him all over me. My free hand gripped his, which was still gently caressing the skin around my neck, and pushed it down my body until he was nearly where I needed him.

"Tell me what you want, Lexa," He whispered into my mouth, his tongue flicking against mine. His hand rested just below the hem of the tunic, inches from the part of me that was desperate for him.

I pressed my behind into him again in answer, eliciting a strained grunt from him. The corners of my mouth lifted into a smile at the effect my body was having on him. And the effect he was having on me.

"I want…" I didn't recognize my voice - this lustful, primal sound that was spilling from my kiss-swollen lips. What did I want? Did I want him to make me forget what happened today? Distract me? No that's not it. Forgetting is a coward's way out of hard situations. The easy way. I want something much more intimate from him. Something at this moment, only he can give me. "I want to feel safe."

His hand slipped beneath the hem of the tunic, and the first graze of his rough finger against my center had me bucking into him. A shockwave of pleasure wracked my body.

"Gods, Lexa…" He growled against my ear as his finger slid through the wetness at my center. Slow, like he was exploring every inch of my most intimate desires. "You've wanted this just as badly as I have, haven't you?" I gasped at his confession. His thumb hovered over the bundle of nerves at the apex of my thighs, I felt it constrict and pulsate even without a single touch.

Gods, what is this man doing to me?

"I thought you said you couldn't be attracted to me?" I teased, breathlessly. I haven't forgotten his cruel remark. But the way he touched me now, the way his body melded to mine so perfectly, I needed to know the truth. Even if it meant this moment would end.

"That's right. I can't be attracted to you, Lexa." His lips kissed the spot of my neck just behind my ear lobe, pulling a whimpered cry from my mouth. "I'm not supposed to. I'm not allowed to. But I am."

"Touch me," I begged. A broken sigh escaped his lips and he lost what little control he had been holding onto. His thumb pressed down into the spot where I needed him, and I cried out at the jolt of euphoria. The moans falling from my mouth spurred him on. He slid one delicious finger into me, powerful and claiming, and my head fell back against his shoulder. My vision blurred at the onslaught of pure, unbridled passion. Every nerve of my body begged for this man, begged to be touched by him. His lips found my neck, and even with the ferocious claiming nature of his hand at my center, he kissed my bruised flesh with a level of care that brought an overwhelming warmth to my heart.

A second finger slipped inside, and I cried out at the welcome intrusion. He slid them slowly, allowing me just enough time to adjust, his thumb continuing its domination of my most sensitive spot. My body lurched at each cautious insertion as his fingers moved within me. But it wasn't enough, I needed more. I began to move on him, rolling my hips to meet his fingers, faster, harder. His body vibrated with laughter behind me, which only pressed his hardening length into me and had me moving with a more frenzied need. His fingers began moving quicker to match my pace, sliding another in to join the others, and I felt the building tension begin to rise, to peak. This was a sensation unlike any I had ever experienced.

"Tell me, Lexa." He panted. His body and mine moved in perfect rhythm as I rode his fingers. I didn't answer for a passion-filled moment, I'm not sure I remembered how to speak. "Tell me…" He said again, this time with an edge of competition, jealousy. I twisted my head just enough to see his emerald eyes dark with desire and another emotion I couldn't place.

"Tell you..what?" I managed, barely, as his fingers moved inside of me hitting a part of my core I didn't even know existed.

"Tell me I make you feel things he never could." He couldn't be serious. Bringing up Chandler at a time like this? I felt the familiar disgust I usually felt in his presence begin to crest, but he slammed his fingers into me again and I arched back into him, the anger fading away with each possessive thrust of his wrist. "I'm waiting…" He taunted me and I tried to speak, but as my mouth hung open, I let out moans instead. "As much as I love that sound, little storm…" he captured my lips with his, drawing another whimper from me, which only had him groaning into me. "And Gods, I love that sound." He moved again, pressing himself forward into me so I could feel exactly how much this affected him. "I need you to tell me."

I nearly protested at the inappropriate line of questioning, but then his fingers curled inside just as his thumb pressed harder, sending a crashing tidal wave of blinding pressure that threatened to drown me in a way I would gladly succumb to. I was with the Warden of The Court of Shadows, an envious Court known for taking what they want. A Court known for seeing the pleasures of others and needing it for themselves. Who was I to deny his nature? To condemn him for embracing his shadow? To deny him the truth. The truth is that there has never been, nor will there ever be, someone who could make my body react the way it was right now. That nobody else could fill me with such an explosion of desire that I fear I'd never recover. He kept up his pace, guiding me through the explosive orgasm that wrecked me.

"Yes!" I screamed because it was true. Because I knew he needed to hear it, even though the reaction of my body was answer enough. His fingers continued moving, slowly, drawing out every last bit of my release as if he knew there was more to be had. I felt my muscles tighten around him as he let out a hum of appreciation. As my heart rate settled and I caught my breath, his fingers stilled within me, but he didn't remove them. I struggled to ignore the feeling of him still inside of me as I tried to regain any inkling of composure I could.

"You are safe with me, little storm." He whispered against my neck, his lips trailing feather-light kisses along the bruise. "You will always be safe with me." My heart skipped a beat at the words. I wanted to believe them, and in the haze of ecstasy, I nearly did. While he has proven, twice now, that he would come to my rescue should I need him, this is still the man who stole my Mythica and used it to rip the most painful secret from my subconscious. I couldn't believe the man who did that was the man whose fingers just dragged every ounce of passion from my body.

I shifted slightly, and he pulled his hand from me. Instantly the absence was noticeable, like the connection between us had filled a hole that had always been there, but now that I knew of its existence, I'd never feel whole again. I felt him, still hard against my back, and I slid my hand behind me in an attempt to graze his length, but he simply pressed against me tighter, closing off any chance of my hand reaching him.

I whimpered. He laughed softly, pressing one kiss against my temple, and snaked his hand around my waist.

"As incredibly sexy as that was, you are still injured and it would be irresponsible of me to allow you to exert yourself." I rolled my eyes.

"Pretty sure you just had me exerting myself," he laughed again, the vibrations moving through my sensitive body.

"No, little storm. Trust me." His lips grazed my earlobe. "Your throat needs to heal because when I have you the way I want to, you'll need it to scream my name."

Warmth spread between my legs, telling me I was nowhere near finished with this man. I wanted to tell him to prove it. I wanted to challenge him, tell him there was no way I would ever scream his name just so I could bear witness to him keeping his promise. But I knew deep down he was right, and the dull ache in my throat served as a frustrating reminder.

"Why do you call me that?" I asked because I couldn't say what I wanted to.

"Your Mythica," he started, his hand lazily traveling up and down the side of my thigh. My body tensed. I didn't want him to talk about my Mythica. I was thankful he couldn't see my face as he hugged me from behind. "I can see it." I didn't answer, and he must have sensed my confusion because he continued. "That's what I can do. I can see the power of others when I'm around them like it's a physical thing that follows them around." Suddenly all those moments when I caught him watching the air surrounding my head made sense.

"For most people, it's a small cloud of smoke that trails behind them, like a shadow. But there are some whose Mythica is more obvious than that. My siblings for example." His hands continued to trail along my bare skin, touching the dagger still firmly in place against my thigh. I listened intently. "Their Mythica is quite powerful. When we're all together, the room is nearly filled with colored smoke. I used to hate it - still do sometimes. It can be overwhelming, all that power in one place, fighting each other for dominance, but even I can admit it's a beautiful thing. So vibrant, powerful." He spoke with a fondness I recognized. A pride one had when speaking about a sibling. Suddenly my heart ached for my twin.

"But you, Lexa." He slid his body back, just enough so I could turn to face him. He propped himself up on his arm again and watched me as I did the same mirror to him. We were no longer in contact, but I felt a tether between us that wasn't there before. My body was begging to be in his embrace again. "Your Mythica is alive, it follows you, protects you, defends you. It's not a shadow, it's an extension of you." I tried to understand his words, but it wasn't making sense. "It's a storm."

My eyes drifted closed then, and I focused on the simmering ability that ran through my veins, the power that got me into trouble, that caused tension between my family and my friends. A power that scared even The Seven. It had always felt like my Mythica had a mind of its own, but to hear Lysander confirm it was almost comforting. To know someone else could witness how irrepressible it felt at times.

Nobody in my Pledge class, Gods, nobody in the entire Verihdian Institute had abilities quite like mine. Sure, there were other powerful people. Chandler for example, though his Mythica manifested differently, his sheer strength was quite impressive. Riley was already healing incredibly difficult injuries and they hadn't even been fully trained yet. Callum was able to locate objects, no matter where they were - even across the veils - and another student in our class could disappear without a trace. They were all incredibly powerful, in their own right. But nobody could do what I could. It was fairly harmless at first when all I was doing was uncovering my classmates' fears and desires, discovering secret crushes, or anxieties about upcoming exams.

But that wasn't all I could do. No, I was capable of something far darker.

I was able to rip open someone's mind, find the guilt there, and watch it play out right in front of me. I could force someone to relive the worst moments of their life while I watched over their shoulder. Stealing their secrets, harboring their guilt. There is a huge portion of my Pledge class, and even some of the instructors, that would never want to be on my bad side for fear of retribution. Not that I ever would do such a thing. But there is a dark corner of my mind where their guilt is filed away. I've tried to forget them, but those memories stay with me. Etched on my soul as if it were my guilt to bear.

I like to think I'm a good person, that it was just a mistake, but even once I had gained control, once I understood the gravity of the power I wielded, I didn't stop. I used it. On Chandler, on those men in my Final Trial.

My heart skipped a beat as the face of the man I sentenced to death flashed in my mind. His empty blue eyes were devoid of any emotion. The face of a man who had given up. I pulled the darkest moment from the recesses of his mind and splayed it out for my viewing. Only to sentence him to death.

Maybe that explains The Forgotten Court result.

Wait, the result!

A dark black ocean raging in a storm. A shadowed and massive figure floating just beneath the surface. A broken building with shattered windows, and moss-covered doors.

'Find Me'.

"The Forgotten Court," I whispered. I didn't realize I had said it out loud until I felt Lysander tense across from me.

"What did you say?" He asked although the fear painted on his face told me he heard exactly what I said.

"My Final Trial result. It was The Forgotten Court." His throat bobbed with a forced swallow.

"I know. I already told you that." He said cautiously, confusion flooding every word.

"That's not what I mean. When I opened the sphere, I saw an ocean in a storm. A dark shadow moving within the water…" My mind was racing, my voice barely keeping up with the rapid onslaught of thoughts. "The thing in the fountain. It said 'Find Me'." I bolted upright in the bed. Lysander followed, watching me with anxious eyes as the pieces to this puzzle fell into place. "I heard that same voice call to me in my results." My breathing became labored, and the tension in my throat was thick and painful.

"Lexa, please take a deep breath." His hands hovered over my shoulders, not actually making contact. I was thankful for that because I felt like at any moment, I may explode.

"The Forgotten Court is trying to kill me, Lysander." It was a whisper. A confession. He studied me, his green eyes filled with worry and … guilt. A rage began to build within me. "What is it?" I asked, my throat throbbing with pain at the exertion. I was doing my healing process no favors right now.

"Nothing…" He spoke quietly, his gaze trailing lower, avoiding my eyes.

"You know something." I accused a finger jabbing into his firm chest. The look flashed across his eyes again. "You're afraid." It wasn't a question. I knew fear well enough to see when someone was experiencing it. But what was he afraid of? Before I had a second to think, to reconsider what I was about to do, the silent question fell from my mind.

Tell me what you're scared of.

I watched the moment it reached him. His eyes furrowed and anger filled his gaze, but his mouth opened and the words spilled out anyway. "I'm afraid you're going to get hurt because of what I've done." His eyes widened as I pulled the truth from his lips his breathing coming in ragged, anxious spurts.

"What did you do?" I asked, a ferocious edge to my voice.

"How did you just…" His face was twisted in an expression of perplexity and embarrassment. I didn't let him finish his question before the darkest part of me was unleashed.

WHAT DID YOU DO?

I reached down into the well of my Mythica, finding that dark, secluded part of myself where the power bubbled. The part I knew better than to touch. And I pulled. The room erupted in a flurry of shadows, filling the space, washing away Lysander's chamber, and welcoming me into his mind. Into his guilt.

I was in a dark room, cold and musty. There was no light except for the simple glow the few torches placed around the room gave off. The walls were damp and the ceiling was low and there was a stone archway that led to a long, unilluminated hall. This chamber looked like it had not been used in years, cobwebs crowding every corner and stone falling. Sounds of rushing water echoed. One singular figure stood alone in the room. Their face was obscured by a dark hood. I knew who it was the moment I regarded him. Lysander. The man whose memory I was living. I tried to study him. I couldn't see his face, but his shoulders were slumped, and his head hung low. Already guilty. But for what?

Then, footsteps sounded from within the shadowed hall, Lysander did not go to move. Instead, he stood stationary, awaiting the arrival of six hooded figures. They entered quietly, shrouded in unrelenting darkness. One by one they arrived in silence, until seven cloaked figures stood, spread about the chamber. Much like the Courting Ball, I did not need to see their faces to know who these people were. But it wasn't just their stature that gave it away.

The room was filled with vibrant clouds of bright colors, swirling around the shrouded heads of each of the figures. Their Mythica. Just as Lysander described it, swirling around their heads, fighting for space. This was his memory, I was seeing what he saw.

I instantly understood what he meant about his own Mythica being overwhelming. Although I knew the smoke wasn't actually there, and neither was I, it made the air feel almost too thick to breathe. He feels this every day.

I pushed the sting of pity away as one of the figures lowered his hood.

Vander Midesues, his bright red hair was messy from the hood, and his eyes were missing the mischievous joy I had come to expect from him. But his golden cloud of Mythica framed his body like the backdrop of a sun. Bright, powerful, stoic.

The others followed suit, slowly revealing their faces. Each of the seven Wardens of Verihdia stood around this tiny, abandoned room, looking disheveled, disheartened, and afraid. My eyes landed on the figure directly in front of me, revealing his face for the first time. The Warden of Shadows. His thick black hair hung in loose ringlets around his face, framing his face as he looked down to the floor. A green shadow of Mythica hung eerily near his hands, small tendrils of power prepared to strike out at any moment. I had no idea how long ago this memory was. Lysander physically looked the same, but there was a missing air of maturity he carried now.

"I trust nobody was followed," Vander spoke, tight-lipped and anxious. The other Wardens nodded their agreement. "Good."

"You know why we're here." Rein said, stepping forward towards the center of the room, trailing a deep red cloud behind him. The others watched him. "He can't be trusted." Murmurs from the other Wardens filled the room.

"He hasn't done anything yet." Miya Moonshackle. They had the same calm expression on their face I saw the night of the Courting Ball, and their blue cloud of Mythica gently embraced them, circling their body in a wrap of protection. They too looked mostly the same, except for the bare skin where I knew they had since gotten more tattoos. Yes, this memory was a very long time ago. There was no doubt about that.

"'Yet' being the operative word, sibling." Rein replied. Miya took a step back, their head lowering in submission and their Mythica tightening its hold around them.

"So what are you suggesting we do about it then?" Ivis asked, her hands crossing in front of her chest. Her Mythica was a pink puff that trailed down her back like a cape.

"Simple," Rein's lips twitched with the beginning of a smirk that never came. "Let me take him to my Prison." A flash of excitement crossed his face, and his Mythica surged in agreement.

"That wouldn't work, he's too powerful," Vander pointed out, his hand rubbing the base of his chin in thought.

"Once he is there he will not be able to use his Mythica," Rein responded.

"How do you know that?" Avalin chimed in. At least, I believe it was Avalin. Witnessing her through Lysander's memory was quite different from the appearance she had in my presence. Here she had short red hair, cropped just above the ear, a thin frame, and stood a solid six inches shorter than she had at the Ball. I tried not to think about the stark contrast between this woman and myself, but I couldn't help but acknowledge this is what Lysander considered attractive, and I couldn't be more opposite.

"You understand my Mythica, correct?" Rein taunted. In books, Warden Mithroar's Mythica is described as being preventative magic. The ability to mute any other power. The legends say he painstakingly crafted each brick of the Sunken Province Prison, imbuing it with his Mythica, so no one who set foot inside could access their powers. That's what made it the perfect place for criminals, Vacants, and Mythica-wielders alike.

"Yes, we're all well aware of what you are capable of brother," Korzich spoke for the first time. Their playful tone, muted though not entirely gone in the face of this situation, their Mythica climbed up their limbs in a delicate, sensual way, moving in constant motion.

"So we throw him in your Prison?" Ivis confirmed.

"Yes," Rein responded, his eyes gleaming with a devilish promise.

"It won't work." The familiar voice caught me off guard. Lysander had remained quiet thus far, much like he did that night in the Observatory. More inclined to watch and listen than to participate unless necessary. Unless it was to get something he wanted. "Are you forgetting our Mythica isn't supposed to work on each other? It's the Gods' little way of ensuring no Warden is more powerful than another." Rein's hands balled into fists at his side.

"That's not true," Rein bit back, his voice laced with venom. Lysander's hand extended toward his brother. His Mythica reached for Reins'. Instead of grabbing hold, it came to a stop just before him, as if their Mythica repelled each other. The bright red storm and the dark green tendril hung in a standoff.

"It is true, brother. Tell me you didn't feel what I attempted just now." Rein snarled, but he did not argue.

"Our Mythica was designed by the Gods to be equal…But that's not entirely true, is it?" Rein's fists closed at his side.

"You don't know anything." He spat.

"I know his Mythica works on us." Lysander's words hung heavy in the small room. The other Wardens looked around, sharing knowing glances.

"He's right. It happened to me." Avalin spoke quietly like she was ashamed of admitting she wasn't as powerful as she claims to be. "He used his Mythica on me and it worked. This is far more dangerous than we initially believed."

"It should have been impossible. But that Warden is proving that impossible means nothing when it comes to him. Your Prison will not hold him," Lysander continued. He paused. "He's too powerful."

"He's right, brother." Vander placed a hand on Rein's arm, and he took a steadying breath.

"So, we can't lock him up. What do you suggest we do then?" Rein asked. They all looked to Lysander. Their eager eyes watched him expectantly.

He ran his fingers through his loose hair, his emerald eyes were dull, devoid of any life. His Mythica moved about the room, coming into contact with the other clouds of smoke, tasting it, testing it. Unable to covet any of it.

"We do what we always do when we are threatened." His eyes traveled the space, making eye contact with each of his siblings.

"You want us to kill him?" Miya's shocked voice startled me. I turned to look at them. Their hands were mindlessly rubbing the spot on their head where their Court Mark rested. I felt bile rise in my throat.

"The others will fight back. The whole Court. They won't let this go unpunished," Ivis reminded them. "And need I remind you, many of them carry similar Mythica? If his Mythica works on us, who's to say theirs won't either?"

"They could overthrow us if they chose to," Korzich replied in a rare bout of seriousness.

"They wouldn't risk their lives," Rein responded.

"Are you willing to risk yours?" Avalin snapped, her eyes burning into Reins and the purple smoke surrounding her grew larger with every word.

"We can't just leave them there without him." Vander speculated, pacing slowly back and forth across the chamber. "It would be anarchy."

"There can be no Court without a Warden." Avalin was right. The other Wardens knew it too. The silence that fell over the chamber was deafening.

"So there will be no Court." Lysander's words sunk into me. Wrenching a sob from my chest. Tears blurred the memory.

"You can't possibly mean…" Miya spoke after a long moment of stillness.

"They cannot remain without a Warden, and we cannot let the Warden remain." He spoke so matter of fact, his tone even as if he was asking a simple question, not suggesting the genocide of an entire Court.

"Ok…there will be no Court." Rein agreed, a wicked glee settling on his face.

I felt the world begin to cave in on me. Shadows folded in on themselves, forcing me from the memory. Within moments, I was back in the quarters with Lysander sitting across from me.

His face contorted in a look of betrayal and fear.

The moment my Mythica released its hold on him, he was up and off the bed and over to the other side of the room in seconds.

"How did you do that?" He ran his hands through his hair, his whole body shaking with anger, fear… I wasn't sure.

"You killed them." It was a whisper. I couldn't muster anything more.

"I am a Warden, Lexa." His voice was pained like he was attempting to muster up the confidence I often witnessed in the man before me, but he fell short. "You should not have been able to use your Mythica on me. It's not possible"

"You killed them…" I repeated.

"You don't understand." He started, a tear sliding down his bronze skin.

"You're right, I don't understand." I stood from the mattress, standing my ground facing him. "I don't understand how you could kill thousands of people." His head fell back and his eyes fell closed. His fists clenched at his side. "Why did you do it? Because you felt threatened?"

"You don't know what you're talking about," He bit back. "You don't know what happened!" He took a step forward, and my hands instinctively gripped the hilt of the dagger. I held it outstretched in my arm, aimed at him. He paused, betrayal painted on his expression.

"I saw it with my own eyes, Lysander!" My throat screamed in pain as I yelled. The muscles were crying against the exertion.

"Let me explain!" He begged, taking more steps forward until my dagger was a mere few inches from making contact with his skin. And just like on that secluded island in my Final Trial, I saw before me a broken man. A man with nothing left. But this time, I couldn't understand it. I didn't want to.

"I don't want your explanations!" I hissed, thrusting the dagger towards him.

He didn't pull back, but fear flashed across his face.

"How did you do that, Lexa?" He asked, his eyebrows furrowed, and his emerald green eyes brimming with tears. His fiery ash scent invaded my nostrils and suddenly I felt weak. But I refused to show him that. My grip on the dagger's hilt was steadfast as I held it aimed at his throat. Veins in my neck bulged as he swallowed, attempting to hide his worry. He took another step.

"Stay back!" I warned, not moving from my place. The tip of the obsidian blade dug into the flesh under his chin, but he didn't fight it. Instead, his eyes remained on me, burning into my skin as if he might find the answers to his questions there.

"Lexa, please..." Tears fell, painting his brown skin with moisture as we stood in our tense standoff.

Could I kill him now, if I needed to? Would I?

His eyes pleaded with me, but the way he looked at me was not the way someone looks at a person they care for, no, he was looking at me the way so many others had before. He was afraid.

A single drop of blood escaped from the skin where my dagger bit into his flesh, and the sight of the bright red trail on his skin sent me into a spiral. At once, I dropped the dagger, returning it to my holster, but took tentative steps back.

Lysander's eyes followed me, waiting for my next move.

I sprinted from the room, leaving this stranger behind me. This murderer. Tears spilled from my eyes as I nearly toppled down the steps to the next floor. Pausing at the landing, I felt my heart constrict. I could leave. Go back to The Living Lands right now, Pledge Uncourted, and spend the rest of my life in the safety of the only home I've ever known. Far away from Lysander, from the threat of The Forgotten Court, from the other Wardens, from the waking nightmares. But my feet wouldn't move. Not the direction I needed them to anyway. Instead, I found myself moving towards my quarters. I couldn't explain why. But something was keeping me here. Something I didn't understand.

Empty and drained, my throat still throbbing from the injury, and my legs still slick with the evidence of arousal Lysander had elicited from me, I opened my door, hoping to fall onto my bed and empty my eyes of the tears and shut out the world around me.

But there was no chance of that.

The smell of paint assaulted my nose, and the sight before me stopped me dead in my tracks. A symbol of a raven's silhouette with a small wilting flower hanging from its mouth was painted on every available surface of the room. The walls, the ceilings, the floor, even the bedspread. Hundreds of ravens, hundreds of brush strokes taunting me, threatening me.

I wanted to scream. I should have.

But I was paralyzed. Lost somewhere between the threat in front of me and the threat behind me. The dark realization enveloped me, blanketing me in a cold embrace.

I wasn't safe.

Anywhere.

Or with anyone.

That's when a pair of arms closed around me, and everything went dark.

ACKNOWLEDGMENTS

There are so many people that deserve a huge thank you for their contributions to this story - I'll start with three very important people. First and foremost, my husband, for reading my words and for always being my biggest supporter. Your brain constantly surprises me, and your ability to see a story for what it is and what it can be is the reason I love to share my work with you. You let me gush about my story, and you constantly tell me how proud of me you are, all while challenging me to improve on my work. It means the world to me.

To Mariah, my creative soulmate, I speak frankly when I say, I hope I NEVER have to create a piece of art without you near, in, or behind it again. You are not only an incredibly smart storyteller but you are the kind of friend every creative needs, someone who pushes them to be better. Thank you, for always being that person for me. (Also, I'm sorry I am seemingly allergic to both commas and hyphens, and that you had to deal with that. Here's, an-excess, of, them-just, for, you-,).

Mom, you were the first person who showed me that I could write a book if I wanted to because I watched you do it. And you did it well! (Seriously y'all, read her book, Sweet Dreams by D.L. Edwards now on Kindle Unlimited). Thank you for listening to me every day at lunch talk about my story and ideas, and for always being the world's best sounding board.

There are countless other people I need to thank for being a part of creating this book. Thank you to my dad, for being my favorite English teacher growing up and teaching me how to write. (I won't tell you how many commas and hyphens I screwed up in the first draft though, that's strictly between Mariah and I…Mariah and me?.. Me and Mariah…). Thank you to Alison Turjancik, for being an incredible artist and bringing my Court Marks to life, Melissa Nash, for the stunning map of Verihdia and Mackenzie Baumhower, Tricia Andel, my incredible first beta readers who gave me such great feedback. And of course all of you, especially those of you coming from #BookTok. In April of 2022, I posted a fun little video about my story idea and it went viral (well viral for me, at least). So many of you were encouraging and practically begged me for this story. You all have no idea how much you inspired me to continue and pursue this novel. Thank you. Thank you. Thank you.

Pronunciation Guide

Buyhay- Boo- hey

Banyad- Bah-knee-odd

Kamatyan- Kah- muh- tie-in

Madillam- Mah-dill-um

Verihdia- Vur-ih-dee-uh

Mythica- Myth- ih- ka

Midesues- Mih- deuce-us

Korzich- Core-zihck

Made in the USA
Columbia, SC
26 July 2023

ec978125-7201-4466-8fcf-08f4e1e060c5R01